Praise for *The Biggerers*

'A dystopian black comedy set in a world where "full-sized humans keep mini-humans as pets." This edgy work of speculative fiction shocks and enthrals with its striking originality.'

Book Riot Best of 2018

'An entertaining, action-filled, and often troubling work of dystopian fiction… Fantasy and speculative fiction fans will enjoy this terrific mix of adventure, social commentary, and dark humour.'

Library Journal

'Lilwall complicates the littlers' gradual awakening to their human ability to love with satiric reflections.'

Publishers Weekly

'Exciting debut weird fiction, which may well become a talking point for book club types all over the world and is ideal for fans of *The Borrowers*, *Munmun* and *The Truckers*.'

Starburst

'It's not simply the dynamic between owner and owned that drives this unnerving and funny dystopian debut. As Jinx and Bonbon develop – the pains of dawning consciousness are brilliantly evoked – everything changes.'

Daily Mail

'I really did enjoy this book. There is something there that begs you to read further… The characters feel very real, with very understandable motivations.'

Looking Glass Reads

'Impressive… One of the things that's most interesting about *The Biggerers* is that there are clear parallels to other genre tales, but it's such an eclectic bunch of influences… Lilwall is not afraid to have moments of dark comedy or to suddenly challenge her readers… It's more than the eye-catching concept, it's fantastic.'

SciFiNow

About the author

Amy Lilwall studied for her PhD in The Contemporary Novel at the University of Kent. She teaches Creative Writing in Falmouth, Cornwall. *The Biggerers* is her first novel.

THE BIGGERERS

Amy Lilwall

In memory of Graham Lilwall

A Point Blank Book

First published by Point Blank,
an imprint of Oneworld Publications, 2018
This paperback edition published 2019

A CIP record for this title is available from the British Library

ISBN 978-1-78607-562-8
ISBN 978-1-78607-356-3 (eBook)

Typeset by Fakenham Prepress Solutions, Fakenham, Norfolk NR21 8NN
Printed and bound in Great Britain by Clays Ltd, Elcograf S.p.A.

Oneworld Publications
10 Bloomsbury Street
London WC1B 3SR
England

CHAPTER I

Bonbon was the first to sit up and look out of the basket. Something pulled at her arm.

'Get off, Jinx.'

'Come back down for a while.'

'No. It's time to get up.'

'Please, Bonbon.' Jinx's voice wobbled and her teeth made a noise like stones being dropped on the tiles on stone day.

Bonbon swung one leg over the edge of the basket and got out to look at the bowls. Both bowls were full. She took three mouthfuls from Jinx's bowl, then began to eat from her own.

They spent the morning gathering dropped thread. Then at lunch they waited for her to come and refill their bowls.

She didn't come.

They crawled through the vacuum hatch to go to Outside. The courtyard was AstroTurf that grew into grey concrete walls that grew into grey bars that Jinx and Bonbon couldn't see the top of anywhere in the garden; except for one spot. Only one of them could stand there at a time and she had to press herself against the far right of the sliding doors where she could hold on to the sticky-out bit while standing on the very ends of her toes. Jinx went straight over to this spot.

Bonbon collected dropped thread from the AstroTurf.

Chips arrived.

'Are you going to get it tonight then?'

'Yep.'

'Well, only if they're in the mood.'

'When have they not been in the mood, Jinx?'

'Occasionally, Bonbon, they are not in the mood.'

'What does that stupid word mean, Jinx? What does it *mean*? Chips! Do you know what it means?'

'No.'

'It means sometimes.'

Bonbon slit her eyes at Jinx before turning her back to her so that she was looking at Chips.

Jinx turned and walked back to the vacuum hatch.

'Yes, we are going to get it tonight.'

'What's it like, Bonbon? Is it good?'

'Chips, I wish you could just try it.'

Bonbon spent the rest of the afternoon putting the thread around their basket. 'Jinx, you're not doing it right; why can't you do it right?'

Jinx went and sat in the toilet box until she heard the front door open. Then she crawled to the edge and stuck her head out.

Bonbon was running across the tiles towards the kitchen door. She stopped at the open side and stood, fluttering her eyelashes. Jinx shuffled along after, kicking at the edges of the tiles. Bonbon was so nasty sometimes, why did she have to be so nasty? And she never said sorry.

She stood next to Bonbon, looked up and fluttered her eyelashes.

The She-one was making noises at them. She bent down and stroked Bonbon on the head, then Jinx, and it was then that they could almost hear what she was saying.

'Little chilly-billies…' And her head went back up in the air.

She filled their bowls, then stayed in the kitchen making the smells that she made until he came home. Then the two of them sat and ate the smells. Then they went into the big room.

They were in the mood.

Bonbon went and got it.

Then Jinx.

Then they went to the basket.

The next morning, they collected paper and AstroTurf and put it around the basket. Jinx helped. She did not point out that it was paper day not AstroTurf day. When they had finished they settled down for a nap.

The front door zjwoomed open. Bonbon woke up and scrambled out of the basket.

Jinx got up and followed.

They waited at the kitchen door, fluttering their eyelashes. She came in, made noises at them, bent down and patted them on the head before filling up their bowls.

When he arrived, they ate the kitchen smells and went into the big room.

They were in the mood.

Bonbon got it.

Then Jinx.

Then they went to the basket.

Bonbon was the first to wake up. She sat up and looked out of the basket.

'Come back for a few minutes, Bonbon.'

'No, Jinx,' said Bonbon, and she got out of the basket to look at the bowls. Both bowls were empty. She went back to the basket and climbed inside. 'It's Saturday,' she said. The bowls were always empty on Saturday, whatever Saturday was… They would be full again after a bit more sleep. She closed her eyes and pressed herself against Jinx.

Jinx smiled, closed her eyes, wriggled into the curve of Bonbon then twitched.

'Bonbon?'

'What?'

'Can we take the AstroTurf out of the basket?'

Bonbon huffed. Not this again. 'No.'

'But it's prickly.'

'What is that word, Jinx?' Bonbon sat up. 'What does that even mean?'

'Bonbon, I explained to you last time. Why don't you ever listen to me?'

'Because it's a stupid word, Jinx; it doesn't mean anything.' Bonbon got out of the basket and went over to the bowls.

'You're so nasty to me, Bonbon,' Jinx called after her.

Stupid Jinx. She never thought about anything except for her stupid self.

Selfish rat.

The bowls were empty. Bonbon kicked one of them and ran back to the basket.

She listened.

Nothing.

'Do it again, Bonbon.'

'Shut up, Jinx!'

Bonbon ran over to her bowl, kicked it hard, then ran back to the basket and listened.

She heard a thump above her.

'Quick, Jinx!' She jumped back into the basket, pressed herself against Jinx's back, then closed her eyes.

Time: 11:57. Oh dear, he was going to be late. He had told Susan he would be back in the morning, but, in fact, it would be early afternoon. But then again, it was *Sunday*. Early afternoon could still be considered morning because, well, everything was a bit later really. It was funny how even though religion had been scrapped since *ages*, Sunday had maintained its Sundayness. Maybe it was because the clocks changed twice a year on a Sunday, leaving it forever tarnished with the panic of being late for something, like, well, *work*, on Monday morning, yet mixed with the pleasure of realizing that it didn't matter, because it was only Sunday. The clocks could never go forward quickly enough to take away a whole Sunday.

Good point actually; when did the clocks go forward?

A photo of his uncle Monty pinned itself to the back of his mind. He was locked into a mock arm-wrestle with a HelpaBot that had been designed to recognize blighted potatoes on an organic potato farm. The HelpaBot even wore a painted uniform, parliament green with the image on the left breast of two leaves rising out of a golden potato. The uniform matched that of Uncle Monty. The article caption read: 'Winning back the working week: employment levels rise as machines banished to Sunday.' From then on, Sundays always felt a bit *anarchic.* They were rebellious, almost *carnival*-like: a once-weekly reminder of how the people had beaten the state. 'But we are fools,' Uncle Monty would say. 'If the state *granted* it, then we haven't really won anything.'

The car stopped at traffic lights and a young man pushed one of those old shopping trolleys across the road, while another young man sat inside the trolley. They lifted half-full beer bottles to Hamish.

He nodded back at them then looked at the time displayed on the WayToGo. 12:01. That whole 'Sunday' thought had taken him from morning to afternoon. Good. The pressure was off; he was into the afternoon and there was nothing he could do about it. It was like talking to someone while a plane takes off.

He cleared his throat. 'When do the clocks change?'

'The time will go back by one hour at one a.m. on Sunday the twenty-fifth of October. In two weeks' time.'

A little panic moth flapped its wings in his stomach: he was almost right to be almost panicked about the clocks going forward – it was, after all, *almost* time.

The traffic lights changed and the car advanced.

Oh, no, wait! The WayToGo had said that the clocks would go back! Ha! Of course they would! Oh well, in that case, no need to panic at all. One extra hour in bed. At home.

Home… Home would be nice. It had been a whole week since he'd seen her. He was sure that she was preparing *something* to win his approval. She really shouldn't do that… She didn't *need* to win anything from him; their themness was just *there*; it didn't need gingerbread and chocolate fondant and what-not… Speaking of which, should he go to Shepherd's? He could pick up some chèvre and French bread to make her trip last right to the end of Sunday. 12:04. No. Better just get home. After all, he'd have to faff about with emptying the car before he could relax.

'Hello.'

'You're here?'

She gaped her eyes and looked around 'here'. 'Yes. I am,' she said slowly.

Bugger. He'd been too excited. He'd been too pleased to see her. And this place was all weird with her in it, and she was all weird in this place. An out-of-work reaction; that was completely appropriate given that he was out of work. But now he'd have to keep up this 'out-of-work Hamish' so that she wouldn't guess that *she* was the cause of his breathy, high-pitched, full-of-eyebrows response to her 'hello'.

'No, it's just…' He grinned, he actually grinned, and he only knew he had grinned because of her not quite mirror-grin and her eyes that flicked down at his exposed teeth as if they were an open wound. 'There are lots of shops in London!' he told her, lilting upwards at the end and slightly shrugging his shoulders. So why should I have to bump into my patients here? it said. Is there no rest for the wicked? it said. Oh dear, he'd fucked that one up. Or had he? She scratched her chin and rocked back on a foot that she'd already placed behind her; when had she done that? Oh no, she wanted to flee… Not good, Hamish, not good.

'I mean…'

'I'm out of context, aren't I?' She said it so kindly that his mouth fell open. Talk about hitting the nail on the head…

A rushing breath puffed out his chest. He put on his normal face. 'A little, I admit…'

'It's okay. I must go anyway.'

'Oh?'

'I have someone waiting for me at home.'

'Ah.' A boyfriend? A date? He glanced down at her shopping bag.

'It'll be like I was never here!' she said, turning away.

'No, that's not…' That's not what he'd wanted at all.

'See you next week?' she called back.

'Yes.' He started to follow her. 'Next week.' Bugger. He stopped. He turned back to the shop, then back so he was watching her again. Following her? *Following* her? Really Hamish…

Her head ducked down into a little white car; something dangled from the rear-view mirror inside but no head leaned across from the passenger seat to kiss her. The car started. He swung his shoulders towards the shop entrance. His legs followed.

* * *

'In the light of the moon, a little egg lay on a leaf…' Drew inhaled and turned the page, and went on to tell the whole story to the child, at the same time flicking glances at his noodle-curls. One little hand rested on the corner of the page and lifted automatically each time it was turned. Skin podged around the knuckles, exactly the same smoothness along the tips, around the fingernails, across the back…

'Ha! How nice; that tiny, baby caterpillar… And then all it had to do was eat cherry pie, and red-and-pink stripy salami, one piece of chocolate cake, an ice cream, a lollipop… And then it built a little house called a…'

'A cocoon.'

'A cocoon, pushed its way out… And…'

'It was a beau-ti-ful butterfly!' they said together.

'Does that really happen?'

'Yes,' said Drew. 'That's where butterflies come from.'

The boy opened his mouth and stared up to the right as he thought about this. 'That was exactly what he needed, that nice-green-leaf, wasn't it?'

'It was,' nodding.

'After that he really felt like building, didn't he?'

Drew laughed. 'He must have done.'

'Sorry I'm late!' A woman strode in with a book bag and a lunch box all hooked around the same finger. 'I was late out of work.'

Drew stood up. 'That's alright. We read a book together.'

The woman tilted her head and mouthed 'thanks' at Drew. 'Lomax, have you been good? What did Drew teach you today?'

'Umm…' Lomax put his finger on his chin and thought.

'Come on… Show me.'

Lomax pushed himself up and walked to the other side of the studio before turning his feet outwards. Then he ran and counted, 'One, two, three…' which was out of time with his four long strides. He jumped, separating his legs as much as he could before landing and striding again. 'One, two, three,' he said. 'Got to keep the back leg straight,' he said.

'Well done, Lomax,' said Drew.

'Who's Mummy's dancing-star then?'

'Me,' said Lomax.

'Same time next week?' the woman asked Drew.

'Actually, next week will be the last one,' said Drew.

'Before the holidays? Yes, of course…'

'No, for good, unfortunately for me…'

The woman frowned at Lomax's ballet shoes.

'I'm being replaced, don't worry, it's just that I have my day job and, well, it's all a bit much.'

The woman's head snapped back up. 'Oh dear, what a shame! You're not giving up dancing for good, are you?'

Drew nodded. 'Hanging up my shoes.'

The woman pulled a sad face and scanned the studio. 'Well, Lomax, we'll have to get Drew a goodbye present. Huh? What do you think?'

Lomax pulled at his elastic ballet-shoe strap and didn't answer.

'No, no! Don't bother… My other half's going to make a cake so that I can say goodbye to all of the children properly at the end of the class – Lomax isn't allergic to anything, is he?'

Drew ran across the car park through the rain, a box-file hugged into folded arms, a sausage-shaped kit bag bouncing on one hip. Watty leaned across the passenger seat and opened the door. Drew landed inside, shiny and pink with fogged-up glasses.

'Thank you for that.'

'For what?' Watty replied, feeding the sausage backwards through the gap in the front seats.

'The door.'

'Oh.' Watty leaned across and kissed Drew. 'Not for picking you up?'

'Well.' Drew dragged a finger under each eye and looked around for somewhere to wipe the raindrops. 'For picking me up and for running me to the lab so that I can check on one weeny thing.'

'Oh God, really?'

'I'll be super quick, honestly; but I must check on this one thing.'

* * *

Susan sat on the arm of the sofa that could be seen from the front door. He would be back soon. What time was it? Midday. He had said in the morning; he would be back in the morning…

Or was he leaving in the morning?

It didn't really matter; the saddest thing about all of this was that he wasn't going to be pleased to see her… Ha! Not one bit. That was the saddest most tragic part of this situation; spending hours, if not days, looking forward to being with someone when, actually, they couldn't give a shit about you being there. Or not being there…

But then again… how could he *not* be excited to see her after a whole week apart? That would not be normal; in fact, would that count as a deal-breaker? Yeah… It would. And she could break that deal; in fact, now would be a good time to break that deal. After a whole week apart, she could manage that. She'd done a week without him – how could a whole lifetime be that much different? Plus, it wouldn't seem so weird to just put it out there: I'm leaving you. *I'm* leaving you. It would seem like she'd had space; one whole week of… space.

She drummed the part of the sofa that stuck out from between her legs, folded her lips between her teeth and stared at the frosted window that margined the front door.

She would be in front of her wardrobe, on her knees, stuffing clothes into a bag; no! Folding them carefully, controlling the situation, like, like it had been thought about. Plopping breakable stuff, lamps and bits of china, into a box of bubble wrap that she'd prepared. She had some bubble wrap in the understairs cupboard… 'What are you doing there?' he would ask. 'I'm leaving you,' she would say. 'I'm packing my things and I'm leaving.' He would glance at the box of bubble wrap and think: Oh… bubble wrap. She's not kidding; she's actually going to do this. She couldn't be going to a hotel for the night, oh no! She was leaving the house for good, with all her little breakable things; that nobody would ever take to a hotel… And their whole five years together would fold into themselves, again and again until they became an oyster shell at the bottom of his mind; and he would kneel next to it, pulling at it, scratching at it. 'It doesn't matter – it's empty,' she would say. And his only pearl would about-turn and stride right out of his life.

She stared at the door. She'd liked that last bit about the pearl.

A shape pixelled into fullness as it got closer to the frosted window and she stopped drumming the sofa. The shape shrank backwards again and it was gone. Of course it was gone. It wouldn't be Hamish… Why would he be acceptably late when he could be really bloody late?

Oh… She was doing this to herself again. It was all her. Her, her, her. It had to be! Normal people weren't like this. She was much too imbalanced for such a reasonable man.

No, it was him. It was definitely him.

But maybe it was her. She'd spend hours being miserable, traipsing through the back alleys of her rainy London estate, looking towards the big pink flowers that peeped over the massive surrounding wall and fantasizing about climbing over it. Knowing that the next day she'd find herself at home again.

It was her. It was definitely her.

What a waste of time.

Perhaps he would be back by one – or at the very latest two. Which would mean that he would have left in the morning. 'I'll be coming back in the morning,' he'd said. Yes, that's to say he would be in the act of returning, which didn't mean that he would have returned.

12:13. Argh. Waiting, waiting. Waiting to be ignored… Disappointed.

Oh stop it. Just stop it.

She leapfrogged from the sofa arm and went to the kitchen.

Surely she had something fun to do. This was all such a waste of… Wait… What was that? Breadcrumbs. Gosh, how many were there? Were they everywhere or just in front of the worktop? Hmmm… She could have easily spread them about over the course of the morning; right through the house…

Right. Vacuum bot.

Ah! The chilly-billies. Better warn them first.

She looked around the kitchen. 'Bonbon? Jinx?'

Nope. Maybe in the living room. 'Bonbon? Jinx?'

Not in there. Kitchen again? 'Bonbon? Jinx? There you are.'

One face appeared at the hatch of the toilet box. The other was on the floor, right next to her socked foot. Oh dear. They'd been fighting. 'Have you been mean to Jinx again? Have you?' She bent towards Bonbon. 'Now you know that you have to be nicer to poor Jinx, she's very sensitive.'

Bonbon licked the bit between her nose and her top lip.

What was that bit called?

Jinx climbed out of the toilet box.

'I'm going to put this on.' She showed them the bot. Their eyes swelled and they ran to the plant and climbed into its pot. 'No, don't do that!' That plant was an original; three thousand pounds worth. Almost half a month's rent. The bot couldn't get into it, that's why they liked it. But there was something else; she was sure that they believed it protected them. As the bot approached, they would look up to the waxy leaves that bowed over them like scooped hands, sort of imploringly. She was sure of it. Otherwise why didn't they just hop into their basket or the toilet box? Ha! That would amuse Hamish. He liked their funny ways; she would tell him that they'd done it again, that they'd jumped into the pot. 'The bot pot' he had nicknamed it.

Yes, she would definitely tell him about this…

Cupid's bow. That's what it was called; the top lip bit. She looked towards Bonbon. 'Alright, you can stay in there. But don't kick at the earth.' With one hand each on the plant's trunk, they eyed the vacuum bot as it weaved through the alleys in the kitchen furniture. It must have had a crystal from the toilet box jammed in its motor because it sounded particularly aggressive.

Actually, the proper name was philtrum, wasn't it? No. Philtrum was the indentation between the nose and the top lip. Surely a Cupid's bow was the outline of the top lip; that was more bow-shaped… Oh well. Who cares? Who cared about things like that when you had to pack up your things and start a new life somewhere else?

She turned and looked at the clock. Time: 12:30. He probably wouldn't notice if the floor was clean, but he didn't like the buzzing noise that the bot made while he was trying to read. 'Can't you do that later?' he'd say; sometimes. It was best to do it now.

Was that acceptable? Was it? Did he think that all she had to do in the world was wait until she had the house to herself just so she could bloody vacuum it?

She opened the fridge and bit her lip at its insides. 'What are you doing?' he would ask. Jumpers would be the obvious things to pack first, because it was October and she would need them. She closed the fridge. There was food; if he was hungry, there was food. Also, jumpers were big and so taking them would make a visible void in her wardrobe… I'm leaving you, she would say. The more stuff she took, the more difficult it would be to come back. The easier it would be to leave. Picture frames were easily packable; they just slotted one behind the other… And furniture, shit! What about her real chipboard chest of drawers? It was sooo heavy. She would hire a removal person for the big stuff. That's what she would do.

Time: 12:42. Oh he had to be back soon. She could make gingerbread! That would make the house smell good and he liked it… She took a bowl from the cupboard.

It wasn't because he was a pig – even though he really, really, acted like one – it was even more infuriating than that. If she was right about his character, he simply believed that she wasn't there to serve him, she was there to serve herself, and she would only do the vacuuming because it pleased her to vacuum. Therefore, he could tell her not to do it while he was there because it pleased him to have a quiet house. She took flour, sugar, honey and spices from the baking drawer. Do whatever you do because it makes you happy; that's the way it always should be. Butter and an egg from the fridge. You should live for yourself and not seek validation through approval from others. She winced at the honey, urgh, made in some lab by those poor freak-bees… Don't expect anything from anyone; just accept people for who they are. One ounce of flour is about one heaped tablespoon. Be yourself, be yourself, be yourself, be yourself… One ounce of sugar is about one flat tablespoon; ounces were so vintage.

'By the way, the house has been vacuumed,' she would say.

He would look up from his book and over his glasses. 'Sorry… Do you want some kind of award for this?'

Bastard… He was a bastard because she sort of did want an award.

She squidged butter, flour, honey and dark brown sugar through the gaps that her fingers made; mostly 'M's, now 'E's, never 'W's. And the little finger, well, that was just the, sort of, tail that you get in whirly joined-up writing. Shit. The oven. She always forgot to pre-heat the oven.

A key turned in the door. She held her breath. He entered and made taking-off-shoe noises without saying hello. What to do? Stand here squidging?

No.

Better at least meet him at the kitchen doorway. But she would keep the gingerbread mixture on her hands. She didn't sit around waiting for him. She did things when he wasn't around.

'Hi!'

Her voice dropped over him like a floaty veil. He kept his head bowed and fought with a finger that was stuck in the back of his shoe. Damn. He didn't actually need to take his shoe off because he still had to unload the car. He opened his mouth to say 'I don't need to take the shoe off because I have, will, still to unload… car', then realized that the *other* shoe was standing on the bottom step.

'Hello,' he said instead.

When had he taken that other shoe off?

Never mind.

'Are you alright?'

'Mmm-hmm.'

Mmm-hmm. She hated mmm-hmm.

She nodded and smiled. Her two gingerbready hands held out like diseased claws. She waited. What the hell was she waiting for? She was not about to dig through all the mmms and the hmms to find out what the hell was wrong with him. A kiss! She was waiting for a kiss! Oh yuk, surely not? But she was still waiting. He hadn't even looked at her. Fine, don't look at me; don't even think about looking at me, you're just making it easier for me to leave you. But he really wasn't looking at her. After one whole week! She turned and went back into the kitchen. God. But she was lovely; she was so bubbly and lovely. He. Had. No. Idea.

He looked up to grin at her. But she had gone.

Right, so… On with the other shoe. And out to the car. What would he do with the boxes? He could put them in the under-stairs cupboard but… 'Open boot,' he said. No! 'Open trunk!' The car boot clicked open; yep, there were too many to put into the under stairs cupboard. He hugged one of the boxes out of the car. They would have to be stacked up for now and he would go through them all later. Susan would like that; stirring up a few old memories. He pushed the door with his elbow and put the box on the floor.

Two little people stared up at him from the living-room doorway. He fluttered his eyelashes at them.

Jinx danced about and waved her arms.

Bonbon screwed up her face.

Susan listened to the hall noises. He'd brought in another load of boxes. For goodness' sake. He'd been to the storage unit again. 'If we get it emptied by the end of the month, that'll be one less bill to pay.' So why not empty it into the tip? Or the second-hand shop? She pressed down another dough-ball. They'd not looked at most of this stuff since they'd moved here, four years ago. More boxes; didn't he know how bad it was to clog up his life with things that lurked in boxes?

And some of it was hers – how was she supposed to leave if she had even more stuff to take?

Maybe she should have washed her hands before going into the hall… Maybe put on some heels and had her eyebrows re-tattooed rather than making bloody gingerbread.

She took a chunk of the dough and rolled it into a ball.

Someone once revealed the secret to a good relationship: 'Never wonder if they are making you happy; always ask yourself: am I making *them* happy?'

She took another chunk.

He was always so miserable…

He came into the kitchen with boxes that he stacked up on the work surface before turning around to get more. She knew he had gone to get more because the front door was still open. Why are you keeping me? She rolled another chunk into a ball and tried not to look at him. With the palm of her hand she pressed one ball into a round.

Miniature Susan-Fairy whispered without moving her lips: 'Come on! You know that he can only think about getting the boxes in from the porch. After that he'll pat down his pockets and stare at the door for a second. Only then can he sit down and love you. We know that's what he's doing. We know it.'

The real Susan blinked. Then shook her head.

Not good enough, Susan-Fairy. If it was as easy as that then she wouldn't feel so sad. She was only asking for a proper 'hello'. Just one sodding 'hello'...

'Ha! And if you got your "hello" you'd be wanting a kiss. And when you got your kiss you'd be wanting flowers; when would it stop, Susan? Some people just aren't meant to be happy.'

The real Susan put a marble-sized dollop of dough into her mouth. Susan-Fairy was right. She was always right.

There were probably loads of useful things knocking around in those boxes that he'd completely forgotten about, he thought as he went back outside. He hugged out another one and scoffed at the neighbours' garden. They had a conveyor belt thing that led from a hole in their house to about halfway down the drive where a car boot would sometimes be waiting. Not today, though, he noted; there was no car there today. He elbowed the door again and felt bad for scoffing. They were quite elderly, the people from next door. He put the box down and went back outside, looking at the belt from this different from-the-house-and-up-the-drive angle. The man must have been about one hundred and eleven now... Was he? The lady was slightly younger, he was sure about that... One Hundred and Thirty flashed up in his mind – the maximum age. Supposedly. He picked up another box and the bottom of it opened up. Shit. He'd put it in upside down. He turned it the right way around and started to place the stuff back inside. Wow; one, two, three, four. Four mobile phones... They must've been about twenty years old! Some pastry cutters – Susan's – she wouldn't need them now she had her fancy shape-lasering oven. A bagful of bottle tops. Bottle tops? Fair enough. Candles, ooo! *Highly* illegal and, what was this? A museum programme? 'Pop-Up Books,' read the title, with dots in the double 'o' to make them look like eyes. He recognized the little picture of a spotty monster at the bottom and remembered an occasion where he'd stared at that same monster so hard *just* to stop his lips from quivering. Five whole years, he thought, dropping it back into the box.

Right. He hugged out two boxes at the same time, 'Close trunk,' then elbowed his way into the kitchen, placed the boxes on the worktop, went into the hall, shut the front door, dragged off his shoes with the toes of the opposite foot, strode back into the kitchen and brushed down his coat.

She pressed another dough-ball, and another, and another, then had to scrape them up with a spatula because she'd pressed too bloody hard. She slid the rounds onto a silicone tray and popped them into the oven. They'd be ready in a few minutes and he would be able to eat a warm one with a cup of coffee. He'd like that, she thought, wiping the oven handle. Her face ached, oh God I'm so lovely. She gathered up all of the dirty utensils and put them in the sink.

She heard chair feet scraping against the tiles and the 'pfff' sound of a bottom compressing a cushion.

He was sitting behind her but she knew he was there. He knew that she knew.

'Well, hello then, stranger,' he said to the back of a woolly hoody.

Her skin puckered up thousands of tiny pairs of lips. 'Hello,' she said to the tap.

Another veil floated down over him and his skin felt happy to be in this coat, on this chair under this veil.

'How was your trip?'

'Fine.' He was being nice. He *always* did this. Well, it was too late for nice. She was leaving. 'I bought you a present,' she said to the tap.

'Ho-ho, lucky me.'

She dried her hands and turned to face him. He still had his coat on and his eyebrows horned upwards at the far ends. He smiled up at his Susan, and saw her eyes twitching from his to where his present was located and back again. 'It's in the gift bag on the table,' she said to the gift bag.

He pulled the bag towards him and looked inside. 'No, it can't be,' he said. It must have been a fake…

She beamed. 'Of course it is.'

'Foie gras,' he whispered. 'But it's… you know.' He turned his mouth upside down and winked one eye at her.

She laughed. Oh he could be lovely! 'Well, you'd better keep it a secret then,' she whispered. And now he'd won her back. With one wink, he had her. She'd gone to the very, very limit of a wet walk through the run-down housing estate and she had just managed to put one leg over the peripheral wall into the enchanted pink-flower land, when he'd grabbed her ankle, pulled her down, put up an umbrella and now was holding her hand to take her home. Bastard.

Just what was the point of the wet walk?

How rebellious. He liked that! Yes! Not many people would dare to smuggle foie gras… He certainly wouldn't. 'How did you manage to get it into the country?' He held the dead-flesh-coloured jar up towards the light, illuminating pools of yellow fat.

'It's not so exciting, I'm afraid.'

He looked at the chunk of peachy liver. It really was foie gras. Really, absolutely, the real thing.

'There are a few farmers who are still protected by heritage laws…'

He remembered The Bookman telling him about the time he had asked for foie gras at Shepherd's and the manager had been called. 'I must make this perfectly clear to you, Sir: we do not sell this product because that would be against the law. As a valued customer, we understand that *blah blah blah*, and we would thank you not to associate our name with this product.' Then he had made him sign something. *Sign* something!

'… and it's perfectly legal to buy from them and bring the product back into the country.'

Hamish swivelled his head back towards Susan.

'Apparently.'

'Right.' Ha! This was absolutely impossible. It was *highly* illegal. She'd obviously been spun a yarn by some struggling goose farmer and smuggled it in without even realizing. That was her to a T. 'No,' he said.

She straightened. 'What "no"?' She saw herself, on the wet pavement, stepping away from the umbrella.

'No, I think you'll find it's definitely illegal.' The Shepherd's thing had happened to The Bookman earlier in the year... It was only October; laws didn't change that quickly. Definitely illegal. Definitely smuggled.

Fuck, why did he do this? 'Well, no, it's not and there's your proof.' She flicked an open hand towards the jar.

'Did you declare it?'

'What?'

He knew she'd heard him, she just hadn't declared it. 'Did you declare it at customs?'

'No.'

'Well, there you go then.'

'Hamish, the average traveller and her suitcase is X-rayed four times before she can even put one toe into the departure lounge.'

She had a point... But no! He would not back down here. He even remembered telling her about The Bookman thing. He shrugged. 'It could have been jam.'

'Jam? Fucking jam? Do you know how much an X-ray costs? Do you really think that airport security would pay out for four X-rays for one suitcase in order to confuse foie gras with bloody JAM?' She could feel herself turning and striding away, back through the puddly streets.

He put the jar back on the table, steepled his hands widely in front of him and looked at her over his glasses. 'Why are you getting cross?' He wanted to say 'Suzie' at the end but hadn't thought of it in time.

'You think you're right even when you're not and, and, moreover, there isn't even the slightest possibility that I could ever be right, even though I'm the one who's had primary experiences with the actual thing, and because you just heard someone talk about someone who might have known something about it, you think you know everything.' She was running now. Back to the wall, back to the pink flowers. Grabbing at jumpers and picture frames and bubble wrap and stuffing them into boxes…

Ah. She hadn't forgotten the story.

But he had double-checked this information. She didn't know that he'd double-checked it, but she should know by now that he would only push his point if he was absolutely sure. 'You don't know that.'

'Know what?'

'You don't know where I got the information from,' he said, brushing one hand across the table as if to underline that last sentence, his eyes fixed on the imaginary line.

This was not fair! Her face went hot and achy again. She had the right to be right about stuff, but, but she was never allowed to be right and she would get all cross and shouty while he… he looked over his glasses at her. 'But why am I not a good enough source?'

Climbing up the wall and swinging one leg over it, she sat there for a moment and started to cry.

He heard the break in her voice and looked up immediately. 'Oh Susan, what's all this?' He got up and crossed the room.

From the wall she felt a tug on her ankle. 'You just make me feel inferior,' she blubbed down at him.

Her confidence. Her confidence had surely been sky-high all week and now she was home and feeling deflated. Inferior, indeed. *Not a good source.* It hadn't helped that he'd been right about the foie gras. He could have let her have that one… She was still clutching the wet tea-towel, crying at it as if it were a creature that had died in her hands. He took it from her; her hands were icy. She always had cold hands. He pulled her into his coat and wrapped the edges around her. She drooped inside the coat like a lettuce leaf between gorilla lips. That's why she made exceptionally good pastry, because she had cold hands; it was better than *anything* he could buy at Shepherd's. 'You are a very good sauce, Suzie,' he said. 'All creamy and delicious.'

Hmmm… That was quite a nice little play-on-words, he thought as he rested his chin on her head. Surely that would have made her smile a little bit. They stood like that until all of her breathy sobs had rolled out of her throat and washed over her tongue. 'A Suzie-sauce,' she hoarsed up at him suddenly.

'Ha, not bad! Sauce-Suzette,' he said.

'A sauce-an,' she batted back.

'A suce!' he triumphed. That was, after all, the obvious combination to follow hers… Although his 'creamy and delicious' comment had been the cleverest. He tightened his arms around her and felt himself still whispering sh, sh, sh well after she had stopped crying.

CHAPTER 2

Pass in hand, Drew flashed the barcode over a scanner and pushed through the turnstile towards the lift. The lift doors opened. Dr Hector stepped out, rumbling instructions at one of the student researchers. Drew straightened and clutched the pass in both hands.

'Drew – bit late for you, isn't it?' said Hector.

'Forgotten items… Again.'

'Right.' The doctor turned his back to the student, his stare wandering down to Drew's pass and back up again.

The student craned to see beyond the window, flicked a glance at Hector, then made slicing gestures at his neck.

'We have that audit tomorrow, don't forget.'

'I know,' said Drew, eyes following the student's gaze towards the window, then snapping back to the doctor.

The doctor looked too. 'Do you have someone waiting for you? You best hurry on up there… Retrieve whatever this forgotten item is…'

'Yes, I'd best be off.' Drew exhaled, both shoulders falling to normal shoulder height. The student started to stammer out his goodbyes to Hector.

'I haven't finished with you yet,' the doctor overrode him. 'Get a pen. Write this down.'

Drew stepped past both of them and jumped into the lift, hoping that the lab was exactly how it had been not four hours before. 'See you tomorrow.' Maybe someone had been in just to make sure that everything was tip-top for the audit. Drew bounded along the corridor with out-turned feet, pushed back the lab door and glanced at the giant fridges that flanked the entrance, in the light of the moon, with their hundreds of surplus children inside. At the back of the room stood three big incubators. 'Hello girls.' Drew stared for a moment at the glass containers in each one, checked the temperature, good, and blinked at the ceiling, once, slowly, chin pressed against clasped hands. The others had never got as far as this. Black thoughts curled into vines about the incubator. No, not this time. Drew would come again tomorrow night, and the night after, and in the early mornings when the buses were cold and empty yet full of all that time to spend guessing at which one would be dead. But after this, that would be it. As soon as they all died they would move on. The dance lessons ended next week. Watty could make cakes anywhere.

Drew's focus fuzzed from gazing too hard. A dot of light swelled in each egg, then vanished in a blink. But one still glowed amber – really? Drew blinked again. The amber dimmed.

* * *

'Where have you been? It's hair day.'

'I know it is.'

'Well, have you been looking for hair?'

'No, Bonbon, I haven't.'

'You haven't been looking for hair? Where were you then?'

'Big room.'

'But they're in there.'

'I know. That's why I went.'

'Why? What would you want to see them for now? It's not time to see them. What would you want to see them for?'

'I don't know why, I just…'

'What?'

'I just needed to.'

'You just needed to. Oh Jinx… Why would you do that? You're so weak. It's too early to see them now; don't you know how early it is?'

'Yeah, I know, but they really seem to like me at the moment.'

'But by the time it gets around to the right time to see them, they won't want to see us. Because you already saw them.'

'Oh no. Do you really think so?'

'Yes!'

'—.'

'Oh dear…'

'What?'

'Now I need to see them.'

'Well, go on then!'

'But it's too early!'

'But maybe they will want to see you because they've just seen me… They'll still be in the mood.'

'Bloody hell. That means I'd better go right now, doesn't it? It's just too… Well… It's hair day, Jinx!'

'I'll look for hair.'

'Even if you don't, I have to go now, don't I?'

'I will, Bonbon, I will.'

'Fine. I'll be back in a bit.'

Bonbon walked across the floor towards the big room, jumping tile gaps every three steps; she didn't want to get her foot stuck again. Why would she go and see them so early? Stupid rat. She never thought about what she was doing and what would happen afterwards. So selfish.

Stupid selfish rat-head.

And it was getting cold. The reason you always did it later in the evening was because in warm-time it was too hot during the day and in cold-time it warmed you up at the coldest part of the day. Also, they were always in the mood in the evening. Well, at least theirs were. Blankey had said that hers were never up for it in the evening; they did it in the middle of the day, and Chips, ha! Chips didn't even know what it was! How weird. But then it wasn't as easy for him…

Because of his thing.

At least Chips got his humcoat when it was still warm-time. That was ages ago. It had been cold-time for ages and they still hadn't been given their humcoats…

Hang on… What was that? Oh bloody hell… 'Why are you following me?'

Silence.

'Jinx? I know you're there.'

'I-I want to watch.'

'You want to what? You want to watch? Why would you want to watch?'

'Oh please. I get lonely on my own.'

'And do I watch when it's your turn? Do I?'

'Oh please, Bonbon.'

'No!'

Jinx covered one foot with the other and looked at it.

Jeez. She was at it again. She was doing that thing. 'Look, please don't do that. You know that makes my ears feel hot.'

'I-I, can't h-help it, Bonbon.' Sniff. 'S-sometimes you are s-so nasty to me.'

'But, I don't even know what you're doing! What on earth is that, Jinx? Stupid ears… Just stop it. Stop it now!'

'Just… So… N-nasty.'

'No, Jinx… No, don't do that; stop it… Look at me, Jinx. Come on, look at me? That's better. It's just that you aren't nasty enough. It's you who's all weird. Everybody thinks so.'

Sniff.

'Listen. I don't want you to watch but you can wait just outside the door if you want, then we'll go back and have a nap.'

'Really?'

'Yes.'

'A cuddly nap?'

Jesus, what was this word? What was this bloody word that she kept on using? 'Whatever. Yes.'

'Okay, Bonbon. I'll wait right here.'

'But you'd better turn around.'

'Alright.'

'And you mustn't look inside.'

'No, I won't.'

'If you do, I'll know, okay?'

'Yes, okay. No, I won't.'

Jinx swivelled on her bottom until she was facing her left, and behind her was her right and what was behind her was her new left. That was how it was, there were specific names given to these specific spaces so that no one could get confused about anything. She knew these names. Bonbon didn't; she just shouted whenever she heard Jinx use them out loud.

Bonbon walked across the last three tiles to the door.

The door clicked open.

Bonbon fluttered her eyelashes. But there was no one.

It must have been the through. They were always talking about that wretched through that opened all of the doors, and it usually happened when someone was arriving or leaving. Bonbon looked behind her towards the front door and fluttered her eyelashes.

But there was no one. Except for Jinx. Jinx fluttered her eyelashes back at Bonbon.

'Ji-inx!' Bonbon whined, bending her knees and holding her cheeks in her hands. 'I just told you to turn around!'

'Are you spying on me, chilly-billy?' Bonbon spun to face the door. It wasn't like she even needed it any more. She didn't even need it. But then they might not be in the mood later, so… She'd better get it now. She stepped through and ran across the wood floor so that she would be noticed. She was noticed. She stopped under the coffee table and looked out from behind one of the legs. She fluttered her eyelashes.

It spoke again. It was the He-one, oh good; she ran over to his shoe and lay across its toe, on her back, arching herself so that her breasts pointed upwards and wobbled above the line of her chin. He picked her up in his hand and set her on his knee. She pulled her hair back and wound it on top of her head. He began to rub the back of her neck with the tips of his fingers. She lay on her belly, across his thigh, and his fingers waved all the way down her back and up to her neck again.

He talked to her. She closed her eyes.

He continued like this for a few minutes then stopped, his hand hovering just above her body, so she kicked his finger, like she usually did, with the heel of her foot and he started to rub her again.

'You got it already? Isn't it a bit early?'

'Yeah. It was Jinx's fault.'

'It wasn't my fault, Bonbon. You're always blaming me. I can't help it if I get lonely.'

'What is this word, what is this bloody word? Do you know what it means, Chips?'

'No.'

'She has so many stupid words like this. They never mean anything.'

'Yes they do, Bonbon. They do! It means that I get sad when I'm on my own.'

'On your own? You're never on your own! That's impossible. There's always the bowls, or the toilet box, or something.'

'No! I mean another living thing; another thing that's alive, you know, that moves.'

Chips and Bonbon blinked at her.

'So you got it already?' Chips said again.

'Yep.'

'And was it good?'

'Chips, I wish you could try it. You'll never know what it's like unless you try it.'

'Yes, but poor Chips has that thing, doesn't he?'

'Shh! Jinx. Bloody hell,' Bonbon hissed, smacking Jinx on the shoulder and looking at her nastily.

'What thing, what thing do I have?'

'Just ignore her, Chips.'

'Jinx, what thing do I have?'

Jinx's eyes glanced down between Chips's legs.

'Honestly, Chips, you can't even see it now you've got your humcoat.'

'W-what? You mean the… My…'

'Brrr… You're so lucky to have your humcoat. It's nearly cold-time, and I'm cold.'

Chips lifted his humcoat. 'But why does that mean that I can't have it too?'

'Well, we don't have them, Chips. Look…'

'Will you shut up, Jinx?'

'I'm just saying, if he tried it, his thing would get squashed.'

'SHUT UP, Jinx. Of course you can have it, Chips. You just have to ask them to give it to you, that's the only problem… I don't know how you're going to do that.'

'Brrrr… It is cold.' Chips let go of the bottom of his humcoat and switched it on. It started to hum. Jinx and Bonbon got a bit nearer. 'I don't know how they can let you walk about like that,' he said as Jinx lifted up his arm and put it around her shoulders.

Bonbon screwed up her eyes. 'I don't know what's wrong with her; she's so, so… I don't even have a word for what she's like.'

'Clingy, Bonbon, I'm clingy.' She took Chips's arm off her shoulders and let it drop. 'I'm just cold.'

They stood, blinking at each other.

'It's no good. I'm going to have to go inside.'

'Right.'

They all turned at the same time and left.

At eight o'clock it was dark. They crept back and went straight to the kitchen where he opened the fridge and she went to check their food bowls. Jinx's was empty. She waited while he finished with the fridge.

'Are you going to eat that now? I thought we could save it for tomorrow.'

He took something else, closed the door, and left.

She reached into the cupboard above the fridge and took out three cups full of dry flakes.

'We should think about putting their humcoats on,' he called from the hall.

She poured the flakes into Jinx's bowl and went over to their basket. Oh they were doing it again! They were doing it again! 'Quick, look; they're doing it again!'

Jinx and Bonbon lay folded together one behind the other with all their arms and legs curled around each other like idle white slugs.

'They're so cute. Look, quick! Come look.'

'It's because they're cold,' he said with his mouthful. 'We really should put their humcoats on.'

'You're probably right,' she said.

'I'll go and get them.'

'No! Don't wake them up… I've been meaning to get them new ones.'

'You've been saying that for weeks,' he said. And then he went.

She crouched down, lifted Bonbon's foot with the tip of her fingernail and put it down again. Then she went.

Jinx opened her eyes and listened to the She-one walking away. She could feel one of Bonbon's hands on her belly, the other one on her forearm, her knees in the backs of her own knees and her breasts pressed against her back. Every other second Bonbon breathed into the little cave between her ear and her neck.

Jinx smiled and closed her eyes.

Bonbon was the first to wake up. She sat up and looked out of the basket.

'Come back for a few minutes.'

Bonbon looked back at Jinx's arm that stretched across the air like it wanted her to pass it something. She bent and sniffed the yellow fingernails. Flakes. Her tongue was slippery inside her mouth; now was eating time. 'Not now, Jinx.' She climbed out of the basket, took a few mouthfuls of Jinx's flakes, then ate all of her own.

They spent the morning jumping on cushions to make the feathers come out. Then they collected up the feathers and went back to the kitchen to put them in the basket.

At lunchtime they waited for her to come home and fill up the bowls.

She didn't come.

Bonbon crawled through the vacuum hatch. Where was Jinx, where was that rat-head? Hmmm… No feathers in the AstroTurf… She went over to the spot where she could see over the bars.

Over the bars was grey. Feather day was long because there were never any feathers in the AstroTurf. She would just have to stand there looking at the grey.

Where was that stupid rat?

'Did you get it yet, Bonbon?'

'Not yet, Chips. It's too early.'

Jinx backed out of the vacuum hatch. Hugging herself. She ran over to the spot where she could see over the bars. Bonbon was standing in it. She started to rub her arms and shoulders while hopping on one leg, then the other.

'But you got it early yesterday?'

'Yeah… All because of bloody Jinx.'

'But it's good, isn't it?'

'Chips, I just wish you could try it.'

'So, if it was good, what did Jinx do that was so bad?'

Jinx stopped rubbing and jumping. Bonbon stopped looking at the grey. They stared at Chips.

'It was too early,' said Bonbon.

Jinx fluttered her eyelashes at Chips.

'But you got it, didn't you? And that's better than not getting it, Bonbon.'

Bonbon turned back to the grey. 'It's better in the evening. In the evening it's colder. But she had to have it in the afternoon. I don't know why.'

'She's… clingy,' he replied.

They both stared at him again.

Jinx reached out one hand and touched Chips's humcoat.

Bonbon turned back to the vacuum hatch. 'There are no feathers out here. There are more feathers in the cushions. Come on, Jinx.'

Jinx turned and followed Bonbon.

Jinx spent the next hour jumping on cushions. Bonbon collected up the feathers.

'Not the shoe one, Jinx. Nothing ever comes out of the shoe one.'

'But it's bouncy.'

Bonbon bent and grabbed at a feather. Why did she keep on coming out with this rubbish that wasn't going to help anyone? All it meant was that Bonbon had to keep telling her to shut up; why should she have to keep telling Jinx to shut up when all she wanted to do was get on?

'And anyway, it's not made from shoes, it's made from some sort of plastic.'

Stupid rat. She should just shut up. She never knew when it was time to shut her stupid mouth. Chips thought she was nasty to Jinx, but it was always bloody Jinx's stupid fault.

'Shoes smell different. Leather smells different.'

Chips couldn't know what she was really like. Chips didn't have to sleep in a basket with her. Chips had nothing to do all day except remember her stupid weird words.

'Leather has its own smell. Once you know the smell, you never forget it. I know the smell of leather now, Bonbon. I'll never forget it. You never forget the smell of leather, Bonbon.'

'I don't care, Jinx! There are no feathers! There. Are. No. Feathers!'

Jinx stopped jumping.

'You're such a weird selfish rat, Jinx. I don't even know what those words mean. No one knows what those words mean!'

'Bonbon!' Jinx held her hands halfway between her eyes and her ears.

'There are no feathers, Jinx! Today is feather day! IT'S FEATHER DAY!'

Jinx crouched down and pressed her face into her hands and her hands into her lap. Bonbon was angry, really angry, and it would only make her angrier if Jinx did that thing that made her ears feel hot. She'd better go away and do it on her own. Jinx slid down from the cushion and ran to the door, still bending as near to her lap as she could. She would have to go and hide somewhere until Bonbon was better. She would find a more secret hiding place than the toilet box. She would hide herself so well that Bonbon would wonder where she was, yes! And then she would come to look for her – when she was feeling better.

She ran out of the room, jumping the gaps in the tiles.

'Jinx!' she heard behind her. She stopped.

'Yes, Bonbon?'

'Come back, Jinx!'

She sounded nicer. But Jinx was still doing that thing. That would only make her shout again. 'I-I'm just going over here for a little while.' Sniff.

Bonbon spent the afternoon arranging the feathers in the basket while Jinx crouched in the dining room between a chair leg and the big glass door. The dining room was nice because it had carpet and she could make big swirls in it just by hopping across it and letting one foot drag behind. Not today, though; today was for hiding and this was a brilliant hiding place. They almost never came into the dining room. She looked out of the patio door. It was near the bit outside where she could see over the bars. She couldn't see over the bars from inside. Just grey bricks. And no feathers.

She'd been here ages.

Bonbon still hadn't come to look for her. Or maybe she just couldn't find her. Maybe if she coughed a bit then Bonbon would come… No! She would wait for Bonbon to find her. Well… Maybe she would wait for a bit; if Bonbon still hadn't come, she would cough. But Bonbon wouldn't come if she had things to do, would she? And today was feather day.

Had she waited long enough?

No. Just a bit longer. She would look out of the patio door.

What was that?! A feather? But there were no feathers outside… Yes, it was! Was it? Yes! And Chips! Chips was outside with a feather! And another! And another! Loads of feathers! 'BONBON!' Jinx ran across the carpet and out of the dining room. 'BONBON!'

Bonbon was sitting in the basket looking at the other end of it. 'What?'

'Chips has got feathers,' she yelled, running to the vacuum hatch and crawling out of it. 'Chips!' She could see him talking to something. 'Chips! Where did you find all of them?'

'On the ground over here. There's something here.'

Jinx stepped forward and felt Bonbon rush past her.

'But there are no feathers outside – how did they get—' Bonbon stopped and looked in the same direction as Chips. 'But… They're all over it!' She ran over to the green box and disappeared behind it.

Jinx leaped after her. 'What, Bonbon? What is it?' And as she got to the other side of the box, she saw it. In the middle of a circle of feathers lay a big, soft head with one long grey tooth and a shiny eye that looked weird and still. Jinx bent down to look into the eye. 'Hello?' she said. 'Hello?'

The eye stared at her.

'Are you having a nap? That's a funny way to have a nap.' She put her hand on its cheek. 'Why isn't it moving? Chips? It should be moving, shouldn't it?'

'—'

'Where did it come from?'

'—'

Jinx turned. Chips had dropped all of his feathers and was looking at the back of his left hand. Then he wiped his eye with his other hand and looked at the back of that too. His hands had wet patches. And his face. It was that thing that happened to Jinx! That thing that made her weird… The thing that made Bonbon's ears feel hot. But… She looked at Chips's eyes then back down to the eye that wasn't moving – it was moving! 'It's moving, Chips, it's moving!' But it wasn't the eye that was moving; it was the head. The head was jerking backwards. Jinx looked at the head, then down the body towards Bonbon. 'Bonbon! Stop!' Bonbon pulled feathers out of its body with one hand, then the other, then the other, so hard that the whole thing jerked 'Bonbon! Stop! Stop it!' Jinx put her arms around the thing's neck and cuddled it, shutting her eyes. 'Bonbon! Bonbon!'

'Shut up, Jinx!' Bonbon shouted, still pulling feathers out of the thing.

'You're hurting it! You're hurting it!'

'I'm not hurting it, Jinx!'

'You are!'

'If I was hurting it, it would say something!'

'It was saying something; it was trying to say something to me!' yelled Chips. Bonbon and Jinx stopped shouting at one another and looked at him.

'See, Bonbon? It was! It really was saying something! And now look at it—'

'Shut up, Jinx. What did it say?'

'I-I couldn't understand it…'

Bonbon screwed up her eyes. What was happening to Chips? Jeez, not this again. 'Don't do that, it makes my ears feel hot. I don't think it's a very good thing to do to other people's ears.' Bonbon looked at Jinx. She was doing it as well. Stupid hot ears. 'I didn't hurt it.'

The thing's head was stuck inside Jinx's cuddle, its still stare fixed on Bonbon.

Bonbon bent to pick up her feathers. She hadn't hurt it. And it was feather day. She turned to walk back to the vacuum hatch. 'I didn't hurt it.' She shook her head. 'I didn't.' She went back inside the kitchen, feeling weird. Oh dear. She would have liked to feel better about what had happened just then, with the feathers. Maybe now would be a good time to go and see if they were in the mood. That would make her feel better. She went to the big room, hoping that the She-one had come home while she'd been outside. Empty. As she turned to leave, the He-one appeared at the door.

'Are you looking for some affection already?' he asked her as she lay across his shoe. He plonked himself down on the sofa then leaned forward to pick Bonbon up.

She would have preferred the She-one this evening. She didn't know why. Maybe because of what had just happened; the She-one would have been better. Oh well. Never mind. She rolled onto her stomach and let the fingers brush up her back.

'I tell you each time that whatever you say here is confidential,' he said without gesturing. Gestures leaked, no, they trickled little bits of personality into an exchange. That was not neutral. Personality was not neutral.

'I know.'

'And so? Why do you keep asking?' The frames of his glasses cut horizontally through his pupils so that he was not quite looking at her; maintaining a barrier; not a barrier, a filter that, well, filtered his gaze.

Barrier indeed. Not in this office.

'I don't know really…'

'Yes, you do.'

She puffed up her cheeks then blew the air out slowly. 'Because I'm worried that some stuff might be illegal.'

He nodded. 'Right.'

'That would change things, wouldn't it?'

'If the authorities needed to know something, I would have to tell them.'

'Okay.'

'But then you knew that, didn't you?'

'Well… Yes.'

'So, how does that make you feel?'

'I haven't really thought about it.'

'Guilty?' He let his eyebrows go up slightly.

'Erm. Yes. I mean, I don't agree with… how they go about things. So I've become a bit of a rebel, I mean, I'd be in so much trouble if they had any idea about… my role.'

'In trouble with the authorities?'

'No!' she grinned. 'No, sorry… In trouble with my employers. Big trouble, though. The biggest trouble, in fact.'

'Why?'

'Well… I have access to some fairly secret stuff and I've been… abusing that privilege somewhat…'

'And would that be the ultimate punishment? Getting into trouble with your employers?'

'I need them in order to do what I do. But I just don't know if what I'm doing is good or bad any more. From a moral viewpoint, that is.'

'You feel responsible.'

'—.' She did a little swimming-duck movement with her head and looked to the side. A lateral nod. Lateral nodding, literally sticking your neck out – but that was a guarded gesture. Or perhaps she was being coy? It was certainly another veiled gesture. Was it because of him that she kept on letting up these veiled gestures? Let's see: was this the eighth or the ninth session of veiled gestures? He would check his notes afterwards… He was pretty sure it was the ninth.

He took the duck movement as a 'yes' to feeling guilty and shook his head. 'You shouldn't.' Drat. His opinion. And a head-shake. Drat, drat, drat. Try again. 'I wonder why you do… Why is that? Tell me.' No gestures. Concentrate, Hamish, for goodness' sake.

'Like I just said… erm… I've abused my situation a little.'

'I know that's what you said but…' His hand wandered up into the air and opened as if to release the question he didn't have prepared. It scratched his ear just in time and laid itself back down on the desk. 'Why don't you just confess? And accept whatever that leads to?'

She shook her head. The clusters of little painted beads hanging from her ears clacked. 'It wouldn't do any good, not when it's just me. I'd be the individual against the system; one of those stories.'

Yes; no. She was quite right. Best not go down that road. 'Some might say that you're in a corner, which means that morally you are… free.'

'No. I used to feel moral, and free. But now I'm starting to believe that I'm not really helping anyone.'

He blinked to switch off a sigh. Little invisible hands snaked out from his body and floated in all directions; some towards her feet and her bottom to lift her out of her chair while others went out of the window to drag back blankets of cloud which they wrapped around her, tucking her feet into the cottony folds and rocking the whole swirly bundle until she dozed off to sleep.

Oh for heaven's sake! How long had that thought taken? These were not his normal thought processes; he understood his normal thought processes; he knew himself. He glanced at her expression, pouty with rearing eyebrows. Concerned. Childlike. That was it! She was projecting caring tendencies onto him. He sucked ropes of air through flaring nostrils. She cared for him.

He'd experienced this before – of course – with many of his patients. It was like being a medium; transmitting messages to the patient from, essentially, their own ghost. The ghost would tip him off about the mortal's feelings towards him, but these feelings had never taken him over. This time, with Emma, it was different… It was like the documentaries about ghost-followers who would be in mid-conversation with a spirit before suddenly bursting into tears; 'Don't make me feel what you're feeling,' they would say to the ghost, 'just tell me your story.'

Sooner or later he would have to have a similar chat with Emma. But that was not for now.

'You think that what you're involved in – which uniquely involves bereaved people – am I right?'

She nodded a normal, non-duck nod.

'Is… is morally wrong – even though you originally thought it was right – and now you're feeling guilty and scared that you'll be found out. Am I right?'

She exhaled and smiled. 'I suppose. I'm not sure…'

His face was hot. Ah. That could mean that hers was too. It

looked like it was. He'd picked up on something; now, this was, indeed, projection and this would have to be brought up… Unless it was relief she was feeling… It was a very relieved-sounding reply she'd given, but, he didn't feel relieved. Did he? If she'd just managed to unload some of her worry then perhaps he did…

This would have to be brought up.

'Why?' he went on. 'What part of what I've just said don't you agree with?'

'I always thought that I didn't care about being found out by the people I work for, as when I originally started to do, erm, what I do, it was to counterbalance their immorality.'

'Counterbalance… In whose eyes? Yours?'

'The world's.'

'You think you've wronged the world?'

'Sort of… There was just this one thing I did that makes me feel a bit panicky sometimes. And it made me start to question… all the other, erm, things.' She let her hand flop at her wrist. 'I'm sure nothing'll come of it.'

A hand-flop. A brush-off. Hamish would have scowled if he allowed himself to do that kind of thing. Instead, he bent forward.

'How would you feel if you could be certain that no one would ever find out about… whatever it is you've done?'

She sighed. 'Relieved.'

'So you'll only really have wronged the world if you get found out?'

'Ha!' She uncrossed and re-crossed her legs. 'And that seems like more of a possibility now, you know, since I went a bit too far… And then, maybe, everything I did would get reversed and all those people would be doubly wronged when they didn't even know they'd been wronged… in the first place.'

He allowed his pupils a rim-free view of the pupils that studied his shoulder. He would get this out of her. 'Go on.'

She half-laughed. 'I don't think I can. I'm used to being so secretive about everything.'

He swallowed and hid his pupils again. 'Shall I help you?'

'You can try if you like.'

'What do you talk about with these bereaved people?'

'Cells.'

'Cells. Okay. And what happens to these cells?'

'—.'

'Do they get used for research?'

'No.'

'Do they get frozen?'

'Sometimes.'

'So they have to be stored for… whatever use they might have afterwards. Like, well, sperm in a sperm bank.'

She went red and half-smiled for a quarter of a breath. Then a nod.

Right.

That confirmed that then. She had sniggered at the word 'sperm' – oh dear. Why oh dear? Did that disappoint him? It was an embarrassed snigger; if she cared about him then she would be particularly vulnerable to embarrassment in his presence. Perhaps he should jump on the desk and shout 'sperm, sperm, sperm!' right into her face. Good God, where on Earth had that come from? The laughing gnome in his head chuckled. When was the last time he had used the laughing gnome? He never felt the need to laugh during his sessions… Next session. They would have to talk about all of this pollution during the following session. It wouldn't be appropriate now… Although… He checked the time; it was already time.

She saw him checking and checked as well then reached for her bag. 'It's already time.'

'Yes.'

'To be continued.'

'Next time, yes. Thank you, Emma.'

'Thank you. Do you want the door shut?'

'No, leave the door.'

He watched as her skirt licked at her ankles all the way along the corridor.

Blankey!

She sat in the middle of the garden all gathered under her humcoat.

Her humcoat was very nice; it was made out of lots of grey cat tails, all sewn together, and she had a thing on her head that was the same as the cat tails, but just one maybe, all curled up like it was sleeping.

Jinx shivered. She hated grey cats. One had chased her from the green box to the vacuum hatch ages ago. It would have caught her but Bonbon grabbed it by the tail and pulled. It made a horrible noise and showed all its teeth at Bonbon, and was just about to swipe her with its hairy hand when Bonbon threw a handful of little stones into its eyes.

Bonbon was so brave.

Good job it was little-stone day – what if it had been feather day?

Jinx shivered again.

Blankey rearranged herself while Jinx watched from the dining room.

'Jinx!'

Bonbon! 'Yes, Bonbon!'

'What are you doing? It's hair day!'

Jinx got up and walked slowly to the kitchen; dragging one foot behind then the other, then the other, then the other. When she got to the door she turned to look at the pattern she had made. A trail of long footprints. Like that picture of the He-one where everything was white and he had long flat feet. 'Skis,' she said. They were 'ski' footprints.

Oops; funny how that happened sometimes. When she was looking at something and she didn't know what it was, a tiny voice would whisper a word inside her head and she was sure that the word was the name of the thing she was looking at… Like the grey-cat day; 'Did you see that? The cat nearly hit you with its hand, Bonbon! It really did, it really did!'

'The what, Jinx? The what nearly hit me with its hand?'

And then there was the death day. The death day had been the most scary of all the days. Bonbon had seen it too. She was the one who saw it first because she knew that she wouldn't hurt it when she started to pull out its feathers. Chips had seen it because he started to do that thing that made Bonbon's ears red. Jinx had been the last to see it, but when she did, the little voice had said 'death' long, long after it had said 'bird'.

'You're right, Bonbon,' Jinx had said afterwards. 'You didn't hurt it.'

'I know, Jinx,' she had replied. 'I don't know why, but I think that nothing could have hurt it. It was already too hurt.'

Jinx knew why.

On the other side of the ski footprints and the other side of the glass door, Blankey and Bonbon stood together looking down at Blankey's feet. Ooo, why was that? Jinx ran out across the hall, across the kitchen, out of the vacuum hatch and into the middle of Outside.

'Jinx, Jinx! Look what I've got.' Blankey stuck a leg out of her humcoat and turned it this way then that way.

Jinx ran over and looked at the end of the leg. 'Oh!' she said.

'And another one.' Blankey pulled up a few little cat tails so Jinx could see the side of the other foot. She was right; there was another one the same. And they were both grey, like her coat and the curly sleeping-tail on her head.

'Just like them!' Jinx shook her head. 'Just like what they wear!'

'Can you walk?' Bonbon asked.

Blankey nodded big nods before lifting her knee to hip height and planting her foot on the ground a long way in front of her. She did it again with the other leg and continued like that around the middle of Outside.

'Oh,' said Bonbon.

'That's not proper walking!' laughed Jinx.

Blankey showed her teeth. 'It is.'

'Shut up, Jinx.' Then: 'Don't listen to her, Blankey.'

'Why don't *we* have shoes, Bonbon? We don't even have our humcoats.'

Bonbon blinked.

'The She-one leaves my humcoat in my room so I can put it on whenever I want.' Blankey put her hands on her hips and stuck her lips out at Bonbon.

Bonbon stiffened. Blankey's room. Lucky old Blankey with her room and her dead-cat shoes. And her stupid dead-cat humcoat and her stupid mouth sticking out like Jinx's bum-hole after she'd eaten a piece of the plant. Bonbon shivered. She wanted her own humcoat so badly. Even if it wasn't made out of fluffy long things all attached to each other like that. Why did *she* get all this stuff? Blankey didn't ever feel like searching for stones and hair and feathers and string, because she had much better things in her stupid room. She had cushions, like the ones they jumped on when it was feather day, but her ones were little and had been made for her basket. She said she had loads of them. She said that she had another thing in her basket, made out of the same stuff as her humcoat, but she didn't put it on; it was just to sleep on so that she didn't get cold at night. And then there was that thing that she stamped on with her foot to make flakes come out whenever she wanted them. Even in the middle of the night.

And now these bloody shoes.

Jinx put her head on one side. 'Can we see your room, Blankey?'

Bonbon looked at her. She just got weirder and weirder. 'What a stupid thing to say.'

'Chips and Blankey come to our Outside all the time.'

Bonbon scratched her elbow and it made her shiver again. Chips and Blankey did come there all the time. She looked up towards the top of the bars. They seemed to go all wobbly at the very top. No… No. It just wasn't right. And anyway, she really didn't want to see Blankey's bloody room. Why did Jinx have such weird ideas? 'We've never been outside of our Outside.'

'We've never tried.' Jinx put her hands on her hips.

Bonbon's mouth opened to answer, then closed again. They hadn't ever tried… But… This was stupid, what was she even thinking of, listening to Jinx? And why was Jinx being so stupid, standing there with her hands on her hips like that? 'No!' said Bonbon. 'We are not going outside of Outside.' She made to leave but turned around and came back again. 'And Blankey and Chips have never, never, come inside the house, Jinx! So you can't go into theirs!' She was really shouting.

'I just don't understand, Bonbon,' Jinx sniffed. 'Why do you have to be so nasty?'

Blankey stroked her cat tails and watched. 'But you don't go out,' she said. 'How can you come and see my room if you don't go out?'

'That's right,' said Bonbon. 'How can we, Jinx?'

Jinx wiped at one eye then licked at a shiny line that ran from her nose and over her top lip.

Bonbon put her hands over her ears. 'I'm going back.' And she turned and left.

'Why are your eyes all wet?' said Blankey.

Jinx sniffed again. If they hadn't tried to go outside then that was the only reason why they'd never been. Her bottom lip popped out and she let it wobble. If they never tried then that was the only reason why they would never go. That was all… But only she thought these things and, and, it seemed like she mustn't; nobody else thought these things. A word popped into her head.

'I'm crying, Blankey.'

'Oh,' said Blankey.

Blankey saw it. Jinx knew that she saw it because she looked at Jinx the way Chips had looked at the dead bird, sort of, frightened. Then she put out a hand and stroked Jinx's face all over, murmuring, 'Oooo… Oooo' as if she were crying too.

'I'm going now, I'm cold.' Jinx took Blankey's hand from her face and squeezed it. 'I really like your shoes.' And she turned and left.

Bonbon was getting it. Jinx didn't feel like it so she went straight to bed. Stupid Bonbon.

Later, she woke up and felt Bonbon next to her. It was dark but not too dark that she couldn't see Bonbon's still, blonde head. Jinx rolled onto her back and went to sleep.

Something ducked down below the edge of the basket just as Jinx turned over. He didn't want to be seen. When he was sure that she was really asleep again, he peeked over the edge and continued to watch her. She had one arm up behind her head and all of her hair was gathered up into it, somehow; he knew it was all up in her arm because there was no hair around her face; he could follow the edge of her face as it upped and downed over eyebrows and cheekbones all the way across to her chin without one piece of hair getting in the way. Then the line started again at her shoulder where it turned into an arm that lay over a tummy; its fingers disappearing around the curve of a waist. He put his hand out for the third time that night but again he remembered just in time. Drawing his hand back he tucked it under his other arm.

Poor Jinx. Bonbon could be so mean to her sometimes. She would get so red and cross. Jinx was just clingy. That was all… She had touched his arm when he said that. She liked it when he said that.

He rubbed his mouth and looked up again at the bits that he liked the most. Her breasts. Even though she never had her humcoat on when she saw him, for some reason, he didn't like to just stare at them; it made him feel… bad. Maybe it was because he didn't have any.

He'd felt strange that time when she talked about his thing like that. He didn't like talking about what was different about them, but at the same time, he did like to think about it. And look at it. She wasn't allowed to know that he liked that. He didn't know why she wasn't allowed to know; but she wasn't. He blinked. Sometimes when his water bowl and his food bowl were empty, he would turn them upside down and think about Jinx's breasts. Although, looking at them now, he realized they were not quite the same. Jinx's breasts were more like… What were they more like? His own buttocks, yes! He'd never thought of that before. He arranged himself so that he was on his knees and sitting on the heels of his feet. Then he sat up straight, reached behind him and started to rub his own buttocks. His eyes closed… Yes, this was what Jinx's breasts were like.

'Chips…'

He stopped and opened his eyes just as Jinx was closing hers. She sighed and turned her face the other way.

Chips froze, hands still on his buttocks. He stared at Jinx without breathing. When he absolutely had to breathe, he thought to himself that it was time to go. Rocking back onto the soles of his feet, he unfolded upwards and crept back towards the vacuum hatch.

CHAPTER 3

'Trish has been replaced and I don't know why.'

He looked over his glasses at her, his eyes two glistening strips. 'Who's Trish?'

'A colleague at work.'

'Does *she* know why?'

'I don't know. I can't contact her.' A laugh. 'I've never met her. I wouldn't have known except the new Trish makes lots of spelling mistakes in her emails.'

'The new woman is also called Trish?'

'It's a work name.'

'—.'

'I'm not called "Emma" at work. I have a work name.'

'And the person that replaces you would… take that work name?'

'Exactly.' A sigh. 'I'm just wondering if she left or if she was made to go.'

'Maybe she was old enough to retire.'

She almost laughed. 'I hadn't thought of that.' They smiled, their gazes running forward and catching each other like two happy children. Hers flicked to the clock then back again, her smile gone.

Bonbon was the first to wake up. She sat up and looked over the edge of the basket. Both bowls were full.

She stood up and stretched.

'Come back for a minute, Bonbon.'

'—.'

'Oh please, I get cold when you're not here.'

Bonbon's chin juddered and her teeth made clicking noises. 'The bowls are full, Jinx,' she managed, swinging one leg over the side of the basket – oh those tiles were cold! 'And it's string day.' She walked on tiptoes towards the bowls, took three mouthfuls from Jinx's bowl and started to eat from her own, but her shoulders shook so much that she couldn't chew properly. The flakes weren't as nice as they usually were; they were too big for her mouth today. Her mouth and teeth shivered as she chewed and the shivering seemed to take up all the flake room. She tried a smaller mouthful. Still too big. The dining room would be warm. She would lie on the carpet in the dining room, that's what she would do. She wobbled from the kitchen and stopped in front of the dining-room door, standing on one foot, then the other. Bugger, it was closed. And usually there was quite a lot of string in the dining room. She hugged herself.

'Bonbon, why didn't you eat your flakes?' Jinx stood at the kitchen door rubbing one eye.

'Too cold.'

'Too cold even to eat?'

Bonbon ignored her and carried on hugging.

Jinx watched as her hands almost touched between her shoulders. 'I don't think it's any colder than yesterday. Look at me, Bonbon; I'm not cold like you, am I?'

'—.'

'I know! Would you like to lie on a cushion?'

A nod.

'Come on then.' Jinx held out her hand. 'Come with me to the big room. We'll find a really good cushion for you to lie on.'

'Not the shoe one,' Bonbon shivered.

'No. Not the shoe one.'

In the living room, Jinx rubbed her chin as she walked below the sofa and its row of cushions. Once she got to the end of the sofa she turned around and walked slowly back again. Hmmm… The heart-shaped one? The sausage one? Wool? Velvet? Cotton? Plastic? Nope, not plastic…

'Which one, Jinx?' shivered Bonbon.

The really woolly one. It would have to be the really woolly one. But she didn't know the word for it. She reached up and pulled at a corner; fluffy rabbits scampered through the inside of Jinx's head. The cushion fell to the floor in a floppy somersault and the rabbits were gone. 'This one, Bonbon. The angora one.'

Bonbon was already leaning against it, eyes closed. 'I don't know what that word means, Jinx.'

Jinx helped Bonbon swing up onto the middle of the cushion and made her lie flat on her belly. 'Better?'

'I want my humcoat,' Bonbon replied, her buttocks twitching.

Jinx glanced around the room for something to put over Bonbon. Nothing. How could there be nothing? Another cushion maybe? No, that might be too heavy. Her eyes rested on a vase in the middle of the small table. What about… Yes! She ran to the sofa and climbed onto it; from there she stepped onto the small table, towards the vase, and lifted out a rose with both hands cupping the underside of its head. She was careful not to touch the long green bit. That was really dangerous that bit. She threw the rose onto the floor then climbed down after it. 'I'm coming, Bonbon!' she said as she pulled handfuls of petals from their base. The Dead Bird watched what she was doing from the inside of her head. She shuddered and started to pull the petals out gently, making a careful pile next to her. 'You know, Bonbon, we should have a petal day.'

'I don't know… that word… Jinx.'

Jinx climbed up onto the cushion with the petals under her

arm. Bonbon was still on her stomach, her face half-hidden in the angora and the one eye that Jinx could see was shadowy and shut. Jinx arranged the petals over Bonbon; there were enough to make nearly three layers! She would feel so much warmer now.

'Hmmm…' hmmmed Bonbon.

Kneeling beside Bonbon, Jinx put her hands on her hips and beamed.

'There aren't enough flowers… to have a petal day…' Bonbon said so quietly that Jinx put her hair behind her ears to hear her.

'Yes. You're probably right. They are lovely and soft, though, aren't they?'

'—.'

'It would have been a good idea, wouldn't it, Bonbon?'

'—.'

Jinx looked around her, hands still on hips. 'Dum-dee-dum,' she said, then: 'I know! I'll just go and get some of your flakes to put next to you. In case you get hungry.' She climbed down from the cushion. 'I'll be back in a minute, so don't worry. I'll come straight back, okay?'

Bonbon could be so sweet sometimes. It was probably because she was poorly. It was so nice when she let Jinx do things for her, because there were lots of things that Jinx could do, but when Bonbon wasn't poorly she had to do what Bonbon wanted her to do. Jinx crossed the hall, leaping over the tiles almost one at a time, trying to fit one whole tile into each leap. So today wouldn't be string day! Hurray! Unless… Unless she collected so much string that Bonbon would be really pleased with her. After clearing two whole tiles in a row, she had entered the kitchen and added a twirl to each leap. Jump, twirl! Then maybe Bonbon would realize that she was good at things too and then she would let her do more things… Jump, twirl! Like the petal day idea. Bonbon had liked that idea. 'There aren't enough flowers to have a petal day,' she had said. That meant that she had liked the idea. Jump, twirl! Maybe there were more flowers somewhere. If only Jinx could find them. Jump, twirl! Jinx stopped just in front of the flakes.

How had Bonbon known that petals came from flowers? Jinx thought.

She said that she didn't know what that word meant…

Jinx bent towards the flakes and caught a big salty whiff.

Bonbon must have smelled them and realized what they were! That was it. They did smell lovely.

She scooped up a handful and started back towards the big room.

Or, perhaps she had opened her eye, very quickly, just to see what Jinx was covering her up with.

Yes, that must have been it, she thought as she skipped across the hall.

Jinx spent the first half of the morning trying to get into the dining room. First of all, she tried to jump high enough to reach the handle. That didn't work. She tried to climb up the door frame. That sort of worked, but she only managed to get a little way up and her foot would get tired. She looked for something to climb on to be able to reach the handle. There was that long pointy thing by the door. What was the word for it? The thing with a spike at the end. She looked at it for a minute. Nope, the word didn't come. Funny that sometimes it did, sometimes it didn't. Anyway, the thing could help her to reach the handle. Jinx went up to it and put her arms around it. It was dry this time. Sometimes it was wet and Jinx would drink the water that collected at its spike. She pulled at it and the spike moved forward. She pulled again and the whole thing moved, Yes! She yanked it, hard, once, twice… The thing started to wobble, she tried to steady it but it was too strong. The wobble turned into a sway. She let go and it fell backwards into a row of shoes.

'Jinx?'

Bonbon! 'Yes, Bonbon?' Jinx ran to the big-room door and looked at the big cushion and the pile of petals, all flat and peaceful except for a little blonde head that stood up at one end.

'What was that?' husked the head.

Bonbon sounded terrible.

'Um. The thing with the spike.'

'Oh.'

'It fell.'

'Oh.' Bonbon put her head back down, then lifted it back up again. 'Are you alright?'

Jinx laughed and ran over to the cushion. 'Yes, Bonbon!' She twirled once in front of Bonbon. 'Look, Bonbon, I'm fine!'

'Alright.' The head went back down. 'You mustn't play with the umbrella. If it fell on you you'd be really hurt.'

Playing? She wasn't playing! 'I wasn't! I just…' She put her hands on her hips. 'Well, someone has to get into the dining room for string, and the only way to reach the handle is to climb up the umbr, umbr, the umbr…' Jinx stopped. 'How did you know the word for it?'

'We both know the word for it.'

'No! No, we don't!'

'Of course we do.'

'I *never* knew that word.'

'Oh, Jinx. Just, go away now please. I'm too tired… Leave me alone.'

Jinx stared at Bonbon. The corners of her mouth started to pull downwards. She could be really mean sometimes. She sniffed and walked towards the door.

Really mean.

Jinx spent the second half of the morning in the toilet box.

At lunchtime, she waited for them to come home to fill up her food bowl. Bonbon's was still full but Jinx wouldn't touch it, not even one flake. She huffed. This was silly. They always waited for her to come home at lunchtime and she never did. Well, she had done when it was warm time, but hardly ever since. But they waited for her anyway. In fact, there were a few things that they did that were silly. Like collecting things. All this string, paper, feathers, hair, stones – what were they collecting them for? For their basket? But the soft bit in the bottom of the basket was far nicer than all of the dirty and spiky stuff they put on top of it, and the big She-one would sometimes come and take all of their stuff away again. Jinx didn't know what she did with it, but sometimes they'd go to the basket at night and it would all be gone and the basket smelled just lovely. Like the petals in the big room. Jinx really liked going to sleep in it when it smelled like that. Bonbon would go quiet. For at least two days she would hardly say a thing.

What was that?

The front door. Jinx jumped up and fluttered her eyelashes. The big She-one appeared. It was really her!

'Hello, Jinx,' she said, bending down and stroking Jinx's head.

Jinx closed her eyes and pressed her head against the hand.

'Didn't you eat your food?' said the big She-one, picking up the bowls.

Jinx opened her mouth but couldn't answer.

'And where is the other little chilly-billy?' Susan took the flakes from the top of the fridge and topped up Jinx's bowl.

Ah yes! Bonbon! She had to go and see Bonbon to know that she was poorly. Jinx opened her mouth. No words.

'Hmmm? Where is she, Jinx?' She took a sheet of Fibre-Web and wiped around the edge of Jinx's bowl without looking at Jinx.

Jinx stood, making shapes with her mouth, before stepping forward and pinching the back of the She-one's leg.

'Ow!' She looked down.

Jinx held out her arm and pointed towards the big room.

'Is Bonbon in there?'

She tried to nod but couldn't, so she pointed again.

The She-one put down the bowl and strode towards the big room. 'Oh my roses!' she said when she saw the cushion. 'These weren't the cheapest things to take apart, you two…' She bent down and lifted off the petals. Bonbon's teeth clacked together. 'Oh no! Oh no, not my Bonbon!' The top of Susan's head creased into lines. Jinx stared at it and took a step backwards. 'You poor things, you've been so cold.'

A scarf, thought Susan, a big scarf would do nicely. She opened the hall cupboard. Honestly, how could she have left them so long without their humcoats, she thought as she unwound a scarf from a coat hanger. Poor things. She turned towards the living room, then stopped and started to unwind a second one for Jinx.

When she returned, Bonbon had curled herself into a ball and Jinx was placing the petals back over her. Susan smiled. 'Okay, Jinx, let's just take these off,' she said as she removed a petal. Jinx glared at her and kicked her hand, actually kicked it; hard. Susan withdrew her hand and gaped for a second. Jinx had never shown any signs of aggression. It must have been because of Bonbon; she was worried about Bonbon. 'Alright, we'll leave the petals; I just want to wrap her up in this.' She showed her the scarf, then started to wrap Bonbon – and the petals – up inside it. Jinx watched what she was doing, leaned forward, and stroked the hand where she had kicked it.

'Oh, you sweetie,' said Susan. 'Look,' she reached behind her, 'I found one for you too.' She held up the other scarf in front of Jinx before wrapping it around her and letting one end flop over her head and face. The top of Jinx's head emerged like a baby bird from an egg. She shuddered, hmmm, this long woolly thing was lovely. She couldn't imagine ever wanting to take it off; maybe she had been colder than she'd thought! She closed her eyes, not as cold as Bonbon, though, and wove her fingers in and out of the little holes that the wool made.

Awake. Bonbon was awake. Whiteness and strange voices and that smell… Like toilet box mixed with wet tiles. Something else was different, what was that? She felt, sort of… still. The shivering had stopped. She held one hand with the other. Warm. Then her tummy with both. Still warm.

'Yes, well, maybe the other one is less active. That would make her less fatigued, a bit plumper, perhaps.'

'And so less susceptible to getting sick like, well, Bonbon did.'

'Exactly. Although they should have both had their humcoats in September, really.'

Susan wrinkled up her forehead and looked at the shape of Bonbon underneath one white blanket and one green blanket in a tiny cot that stood on a table between herself and the doctor.

'Did you… Have you had them for a long time?'

'Seventeen months.'

'Did you put coats on them last year?'

'Yes, yes, I did. It's just that, they got a bit worn, and so this year I was hoping to get new coats and, well, time got the better of me… And I didn't realize they could get outside until quite recently. It turns out that they've been climbing through the vacuum hatch. I should have realized with all the stuff they collect and bring in… I've been rather a bad mistress.'

The doctor eyed Susan and smiled mimicking the same curve as the mask that hammocked her chin. 'Gosh, I've seen worse cases than this.' She let one hand flop at its wrist. 'If there's one thing that this job has taught me, it's that people can be shitty. I've seen chopped off ears from "haircuts" gone wrong, I've seen mangled limbs from cat and dog attacks because all the "pets" are kept in the same room – can you imagine that? Deep bloody rings around the buttocks – which is actually quite common – from where owners tie them down to toilets while they go to work. I've dealt with some gruesome situations, this is nothing but a teensy cold.' She gestured towards Bonbon.

Susan stared, mouth open. 'So, the ones that have been, erm, maltreated, what happens to them when they come here; do they get taken away from their owners?'

'Depends. Sometimes, yes.' She rubbed her temple with the back of her wrist and frowned at Bonbon. 'Hmmm,' she said.

'What is it?' Susan frowned in the same direction.

'That ear could do with pinning.'

'Oh, really?'

'Hmmm,' affirmed the doctor.

'Which one?'

'The one on the left.' She put her hand in the cot and, with one finger, pushed Bonbon's face so she was looking to the right. 'You see?'

Susan nodded then shook her head. 'No, not really.'

'It's subtle. It will disrupt her balance, though.' She withdrew her finger and Bonbon's head snapped back to the centre. Bonbon showed her teeth. 'Is she a bit wobbly on her feet?'

Susan upside-down smiled and looked to the left shaking her head. 'No,' she said.

'Slow? I mean, not agile.'

'No.'

'Clumsy?'

'No. In fact, she's very nimble.'

'Grumpy?'

Susan's pupils snatched back to the centres of their eyes. 'Yes! She can be really grumpy.'

'Ah.' The doctor flung a hand towards the sticky-out ear. 'That's what's causing it.'

'Seriously?'

'Yep,' she nodded. 'It might seem unimportant to you but,' she took a ruler from her front pocket and bent towards the ear, 'it makes a big difference to missy here. Can you imagine feeling constantly unsteady?'

Susan frowned at Bonbon's ear. 'Can we do something about that?'

'Oh yes!' said the doctor. 'It takes ten minutes, spray anaesthetic, no incisions; just a couple of stitches.'

Bonbon sneezed.

The doctor pulled her mask up over her mouth and pressed a button on the wall. 'I'm going to need another blanket for my patient, please.'

Susan jumped. A door whirred somewhere behind her. A woman came in with a small blanket, tilted her head and smiled at Bonbon, put the blanket on the table and left. The doctor tucked the blanket around the edges of Bonbon. 'You really are quite chilly, aren't you?' Then she stood back with her hands on her hips and looked at Susan.

'When can she have it done? The, erm, pinning.'

'I'll have to check with my secretary.'

'Would she have to stay overnight?'

'Usually, no. But given her condition… We wouldn't want to take any risks with infection.'

'Yes, of course.'

'Would you like to go ahead with the procedure?'

'If it's the best thing for her…'

* * *

'Tell me, what is it? I've been *so* excited!'

Watty smiled and dragged a round hat box into the door frame.

'What is it?'

The other snorted. 'A toaster.'

Drew eyed the box and frowned.

Watty sighed through half-closed eyes, then pronounced slowly: 'Why don't you come and have a listen?'

'A listen?' Drew jumped up from a large triangle-shaped beanbag on the floor in front of the fire, dropping some papers and showing off a woolly knee support; like a tree stripped of its bark, thought Watty. 'Oh yes!' And with movements so miniature, even when hurrying, that there couldn't possibly be any sound – just a swish-swishing of one bandaged foot and one almost socked – Drew padded over to the box. A manipulator of physical laws, thought Watty, watching Drew shake off the loose sock. Even when shaking off loose socks, the energy triggered by the jolt of a shoulder blade would send the shoulder through little, tiny movements, all seriesed together like one of those spinning wheels with a flickery horse galloping around its inside; yes! That was it! The shoulder was flickered into going up and then down again, like slow motion, like little men were building up slices of shoulder until they really couldn't reach any higher and so, piece by piece, they took it all down again. With one hand, Drew pulled aside the curtain that divided the studio. The little men worked on, building upwards, then down again, calling upon every member to build up its part into a crescendo, tympani drums boomed, the notes curled out of the curtain-pulling hand and flutes tinkled the hand back down to its side. All was still. Watty patted trouser pockets, breast pockets, the little zippy sleeve pocket and glanced about the floor. All of that would have to be written down later, especially the little men and the pieces of shoulder.

'If you picked your feet up, you wouldn't get splinters.'

'Can't get splinters with socks.' And as if to prove this, Drew twirled on the ball of a foot, sending out ripples of music…

'You're not wearing any. You're wearing a bandage and you just kicked the other sock off.'

Drew picked up the non-bandaged foot and held it up at head height, then swivelled over, heel, ball, heel, ball, on the protected one, laughing.

'You really must be careful when bending your knee like that…

You know, I don't think you're switched on enough to deserve this present,' Watty said. 'If you bugger yourself up any more, you won't be able to run after it.'

The foot now back on the floor, and hands now on knees, Drew bent forward to put one ear to the box. 'Run after it?'

Damn. The cat's, *dog's*, nose was peeking out of the bag.

'I can't hear anything.'

'Maybe it can hear you and it's silently worrying about its future.'

Drew's eyes gaped suddenly. 'You didn't?'

'Say "Jas-per",' mouthed Watty.

'Jaspa?' queried the other.

'WOOF!' said the hatbox.

'Oh! Oh!' Jumping backwards, hands on chest. 'You did! You bought me a dog!' Mouth corners climbed cheeks. 'I don't believe it!' Tearing the lid from the hatbox.

Short biscuit-coloured fur turned inside the box, glimmering golden and shadowing ecru. It jumped once, then again and knocked the whole box onto its side. A tongue dangled from black-lined lips as it ran towards Drew and black padded paws landed on the knee support.

'He's lovely! He's *beautiful*! Yes, Jasper, you are *so* beautiful and you like being fussed, don't you? Yes, you do...' Looking up. 'Is he really mine?'

Crouching down. 'I think he's decided that *you* are *his*.'

Jasper marched all over Drew, who was now lying flat to facilitate this; his tail seemed to become three tails, his nose explored the back of a leg or the hollow of a cheek. Then a bark. Then another.

Drew looked up as Watty produced a plastic tube, opened it, and pulled out a wet wand with a gooey loop at one end. Watty blew. Five or six bubbles, each smaller than the one before, waddled out of the wand like a duck family.

The biscuit-coloured legs skid, skid, skidded towards the duck-bubbles that seemed to want to land anywhere but into the mouth of the puppy. But more appeared. And more. And finally he got a big one that made him sit and blink and lick his own nose for a moment before barking for more.

Drew, laughing, had rolled over to watch it, head shuddering between its shoulders, a ping-pong ball between two hairdryers.

Watty took a deep breath. 'Would you like to keep him…'

'He mustn't eat those bubbles, though, he'll get stomach ache…'

'Even if it means being a responsible adult, taking him for walks, picking up his *poo*…'

Drew wiped at the puppy's mouth with the fallen sock. 'He's staying. He'll be my confidant when you're all mean and grumpy.'

Watty squatted in front of them. 'Now, don't get cross.'

'Why?'

'I think we could be happy. The three of us. I think we should try to be just the three of us.'

'—.'

'Drew?'

Jasper gnashed his teeth at each wipe of the sock.

'I couldn't let you keep him and then tell you *why* I'd bought him. Better to be honest from the off—'

'Ow!' said Drew, tapping the black nose before tickling the groove between Jasper's eyebrows. 'The thing is, I can't give up on Isabel. Not at this stage in her development.'

They sat for a moment, their faces angled towards the little bean-shaped being in the next room, suspended in its artificial womb.

'Will you at least think about it?'

'Apart from anything else, what would I *do* with her?'

Watty's eyebrows flicked up.

'We've been through this.' Drew clasped a golden ear in each hand. 'I just couldn't.'

'Alright.'

'Please don't ask me that again.'

'Alright.' Watty reached forward and shook Jasper's paw.

'I just need some support,' said Drew. 'I know what I've done and how serious it is… But I'm not very sure about it.'

'I know,' said Watty. 'I know you.' Then: 'Don't worry, I'm here.'

* * *

Awake. Jinx stretched her arms out in front of her even before she opened her eyes. They couldn't stretch very far as they were wrapped in the toasty warm thing that the She-one had given her. She hadn't moved one tiny bit since she'd been wrapped up inside it.

Sitting up straight, she reached behind her and scratched her shoulder; then, with her eyes still closed, she settled back into her slouchy position, like a fat pigeon.

Bonbon! Her eyes pinged open and looked towards the angora cushion.

The petals were gone. There was no blonde head sleeping at one end. 'Bonbon?' she called. No answer, maybe she was very asleep? Or had she been taken to a different room? Holding the warm thing around her, Jinx got up and swish-swished over to the angora cushion.

Empty.

She turned and looked at the door. 'Kitchen,' she said out loud, and shuffled towards the big-room door to cross the hall. If she was in the kitchen, she'd be in the basket. Oops! Jinx tripped on a corner of the scarf, shook her foot and carried on walking. And if she was in the basket, she'd probably be wrapped up in a long thing like Jinx was. Ah ha! The dining room! Jinx stopped at the dining-room door. It was open. It hadn't been open earlier, could she be in there? It was always lovely and warm in there because of the nice carpet. She stepped inside. 'Bonbon!' she said. Nothing. 'BONBON!' she shouted. Nothing.

Jinx's mouth felt all dry. She wasn't at all sleepy any more. Bonbon must be in the kitchen, she must be, she thought, hurrying towards the kitchen door. 'Bonbon!' she called, as she passed the food bowls. 'Bonbon! Wake up now!' Nearing the basket, she peeped over the edge. Empty. Empty! Well, where was she then? She glanced around. Yes! Toilet box! She swished over and looked inside. Nothing. Where *could* she be? She had to be in the dining room. That was the only other thing that had changed since she'd been asleep. Perhaps they had put her up on the table?

Jinx made her way back. Her head felt big and poundy and her legs were all springy, but not a nice springy; she wondered if her feet would keep her up each time she put one of them down in front of her. Maybe they had things up on the table; things to make Bonbon better and so it was just easier to keep her on the table. With the things close by.

Jinx's ears thump, thump, thumped and her eyes were dry from looking about everywhere. Then she was there, at the dining-room door, but she couldn't remember getting there and then couldn't remember getting to the table but she was there and so shouted up at it: 'BONBON!' No answer. 'BONBON!' No answer. 'BONBON!' The table was black today. They'd changed its colour from see-through to black. She swish-swished underneath it deciding which chair to climb before choosing the one that was sticking out slightly, as if someone had been sitting there and had not put it back afterwards. Jinx dropped the scarf, stepped out of it, pulled herself up onto the chair and closed her eyes. Please be there, please be there, please be there…

She squinted her eyes over the edge of the table, too frightened to open them fully. The table was all fuzzy from the squinting.

But there was no Bonbon.

'NO!' she shouted. 'NO!' And she slumped back into her pigeon position, this time with no scarf. She was a naked pigeon. She shivered. Her face ached and went all bendy. Mustn't do that. It makes Bonbon's ears get hot. Oh! But Bonbon wasn't there! She let herself cry. How could Bonbon's ears get hot if she wasn't even there? Jinx fell forward and cried into her knees.

Ages later, Jinx was still folded into a flattened 'Z'; one red eye was open and had stopped leaking. The other one was buried in her knee, closed and not yet needed. Her breathing had slowed down. Her mouth made the shape of Bonbon's name. She could feel the stuff that the chair-top was made out of making lines in the fronts of her legs. She shivered and thought that she should really get down. But what for? There was nothing down there… And she only needed one eye to look out of the window.

The scarf would have been nice, though.

But then maybe if she got really cold, they would take her away to the same place that Bonbon went to.

The Dead Bird lay inside her head and she let herself look at it. Probably with the other eye. That's what eyes did, when they were closed. She got closer to it, put her arms around its neck, like she had really done, and put her mouth on its head.

'A kiss,' said her real mouth, on the outside of her head.

A piece of something licked at the edge of the glass doors. What was that? Bonbon!

She sat up. There it was again! It was the colour of humcoat! The She-one had given Bonbon her humcoat! Bonbon! She climbed off the chair and ran to the window. 'BONBON!' she shouted and banged on the glass.

The humcoat moved towards the window. At the top of it was Chips's head.

'Chips!' yelled Jinx. She turned and ran across the carpet, the hall tiles, the kitchen tiles and through the vacuum hatch. 'Chips!' she said.

'Jinx!' said Chips, his head whizzing around to face her. 'What happened to your legs?'

Jinx glanced down at her legs. 'The chair did it,' she said. 'Where's Bonbon?'

Chips put his mouth on upside down and shook his head.

'She's not inside.'

'Oh.' Chips glanced around at Outside. 'She's not here either.'

'I've lost… Bonbon,' Jinx sniffed.

'Why?' said Chips.

Jinx wrinkled her eyes. They looked at each other for a moment.

'Well, she was very cold; very very cold. Then the big She-one came and put a scarf around her…'

'A what?'

'A thing to keep her warm.'

'Oh.'

'She put one around me too… and… it was so nice that I went to sleep and when I woke up Bonbon was gone.'

'Oh,' said Chips. 'Is she in the kitchen?'

Jinx shook her head.

'What about in there?' Chips poked the glass door.

'No.'

'Oh,' he said again. He stared at Jinx, then looked towards the green box. 'What about behind the green box? I haven't been over there.'

Jinx raised her eyebrows at the green box, then made her way towards it with long careful strides across the prickly AstroTurf. 'Come on, Chips!' she called. She circled the green box; no Bonbon this side, no Bonbon that side… But then…

Chips heard Jinx scream just as he cornered the green box. He stopped right next to her, right in front of the pile of feathers. The Dead Bird lay staring at them with its now empty eye socket, its face blackened and oily; its beak lay open in the shape of a cry and little wormy creatures crawled into its mouth and out of its eye.

Jinx turned to Chips. She was shivering and naked and her bottom lip stuck out. What a horrible, horrible day this had been. Chips turned too. They both faced the same way. 'I don't know why, but I don't want to look at that,' he said.

Jinx let her mouth open wide and go all wobbly. Chips, now in front of her, reached behind him for her arm and led her to a different side of the green box.

'You're all shaky,' he said, turning to face her and her wobbly mouth.

'—.'

Jinx held her own hand and pushed the fingers back. One of her feet covered up the other. Chips's own lip started to jut out and wobble. He took off his humcoat, pulled it around her, and started to button it up at the front even though she hadn't put her arms through the holes. The cold tickled and pinched his back. 'How do they let you walk around like that?'

Jinx watched as the tiny thin-lipped mouths opened and spat out their buttons, the cold bits of her all happy and tingly as all the warm he'd left inside the coat rubbed over them. Chips was so nice. He was one of the nicest littlers ever. Except for Bonbon. But then… Bonbon would never button her into a coat like this – would she?

Yes, yes. Of course she would.

Was Chips even nicer than Bonbon?

Bonbon… Her stomach bubbled. The Dead Bird lay inside her head again. She didn't feel like kissing it, like she did last time… Not now that it had changed.

Chips did up the last button, just under Jinx's chin; his teeth clacked and his fingers wobbled. He was so nice… She wanted to do something nice like put her arms around him; that would warm him up. But she was trapped inside the coat.

'You're cold like Bonbon was,' she said.

He nodded.

She opened her mouth to say something, then noticed the pointed things sticking out of his chest. What were they? She looked down his body. Bluish skin stretched over thick lines with dents between them that grew around his chest. She had them too, those liney things. But she could only feel them when she lay down; she'd never seen them like that, like that sleeping spider she once saw, with all its legs bent towards its body. 'Not sleeping,' said the inside of her head, 'dead.' She screwed up her mouth. His tummy was so empty that she could have put her whole head inside it and tucked it under his… his… 'Ribs,' said the inside of her head.

'What are you looking at?' Chips tucked his thing between his legs and crossed them.

'You look weird,' said Jinx. Chips's cheeks went pink and he looked at the floor. Oops. 'I mean,' she tried, 'you look cold, like Bonbon did.' It was true, but she had said it to cover up the 'weird' thing. Oh she'd ruined it now… He would go and she would be alone. She bent to look up into his eyes.

He looked back, but kept changing the foot he was standing on and glancing towards the hole in the fence.

Jinx had an idea: 'Will you come into my house?'

Chips widened his eyes. 'Yes.'

'Come on then!' she grinned, and started to walk towards the house, twisting at the waist as she did, twist, twist, twist, making the empty arms of the coat flap around her. Chips scampered after her, hugging himself.

Once through the vacuum hatch, Chips stopped scampering and gazed about him. It had always been dark before, now it was daylight and different. He'd been invited in. He was allowed this time…

Jinx made him sit down on the edge of the basket. This was a bit strange; what would Bonbon say? Bonbon… Her stomach felt bubbly and floaty – maybe Bonbon would get cross. Or maybe… Maybe Jinx would be really naughty and not even tell Bonbon. The idea made her feel smiley. She watched Chips watching the fridge, his head tilting as his eyes climbed to the top of it. Chips was in her house!

What could she do with him? 'Would you like some flakes?'

'Flakes?' Chips stood up.

'Undo these buttons and I'll bring you some.'

He did. She shook off the humcoat and went to fetch him her bowlful of flakes.

He fell into the bowl with his mouth open and made loud munching noises, his hands pushing small piles towards his face.

Jinx watched with her hands on her hips; it wasn't nice to eat like that, she thought as he licked at the empty bowl. She brought him Bonbon's flakes and he ate them too. She bent to sit next to him; it would have been nice to stroke his back or his leg or something… He looked up at her with eyes squished into black lines by full cheeks, his arms cuddled around the edge part of the bowl.

Jinx backed away and sat on the tiles, fiddling with things that had got stuck between the basket and the floor. A feather, a comb, a crystal from the toilet box…

'Why were you so hungry?' she asked when he'd finished eating.

He wiped his mouth.

She looked at the top of his head and thought about that for a minute.

'Can I comb your hair?'

He nodded.

She knelt behind him, catching and combing the orange glints that grew at the back of his head. Brown water rose behind her eyes with big orange flashes that turned inside it. What was that, head? She combed the hair in all different directions, glint, flash, glint, flash, until Chips slept in his hands, elbows on knees. 'Stay here with me, will you, Chips?' she said, twirling the curls on his forehead around the teeth of the comb.

'Alright,' he said, eyes closed.

In the middle of the night, Jinx woke up. A rumbly noise blew through the hair on top of her head. It sounded like that nasty vacuum bot – stopping and starting and stopping and starting... Yes, exactly like the vacuum bot but when it would get stuck in a corner; or between two things. Something was pressed against her cheek. It was warm and skinny – that's to say, it had skin. And spider-ribs. Of course it was skinny, ha! It was Chips! Although... she mustn't say that to him. He didn't like it when she said things like that. She felt the dum, dum, dum of whoever that littler was that knocked at the inside of his chest. 'Do you want to come out?' she whispered to the knocking littler as she peeked out into a room of dark shapes over the bend of a shoulder that grew into a neck.

'Heart,' said her head. No... That was wrong! A heart was the thing that one of the cushions was shaped into. That couldn't be right...

Jinx closed her eyes. It was nice to be with Chips like this – with Chips this way round. She was so used to cuddling Bonbon's back. That was nice too. But there weren't as many noises in someone's back. There was no stuck vacuum bot, or dum, dum, dum, or the sound of lips separating and a mouth swallowing and then there was the filling up and emptying of a chest and belly and the heat that got trapped between two tummies and two chests and a cheek and a shoulder. All that warmth and noise just for her.

Chips was so nice.

'Heart,' insisted her head. Hmmm... Her head could sometimes get things wrong.

Chips swallowed and the vacuum bot noise stopped. Then it started again, quietly. Jinx giggled and hushed herself, listening to see if she'd woken him up. She hoped that Chips would stay tomorrow too, if Bonbon wasn't back. Oh but... What if Bonbon came back in the morning? She would find them like this. What if the biggerers found them together like this? What if they brought Bonbon back and all three of them found her with Chips? Jinx's tongue prickled and dried. They would stand around the basket, looking at her crossly; picking Chips up and throwing him outside.

She thought.

Chips carried on making strange noises, whatever they were – the word didn't come.

She thought again.

She would get up early and make him go home. Yes! She would wake up before everybody else and he would be gone before anybody could know. Ha! Easy-peasy!

She pressed her nose into Chips's neck, yawned and her eyes closed.

What time was it? Susan peered at the wall, at the big blue projection of numbers; 03:50. That noise! God, it was deafening! Her head felt, kind of, scrunched up, as if her neck had been pressed in like a snooze button under a sleeping hand. She tried to stretch it out but there was something blocking her. Had she been properly awake, she might have known what it was... But she was still asleep. She *should* have been asleep, she thought. Hamish's arm cut through the bottom half of her pillow. Again. He *knew* he shouldn't sleep on his back. How many times had she asked him either to sleep on his side or to get one of those funny sticker things that would hold open his nostrils? He was so selfish. There was no way that he would accept this kind of behaviour from *her*. He would grump and huff when she used the SuckAway on the toilet, or accidentally set the clock figures to disco mode so that they'd flash and twirl about the bedroom at 2 a.m. Noiselessly, though. And she only knocked the buttons because her pillow was occupied by the arm. She pushed the arm further upwards, but it sprang back down again. This was so unfair. It was because she was little and he was big. If she had been on her back making noises like some kind of dying, pig-monster thing, then he would have rolled her over…

Oh fucking shut up!

She blinked in the blue and considered the processes that the air had to go through to make that kind of noise. It would dislodge, perhaps, from its rippled mould like a rocket shuddering out of its launch… For a moment, all around her twinkled with hundreds of mini rocket-snores, all the same blue as the clock light. Hmm. She had such a charming imagination.

She closed her eyes.

It never made the same noise twice. It peaked and faded and exploded and her brain would try to predict the tone of the next explosion. Was it going to crescendo here? Would it be long or short this time? And then he would swallow, or twitch, or something and her brain would think: is it going to stop now? And for a few seconds he would stop breathing altogether and she'd say *good. He's dead.* But gently, gently, it would start again.

For fuck's sake.

She winched herself up on her elbows and flopped back down again.

The noise stopped. Ha!

But the arm was still there.

She heaved the arm up into the air and threw it towards him. He caught it before it could fall back down on her. Good! He snatched his arm away, and twisted himself onto his side. The whole bed made spring noises.

Now they both lay awake and angry.

It was his fault. *He* bred all the negative energy in this house.

She swung her legs out of bed and got up.

'Where…' he said.

'Toilet,' she whispered back.

She went downstairs. There was that documentary that she'd recorded on – what was it called again? *AISD*? No. It was like 'said' but with the 's' at the end. *AIDS*. That was the only way she could remember it, ever since she had learned about it at school… There was also that other documentary. *The Mini Human Phenomenon*. That would be easy watching, and more relevant to her life than bizarre historic diseases. A sleeping pile of Jinx and scarf swelled and shrank inside her mind. She went over to the kitchen door. Poor little Jinx, all on her own. She'd forgotten to see how she was, having left her all wrapped up in the living room. But what was that noise? Was it… Was it coming from inside? Yes, yes, it was! It sounded like… snoring. She ran her thumb across the skin on her wrist and it lit up. Shining it over towards the basket, she could just about make out Jinx's loopy dark curls, even darker against her white back and… There was another back. Who the hell was that? She crept closer. A boy; it was a boy! Ha! The little *floozy*. The boy screwed up his closed eyes, slid out of Jinx's hug and climbed over the side of the basket.

'Oh no!' said Susan. 'Sorry. *Please* don't go. I didn't want to…'

Short grey eye-slits prised themselves apart. He glinted at her, turned and bolted towards the vacuum hatch.

Susan covered her mouth and grinned through her fingers at Jinx, who shivered for a moment before putting her arms around her own knees; eyes closed, apparently still sleeping.

Susan turned back to the door. Bless little Jinx. She could have let her sleep in the bedroom just this once, but instead she'd left her to go and pick up some *stray* for company. Pasty little thing, he did look very skinny. And Susan had scared him away from a warm bed. She flopped onto the sofa and looked at the angora cushion on the floor. What if Jinx had caught something from him? Could they even catch infections from one another? She was only *hugging* him – that was all she *could* do really. They weren't programmed to have sexual feelings, were they? No. No, they weren't because they were *supposed* to be for children. And anyway, they certainly couldn't reproduce. She leaned towards the coffee table and tapped it twice. It made a noise that Susan spelled out in her head: Z-J-W-E-E-M, as she imagined a pathway of letters curving upwards like music notes released from their noise. She tapped the icon that read 'TV', then 'Playback', then 'The Mini Human Phenomenon'. The mirror above the fireplace shimmered: activate holographics? No. No, that would freak her out too much.

'Customize programme narrative?'

No, thank you.

'This programme has been classed as unsuitable for children under twelve; customize programme contents?'

Nope. Just 'play'.

'This documentary has been sponsored by Billbridge & Minxus.'

Good.

'Ten years ago, Billbridge & Minxus stunned consumers with what was considered to be a perfect prototype of the "Littler", so called after the failure of its predecessor's pocket-sized model, "Teeny", twenty years before. Billbridge & Minxus bought the rights to the idea in 2103, and has been making happy additions to happier families, ever since.'

This wasn't really a documentary. This was some company-sponsored advertising *shit*. Oh, she would tell Hamish about this. He would *love* this. She reached over and pressed the steaming cup icon on the coffee table. 'Chocolate,' she said. At the end of the sofa the coffee machine buzzed, frothed and told her that she had recycled seventy-eight beakers that month.

She took the cup that appeared next to her on a long glass tongue. In a month? Wow. *And* she'd been away for one whole week of that…

'We believed that the fall of our predecessors, whose company name has since been discontinued, identified what could potentially be a fatal failure in the effort for re-humanization. Its idea of *breeding* empathy back into what was becoming a *dangerously* individualist society was just *too* important to give up on. So, ex-adoption agency Billbridge & Minxus picked those reins straight back up and by 2104, the "Little Love" programme was kick-started with the Batch Eight model. Batch Eight was an *instant* hit. Of course, we were fairly limited with its functions at the time – there were certain genetic settings we were unable to change: like the anti-ageing, difference of appearance… As well as the fact that they were all female.'

Jesus, 2104? It only seemed like three or four years ago that the old company was all over the news. She licked the chocolatey foam from her drink and watched as images labelled from Batch Eight to Batch Twenty-One slid across the screen. 'What a wonderful journey,' spouted the narrator, 'culminating in a love-balance that is allowed to prevail in every home.' A tag appeared in the bottom right corner. 'Tag!' she warbled over a tongueful of chocolate.

The image froze. 'Tag selected,' replied the TV. The image changed. A man appeared in an interview room with a microphone. Another man sat opposite him with one leg crossed over the other, his index finger playing with his top lip.

'We are here with Dr Peetzwelt, deputy head genetic engineer at Billbridge & Minxus, who is going to clear up several ideas surrounding a fairly *controversial* topic,' said the microphone man. 'Dr Peetzwelt, there has been much speculation over the *origins* of these *fascinating* little creatures. Obviously, the first word to appear on the lips of conspiracy theorists is clo—'

Dr Peetzwelt snapped his index finger down from his lips. 'Yes, *goodness*, don't say it out loud! It's best that we avoid that word completely, I think.' He smiled with his mouth.

'To clarify, cloning is illegal.'

'*Largely* illegal, yes. We can, of course, clone body parts and use them for transplantation. This is common practice and makes perfect medical sense. But they are just *parts*, that's the thing.'

'Let's talk about that for a moment. Can you explain to us how this system works?'

'Well, this process started about seventy-five years ago; people who had a problem with a certain body part could request that a replacement body part be *grown* for them. Not only was this an incredible breakthrough, shall we say, rendering some incurable conditions curable, but there was also very little after-care involved; the danger of rejecting the transplanted body part was side-stepped completely. Anyway, eventually the system changed, as it does, and rather than waiting for the illness to start before growing the replacement part, the health authorities put together a screening programme that could predict any future flaws in an individual's health. In short, people were having body parts "prepared" for them, just in case they got sick.'

The interviewer leaned in closer. 'And so, what was pivotal about this?'

'I'm getting to that.' He coughed. 'Well, everyone who went for it had at least one body part cloned. But during the first twenty-five years of the study, only twenty-six per cent of participants needed their body part.'

'That's quite a big number.'

'I'm not disputing that. At no point has anyone asked themselves if it was all "really worth it"; it has changed the lives of millions, *millions*.'

'But it all stopped. Why?'

'Four billion people went for the initial screenings. Each one had at least one body part cloned, and only a quarter of those people needed them.' Dr Peetzwelt looked at the interviewer with his eyebrows up, waiting for him to understand. The interviewer said nothing. 'Well, in short, the International Health Care Corporation was left with a bank of just under 7.5 billion excess body parts from that initial screening programme; that's not to mention the others that resulted from subsequent screenings, and those that were still in development. Nobody knew what to do with them.'

'Right.' The interviewer licked his lips. 'Couldn't they just be disposed of?'

'This is *the* subject of the hour, you see; especially since certain practices, such as sperm and egg-cell stockpiling, have recently been banned. Now that some of the first patients to be scanned have passed on, just what do we do with their body parts? The idea of storing bits of people away "just in case" is all very well but it's expensive, and space-consuming. Of course, unlike the sperm and egg cells, and embryos, the body parts could never live autonomously but *potential* is the ethical, er, *buzzword* of the century – could they potentially save a life? Yes. Could they potentially live? Yes. Could keeping them potentially harm life as we know it? No. Well. Unless the world turns on its head, cloning entire beings is made legal and people start *demanding* that we use these body parts to clone the *whole* of their deceased loved-ones… And then, of course, the big question is, just *how* would we ever dispose of them? They are, after all, *human* "remains".'

'The viewer can rest assured that this is certainly *not* something that the authorities take lightly, shall we say.'

'*Cloning* is something that *humanity* doesn't take lightly.' Dr Peetzwelt pinched his nostrils together.

'Switch off,' said Susan, realizing that she was suppressing a yawn when she didn't have to. The TV blinked back into a mirror, then shattered into snowflakes that gathered on the tiles before fading into nothing. Snowflakes already? Hamish had obviously got rid of the Autumn leaves. Her mouth yawned so much that she imagined the top three quarters of her head rearing backwards as if on a hinge. Time for bed. She put the cup back on the glass tongue, which disappeared into its mouth. She watched it and thought of the initial screening participants who had 'passed on'. *Death.* That was it. *That* was the problem. In fact, that was the *only* problem. They knew how to do it. Cloning. But, if Hamish died, nobody would rebuild him… And even though he was a pain in the neck, she'd really want them to. Rebuild him. How about that? A stonking realization, pushing her through the membrane of this, comfort, this… chocolate sofa *bubble* where Hamish would piss her off with his snoring and his pillow-arm but, outside of that bubble, life would happen anyway, grand and powerful, and she was hurtling through it with him. Because people rarely hurtled alone… And no one cared about snoring while they were hurtling. Then her brain would connect to the first thought: *if Hamish died, nobody would rebuild him for me.* She got up and crossed the living room slowly. *All of those pillow-arms would just float away in chocolate sofa bubbles, and I would try to grab at them and gather them all up again, and wake up hoping to feel an arm on my pillow. On my own in powerful grandness.* She stopped at the kitchen door and lit up her wrist; Jinx's hair slept alone. She turned and pulled the door almost shut. Then watched as each foot stepped upwards into a patch of wrist-lit stair. Hmm… That was quite a clever thought about bubbles and, and life. Her slippers fell perpendicular to each other, one rolled onto its side. She slid into bed with her non-dead Hamish, wrapping her arms all around him, looking for holes under the bits of him that he was sleeping on so that she could pass her arm through and hold all of him in one hug.

'Are you constipated,' he mumbled, 'or did you fall in?'

She laughed and kissed him in his hair. 'You're silly,' she said.

CHAPTER 4

Bonbon had understood everything. Except for the word 'pinning'. And it didn't really matter what she had and hadn't understood because her sleepy head let in and kicked out all of the words, one after the other. But it kept pictures. Like the She-one talking to another she-one, who had pushed her face to one side and covered her up with a blanket, and on waking up in the middle of the night, the smell of toilet box and clean tiles reminded her of these pictures. She was still 'there', but she didn't know why, or where 'there' was. She opened her eyes and sat up. Then closed her eyes again and reopened them. She waved a hand in front of her face. There was no difference between having her eyes open and keeping them closed.

Something was making horrible noises.

The side of her head felt like she had fallen on it.

She pushed herself up onto her knees and listened.

'Aaaah!' said the voice in a way that made Bonbon's stomach bubble. 'Take me home!'

Whatever it was made quick breathy sounds. Bonbon's ears got hot. 'Take me home. Oooh, take me back to my She-one. Take me back to my She-one. Aaaah!' She put her hands over her ears. Horrid sound, jumping through the black air and wrapping itself around her head. 'Aaaah! Aaaah!' What on Earth was it?

A white light stunned Bonbon into shutting her eyes. Whispery voices made her open them again. She realized she had been facing a wall.

'Lawnmower?' asked one of them. 'People still have lawns? Okay, Champ, I know, I know…'

'Did you give him a shot?'

'I'm just doing it.'

She turned at the waist and slit her eyes at the voices. Two biggerers stood all in white. She could see the tops of their heads. That was weird. She looked up. If she wanted to, she could easily touch the ceiling… And she was sure that if she lay between the walls of this box thing, she could touch both ends; one with her toes and the other with her hands. But the front of the box was open. She could have climbed right out of that thing had she wanted to. She didn't want to. She held her breath and inched herself around to face the head-tops.

'They can afford a lawn but they won't pay for an amputation,' said one to the other. He held up a tube thing, looked at it, flicked it, then brought it down to, to… Oh! Bonbon twisted back round to face the wall and covered her eyes with both hands.

'They got insurance?'

'Ha!'

'Right.'

With her hands still over her eyes, Bonbon slowly, slowly turned back around.

'Utterly selfish.'

'They're in the waiting room. I think I'll go and have another talk with them. I'm so fed up with this.'

'I'll come with you. It's okay, sweetie; we'll be back in a little while.'

'Who mows their lawn at two o'clock in the morning?'

'I know, right?'

Bonbon watched as they did something to the thing on the table – touched it or poked it. She wasn't sure. She kept her eyes fixed at their shoulder level until they had left the room and there were no shoulders. The light was still on. The thing made no noises at all now. Bonbon dropped her eyes, quickly. The thing stared around it, its mouth breathing too fast and too, too hard. And its eyes were weird; very open and dancey. Bonbon edged forward and butted the glass in front of her, ouch! It was a door! She was shut in! She was shut in! She pressed around the glass hatch with her hand to see if the glass was everywhere; it was, but… The thing was watching her. She stopped pressing and watched it back. Her eyes flicking further down the thing's body, letting themselves glimpse a bit more horror each time. Bonbon had never seen blood so crusty and dry that it had turned black. She didn't understand the idea that tummies could be cut open like that and fold and flop around bits of leg and hip and dry out and scab over, and that from a distance, what looked like pink was actually bright red and white if you were very close. She didn't know what she was looking at when she saw a leg bone protruding in two places. The pinkness reminded her of the inside of Jinx's mouth, or that bit between her legs. The Dead Bird lay in her mind with its patch of pink and bumpy flesh that got bigger every time she pulled out a handful of feathers. The Dead Bird thing had been strange. But here the strangeness was bubblier. It bubbled in her stomach, all the way up to the back of her throat and out it came, running down her chin, her breasts, her tummy, and over her thighs. The smell of it filled her nose; the bubbling started again. She crouched down and retched over a little space that she could hide her head inside. But then her head was too upside down and the bubbling burned the inside of her nose. She sat back up, wiping at her chin. The thing had raised itself up onto one elbow and was looking at her just like Jinx did, sometimes.

'Are you sick? You've been sick. Are you alright?' it said.

The words knocked Bonbon's eyebrows up and her head backwards as she took in his Jinx-face and his bloody body. You, she thought, you are not alright. You shouldn't be asking me if I am alright.

'Do you feel bad in your stomach?' he said. 'Does it feel funny?' he said. 'Hello?' he said. 'Hello?' he said. 'Hel—'

But he couldn't finish. The two white big-ones came back into the room.

'It's because they don't want one if it's only got one leg.'

'But we can make him another leg. That's the bit I don't get.'

'The little girl let it slip I think. The new model is out next summer and she'll be able to design her own.'

'That's exactly what I thought. Makes you sick, doesn't it?'

'What batch is he from?'

'Um… He's an old'un. Batch Eleven.'

'Batch Eleven?'

'Yep.'

'Wow! Have you ever seen a Batch Eleven?'

'We got a Batch Eight in yesterday.'

'You're kidding?'

'No, she's up there.' He nodded his head towards the other end of the room. 'Take a look.'

'You'd have thought…'

'He's bleeding pretty badly. Are you alright, Champ? Does it hurt?'

'We should sort him out.'

'I was rather hoping it would all be over by the time we got back.'

'Gosh, I wasn't! Too many forms.'

'He's completely fucked either way. Come on, Champ. Let's lose you a limb before you run out of juice.'

Bonbon watched as Champ's eyes started to close. One of the white big-ones put him on a tall, narrow bed with wheels. The other held the door back.

'Dorothy!' said Champ. Both biggerers looked at him. 'Dorothy!' he repeated.

'Shit,' said one; and they hurried out with the trolley.

Bonbon's mouth dropped open; he had said 'Dorothy' in front of them. How had he done that? They had heard it, they both looked at him when he said it. But what did it mean?

'Dorothy,' Bonbon said to herself. 'Dorothy.' She gazed at the door. What did 'Dorothy' mean? She scratched flakes of vomit from her knees. Maybe she would try and say 'Dorothy' to the She-one…

The door blurred open and Bonbon jumped. Her arms and legs were sleepy and stiff – had she been sleeping with her eyes open? She'd never, ever done that before. 'Aaahh!' That same horrid noise. A different voice. Bonbon covered her ears. Something soft was stuck to the achy side of her head. As she squeezed it, two different biggerers, a she-one and a he-one, pushed through the door. Bonbon's eyes danced over the white-coated back that hid the littler. 'Aaahh!' it screamed again; how was it screaming?

'Alright, little miss,' said the she-one. 'I hate it when they scream.'

'What is it this time?'

'I can't even say it, it makes me so angry.'

'Tell me.'

'An operation.'

'What?'

'The kid was playing doctors.'

'Really? At this time?'

'Earlier this evening.'

'For fuck's sake. Where were the parents?'

The other one shrugged. 'He hid her away in a cupboard somewhere. He must have been ashamed.'

'Insurance?'

'Nope. They're going to pay.'

'Instalments?'

'No.'

'So, they'll get to take her back again.'

A different he-one opened the door and brought in a bed with wheels. 'We're ready.'

The bed wheels squeaked as they started to take the screaming thing away. 'Joshua,' she said.

Both biggerers stared down at her.

'Oooh no you don't,' said one of the big-ones. 'You're gonna be the only one today with any money in you, missy.'

'Joshua,' said Missy. They wheeled her away.

Bonbon stared at the door again. Words sharpened and dimmed inside her head. Operation. Kids. Insurance. Joshua. What was 'Joshua'? And how had she managed to say that to them? How had they heard her? What if Bonbon tried to say something; would they hear? Maybe she had to be on that wheelie thing. Maybe the wheelie thing meant that they would be able to hear what she said. They had both been on it when they had been heard, it must have been that…

The door opened again. Bonbon's eyes scrunched shut and she turned her head away. That thing was so broken… She looked back and half-opened her eyes. Exactly like a pile of rose petals, it was. The ones that her She-one put in the big room. The peach ones with pink lines. Rose petals were nice, but it wasn't right to look like a pile of them.

This time there was no screaming or speaking. The two white biggerers looked like the same two that had come in with Champ.

'Deep fat fryer.'

'Not again.'

'Yep.'

'Very retro. When will people start eating healthily?'

'Right… Gosh, she doesn't look good at all.'

'Can they pay?'

'Nope.'

'Insured?'

'They don't know.'

'Great. Okay, sweetheart. Stay with us, we're just waiting for a room.'

The door opened but the person who had opened it stood outside, looking behind her as if she was finishing a conversation. The other two watched the door for a few seconds before speaking.

'Are we ready, Nurse?' The door swung back, shutting the next sentence and the two big-ones outside with Nurse.

Sweetheart's eyes were forced shut by the four milky bubbles of eyelids. Glittery lines ran from the inner corner of each eye down to her flaking mouth, which opened just wide enough for a tiny bit of voice to climb out of it. 'Mum,' said the voice. Bonbon blinked. 'Mum,' it said again, and the face got redder and screwed itself up. 'Aaahh!' cried Sweetheart as she scrunched up her own rose-petal face and made it bleed.

She didn't say 'Mum' again. The white big-ones came back and took her away.

Bonbon thought about this word. Mum. She let her mouth say it: 'Mum, Mum, Mum…' But it made her eyes feel sneezy and her ears get hot. She looked down at her fingers and counted them all. Then she did the same with her toes. 'Mum,' she said again afterwards.

'I noticed the last time we came in. She's vomited all over herself, look.'

Her glass door was opened and a rubbery hand came in and lifted her out. Bonbon tried to scream but couldn't. She turned and bit one of the fingers.

The rubber hand dropped her.

'She bit me.'

'Oh… Has she done this before?'

'Not while she's been here.'

Bonbon stood up to run, slipped in the vomit and landed

chest-down. She shuffled onto her bottom and pushed herself backwards until the cold wall pressed against her back. Four big eyes stared at her.

'Aggression?'

'Don't know. Which batch is she from?'

'Um.' The biggerer touched the glass door with one plastic finger and squinted his eyes at it. 'There.' He touched it again. 'See for yourself.'

'Batch Twenty. A newbie.'

'The latest batch.'

'Zero aggression.'

'Apparently.'

'Do you think she's just scared?'

The other biggerer pressed the door again. 'Fear was excluded as a characteristic for Batch Twenty.'

'Kids probably complaining that they couldn't play with them because they were always hiding.'

'I seem to remember that that was the reason.'

'So, do we report her as an anomaly?'

The other one looked at his bitten finger. 'She didn't draw blood,' he said. 'I think she was scared. Can you imagine witnessing all this for the first time? Then having a massive hand drag you from your cage? I wouldn't care if fear had been excluded from me, I'd crap myself.'

'Maybe that's why she vomited.'

'Maybe.'

'Hey, sweetheart. Come here; we won't hurt you. We just want to clean you up a bit.'

Bonbon sat in her corner, shaking. She wasn't called Sweetheart.

A hand came back in and lay on the floor next to her. 'Come on.' She didn't move, but allowed it to get nearer and pull her to the front of the cage.

'You see, she's shaking. She's frightened.'

'I know. But she shouldn't be; not according to her make-up. We'll have to keep an eye on her just in case,' said the hand as it lifted her out of the cage. 'She's petrified!' He shook his head. 'Excluded as a characteristic indeed… Marketing bullshit. You know, there was "zero aggression" in Batch Seventeen, and what came out of Batch Seventeen?'

'The Toe Biter of Michigan. Seriously? That was a "zero-aggression" batch? They kept that quiet.'

'Of course they did.' He reached behind Bonbon's head again towards the glass door. Her eyes followed the hand. Squiggles and lines glowed green across it. 'It's noted. The "scared" part anyway. I don't want to get her into any trouble.'

Something moved at the side of Bonbon's eye. She tilted her head back to see what it was. More glass doors. She tilted her head further, her eyes climbing up her forehead until she could see twenty glass doors and twenty tiny faces staring out from them. Maybe it was even more than twenty… Were there any numbers after twenty? There seemed to be more than one face for each of her fingers and toes; each one looked at her, blinking, a tiny white cushion thing stuck to the same side on each head. She put her hand to her own ear, it was still there, the thing. She screwed up her eyes and patted it softly.

The big he-one looked at her and laughed. His mouth smelled like the brown stuff that covered up the plant's legs. 'Targets are evil things, sweetheart. Believe me, that's not why I'm here; we don't like targets, do we, Mac?'

'Not one bit,' said Mac, shaking his head at each word.

'Be thankful that the other one is on holiday,' said the one who wasn't Mac. 'You got Dr Lilly; she's got a conscience.' He opened the big door. 'That other one – what's her name? The one with the hair… She prefers more profitable procedures.'

'Breast reduction: last month's thing,' said Mac.

'Yep. And before that it was rib removal.'

'It'll come back around.'

'It always does.'

'Tell him that I've got an hour free at one – he can come back then if he likes.'

'Okay, Hamish.'

'Thank you.'

He clicked off the tablet that was propped up on his desk and swivelled to face his bookshelf.

His bookshelf.

The newest one, well, the latest edition shined in its plastic cover. It looked very young compared to its leather-bound colleagues. Another one from The Bookman who shopped at Shepherd's – they had started chatting after being the only ones standing at the big glass-topped barrel with plastic vines twisted around it, grimacing over polystyrene thimbles full of melon-flavoured cognac.

He pressed a button and the glass screen hummed aside letting out the smell of old paper. He flexed his feet as his calves tingled. Thirty-six books! Whenever his work colleagues dropped by for some reason or another, they were always looking past his shoulder at the bookcase.

He spread a sheet of plastic over his desk and tugged his latex gloves. 'Filters!' he called, and the lights faded to a dim yellow.

Now then, if he had a client at one, that gave him two hours of reading. Calves still tingling, he wiggled his toes and opened the book.

'Oh… You're in darkness.'

He looked up. 'Emma!'

'I'm sorry I'm late.'

He fumbled for the on-switch on the tablet. 'I didn't think we had a… Lights! I didn't think we had an appointment today?'

She squinted through the now white lighting. 'Yes. I changed it… I couldn't make next Friday so I changed it.'

'Oh?'

Did you feel that? Your tablet booted 132 per cent faster than before you installed Hug Virus Protection. Ah good… Yes, he had felt that. He looked about the screen for somebody to thank before tapping on 'Agenda'. A blank white rectangle stretched from 11 a.m. to 1 p.m. Never mind, he wasn't about to send her away. 'So you did. Well, do come in.' He closed the book and swivelled to place it back in the cabinet.

She smirked. 'A tablet. Very retro.'

He swivelled back and blinked, trying to work out what his face was doing and how to answer her at the same time. His mouth was open. He closed it. Why was she here? Why had no one told him that she was coming? 'Oh, um… Yes. Actually. It's for confidentiality reasons. You know… So you can't see what, erm, I've got on, you know; my agenda.' He pursed his lips and sniffed. 'I do have the new stuff as well.' He tapped the centre of the desk. Transparent green and blue pixels swarmed upwards to form a face just in front of her stomach. It opened its mouth then fragmented and disappeared back into the table. Hamish had turned it off. He breathed in through his nose and clasped his hands in front of him. This was not supposed to be a show-and-tell.

'You have a lot of books, I never noticed before.'

'You didn't?' He flicked a look at the bookcase. Why did that disappoint him?

She shook her head. She was wearing the same earrings as last time. Oh dear! This time she only had one; she must have dropped it – 'You, erm…' No. It was none of his business if she wanted to go about with one earring. 'Do sit down, Emma.' She sat and bent forward to put her bag down. It was bleeding; there was blood coming from her ear! 'Oh dear… There's blood coming from your ear.' She stuck a finger in her ear and he handed her a sheet of Fibre-Web. 'I mean – where your earring should be, not your *ear* ear.' He made circles with a pointing finger to indicate the bit around her ear ear, then tucked his hand back inside the other one that waited alone on the desk.

She scrunched her earlobe and the Fibre-Web together. 'Oh – I knew he had pulled it out but I hadn't realized it was bleeding.'

'Are you alright?' No gestures.

'Yes! He, um… I have this um, pet – kitten actually – and, well…' She pointed to her ear with her free hand.

He wanted to say that cats were very 'retro' accessories. Instead, he said: 'Ah.'

'Yes,' she agreed.

He wanted to say that this kind of thing is part of the 'pet package'. Instead, he said: 'Well…'

'Yes.' She laughed and cast her eyes down. Her eyelids were powdery brown.

He didn't bring it up this time; that problem he'd thought about the time before last. There was too much of it in the room to talk about it. Little sparks of it made the air twinkly and dizzying and so it was better just to ignore it. He tried to bare his pupils again, to focus on something that wasn't blinking about in front of him in a million fragments, but his eyes searched her so thoroughly that his ears began to ring. This was 'being alert' he thought, before some sort of reaction. But what was the reaction? Was she reacting and so he was reacting to her reaction? And then she to his? This could go on for the whole session; looking with exposed pupils was really not helping. There had to be a 'filter'. He decided to take notes, typing faster than the air could blink and asking himself every few sentences if this was real life… Was he really living this? And every time he asked himself, his typing hands got shakier and so he typed faster.

By the end of the session he was sweating.

He had typed up every word she'd said.

Jinx was the first to wake up and roll over. Oh! Bonbon was already up! That was strange… Usually Jinx woke up at the same time as

Bonbon. She sat up and stretched her arms so high that her ears touched the knobbly bit on her shoulder, then crawled to the edge of the basket. One of the bowls was full. Bonbon must have eaten hers…

Oh, but… Bonbon wasn't there. The basket bottom stretched beside her, wrinkled and empty; feathers and AstroTurf gathered at the corners. Bits of fluff that had started out big and floaty were now dark and flattened. She rubbed one eye. Chips had been there. And now he was gone. And there was no Bonbon.

She slumped against the side of the basket and wrapped some string around her thumb. She should be eating, not wrapping string. Then she would say to Bonbon: 'What day is it today?' and Bonbon would say: 'It's… It's…' Oh dear. Jinx couldn't even remember what day it was. Not without Bonbon.

Her mouth pulled at the corners. It didn't really feel like eating now.

Her eyes flicked up towards the kitchen door: had the She-one filled up her bowl before or after Chips had gone? Jinx sat up. If it was before then… the She-one must have seen Chips and scared him into Outside.

Jinx jumped up, climbed out of the basket and ran towards the vacuum hatch.

* * *

'Goodness me, what's wrong with you? Do you want a biscuit? Is that what you're after?' Drew slouched back against the worktop. 'You're going to turn into a right little porker, Mr J.'

Jasper put his backside on the floor and bent his head to one side. His ears swelled and drooped like wind-filled spinnakers as they sorted through the air for tasty-sounding syllables.

Drew bent and looked into the cupboard that had been cleared of stained Tupperware, dusty packets of paper cupcake-cases, a beer-mug full of takeaway chopsticks and a pond-coloured 1970s fondue set, to make room for the treats that Watty and Drew shared with Jasper. 'Right; let's see if we can find you something doggy.'

The dog danced his front paws and squeezed out the highest little moan.

'Oh no. Not this as well! Have you seen this, Jasper? This was one of my favourite bloody brands.'

Jasper barked and gazed at the blue packet that was being waved about.

'You'll just have to wait, I'm afraid. I know you want one but…'

Drew stood, phone to ear, mouthing 'sshh' at the dog. 'Oh hello, um, I was reading the ingredients of your Wholegrain Organic Bear Bars and I was wondering if you could explain to me what is meant by hydrogenated vegetable oil? Mmm-hmm, right… Yes, I know what hydrogenated means, sorry, I should have been clearer; what vegetable oils do you use? Right. Mmm. Palm oil? It is palm oil or it isn't? It is. Right. Thought so. Oh well… Thank you. B-bye.'

Drew pressed the red phone button on the handset. 'This really pisses me off, Mr J. Look at this lovely packaging, look at these silver bears gazing up at their snowy bloody mountain,' waving the blue packet again before tucking it under one arm. 'It's all so dreamy yet… They use cheap, poisoned oil,' letting a hip fall against the worktop and staring into nothing. 'I love Bear Bars.'

Jasper marched his front feet again and moaned, staring at Drew's underarm.

'Loved Bear Bars.' Drew slouched back against the worktop and thought for a while before putting the biscuits down and walking away.

Jasper looked between Drew and the worktop until the gap between them got so big that he had to push up a bark.

'Oh right,' swivelling round. 'Sorry, Mr J. Let's see if we can find you something a bit more doggy.'

Another loud, high-pitched noise cut through the air. Drew and Jasper turned their heads towards it.

'Drew! This thing is bleeping! Drew!'

Drew leapt across the kitchen, toes turned out. The outline of Watty could be seen through an open door, standing over a giant incubator with a great transparent egg inside. Drew swished through the door and slotted into the gap between Watty and the incubator.

'What is it, Drew? Is there something wrong with her?'

In the middle of an egg-shaped container, a tiny person bobbed in liquid, a red tube attaching her to the wall of the egg. Other tubes and wires anemone-d out from various parts of her body. 'I think… I think she might be ready to come out.'

'Oh!' Shit! Watty's head flicked around as a search-for-help reflex, or a run-away reflex, or maybe a hope-nobody-is-watching reflex. Jasper watched from the doorway, his halfway-up tail hammocking lazily. 'But she's not due until next Wednesday!'

'I know!'

'Was that a sort of oven-bleep then? To tell us that she's ready?'

'Yep.'

'But how does she know?'

'She doesn't. The womb does.'

'How come you don't?'

'I thought I did. I had planned to get her out on Wednesday!' Drew bit a lip at Watty. The busy hands had stopped and rested on the surface of the liquid-filled oblong.

They blinked at each other, the loud bleeping continuing in the background. A bang came up from the floor below them.

'Old Beverly's broom,' said Drew.

'Right.' Watty snapped out of the mutual stare. 'What can I do?'

'Um…'

'Can you shut that bleeping off?'

'Not yet, well, I could… I…' Two strong hands climbed through the air and hung like creamy stars, one at each side of Drew's head. 'Nothing about this procedure should be rushed.'

'Okay… How about I go and tell Old Beverly that we're having a problem with… something. I'll think of something.'

'Yes… Do… before she calls the police. And make sure you lock me in, won't you?'

* * *

Awake. Bonbon opened her eyes to the ceiling of her cage. The light was bright and everywhere, not like normal light. She was still there but couldn't tell if it was daytime or night-time. Was she hungry? She swallowed and thought about her stomach. It fizzed and got smaller. No. Not hungry. Maybe it was still night-time.

'Hello, sweetie!'

She turned her head. The She-one! Oh! It was the She-one standing in the doorway! She sprang up and threw herself at the door. The She-one's face got all wrinkly and blinkey as she looked at the other cages.

'We'll bring her out to you. You can't come in here,' said another she-one from somewhere that Bonbon couldn't see.

'I'll see you in a minute,' waved the She-one, wiggling her fingers at Bonbon before opening the line in the door and going through it.

Bonbon stared at the line. A hand appeared at her glass hatch, opened it and caught hold of her, pulled her out, dunked her up to the neck in warm tile-smelling liquid and wrapped her in a blanket. 'Stain… Oh crap, that won't do.' She was unwrapped and rewrapped in a colder blanket. A giant finger and thumb held her eyelids back, shone a light into each eye and then into her 'good' ear. A comb was pulled through her hair three times and then: 'Right, kiddo, you're good to go'. And they were leaving the room.

Bonbon looked back towards all the little faces, her eyes jumping to one in the top corner. The 'right' corner, Jinx would say. Or the left. It must have been the left. Left was a nicer word… the face's hair was white; its skin was weird; floppy and lined and… Weird. One green eye and one brown eye stared out from the lines and flops. The head nodded at her and was gone. No! Bonbon tried to say, reaching out of her blanket and back towards the room, scratching at the air.

'Bonbon! Oh my Bonbon.'

She spun around. It was the She-one! She grabbed handfuls of the fingers that held her and lunged towards the shoulder, taking mouthfuls of hair and breathing long breaths of She-one smells… Hmmm… 'I think someone's pleased to see you.' That voice. The first voice that she had heard when she came here yesterday and her hands clutched even more tightly to their clumps of finger.

'As I was saying, Batch Mode is the one I normally go to.'

'And do they have an actual address or do I order online?'

'Yes, absolutely; they have an address.'

'Wow. That's a rarity.'

'Tell me about it! I was thinking about this last week because my *plant*-food provider has kept their address a secret for years…'

'Like the banks?'

'Yeah, like the banks, except they've gone one step further: just recently, they've even taken the contact number off their emails.'

'So you can't call them?'

'I can't call them, no.'

'Even if you have a… a plant-food crisis?'

'Nope. Can't call them.'

Susan smirked. 'Banks I can understand but…'

'I know, right?'

They looked at each other for a moment, smirking and nodding.

'So you usually go to Batch Mode.'

The doctor's face was serious again. 'Usually, yes.'

'Not Mini-Me's?'

'Mini-Me's is good, but I normally go to Batch Mode.' The doctor nodded slowly and closed one eye.

Ah. Of course… 'Slander' ruined people like her all the time. 'You should get one of them to sponsor you, then you could relax about giving recommendations,' Susan offered while stroking Bonbon's head.

'We have a contract with our suppliers,' said the doctor. 'Their competitors are also *very* good but unfortunately, they don't make humcoats.'

'Not *yet*.'

'I'm not at liberty to say.'

Susan breathed back a giggle. 'Righto.' She picked up her bag. 'Thank you for everything, Doctor.'

'My pleasure.'

She would enjoy telling Hamish about the 'liberty' thing, Susan thought as she strapped Bonbon into the car. He would growl out a low chuckle; the one he used when he heard a dirty joke. 'Oh Bonbon…' She looked at the white bandage on the side of Bonbon's head. 'I'm *so* sorry.' Bonbon caught one of the charms on Susan's bracelet in one hand and rubbed it with the other. 'Right,' Susan smiled down at her, 'let's go to Batch Mode because it's *better* than Mini-Me's.' She rounded the car and strapped herself into the front seat. 'Batch Mode,' she sang to the WayToGo, 'because Mini-Me's is totally *shit*,' she laughed.

Bonbon's ears rose. Her eyes danced over Susan.

'First destination: Batch Mode Store. Twentieth borough. Located,' said the car. Oh dear. She hated the twentieth. A mass of super-rises and no outside. Like a car park that covered the entire borough, as tall as it was sprawling. And grey. Elephant-foot grey. 'Second destination: Because Mini-Me's is Totally Shit. Non-identifiable. Continue search?'

'No,' said Susan.

The car started and drove away.

Soon, they were filtered on to the highway belt. 'Highway belt,' said WayToGo. 'Engine will disengage in three seconds.' And after three seconds they were gliding along in silence, accept for the tiny clicks of the belt as the sections under the wheels lifted and swivelled and fed them onto identical sections in the next lane. They were eased onto a third lane. Susan bent over into the passenger-seat footwell and took out the Shaker from her handbag. Bonbon clapped her hands.

'Okay, okay. Here you go.' She turned to Bonbon who took the Shaker, shook it, then turned it upside down over her mouth. Two flakes fell onto her tongue. She closed her eyes and sucked them. 'I knew you'd be hungry.' Susan leaned on her hand and watched Bonbon in the rear-view mirror. Funny how she only ever clapped her hands when she saw the Shaker – not food in general – just the Shaker; and she hadn't seen it very often. This was probably the fourth time… The *Littlers Advice Manual* had said that they were 'brought up' to understand basic English, but communication between a 'full-human' and a 'littler' had been blocked in order to maintain the established, intended roles. Animals could not communicate verbally, the manual had explained, and this was the main difference between humans and animals. 'Littlers' were by no means to be considered animals, although it would be unethical to demote a 'verbally capable' being to the role of 'pet'. They *did* try to talk, Susan thought; on several occasions she had seen one or other of them open their mouth but nothing would come out. Susan looked at Bonbon for a moment.

'We're going to Batch Mode, Bonbon.'

Bonbon stopped shaking the Shaker and blinked at Susan.

'Batch Mode is a shop that sells *nice* things for littlers.'

Bonbon squinted. Shop. Sells. Batch Mode? There were a lot of words she didn't know.

'We're going to *Batch Mode* to buy a *humcoat* for *Bonbon.* For you.' Susan's reflection pointed at Bonbon.

Bonbon widened her eyes and licked her top lip. Blankey's humcoat lay on the floor inside her head. She pictured herself putting it on and rubbing bits of it against her cheeks and chin. 'Humcoat for Bonbon,' Susan said, and then started to clap.

Bonbon dropped the Shaker and clapped back.

'Humcoat for Bonbon?' Susan repeated; this time she didn't clap.

Bonbon clapped again.

Susan clapped back; just once.

Bonbon watched. Then clapped back again.

Susan clapped three times.

Bonbon repeated. Three times.

Susan clapped out a slow, slow, quick quick, slow.

Slow. Slow. Quick quick. Slow.

Susan grinned. They were communicating! She put both thumbs up.

Bonbon looked at her thumbs for a second then copied.

Yes! Ha! They were communicating!

'Leaving Highway Belt in ten seconds.'

Big purple numbers counted backwards from ten on the WayToGo.

'Engine start: unnecessary,' it said when it got to five.

Yep, thought Susan, Batch Mode was in a bloody super-rise. When would the powers-that-be tear those stupid buildings down; grey, concrete, smoke-spewing eyesores. They were so *against* everything that teachers preached to kids during their Green Practice classes. She scowled as the car was loaded into a glass lift and rolled her eyes when the lift said 'Fifty-ninth floor.' Clapping snapped through the air and she spun around.

Bonbon pointed out of the window towards the city-bed that was quickly shrinking as they soared upwards. Susan blinked. Bonbon had clapped her hands to get her attention after not even a *thirty-second* lesson in hand clapping.

Susan peered into Bonbon's face. 'Would you like a humcoat, Bonbon?'

Bonbon clapped.

Susan nodded her head. Then clapped once.

Bonbon wrinkled her eyes.

'Would you like a humcoat, Bonbon?'

Bonbon clapped madly.

'Yes,' Susan nodded and clapped once. 'Or *no*.' She clapped twice.

Bonbon blinked. Then clapped madly.

'Destination,' said WayToGo as they slid into a parking bay. 'You've been brought here by WayToGo.'

'Okay. Thank you, WayToGo. Let's go get you a humcoat.'

Bonbon allowed herself to be lifted out of her car-seat. That whole clappy thing had been really… new. She had never clapped at the big She-one before. But now she was confused: was she going to get a new humcoat or not? She hoped it would be just like Blankey's… But that bit at the end where she had said 'yes' clap, then 'no' clap… Did that mean she wasn't going to get one? Hmmm. It was all very unsure. She sat on the roof of the car as Susan's bottom bobbed about below, the top half of her searching around for whatever it was she was looking for. Maybe she would pick up her Shaker… Yes clap, no clap, yes clap, no clap. Bobbing bottom. 'Bugger, it must have gone between the seats,' came wafting up word after word. If only Bonbon could catch the words between her hands and let them go when she wanted to use them. Yes clap, no clap, yes clap, no clap. Then she might be able to say something to the big She-one. Yes clap, no clap, yes clap… No! It was 'no' clap-clap. That's what she had meant. She was trying to tell Bonbon how to clap 'yes' and 'no'. Bonbon stared at the bottom without blinking: that meant that she was *definitely* going to get a humcoat.

'Got it!' Susan said, backing out and popping the Shaker in her handbag.

At the entrance to Batch Mode, the doors parted and hot, strawberry-smelling air blew onto their heads. A screen formed over what was just normal air to reveal a woman in a long black humcoat. 'Welcome to Batch Mode,' she said as her black coat changed into a grey one then into a shiny white one with a funny collar. 'An assistant will be with you shortly.'

Bonbon took mouthfuls of the blowy, strawberry air.

'Bonbon, look at that!'

She swivelled around, mouth still open. There were three of them, just like her – but really like her; not broken and making noises like the ones she had seen the night before. Each one was arranged on a, a… What was that thing? A table? But there was nothing to keep it *up*, even though it *was* up. It seemed to turn around and the one that was just like her stood at its centre and turned around with it. All *three* of them had their own turny-tables.

'What do you think of that one, Bonbon?' Susan nodded to the one on the right.

Bonbon looked at where the She-one was looking. It was weird. It just stood there, going around and around. Its face was weird too, it didn't change *at all*. Bonbon waited for the face to come back around and showed her teeth to it. It ignored her.

'Would you like a humcoat like that?'

Bonbon looked down at the coat. It was nice… Black, like her one at home. Inside her head, she walked about in Blankey's grey one.

'We also have that one in khaki.' A she-one appeared next to them. Bonbon held on to Susan's coat and stared.

'I think this is the same as the one I bought last year. I was *hoping* to go for something a bit, well, *fancier*.'

'I see. Does Miss belong to a child?' The woman nodded towards Bonbon.

'No, why? Do you have a kids' collection or something, like dolls' clothes?'

The woman, who up until this point had neatly stored her arms behind her back, shook them out and deployed two heavy-looking bat wings. Susan glanced from one to the other, then back up to the woman's face. 'Absolutely not,' the woman said with one wing in the air; in its hand was what looked like a remote control. 'Littlers are *not* dolls.' The other hand gestured towards Bonbon. 'This is why I'm asking you, actually. The safety of our customers is something we have to monitor.' She folded her bat wings in front of her. 'Safety is rooted in *attitude*.'

'I've *never* treated Bonbon liked a doll.'

The woman de-wrinkled her face and put her wings back into storage. '*Bonbon* is a littler. Littlers do not wear clothes because they are not people. However, they have to wear *coats* because they are not animals. I can understand you wanting to buy a *chic* model, but I just have to make sure that it's for *her* benefit and not yours.'

'Well… Why do you have *better* models on offer?'

'Ah ha. *Very* good question. There are many reasons really, but the main one is skin sensitivity. You know… and allergens.'

'Allergens?'

'Yes, well, that's to say that each model is designed for a different skin type. It's a very well thought-out system.'

'But you have different colours as well?'

'Well, yes. Mainly to avoid confusion between coats *in the home*,' said the woman. 'But there are other reasons; black doesn't stain, white doesn't get too hot, khaki is good for camouflage.'

Oh, Hamish would *love* this. 'Very practical,' Susan replied. 'How about if I let Bonbon choose?'

'That's how we would recommend you do it. Of course, only if she's capable. Let me show you the khaki model I was talking about.' She unfolded one wing towards a button on the remote control and pressed it. A platform whirred towards them and stopped just next to the other three. 'Here we are – what do you think of this one, Miss Bonbon?'

Bonbon blinked. Yes, it was nice…

'She's staring. She likes it,' said the woman, smiling.

'Really? Bonbon, what about this one?'

It was the black one again.

Bonbon blinked. Yes, it was nice…

'And this one?'

Another black one. She looked closer then reached out and touched it. Made out of shoes. No. She didn't like that one.

'She touched that one,' said the woman. 'A good sign.'

'She did, didn't she?' Susan turned, and looked at the other different-shaped floating platforms then back to the coat that Bonbon had touched. 'We'll probably go for this one then; yes, Bonbon? Would you like this one?'

Bonbon's eyes flicked from Susan to the shoe-coat and back again. No. She did not want that one.

'What's it made from?'

'Leather.'

'Ah. Where is the leather treated?'

'Scotland.'

'Good. Sorry to…'

'Not at all. Most customers do ask. There are still a few places that outsource their factories. You can never be too careful.' The woman started to take the coat off the display platform.

No, Bonbon thought. No, she did *not* want that one! That one would be *horrible* to wear. And anyway, it belonged to the one-like-her who was wearing it, surely? But what was wrong with her? Why was she not moving while they took the humcoat off? Why didn't she have any nipples? Bonbon leaned forward and touched its belly. It was cold and hard.

'Oh, look at her! Yes, that's right, this is for you, Miss Bonbon; she's very eager, isn't she?'

'She seems to be,' Susan laughed.

No! She didn't want this one! Bonbon clapped her hands. Both women turned to stare at her.

'Ah, now, did you see that? She only does that when she really, *really* wants something,' said Susan.

But she didn't want it at all. Not. One. Bit. She clapped her hands again.

The woman hooked a finger over her lips and considered Bonbon. 'Shall I wrap this for you?' she said, straightening the finger and pointing at the leather coat.

No, no, no! thought Bonbon. Clap-clap.

Susan looked at her.

Clap-clap, again.

'She just said "no"!'

Clap-clap.

'She's saying "no". Once for "yes", twice for "no". She's got it! She understood!'

'Interesting…' said the woman.

'Bonbon. Do you want this coat?'

Clap-clap.

'You see? Did you see that? Bonbon, do you want a *different* coat?'

Bonbon thought for a moment then: clap.

'Ah!' Susan cried. 'Did you see that?'

The woman stood with her mouth open. 'I did.' She slit her eyes at Bonbon. 'Would you like some flakes?'

Bonbon looked right at her. Clap.

The woman shut her mouth, swallowed, turned and strode over to another floaty thing that hovered underneath a 'Please Pay Here' sign.

'I have to report this. And if it's what I think it is…' The woman tailed off as she retrieved a telephone handset from a nook somewhere inside the floaty thing.

'What?' said Susan.

'Littlers aren't meant to communicate. They are not people. I'm obliged to report any anomalies.'

'Oh… But… Whatdoesthatinvolve?' Susan blurted.

'Oh hello? Yes, Batch Mode, yes, that's right. I'd like to report a case of successful communication. What's that? Nope, no speech – through clapping. Uh-ha.' The woman fixed Susan with her stare. 'Oh really? Right. Ten minutes? Okay. I'll tell the owner to wait. Thank you, have a good day.' She hung up. 'You have to wait here now.'

'Have to?'

'Well, no, but you are *strongly* advised to.'

'I really can't. I just wanted to stop off here quickly. I should be gone by now, really.'

'I'm sure it won't take very long, you should probably stay.'

Susan took a step back. 'Tell whoever-it-is that I really couldn't stay.' She turned and strode towards the doors.

'It won't take very long, Madam…'

The doors parted, the strawberry air blew her out into the car park. She bundled Bonbon into the car. 'That woman was weird,' she said.

Clap, came the reply.

'You understand "weird"?'

Clap.

Susan giggled at her in the rear-view mirror, then thought for a while. What was the big deal about communication? Apes and chimps and gorillas did it without any hassle from anyone… Susan leaned forward and pressed the ignition button. And dolphins. And parrots… 'Mini-Me's,' she said to the WayToGo. They probably wanted to ask a few questions. Maybe just to see if she was all right;

they weren't allowed to take any chances now, not after the Toe Biter of Michigan.

'First destination: Mini-Me's,' said the WayToGo.

'Okay, Bonbon. Let's try again; somewhere different.'

CHAPTER 5

'I lost my brother when I was twenty-two.'

'Lost him?' Hamish stopped the smile just in time. Shopping mall in the twentieth, he was sure. Susan had lost her sister in there once.

'He died.'

His eyebrows sprang upwards.

'He was only nineteen.'

Nineteen? Was it even possible to die at nineteen? 'I'm sorry… you've thoroughly startled me,' he said, his voice high and weird. Nineteen. Nineteen! But this wasn't 2017! People could be cured of anything, vaccinated against anything, brought back to life within hours of dying, have any body part replaced…

'Burned to a skeleton. They couldn't bring him back, there was nothing to work with.'

Hamish gulped, wanting to wail 'how' but choosing instead: 'Would you like to explain what happened?'

'He fell onto a bonfire, drunk. Camping out on the cliffs in the South with a friend. The friend had passed out too…but not in the bonfire.'

Hamish covered his mouth. She was too calm… 'Steely' was the word. He imagined the fibres that linked her thoughts, thickened and frayed by the fact that death had happened. He'd only ever read about what it was like to lose someone. His gaze floated up to the reflection of the window in a framed brainful of cogs that hung on the wall behind her. The outside world shone between the cogs, super-rises, post-drones and advertisements beaming off clouds; rows of people on escalators, crossing roads, in cars, completely ignorant of their own precariousness.

'I'm quite sensitive about death,' she added, as if she were quite sensitive to the cold.

Jinx had spent ages arranging her hair so that it was all around her shoulders. She had used the dining-room doors to watch herself doing this. Big blue birds with long green, spiky tails traipsed through her head.

She closed her eyes and watched them for a minute.

Her hair had given her something to do and it meant that her shoulders were now warm. She had been standing outside for what seemed like hours and the rest of her was bumpy and shaking.

'Chips,' she mewed again, looking at the fence. 'Come back, Chips.'

Nothing. Except more blue birds, walking and turning and walking again.

She turned around, looking at herself as much as she could in the glass doors. A weird thing had happened on the inside of her head since she had slept next to Chips like that. Every time she thought of him she, sort of, forgot that she was cold and her stomach went all bubbly. This was good because thinking of him kept her warm. But the inside of her head was doing even weirder things than sending out blue birds and making bubbly stomachs. It kept playing back a bit of the night when she had been sleeping under his chin and it was all warm and Chips-smelling and then, all of a sudden, his arms had pulled her really close so that his chest was pressed against her cheek and her breasts were against the top of his stomach and his stomach was against the top of her stomach and his thing was against her belly button and their legs were all kicked over and under each other, right down to the toes. Jinx had liked that. She could have spent the whole day like that; warm and lovely. Her mind played and replayed this bit of the night, from the moment he had pulled her close to the moment she had fallen right to sleep.

She heard a noise behind her and turned: 'Chips? Is that you?' It wasn't. But she just had to wait, even though it was really difficult, she would wait and he would come like he did almost every day.

At least her shoulders were warm, she thought. Then she would think that her shoulders had slept against the top part of his arm as it bent around her and then she would think about Chips and her stomach would bubble and the cold would go away and when the thought had finished she would shiver and think to herself: at least her shoulders were warm...

And then she would think about Chips.

After a while, her mind stopped playing back The Big Cuddle and started to play with things that hadn't happened. On the inside of her head, she had kissed Chips on his chest while she was sleeping in his Big Cuddle. On the inside of her head, they had woken up together and talked about The Big Cuddle. They had both agreed that it was lovely and had decided to do it again. So they did it again, but this time they were awake and could hear each other breathing. On the inside of her head, Jinx kissed Chips's chest again and Chips kissed the top of her head. But after thinking this thought, the inside of her head was disappointed. 'But it didn't happen like that,' it said to itself, and she would wonder if Chips would ever come.

Of course he would. He came every day!

But what if he was too frightened? What if he had been scared away?

No... He had to come back to... well... to talk about The Big Cuddle. Surely he would want to talk about that.

She stood for another few minutes, looking at her hair. Thinking about Chips, feeling warm, talking to him about The Big Cuddle, feeling disappointed, wondering if he would come, wandering over to the part of the garden where she could see over the bars, then thinking about Chips all over again.

But wait! She twisted a strand of hair around her nose as her head thought about the best idea she'd probably ever, ever had; what if she went outside of Outside to, well, look for him? That made her feel very bubbly in her stomach; what would Bonbon say? Huh! That was the first time she had thought about Bonbon since waking up that morning… Because Bonbon wasn't there…

She'd be ever so cross, though.

But she wasn't *there.* And anyway, maybe Jinx wanted to see Chips even more than she wanted to see Bonbon.

Maybe…

She strode over towards the part of the fence that Chips went through whenever he left the garden.

No.

She turned and walked back towards the house.

But… he *had* been in their house…

And anyway, what if Bonbon didn't come back tonight and she had to sleep on her own?

That thought made her all shaky. She turned again and headed back towards the fence. Funny, there were no holes, marks or even scratches on the great grey fence. A dark shape caught her eye. A stone. She went over to it, maybe she had to lift it up? She couldn't lift it, she could only push it. She clenched her teeth and pushed. Behind the stone was a tiny gap between the fence and the ground.

Jinx squatted down; Chips was very skinny but he wasn't that skinny. She put her cheek to the ground and looked through the gap. Maybe, if she tried, she could get her head and shoulders through.

She tried.

She couldn't.

She stood up and walked right to the end of the wall, dragging her hand along it. At the very end, when she reached the bars where she could see the outside of their Outside, she found a gap where the two walls should have touched. Oh, that was a much better gap! She could fit through that easily.

She jumped from foot to foot for a moment, stepping towards the gap only to jump back again. A picture of herself emerged on the inside of her head, alone in the dark basket with the squashed fluff and stones. She closed her eyes and marched straight through the gap. It was really long… and low. 'Tunnel,' said the inside of her head. Yes, that's what it was; a tunnel. She bent forward and started to walk. Ahead was a patch of light and as she got closer to it, she realized that there was a hole to her left. She poked her head out of the hole.

Another Outside, the same as their Outside, stretched out all the way towards a house, the same as their house, but also very different. Where their house was grey, this one was white, and where their house had a green box, this one had fishes that spat out water, and where their house had a dead bird, this one had a pot of flowers. The dining-room doors were the same, except that they had curly black handles. Their dining-room doors didn't have any handles.

Jinx stood, half in and half out of the tunnel. 'Chips!' she shouted. 'Chips! Are you here?' She waited for a moment then shouted again. 'Chips!'

'Jinx!'

Jinx flicked her eyes towards the direction of the noise. 'What?' she said.

'What are you doing here?' Blankey swished out from behind the water fishes in her grey coat. She had a bright pink flower on her head.

'Peacocks,' said the inside of Jinx's head as another four blue birds ran from her left ear to her right one.

'Oh!' Jinx gasped.

'What?'

Jinx didn't know why she had gasped like that; she stared at the flower and thought that she would also like to put a flower on her head.

'But you never go out,' said Blankey.

Jinx grinned. 'I'm looking for Chips today.'

'Oh. Why?'

'Because he stayed with me last night.'

Blankey's eyes got bigger. 'Why? Why did he stay with you?'

'Because Bonbon wasn't there.'

Blankey screwed up her face and folded her arms.

'Is this your house?' asked Jinx.

'Mmm.'

'It feels lovely,' she said, pointing her toe as she stepped out of the tunnel. Brrr… It was chilly. She pulled her hair around her shoulders while Blankey watched her. At least her shoulders would be warm… 'Do you know where Chips is?'

'It's weird,' said Blankey.

'What's weird?'

'I don't want to tell you.'

'Why?'

'Because I've always wanted Chips to stay at my house.'

Jinx blinked. 'Well, ask him! That's what I did.'

Blankey stared at Jinx's belly button. No. That still seemed weird, but she didn't know why.

'Please tell me where he is, Blankey. I'll ask him for you if you like… I'll ask him if he'll stay at your house.'

That seemed even weirder.

'I just don't want to be on my own, and Bonbon's not here and… Please, Blankey.'

Blankey unfolded her arms and lifted the inner ends of her eyebrows. Feeding a cat tail through one hand until she got to the end of it, she stroked the tip with her thumb; oh dear, she thought. Poor old Jinx. She just didn't want to be on her own… 'You have to go all the way through the gap. Right to the end.'

'Tunnel?' said Jinx.

Blankey screwed up her eyes, 'Yes, tunnel. All the way to the end.'

'Right.' Jinx turned around and climbed back through the hole.

'Where is Bonbon?' called Blankey.

'Don't know,' Jinx replied. 'Bye, Blankey.' And she was gone.

'Right to the end,' Jinx said to herself. 'Right to the end.' It wasn't very far. 'Oh!' she said when she walked straight out of the end without realizing. But… This house was not the same. At all. It was all dark grey; the floor, the walls, the fence. The walls seemed to grow upwards so high that the light couldn't reach down to the floor and so she stood in the dark. There were no marks or lines or green boxes or flowers or curly handles. There were no dining-room doors; just one small window in the centre of the house that looked at her like a black, shiny eye. And everywhere smelled strange. Like the water that the roses stood in, after a really long time.

Jinx saw a patch of light on the floor over by the house. She tiptoed over to it. 'Chips!' she hissed. 'Chips?'

Nothing.

'Chips?' she called a little louder.

Nothing.

She stood in the middle of her patch of sunlight and watched as the edges went dark grey, and the dark greyness rolled towards her and climbed up her feet and legs until she was all dark and cold.

It did not feel lovely here.

She turned to the tunnel, it would take her back home, back to the basket.

Alone…

'Right,' she said out loud, looking back towards the house. Ah! There it was! Exactly the same as their house. She marched over to the vacuum hatch and climbed her head and one leg through, then stopped. In front of her, around the thing where the water came from, piles of biggerer bowls covered the floor. Some of them looked normal, others had green furry patterns inside them. She bent towards one and sniffed it, wrinkled her face and walked away.

Biggerer bowls were never on the floor in her house.

'The sink,' said the inside of her head. 'Where the water comes from.'

In front of the round window, where her big She-one would sometimes put the bottom of their basket so it would come out smelling lovely, were piles of biggerer things, all different colours. They were probably waiting to go inside the window and come out smelling lovely.

Jinx covered her nose. These ones did not smell lovely. Oops! One foot had trodden in something wet and squidgy, and the other was stuck to the floor between one and a half slices of green bread and an open sheet of Fibre-Web with yellow slime shining inside. She pulled on her leg. Hard. So hard that she fell sideways and landed on the bread, coughing as the green stuff clouded up in front of her. She got up quickly and brushed herself down. There was a giant pile of grey fluff on the floor in front of her. That was nice. Bonbon would love that for the basket, it was just massive. Maybe she could take it home for her; fluff was quite easy to make small. As she got closer she noticed crumbs trapped inside the fluff. Bonbon hated crumbs in the basket. Maybe she wouldn't bother.... Ahhh! She ducked down. There was one of them. Waiting for her. Mean little thing. The start of a cough tickled her throat. Oh... Not now; it would hear her. It was all that bloody green dust that had floated into her mouth and... She coughed. Then held her breath.

'Jinx?'

Chips! 'Chips! Where are you?' She stood up then remembered the thing and ducked down again.

'Are you in my house?'

'Come and help me! There is a vacuum bot!'

'I can't.'

Oh no. 'Well… What am I going to do?'

'Don't worry, Jinx, it just sleeps all the time. It won't chase you.'

'Really?'

'Yes!'

Jinx stood up and eyed the vacuum bot. It lay sleeping; its blinking red eye was black and it looked like it needed a bath. She hoped her head would say 'it's dead' but it didn't.

'Where are you?' she called.

'I'm here! I'm here!'

She walked towards 'here'.

In the corner of the kitchen stood a small cupboard with a jagged hole in its door that Chips had managed to poke his head through.

His head was smiling.

Jinx ran over and stood just below. 'Can you come out of there, Chips?'

'No.'

'Why not?'

'The big He-one wants me to stay in here… While he's out.'

'Why does she?'

'He.'

'He.'

'Because of my humcoat.'

'What happened to your humcoat?'

'I left it at your house. He doesn't want me to get cold.'

'Why did you go away from my house?'

'Your big she-one found me in the night.'

'Did she put you into Outside?'

'No. I got frightened and ran away.'

Jinx wrinkled her face and stood on tiptoes.

'Is it nice in there?'

'Yes. It's nice.'

Jinx smiled up at Chips then sighed. If only he could come out. She thought of The Big Cuddle… Then started to look around the cupboard for a handle. Two big silver loops, one above the other, were caught around two big silver sticky-out things that were sticking out of the door. Jinx reached up on tiptoes and managed to brush the lowest one with the end of her finger. 'Nails,' said the inside of her head. If she could just find something to stand on… She looked around.

'I can get you out of there!' strained Jinx as she stretched again.

'No!'

Jinx stopped stretching and stepped backwards. He had really shouted just then. She glanced round at the vacuum bot but it hadn't woken up. 'Why not?'

Chips pulled his head back inside and hid. 'Don't know.'

'Chips?' She twisted her arms together in front of her and felt her face go hot. 'Did you like The Big Cuddle?'

'—.'

Jinx stared at the hole. Why wasn't he answering? He had hidden his head inside the cupboard and he wanted to stay in there. She put one foot over the other and dipped her chin so that it touched the part where her elbows crossed as each twisted arm slid further along the other until her hands were holding her shoulders. Why was he being so weird?

'Yes,' said Chips.

Jinx's head snapped back up. 'Really?'

'I keep thinking about it.'

She opened her arms out as far as they would stretch and started to spin.

'I can hear you laughing. Why are you laughing?'

'I'm happy!' sang Jinx. She stopped spinning and squinted over at the bot. Still sleeping. 'Why won't you come out, though?'

'I'm not sure.'

Jinx nodded. Sometimes she had feelings that she wasn't sure about… She thought very hard for a moment about all the reasons why Chips would want to stay in the cupboard but wouldn't be able to explain.

'Is it your big he-one? Is it because he doesn't want you to come out?'

'—'

'Because, you know I can shut you back in… after…'

'Yes. You would have to shut me back in.'

'Well, that's fine then!' She started to climb the side of the cupboard.

'No!' said Chips.

'What is it? I can shut you back in, I really can.'

Silence. Then: 'I've done a poo.'

Jinx stepped down and put her hands on her hips. 'What?'

'—'

'Shit,' said the inside of her head. Jinx started to laugh.

'Why are you laughing? Stop laughing. I don't like it.'

'But Chips, who cares? I do poos all the time. So does Bonbon, and Blankey—'

'No,' said Chips. 'Blankey doesn't poo.'

'She does. Everyone does.'

'Not Blankey.' Jinx stopped laughing and started to feel cross about this. Although she didn't know why. Blankey appeared on the inside of her head on the back of one of the peacocks. 'I want Chips to stay with me,' she said without moving her mouth.

'Jinx. If you pass me something through the hole to cover it up with, then you could come in.'

'Cover what up?'

'My… poo.'

'Oh.' Jinx looked around her. Then ran over to the Fibre-Web and picked it up. Yuk, she put her thumb in the yellow slime.

She dropped it, folded it so that the slime was on the inside and reached up to poke it through the hole. 'Will that do?'

'Yes. Wait a minute.'

Jinx looked around again for something to stand on; what could she use? Maybe the bread. No. That had been really nasty when the powder went in her mouth. Oh, what about a plate? Or a bowl? She ran over to the sink and found a small bowl on the floor, turned it onto its side and rolled it back to the cupboard. The vacuum bot didn't move one bit.

'I'm coming in now.'

'Alright.'

The door swung open. Chips stood squinting at the other end of the cupboard. 'Chips!' she said, bounding over to him, then covering her nose. She stopped and looked around the cupboard. 'Is this your room?'

'Yes.'

The cupboard walls were chipped and covered in black patches. A square of fabric with cloud-shaped brown bits on it wrinkled over one corner of the floor. The rest of the floor was shiny with smears. Two bowls lay upside down and their undersides were rough with flake-coloured scum. Jinx flicked her eyes over the Fibre-Web in the corner and looked away. A long chain with a loop in it swung from the ceiling.

'What is that?'

'That's my lead. It's for when my big He-one leaves the door open for me but doesn't want me to come out.'

'Oh. How does it work?'

Chips took the loop, which Jinx thought might just fit over his head; stepped into it, pulled it up over his knees and his hips and set it on his waist. 'There,' he said.

'But you can get out!' she said, looking at his stomach.

'He doesn't think I can; he's the one who puts it on me.' He pulled the loop back down again and stepped out of it. 'This is when

I come to your Outside; when he's out and I'm on my lead.' He kicked the loop to the back of the cupboard and smacked his belly with one hand. 'I was too big to get out of it, when I first got here.'

Jinx looked at the food bowls. Then at Chips. 'Don't you get thirsty?' she said.

'Yes.'

'Where is your water?'

'I drank it all.'

'Oh,' wrinkling her eyes. 'Is your big he-one bad to you?'

'No.' Chips shook his head. 'Not at all. I have my humcoat. You don't have yours. But I have mine.'

This was true. And weird. Why didn't he have water, though? It was a bit strange to give someone a humcoat but not give them food or water… She looked at Chips, standing in front of his piece of fabric, next to a big black stain on the wall, one of his feet covered the other and she couldn't tell if it was blue from the cold or just dirty. Chips crossed his arms over his belly, still shaking his head.

'He's not bad to me. He would never be bad to me.'

She walked over to him and held both his hands, then kissed him on the chin like she had in her dream. This house was horrid. And her lovely Chips was living here. 'Come and live with me.'

'I can't,' he said. 'He'll be back soon.'

'Really?'

'Yes.'

Jinx let go of his hands. 'Oh.'

'Why did you drop my hands? Don't do that.' He picked up her hands in his own. She beamed. 'He'll be gone again tonight. He'll be gone and he'll be sad. And I'll know he's sad because I'll be sad too…'

'Why will you?'

Chips shrugged and looked at their four hands all knobbly and joined up. 'Will you come back tonight?'

Jinx let her head flop right backwards and laughed. 'Yes, Chips. Yes, I will!'

Right. Best take his humcoat… Oh, she could probably wear it on the way. That would be the easiest way to carry it and it would keep her warm. What else? Hmm… Some flakes. She would take a bowlful of flakes. Jinx stood with her hands on her hips and gazed about the kitchen. Ooo, what was that thing? It was sticking out between the fridge and the cupboard. She had seen one many times but she'd never touched one. She dragged it out and tried to pick it up. It was quite light! With its fat end, she scooped up a big helping of flakes, then put them back again as she realized she couldn't hold the thing full of flakes and put on the humcoat at the same time.

It wasn't the easiest way to carry flakes, but if she was careful, she was sure that she would be able to get it all the way to Chips's house without dropping any. Jinx took large strides across the garden. It made her think of the way that Blankey walked in her new shoes. She giggled. A few of the flakes shuddered off, dissolving into the AstroTurf. She shut her mouth, tight. Stupid thing…

'Spoon,' said the inside of her head.

'Spoon,' she said out loud. 'Stupid spoon.'

By the time she'd reached the tunnel, she'd already lost quite a few of her flakes. The wind hadn't helped. Bloody wind. It puffed the flakes up into her face and they floated about her like little yellow flies. She blew at them so that they wouldn't get into her eyes and carried on through the tunnel. 'Nearly there, Chips,' she said to the tunnel. Wait a minute… What was that? Over on the right, a plastic tube lay on its side. She hadn't noticed it when she had come through earlier. It was right at the end of the tunnel near the opening into Chips's garden. The tunnel seemed lighter now, even though it was evening… That was weird. Jinx stuck her head out. Chips's garden had a light in it. But this one was really, really bright. She ducked back into the tunnel and tried to blink away the white blobs that swam about in front of her. The tube thing had a, sort of, lid, as if it were a little box of some type. That would be much better for carrying flakes. She laid down the spoon and another sprinkling of flakes fell onto the floor. Oh bugger! What a stupid idea it was bringing that silly spoon. She pulled off the top of the tube, yanked out a rolled-up plastic thing that was inside and started to stuff the tube full of flakes. She started with the flakes from the spoon, then around the spoon, then realizing that there was still loads of room in the tube, retraced her steps, picking up flakes where she could see properly and adding them to her little harvest. She imagined that the tube was Chips's dead-spider belly and that each flake was helping to make it full and better and this thought pushed her back along the tunnel and to her Outside, her fingers picking through the dirt then the AstroTurf. She got closer and closer to the green box, the light getting better as she continued, picking and putting, picking and putting, when…

'I asked her where you were and she said she didn't know.'

Blankey.

Jinx stood up straight and looked around the side of the green box.

Blankey, backlit by the outside light bulb, stood with another littler who wore the same humcoat as she did. She looked at the other littler's hair, curly blonde with a pink flower, no! That one was Blankey!

So, who was the other one? Jinx started to walk towards both of them. The other one spoke.

'Where is she now, though?'

Bonbon! Was it? No… Jinx froze; then shook her head and looked at the ground. Then looked back up again, yes, Bonbon was definitely there, but… she… she couldn't really be here, could she? She shut her eyes and shook her head again, then reopened her eyes. Bonbon was still there. It was her Bonbon.

'At Chips's, I suppose,' said Blankey.

'Bonbon!' Jinx's tummy filled up with bubbles and her legs wobbled as she ran towards the two humcoated shadows. Bonbon was here! 'Bonbon, oh Bonbon!'

'Jinx!' Bonbon spun around, the skirt of her coat swinging like the thing that covered the light bulb on the ceiling in the big room. 'Where have you been?'

Jinx stopped. Bonbon's voice was a little bit nasty… All of her little belly bubbles turned to pebbles and dropped down through her legs to her feet. Oh no, why did she have to be like that? What did it matter where she had been? They hadn't seen each other for two whole days! That had never ever happened before. Why did she have to be so mean and nasty all the time? 'Oh dear…' Jinx managed, looking at her feet.

Bonbon stared at her with still eyes and a mouth that looked like a short straight line; her hands were scrunched into fists at the side of her coat.

'Aren't you happy to see me?' Jinx said more angrily than she had wanted to, and surprised herself with her new, angry voice.

They stared at each other. Bonbon's eyes widened and her fists got tighter. Her short straight line was wobbling a bit. That wasn't like Bonbon, thought Jinx, Bonbon never had a wobbly mouth.

'I…' started Bonbon, but couldn't finish because she was too wobbly.

Jinx didn't like that mouth, not one bit; it was making her ears feel hot… She flicked her eyes downwards at the downy bits of fur that waved at her like millions of tiny fingers. Oh she looked so nice in that new coat with her white-blonde hair spread out all around it. 'You look so lovely, Bonbon,' she couldn't help.

Bonbon swished across the three steps that separated them and put her arms around Jinx.

Jinx squawked and let her mouth hang in that shape while Bonbon held on to her. 'I was worried about you, Jinx.'

Jinx laughed again. 'I'm fine, Bonbon.' Then: 'I was worried about you too! Where did they take you?'

Bonbon thought for a moment. Why was that important? She was home now. That was all that mattered. 'Doesn't matter.'

'Oh, alright,' Jinx replied. Then: 'Yes, yes, it does matter, Bonbon. I want to know.'

Bonbon blinked as she looked at the buttons on Jinx's humcoat. She hadn't been wearing it when Bonbon last saw her... And it smelled funny. Oh... Everything had changed! Everything. It would take ages to change it all back to the way it was.

Jinx opened her mouth. Then closed it again. Then reopened it. 'Don't you want to know about Chips's house?'

No. No! Of course, now that Bonbon was back, Jinx would never ever go there again. Bonbon frowned and shook her head. 'It doesn't matter. You're back now.'

'But I have to go to Chips's house. Tonight. I promised him.'

Bonbon's mouth fell open. 'No!' What was she talking about? Nobody had to go anywhere!

Jinx pulled her shoulders up around her ears and blinked at Bonbon from the side of her head.

Bonbon pressed her lips together and looked at the floor. 'No,' she said, really quietly. 'Please don't go.'

Jinx's head rose out of her shoulders. Where was all the nastiness?

Bonbon danced her eyes backwards and forwards at the ground; what could she say to make Jinx stay? Jinx wanted to know where she had been... But it was all so unimportant now that she was back. She squeezed her eyes shut and thought really hard; what could she tell Jinx? What could she tell her? An image flashed up in her mind of her own fingertips at the end of her own arms held out towards the green eye and the brown eye in their crumples of skin. And all that white hair. White and crumpled with funny eyes, how did it get like that? Because Bonbon was sure it hadn't always been like that. Thinking about it again made her want to go back, to the tile-smelling place. She must go back and find out who the white and crumpled one was. 'There was a…' she began, then took a deep breath… Oh, it was no good! She sniffed. So many things happened on the inside of her head that her mouth wouldn't tell.

It was like that time she made a nice pile of feathers in their Outside and the wind picked them up and threw them around the sky and every time she put them back into a nice neat pile, they would blow away again, all in different directions. Just like her words were now. She tried again. 'There was a…' and again they scattered like feathers in the air.

Blankey started stroking the side of Bonbon's coat and making funny noises the way she had done when Jinx had cried. Surely Bonbon wasn't going to… Not her Bonbon; angry, strong Bonbon. 'It's alright, I'll stay, Bonbon. Don't get sad. I'll stay.'

Bonbon dragged a finger under her nose. 'Will you really, Jinx?'

'What were you trying to say, Bonbon? There was a… what? What was there?'

Bonbon put her arms around Jinx again, her mouth trying to make words over Jinx's shoulder.

'Do you believe in the soul?'

'It's a, sort of, trend these days, isn't it? Linked to this prevailing fear of death that characterizes, to some extent, our generation.'

'Yes, but do you believe in it?'

Hamish inhaled as he thought about this. 'I like that there are still ideas we can choose to believe in, or not.'

'It was never a choice for me. It's always been as real as… my own face.' She smiled and placed her fingers on her brow bone. 'And to some extent, I've allowed myself to be driven by it.'

'You never know, we might be the last ones… with this fear.'

'Yes.' She twinkled her eyes at him. 'Death might die with our generation.'

Jinx twirled around, then stretched her arms out to the sides and pointed one foot. If she balanced her hand just over the very tips of the millions of fingers that made up the cat tails, it felt like, well, like the way *air* would feel if it could tickle her. 'You're so lucky, Bonbon.' The inside was silky and slidy. Jinx twirled again. 'Where did you get it from?'

'Mini-Me's.'

'*Oh*,' said Jinx, seeming very impressed. Then looking up to the left and screwing up her face; what was Mini-Me's? 'Did the She-one get it for you?' she asked, finally.

'Yes.'

'So, it's a shop then?'

Bonbon frowned.

'Mini-Me's; is it a shop?'

'Yes, it's a shop.'

Jinx held the end of a tail in each hand. 'I've never been to a shop…'

'Don't be ridiculous; we *came* from a shop.'

Jinx dropped the tails. 'What?'

'Remember, where we were before we met the She-one? That was a shop.'

'But… No… *No*, Bonbon. We've never lived anywhere other than *here*.' Jinx squeezed her eyes shut just to ask the inside of her head about all of this. Images flared and faded; glass boxes and funny woolly stuff on the ground, bowls of water and the smell of a toilet box. A pile of littlers huddled over each other, sleeping, in one corner. 'No…' Jinx shook her head. 'Why would we come from a shop, Bonbon? You're being quite weird, you know. You've never *ever* talked about that before. Fancy saying such silly things about living in shops…' Jinx held her shoulders with her own hands and took a step back; *oh dear*, she'd been a bit nasty there. She'd said that Bonbon was weird and silly; that would definitely make her cross. She would say something like: 'Leave me alone,

Jinx; you're making me tired.' Or: 'Me? Weird? You're the weirdo, Jinx. *No* one is as weird as you.'

Jinx held her breath.

Bonbon said nothing.

'Why do you think that we came from a shop, Bonbon?' she said in a nice voice. 'Why?'

'I don't know.' The white and crumpled one appeared inside Bonbon's head with her hands held behind her back. She smiled at Jinx and bowed a little. 'I'm *trying* to know but, but I… I just don't.'

'We come from here. We've always been here. What's happened to you?' As she said it, she felt the heat coming from the bodies piled up in the corner of the glass box and the smell of flakes and toilet box grew thicker inside her nose. It couldn't… Could it?

Bonbon looked at Jinx. 'Can we go to bed now?'

'Why are you asking *me*? You always decide when we go to bed.'

'I – I just want to go to sleep.'

Jinx bent to look up into Bonbon's eyes. Maybe Bonbon was still ill. 'Do you feel weird?' she asked. 'Do you feel bad in your stomach? Does it feel funny?'

Bonbon jolted. Champ had said that to her. With his little Jinx-face and his legs all… all… poorly. Looking up at her just like Jinx was doing now… Bonbon's eyes started to feel hot like they would overflow, and then, perhaps they *did* overflow, they felt all blurry. 'No, Jinx,' she croaked through lips that had gone all weird and bendy, 'my stomach is fine.'

Jinx's mouth fell open. She looked to her left, then to the right, then back at Bonbon. Bonbon had *never* cried before. Never *ever*. 'I'll get the She-one.'

'No!' Bonbon thought of the car, the road, the super-rise, the horrid place where she'd seen all those horrid things. The horrid shoe-coat and that weird shop-woman. If the She-one thought there was something wrong, she might take her back again… 'No, Jinx. Please can we just go to bed?'

'Alright, Bonbon,' replied Jinx, moving a string of blonde hair out of the wet eyes and tucking it behind Bonbon's ear… A big, white pillow-thing was attached to Bonbon's ear. It had a brown spot in the middle of it. Jinx stared. 'Bonbon, you've got…'

'I don't know what that thing is,' Bonbon sobbed.

'Don't worry, Bonbon,' still staring at the thing. 'Let's have a nice sleep. A nice *cuddly* sleep.'

'Yes.' Sniff. 'Yes, let's do that.'

She'd promised him. She'd *promised* him.

Maybe when she'd let go of his hands it meant that… Well, it meant something. It was a *thing*. He hadn't liked that. It was like when she put her hands on her hips while she talked to Bonbon sometimes. It was that kind of thing.

Although, he liked it when she told Bonbon off. She needed to do that *more*.

Bonbon. Bonbon who was *back*. Maybe that was why Jinx had broken her promise. It *had* to be that. They had both discussed The Big Cuddle. They had both agreed it had been really, *really* nice…

Chips looked at Jinx's nipples. Her arm lay above her head so one nipple was pulled up nearer to her chin than the other. The chin nipple was right in the middle of its breast like a star in the sky. The other one hung off the end of its breast like a bag with a knot at the bottom.

He couldn't decide which one he wanted to lick the most. Oh! He put his hands over his face; what a terrible thought! Had he *really* just thought about putting her nipple in his mouth? Lowering his hands, he looked back at Jinx from under his eyelids. His Jinx, who he wanted to cuddle *so* much. 'Sorry,' he mouthed, bowing his head. 'Sorry,' he mouthed again.

It must've been because Bonbon was there. That's why she hadn't come to his house. She'd been *so* worried last night when they went looking for her behind the box... When they found the Dead Bird again.

Jinx was always so nice to Bonbon. *Too* nice.

Chips felt every part of his face droop towards the floor. Never mind. He would come and see her in the morning. Never mind...

He rocked back onto his heels and stood up, putting on his very old humcoat that the He-one had found in a box somewhere. The sleeves of it swallowed up his hands. The hum didn't work any more and it smelled like... Well... Bad. He would have to take it off again before he saw Jinx. Now that his He-one was gone away, he could come and see her whenever he liked.

He looked back at her, sleeping on her own arm with her mouth pressed up against it as if she were kissing it. 'Bye,' he mouthed, thinking about her arm.

Lucky old arm.

'Oh!' he heard and froze. Where had that come from? It didn't sound like anywhere *near*.

Maybe it was Blankey. Could it have been Blankey following him about again?

Laughter.

His eyes shot a look at the hall door. It was coming from further inside the house. Was she laughing at him now? He glanced at Jinx, still unconscious and kissing her own arm. If she wasn't careful, she'd wake everybody up! Silly Blankey, he thought as he made big careful steps towards the hall door.

'What are you doing here?' he whispered into the black.

Nothing.

He stuck his head further into the darkness. Then snapped it back again as the ceiling thumped above his head.

What was that?

It thumped again.

And again.

And again.

And now it was getting quicker. So quick that the inside of his head no longer had time to say 'and again'.

'Stop. No. Let me turn around now, let me… Let me turn around…'

It was Jinx's she-one. The voice was breathless and quivery, but not in a frightened way… In a way that made Chips feel warm and shaky in his legs.

But not in a *frightened* way.

Chips licked his lips and crept closer to where he thought he would find the stairs. Yes! Just as he had thought – they were in the same place as his house. But instead of being sticky and rough, they felt soft and strokey. He put his cheek against the top of the first step and closed his eyes.

'Oh!'

His eyes pinged open and he pulled himself onto the second step, and the third and… 'Uh!' And the fourth and the fifth and… 'Mmm!' And the sixth and the seventh and the eighth. That voice pulled his achy arms upwards, not by his arms but a hot patch at the bottom of his stomach. With every step the strokey softness brushed his body and made him want to climb the next one and feel it all over again, why was that? 'Uh! Mmm!' The ninth step, the tenth step, the eleventh step. The 'oh's' had turned into a funny sound now, like when he smacked his own leg; but over and over again *really* quickly. As he heaved himself over the final step, he saw into another room. Some sort of night-time lamp was spying through a window. Spying on what? What exactly was that thing? All breathy and bumping up and down. It was so weird that he couldn't look away from it; he crept closer, his eyes getting used to its shape, he saw three legs, two heads, two arms, no, three arms… Four legs and… 'Let me roll over…' Chips ducked back as two arms pushed one head and one back up above another back that rolled over to reveal two breasts, one tummy and two legs *wide* open, and… What was that thing? That was a, a *thing* but why was it like that?

Chips put his hand over his own thing. His thing wasn't like that…

The big he-one lowered himself gently onto the breasts and after a second or two, the she-one 'mmmmed' again. The two-headed, four-armed, two-tummied thing started to rock, getting faster and faster, the 'mmmms' turned into 'oh's' then 'OH's' then 'AHH's'. Chips watched, mouth open. His hand was still on his thing, but it didn't feel like his thing any more. He squeezed once, twice, his other hand flying to his mouth. What on Earth had happened to it? The same thing as… as… Jinx's big he-one. But why? Chips turned and ran across the landing, his thing boing-boinging against his belly. He scrambled down the stairs, aware that he could crush it at any moment… Or even trip over it… What if it got so big that it turned into a leg? It wouldn't do that, would it? And if it did, everyone might know what he'd seen, that he'd been spying.

As his foot inched down from the bottom step to the hall floor, he put his hand on his thing to hold it out of the way and… it was back to normal. Little and squidgy.

Phew!

He stood and listened for a moment. The noises had stopped. He cupped his ear just to make sure.

Yep. Silence.

Oh! Phew. Everything seemed normal again. He would just stand here, against the bottom stair, just for a minute until he was sure that everything was normal again. A leg, huh, of course it wouldn't turn into a leg… At that moment, the middle of his leg, just above his knee, started to tingle so much that it pushed up an 'Ow!' from his belly. He shut his mouth and looked around him, then, holding the middle of his leg, he crept across the hall and through the kitchen. Jinx lay on her back with both arms stretched above her head; both nipples like stars in the sky. Her big she-one appeared on the inside of his head, as she had been just a moment ago, with her legs wide apart. The tingling had stopped. Chips crouched in front of Jinx, imagining that she was the big she-one, and he the big he-one, and that he would lower himself onto her and she would say 'mmmm'.

As he thought this, his thing felt weird against his humcoat. His hand swooped to grab it and… Oh no! It had happened again! Oh no!

He got up and ran to the vacuum hatch.

What if it didn't go down this time? What if he'd been lucky last time? Oops! He tripped as he ran across Jinx and Bonbon's Outside but kept on running. Dear oh dear! What if this happened to him *all the time*? He should never have spied on the biggerers… Stupid Chips… He should *never* have gone up those stairs… Where could he go, could he go home? But everything seemed so weird. He didn't want to take all of that weirdness back *home*. It would wake him up in the night and make him frightened. It needed to be gone!

He went over to the green box and hid himself behind it, sitting with his back up against it and his hands over his ears. That was better; he would just sit here for a few minutes. Everything would be normal soon. He would just wait here, with his hands over his ears, and listen to his own breathing. In and out… In and out… Until everything was normal.

Blankey looked *lovely*. Much nicer than those other two…

She gazed into the glass door and turned all of her body around except for her head until it really had to catch up with her body. Then she whipped it around to look back into the door.

She had managed to do something funny with her hair. She'd twisted it up the back of her head, then stuck the green bit of her flower through it so that it stayed up. All her blonde curls made a, sort of, cloud on top of her head.

She shook her head really hard to see if it would all fall down again.

It did. Oh bugger… She'd just have to put it back up, but this time she'd be really, *really* careful to properly stick in the green bit of the flower.

She'd put Chips's humcoat in a grey bag that her biggerers had given her and slipped a rose petal inside to make it smell nice. She'd kicked the dirty blue thing right under one of the kitchen cupboards. Dirty thing! But then she realized that she had nothing better to carry the flakes in, so she took off her humcoat and her shoes, and scrambled underneath the cupboard to fetch it back again.

What was it she had to say? Word for word, Jinx had said. You must remember this, word for word. 'Word for word,' Blankey repeated aloud. 'Word for word.' Maybe she would stop at her house to get some nice new flakes. This wasn't something that *she* would give to anyone, *even* Chips, who had told her that he had once tasted his own *poo* because he had been hungry. He was so funny after that, he kept shaking his head and saying: 'I didn't mean to say that. That wasn't a good thing to say to you.' Blankey had thought that this was disgusting until she saw Chips at the end of the summer, without his humcoat. No wonder he was always hungry.

The underneath of the cupboard pulled the flower out of her hair, bugger, bugger, *bugger*, so she had to put it up all over again *then* wash the blue thing *then* dry it and fill it with flakes.

She often thought about how the other three never seemed to mention washing. Not even them*selves*, let alone their things. Blankey had got used to having a nice-smelling bath twice a week, while they were sneaking about collecting stones and feathers and other dirty things…

She turned sideways to look at herself in the glass door again. Well, it was actually a good thing that the cupboard had pulled her hair out because it seemed to look even lovelier the way she'd done it this time.

She slid into her humcoat. 'Word for word,' she said again.

She liked that word 'sneak'. She couldn't remember where she had learned it. But she liked it. She liked the way that Chips *sneaked* about. Once she had caught him *sneaking* into Jinx's house. It was quite late at night, she had also been *sneaking*. 'What are you doing?' she had called to him from across her Outside.

'Don't know,' he had replied. Then he *sneaked* off and was gone! Just like that.

'Word for word.'

How could they live with themselves knowing that they never washed?

Then she put on her shoes.

They weren't *animals*. Her She-one always told her that she was a little lady and ladies *should have baths*.

She picked up the bag with Chips's humcoat inside. Yes. Chips could be excused, but Jinx and Bonbon *weren't* very ladyish. Ah flakes, mustn't forget them, she thought as she bundled the blue box under one arm. Flakes for her favourite sneaker. She had brushed up his humcoat a bit, with that lovely soft brush in her bedroom. She used it to make all of her little grey cat tails really shiny. It had worked very well on Chips's coat to get rid of the bits of fluff and AstroTurf. Yes, she had made it nice for him again. *And* got him more flakes. And maybe she would *tell* him that she had done all of this, before giving him the message. 'Word for word. Word for *word*.'

She pressed a pink gem-like button that sat inside a chrome ring on the wall and her glass door slid back to let her out. She crossed the garden and disappeared into the tunnel.

CHAPTER 6

It was very late. Jinx closed one eye and opened the other. Then did the same thing but the other way around. She did this again. And again. Until a big puff of air ffffed out of her mouth and her fingers started to drum on the floor of the basket.

'Just go,' she whispered to herself. 'You could get up and go and be back again before Bonbon even realizes that you've gone.' She whipped her head to the side to watch Bonbon for a moment.

Bonbon slept with her back to Jinx. They weren't touching even the tiniest little bit; it would have been so easy to get up and sneak out.

Poor Chips. He'd probably been waiting for ages… Jinx's heart started bouncing, what if his big he-one hadn't let him out of his cupboard? She sat up. And, what if Blankey hadn't gone?

Her shoulders relaxed slightly. Of course she had.

But what if she hadn't?

She'd said she would. She had promised.

Jinx looked back at Bonbon. What if Blankey couldn't keep her promise?

Hmmm… She got up, slowly, slowly, and ran on tiptoes to the vacuum hatch, stooped and climbed through it.

Everything seemed all right again, he thought as he wandered back through the tunnel. Tomorrow, in the daylight, and after a long sleep he might even feel silly about panicking so much.

Squinting through the outside light, he crossed his Outside and went into his house. That horrid smell hit him straight away. Gosh, this house was so different to Jinx's. He felt it a little bit more every time he came back from hers. It hadn't been this bad when he first moved here, had it? He stopped and leaned in to sniff the grey and black specks that spattered the bottom of a bowl. It looked like someone had turned his chin inside out. He rubbed his chin. That poor He-one. Some other biggerer would come and help him sometimes, to clear all this mess… His eyes jumped to the vacuum bot, the green bread, the cupboard and, oh! A foot! A foot was poking out of his cupboard!

Whose foot was that? It couldn't have been… He'd just left her sleeping with her… starry breasts… It, it couldn't have been… 'Hello?' he yelled at the foot.

'Chips!' Jinx stuck her head out of the cupboard and threw the rest of herself out afterwards. Running towards Chips she repeated his name, 'Chips, Chips, Chips!', and she was in his arms, pressed right up into his humcoat and kissing his face. Then she put her arms around his neck and leaned her head on the bit where his chest became his shoulder. 'Bonbon came back today.'

'I know,' he said, thinking that he was so happy he was shaking.

'Oh,' she said, then, 'Your humcoat is smelly.'

Bugger. His humcoat. He pushed Jinx gently away from him. 'I'm going to take it off.' Then in one movement, he let his coat fall off and let Jinx flop back onto his shoulder. 'It's old… I got my old one back because the other one is still at your house,' he said. 'But the hum doesn't work.'

'Oh,' said Jinx. It didn't matter if his humcoat didn't work. They were all warm in this cuddle. Toasty warm. Mmm… It had been the best thing to do, to leave Bonbon sleeping so that she could come and see Chips. She breathed in the smell of his shoulder; it smelled lovely and cuddly, like last night when she had woken up breathing in shoulder. Yes, yes, it had been the best thing to do…

But... wait... hang on... She lifted her head. 'Blankey gave you your humcoat today.'

Chips scrunched up his eyebrows. 'Why?'

They looked at each other for a moment.

'Because I told her to. And I gave her a message for you. And I sent flakes... Didn't she come to your house tonight?'

Chips wrinkled his face. Then his eyebrows pinged back up again, and he was about to say that she may have come over while he was at Jinx's house but... Whoops! He re-scrunched his face; he couldn't tell her that, could he? His cheeks got hot and weird as he thought about what had happened to, to his thing and, and what he had thought about doing with Jinx and... Oh... He shut his eyes tight. Oh, it was all just funny feelings inside his head, and now that she was really here, in front of him, those thoughts just couldn't stay! He felt all horrible, no, disgusted... He didn't know where that word had come from but that was exactly how he felt: disgusted with himself. 'Oooh...' he groaned, eyes still shut.

'What? What is it? Why have you gone all weird?'

He made slits with his eyelids and peeked out weirdly. Jinx had crouched down so that she could really look up at him and it felt like she was looking up his nose.

'No,' he said. 'No. She hasn't been here,' he said to her nose.

'Really?' said Jinx, standing up straight and putting her hands on her hips. 'She promised me she would.'

Chips folded his lips inwards and looked at his feet. He should have said that he hadn't seen her, not that she hadn't been here. But anyway, it didn't matter; it was only a little thing. And at least Jinx would be cross with Blankey instead of knowing about... the thing. That was funny – he could just say something, just like that, and Jinx would stop asking questions, because, well, because she didn't know that it could be any other way.

'Never mind,' said Jinx, putting her arms back around Chips. 'We can get your humcoat back from her tomorrow.'

Chips nodded, then his eyebrows shot up again; they couldn't see her. Then she'd tell them that she'd been here and couldn't find Chips. 'No!' he said.

Jinx giggled at him. 'Why?'

He flicked his eyes all over the kitchen. 'Perhaps she came and, and left it here somewhere.'

'Oh yes!' said Jinx, also looking around. 'But wouldn't you have seen her?'

'I was… erm… asleep, for, for quite a long time… erm… this evening,' he replied.

'Well, maybe she did just leave it somewhere then.' Jinx started to prowl about the room, squatting to see underneath things then stretching upwards on tiptoes to see on top of them.

Chips watched, disgusted, really disgusted. She was doing all of that for no reason. No reason at all.

But then again… Maybe Blankey had left it here. Everything could be all right, this hunting high and low for his humcoat. Maybe she did come and leave it somewhere. Yes! He started looking as well, under cupboards and inside bowls; yes! Then he could just say that he had been hidden away somewhere sleeping for that whole time. If Blankey had come: he'd been sleeping. If Blankey hadn't come: he'd been sleeping. Had he been to Jinx's house? No! Because he'd been sleeping. It worked for everything! It would all be okay. He looked around behind the fridge and promised himself he'd never say something that wasn't okay, never ever again.

'A lie,' said the voice inside his head. 'Liar,' it said, rather nastily, making the middle of his leg tingle.

He kicked the tingle out of his leg. Everything would be okay this time, he thought as he looked underneath another cupboard, and froze. Next to a blue tube, the collar of his humcoat poked out from a grey bag. A pink flower lay on the floor. He covered his mouth with one hand but it was shaking so much that he brought it down again. He opened his mouth into the shape of Jinx's name…

'I don't think it's here.' Jinx spoke just before he could. 'Let's stop looking, shall we?'

Chips tried to reply but his mouth closed up. His body was doing so many strange things, shaking and getting really hot, and thinking about what would happen after he did tell her, and… He would have to say that he had been sleeping. He would have to tell the lie again and then tell it again in front of Blankey tomorrow. Jinx's big she-one appeared on the inside of his head. She was lying with her legs wide open like before. She closed one eye at him. He jammed his eyes shut and backed out from underneath the cupboard.

'Chips? Chips? Where—'

'Let's stop now,' he said, emerging from under the cupboard and standing up. 'We might as well stop.'

Jinx bounded over to him and grabbed his hand and swung it, hard. 'Come on!' she sang. 'Where can we…' She stopped swinging his hand and put one foot over the other. 'Where can we do The Big Cuddle?'

Chips scratched the back of his head, then looked at the fridge, the ceiling, the cupboard, the floor; everywhere except for Jinx's face, until it was the only place he could look. She stood, blinking at him, sticking her breasts out while she twisted her arms behind her back.

The Big Cuddle could never be the way it had been the night before. Now that… Now that he had told her a lie and, and especially now that he had imagined himself over her like that and that thing had happened to his thing… Oh no! He scrunched his eyes shut again, so tightly that his head juddered.

'Why do you keep shutting your eyes like that?'

He peeped out at her through one eye. Maybe he should just tell her. He had told her that he had done a poo… Surely he could tell her this.

'Are you cross because I broke my promise?' Jinx wrapped her arms over her belly.

Chips opened both eyes wide. 'No!' Not at all, he couldn't imagine ever being cross with Jinx. 'No, Jinx, I'm not cross, it's just… it's a bit dirty here,' he said. 'It was better at your house.' The words 'your house' felt lumpy in his mouth. He folded his tongue and held it between his teeth.

Jinx grinned. 'Doesn't matter! Cuddles can happen anywhere.' She looked around. 'How about right here?'

Chips swallowed. 'Alright then.'

They looked at each other.

Jinx scratched her head. 'So… should we lie down first and then cuddle or…'

'Yes. Let's do that.'

They both lay down on their backs with their arms straight by their sides. After a while, Jinx rolled onto her side to face Chips. Chips copied. Jinx giggled and pulled herself closer to Chips, putting her head under his chin and squashing herself against him, at the same time picking up his arm and flopping it over her shoulder and behind her back. 'Mmmm,' she said, 'this is nice.'

'Mmmm,' said Chips. It was nice.

He heard the door creaking open behind them and his head popped up. The door shouldn't creak open, that only happened when the He-one was at home. Why would the… Blankey! He sat up. It had to be Blankey! She'd obviously been looking around the house for him.

The toe of a great big boot thumped down at the opening of the door. Chips scrambled up, opening his mouth to tell Jinx to leave, but his voice wouldn't work. So he dragged her up by her arm and pulled her towards the vacuum hatch.

Jinx screwed up her face and tried to ask why was he dragging her up by the elbow, weren't they enjoying their Big Cuddle, but, oh no! A huge biggerer was covering them up in his shadow. He walked towards them; one of his legs seemed to take longer to hit the ground than the other. 'What's going on here, then?'

Jinx turned and ran.

Chips stood, staring up at his He-one. What was he doing here? He was supposed to be gone.

'Well, Little Chips, you seem to be a bit of a ladies' man, don't you?' he laughed. 'Now, at least, I know what you were up to when I came back earlier.' He bent towards Chips's cupboard. 'Come on then. Back inside. And this time I might tighten your lead.' Chips climbed into the cupboard while the He-one fiddled with the fastening on his lead. 'My my,' he said, running a finger down one side of Chips's chest. 'You are getting skinny, oh dear, that won't do.' He dropped the lead and shuffled over to another cupboard. Chips jumped down and ran to where he had found Blankey's bag. He hoisted out his humcoat and dragged it back into the cupboard. 'We don't have many left, I'm afraid,' tipping the rest of the flakes into Chips's bowl and putting the box on the floor. 'What's that you got?' He pulled a one-armed pair of glasses out of his top pocket and stuck them on his nose. 'You found it then?' he grinned, rubbing Chips's head. 'Good boy. We can get rid of that smelly one I think,' poking him in the stomach. 'But we need to keep an eye on our weight, Mister.' How had he become so skinny? He picked up the empty flake box to read it and knocked the cupboard door really hard with his elbow, bang! Oh dear, putting the box back down, had that come off its hinges? No. No, it hadn't… Now where was he, ah yes… Ah no… No… It was no good. He couldn't remember. Something was drawing him to upstairs. Yes! Tilda! Tilda was upstairs waiting for him. 'I'm sorry, old chum, I have to go.' He recognized a throb in his elbow and looked around to find what had caused it. The cupboard door hung open so he closed it; why was his elbow throbbing? Probably bashed it on the way down the stairs. Oh well, he'd live. He took another look at Chips and tried to think of things that he had forgotten. Food? Yes. Just done that. And water? He glanced at the empty water bowl, his mind still thinking of the food bowl, said 'yes' again. 'Righto. Bye-bye then. Did I tell you I'd be gone tomorrow?'

Chips looked at him. Yes, he'd said that yesterday.

'Nadia's coming to pick me up. I'll be back in a few days,' he said as he walked away.

Chips looked down at his lead. Whenever he talked about Nadia, his eyes went all shiny and wrinkly, as if he'd got stars stuck inside them and all the sharp corners were making him wince. Nadia hardly ever came, though… Chips felt his own eyes grow hot and sad. The He-one hadn't even tied his lead after all that. It was probably because he'd thought of other things and forgotten that he'd wanted to tie him up. Or maybe it was because Chips had found his humcoat. Usually, when Chips showed him his humcoat he didn't tie up the lead. Chips had worked that out; the lead was only put on him to stop him from going outside and getting cold. Huh. What was that? As he slipped his humcoat on, a pink, flat thing fell out of it. He squatted in front of it and sniffed it. It was one of those coloured leaves that grows on flowers. He scrunched it up in both hands and pushed it into his mouth, before turning and falling onto his bowl; crunching and snuffling loudly through his nose until the flakes were gone and he lay on his cheek, panting, his eyes falling on the blue tube. He opened it and tipped the flakes into his bowl, taking big handfuls as they tumbled out and stuffing them into his mouth.

Only afterwards did he think of Jinx.

His Jinx.

They were just about to enjoy their cuddle.

Never mind, he thought, yawning and feeling all warm in his humcoat and full in his belly. He'd had a lot of things to think about today and he needed to make them all, well, calm down a bit before everything would go back to normal. She would still be there tomorrow, he yawned again, and it would be better because things would be more normal… Yes, he would see her tomorrow, eyes closing… He would go and find her first thing tomorrow.

She was in a foul mood, this morning.

Hamish rubbed at his eyes and went over the lead-up to his error, just once more, to make sure that it had been him.

But he knew it was.

Yesterday was Saturday. She had been to collect Bonbon from the vet's – sorry, doctor's – and then she had gone to one of those specialist places, to buy Bonbon a new humcoat. About time too. When she came home, she was in an okay mood because of, well, some drama at the specialist store that hadn't turned into a drama, but had obviously pumped a bit of adrenalin around her.

He had just squeaked the cork out of a niceish Bordeaux.

She collapsed on the sofa: 'Well, this is a nice surprise!'

Ah, she'd thought it was intentional. 'It wasn't intentional, I just fancied a glass,' he said.

She was in a good mood. She laughed. 'You are funny.' Then she leaned right back into the corner of the sofa and yawned. 'Seriously, though, thank you. It is lovely to come home to a little treat like this.' She nodded her nose towards the wine.

Ah. Well, he wasn't going to push the point. Instead, he poured some wine into the only glass on the table and decided that he'd been dealt a good hand that evening. 'I'll just go and get some olives.' And he did. As well as another wine glass.

She didn't notice. She had lots of things to tell him about the vet – doctor – being so guarded when recommending a store, and then the same thing with the shop assistant slipping up by telling Susan that she had to wait, when really she didn't have to do anything! And then the fact that she had learned to communicate with Bonbon, and that she had since told Bonbon that they mustn't communicate in public any more but, having been in the other specialist shop that seemed much more chilled out, she'd probably been a bit paranoid. Wasn't it crazy how this dog-eat-dog world could provoke these bouts of paranoia?

Yes, it was. All of this had been quite interesting, actually. When she was in the right mood, and had something in particular to talk about, something that had lit her wick, she became animated and her hands would fly all over the place. He loved the way she'd beaked both of her hands when she'd said 'dog-eat-dog' and made one bite the other...

But anyway, what did he think about all of this? Did he agree with the communication thing? He answered, and she listened, and she reminded him of every time she had ever listened to him, with those eyes that looked right to the back of his... Eventually one shoe came off and one of her legs was resting over one of his. He broke off his sentence to say: 'You know, this reminds me of when we were first together, and you used to listen to me. I always had to concentrate on something to stop my lips from quivering.'

'Really?' she said, surprised. 'Like talking even more?'

And it was all uphill from there.

Until, and he knew it as soon as he had said it, they were both in bed, on their backs and naked and she had said, that was pretty good, and he knew he had to say something nice, to keep the mood buoyant, even though his eyes were closing. Oh he couldn't, he just couldn't... So instead he rolled over, tucked himself under her arm, put one hand over her breast and kissed the part where her ribs were or where her armpit was or somewhere around there...

'Did you think that was good?'

He'd heard it, echoey, as if it were far, far away. But he knew that this time he had to answer.

He could have said anything, anything at all. Or even nothing! Nothing would have been much better. Instead, his hand slipped down from her breast and on to her stomach where he shook it a little with the palm of his hand and said: 'My little holiday belly.'

Oh no. Too late. He'd said it. That had woken up his eyelids.

She was silent for a minute, and thinking back now, that must've been a disbelief silence.

'What?' she said eventually.

'Oh Susan,' he said in a come-on-you-know-I-didn't-mean-it voice. He could have retracted it, right then and there. He could have fallen on the holiday belly and pretended to eat it, making her scream with laughter. He could have moved his hand all over her body saying 'my little holiday arm, my little holiday leg…' He could have even said something like: 'I absolutely forbid you to get rid of it. It's the sexiest thing that you've ever, ever acquired…'

Instead he said: 'It's normal, Suzie, it'll be gone in a couple of weeks.'

He couldn't apologize. Then he'd be all sheepish and practically admitting the fact that her holiday fat should have remained something that they could both know about, but mustn't address.

So… He told her that he loved her, kissed her again on her ribs/armpit and pretended to go to sleep.

Yes, it might have been ever so slightly his fault. In fact, he knew that it was because he was wincing.

So now, even though she claimed to dislike Shepherd's, because he was 'obsessed' with it, and would sigh and huff whenever he said he was going there, he'd slipped out of the house with a big shopping list in his ScreenJotta. He read through it as he walked from the drive to the car… Ice cream, goat's cheese, sushi, she'd love the sushi. He had to get the right balance; if it was all mung beans and celery, then she'd think he was trying to feed a diet. That wouldn't do… He was right to go with cheese and ice cream. In fact, it was a roundabout way of saying sorry, wasn't it? It said: 'I believe that there is no reason for you not to eat this.'

And flowers. He'd get some flowers; just in case.

'You're lovely the way you are,' was all he really wanted to say. She would realize the message. She would say to herself: 'Shepherd's is his way of showing me that he loves me.' And she would roll her eyes a little because 'Men love you in their own special way; you can't expect them to be very original'. And he would ignore the fact that she would be essentially plopping him into a box marked 'Experiences with Men' – including her father – and tying a big social cliché ribbon around it. At this point he would lead her into the dining room; for the plan didn't stop at cheese, ice cream and sushi; heavens no! He had planned to fish out the candles that he'd found last week and prepare a nice, restaurant-like table.

Fish out the candles. Sushi! Ha! That was good.

'Hello there.'

Hamish looked up. A small lady floated towards him across the neighbouring driveway, the dividing fence covering up her legs. Her eyes smiled at him through skin like autumn leaves, her mouth showing off all of her veneers.

'Hello,' he said with no emotion.

Usually she would stop and put her hands on her hips, leaning back slightly, and look out towards where the driveway ended and the world started and say something like, 'Off out?'

This time, she floated right up to the fence and put her hands on it. They seemed a bit shaky and in one of them she held a handkerchief. Barriers. She was handling the barrier. She wanted something from him.

'Yes… Hello,' she said. Not quite able to ask him.

He put his ScreenJotta under his arm and looked over his glasses. He could break barriers. 'Is everything alright?' releasing some emotion into his eyebrows.

'Erm… I was wondering… Are you going to the supermarket?'

'Yes, I'm off to Shepherd's,' he replied, surprised, as always, about how old she looked. 'Do you know it?'

'Yes,' she enthused, 'it's Jerry's favourite.' She looked to the side, folding her lips and licking them at the same time. 'The thing is, Jerry's in hospital, and… I can't get out really. I wondered… if you wouldn't mind—'

Hamish cut her off, striding towards the fence, emotion now yanking his face in all directions. 'Yes, of course!' he said. 'Of course.'

She beamed, giving the fence a little squeeze before scrunching her hands up under her chin. 'Oh you are kind!' she smiled. 'Now, shall I jot down what I need?'

Hamish was surprised; 'Oh, wouldn't you like me to take you there?'

'Well!' she said, looking at her house with one finger in the air. 'I would have loved to come with you but…' She looked at him from the side of her head. 'My little Blankey's been missing all morning and I'd like to be here when she comes home. Silly, isn't it?'

Hamish put his mouth on upside down. 'Blankey?'

'Ah,' she said. 'My littler.'

'Oh, right!' he said. Jinx stood inside his head with another littler that he didn't recognize. Was that a memory? Or had his brain just made that up? 'When did you last see her?'

'Yesterday evening.' With her handkerchief hand she pushed her other sleeve up and scratched, revealing the scrunchy bird-like bottom of another handkerchief. 'What with Jerry and, and now Blankey…'

'Of course,' Hamish said again. Then still gripping the fence, swung backwards a little. 'Is it… Will, erm… Do they think he'll be coming home soon?'

She looked straight at him. 'He's one hundred and thirty-four years old.'

Hamish stopped swinging; his mouth fell open.

She laughed. 'That's about one hundred years older than you, is it not?'

The maths had shocked him – one hundred years older? 'That means he was born in…'

'Nineteen eighty-two,' she smiled. 'In the house next door

but one from mine.' She gazed at nothing for a moment, sadly. 'Yes...' she tailed off out loud a private thought.

'Wow,' Hamish said cheerily. 'That was before... before tablets.'

She laughed again. 'That was before everything. That was before personal computers and, and internet in the home, Wi-Fi, oh yes! Certainly before Wi-Fi.'

Hamish's cheek twitched. It was one of the things he knew about but could not imagine. He was incapable of visualizing a world without Wi-Fi, *incapable*. It was well known that only very intelligent people were able to do it.

'We've seen a lot!' she chuckled again.

'I can certainly imagine.'

They were silent for a moment. 'Anyway,' she said eventually. 'To answer your question, I don't think he'll be home soon.'

'But what will you do?'

'I'm going to my daughter's this weekend... I'll stay with her for a while. I was supposed to go today but,' she looked about her, 'what with Little Madam going off like that...'

'Well, just you remember that we are here. You mustn't hesitate, if you need anything.' He looked at his wrist. 'Networks,' he said to it. A list streamed up in front of him. 'Lucas,' he said. Mr and Mrs Lucas were highlighted in the list – request action? 'Business card,' he said. Business card sent. The screen faded back into a ticking clock face. 'I've just sent you our number so you don't even have to come out of the house if you need us...' He stopped. 'I'm sorry, do you know how that works?'

She dipped her chin and raised her eyebrows. 'The telephone?' she asked.

'No, the...' Then he blushed and let out a smirk. She was making fun of him. 'Sorry about that.'

'One becomes accustomed to ubiquity.'

'Hmmm,' he hmmmed. Nobody said 'one' any more. Hearing it was like hearing a chord played on a harp.

'I'll just get a scrap of paper, and I'll jot down what I need.'

'Paper,' he smiled. 'Righto.' Many elderly people were still in the habit of saying 'paper'. He remembered his list under his arm. 'Oh but… I have my ScreenJotta here if it's easier.'

But she'd shuffled off towards her porch.

Hamish looked up at the house. He'd left Susan upstairs trying to get into a pair of white jeans that she'd had since she was about fifteen. His eyes wandered up to their bedroom window. One hundred years… he thought to himself. And to his surprise, she was looking back at him. Her face, behind the tinted window, was blank and puffy, and a little grey. Lifting his hand to his mouth, he decided to do something he had never done; he didn't know why… Just to try it maybe… Just to be original… Just because he'd done something nice for Mrs Lucas and that had felt good… He kissed his fingertips and blew the kiss up to her, imagining it like a jellyfish climbing through water. Behind the window, her face flooded with redness that contrasted with the gleam of her teeth. Her mouth pushed up her cheeks and forced her eyes to squeeze out a little twinkle. She opened the window, put her opened hand out and snapped it shut around the jellyfish.

He took a step back to get a better view of the new Susan, the real Susan. In that moment, he had changed her back. And it had been so simple!

He decided to continue with his experiment and strained his cheek up towards the window, tapping it twice with one finger. She laughed and kissed the palm of her hand, for quite a long time; in fact, she even closed her eyes. Then she held her fist outside of the window and opened it, palm upwards yet tilted towards him; she gave her hand a little bob as if she were releasing a bird.

He let one hand out of its pocket to reach out and catch the kiss. Hearing the scrunch of driveway footsteps, he smiled and tipped his head at Susan, baffled at how he'd just managed to brighten up what had looked to be a pretty grim day.

'Here we go.' Mrs Lucas gripped the fence with both hands; something was tucked between the finger and thumb of one hand. She steadied herself and gave it to him.

Immediately he was alone in his office, having just pulled on his gloves and opened up his cabinet. The woody, almost burnt smell crawled up his nose and back out again, over his face, his shoulders and kicked up goosebumps along each arm. It was as if she'd given him an opened jar full of ants.

'Where did you get this?' he stage-whispered, letting his eyes glance left and right.

She laughed. 'From my notebook.'

'You've got a whole book of these?'

'My dear… I've got a whole cupboard full of boxes, all packed to the brim with notebooks.' She let one arm fan out a veritable plethora in front of her.

'Shhh!' he hissed, looking left and right to make her laugh again.

She did laugh. Then she put one of her hands over his and squeezed it. 'When you come back, I'll have one waiting for you.'

Hamish held his breath and let his hand be touched by this person who he didn't really know.

She quickly withdrew her hand and folded her arms.

'I could never accept a… I mean… Do you know how rare this is?' He looked down at the sheet of paper while she waved his protests away. 'Seriously, do you know how rare…' He stopped and read. Fig jam, unsalted butter, skimmed milk, egg noodles, mature cheddar, carrots… 'Who wrote this?'

'Who wrote what?' She looked confused.

'This writing.' He indicated towards the paper with his right hand as he cradled it in his left. Black loops and angles, thick and thin in different places, grew across the page like an old vine curling up the side of a house.

'I did,' she said. No longer confused. 'But, you know how to write, don't you?'

'Not like this.' He shook his head, one finger curled over his lips as he contemplated the evenness of the black shapes.

Sometimes he practised writing when he had the time for hobbies. He had an app that would trace out a letter and then he had to write over it using the same method; then he had to have a go on his own. It was a bit tricky, but he was fairly confident with about twelve letters now. 'Did… did this take you a very long time?'

'Ha!' she scoffed. 'You saw me do it!'

'Just then? In the porch?'

'Yes!' she nodded. 'You can keep it if you like.'

'Really?'

'Of course.'

As he told the WayToGo to take him to Shepherd's, he vowed that he would, he absolutely must, learn to write. Shepherd's was open and busy. They had even sent out their parking attendant today. Because it was Sunday, it was only a machine. As he advanced and indicated right, the HelpaBot pointed towards the left. No! He didn't want to go that way. He wanted to turn right. Paying no attention to the machine, he turned right and drove on to the area where she usually parked. It was unlikely he'd bump into her; he'd never seen her here on a Sunday… Oh! Sunday samples; he craned to see what the machines were handing out at the entrance to Shepherd's. Small plastic packets of yellow. Hmmm… Probably cheese. A white car caught his eye. Nope. Too square. He continued past the others, all parked neatly in their bays. Red, blue, silver… white! Too big. Red, red, black, pink, black, white! No, a van. White again! Was that it? No, too many accessories.

He sighed; only a little bit. It wasn't just because it was Sunday; he didn't really see her here at all any more. In fact, the sighs got smaller and smaller each time he came. And today lots of other things swam in his head, like jellyfish kisses, loopy letters, sex and sushi. She only occupied a small part of it, maybe a square centimetre, and that was only because he was here.

Then again, he had wanted to see her enough to turn right.

It wasn't healthy, this spying. But really, how could it hurt anyone? He was only looking out for her car.

Association, he reasoned as he pressed the 'park' button and the car started to reverse into a bay. Conditioning. He had learned to associate that right turn with past feelings of excitement, rather than the act of discovering her. Now, where had he put that list? Top pocket. Wonderful! Fancy pulling a sheet of paper from your top pocket! No. Fancy pulling a piece of paper from *one's* top pocket!

He got out of the car and headed towards the entrance, the thought of cheddar moistening his mouth. Mmm… 'Welcome to Shepherd's! Please help yourself to one of our free samples.'

'Yes, thank you, I'll take one from you,' he turned to the other machine, 'and one from you, Sir, and…' He turned back to the first machine.

'Welcome to Shepherd's! Please…'

'And another one from you. Ha ha!' He flicked the plastic-covered rectangle up in the air and caught it on the back of his hand. Red red hair and bangles stopped at the opposite machine and slipped two bags of shopping onto one wrist before helping herself to a sample.

'Cheddar… Yum,' said Emma.

Or was it Emma? He had seen that back walk away from him so many times, why couldn't he remember it? He blinked. Was it her? He couldn't be sure… Yes, yes, it was! Or, was it… Damn! If only she would turn around. If only he could see a little bit around the side of her…

'Excuse me.'

'Oops! I am sorry.' He was blocking the entrance and he still had the cheese on the back of one hand and the list in the other. Stuffing both items in his pockets, he turned back around to watch her again, but she was gone. He stood on tiptoes for, well, whatever reason, then walked towards the car park, his head owling this way and that, but no – shit – he'd let himself go. Damn! This wasn't the reason he'd wanted to see her. There was no reason. He couldn't see her… He had only ever wanted to glimpse her, and now he was chasing after her…

He turned quickly, shoved his hands in his pockets and went back to the entrance.

'Welcome to Shepherd's! Please help yourself to one of our…'

Through the doors and he was in. He wouldn't look back. Not even to check if he should have held the door for the person behind. Not even to wonder if it was actually a sliding door and so there would've been no reason to hold it. Not even to see if he'd dropped anything when he pulled his hands back out of his pockets.

He retrieved the list. Well, at least he was sure that he hadn't dropped that. The same feeling, only a little diluted, the burnt jar of ants, filled him up again as he straightened the list out and re-read it. The spaces in his head that had reopened, the Emma spaces, cavities that yawned empty and dead now crawled with busy burnt ants.

'Fig jam,' he said to himself. 'Unsalted butter. Egg noodles. Carrots…'

'They used to call me Carrot-head.'

'Right.'

'I think they meant "Carrot-top". I never really hear anyone say that any more… Do you?'

'I don't know what it means.' He kept his hands clasped in front of him, the lenses of his glasses well and truly displaying his whole eyes.

'Really? Well, it's because of my red hair.'

'Right.' A line of carrots rose out of her head; one by one they collapsed, sighing, and dangled at the side of her face. He wanted to grab up handfuls of her carrot hair and bite it. 'How did that make you feel?' careful to keep his tone neutral; not to show the fact that he already knew the answer. He already knew that she would laugh because she didn't care…

She laughed. 'I didn't care. I was… What? Seven?'

'Nothing else?' he said, to stop himself from saying something like *of course you didn't care!*

She thought for a moment, taken in by this false importance he had built up around her hair.

'It's funny. I've always behaved a bit differently to other people, and I tend to blame it on my hair.'

'Why?'

'Well… The cliché goes that redheads have fiery characters… So… Um…' She smirked at her knee. 'I don't actually know what I'm trying to say.'

He smirked with her. Damn! Casting his eyes down, he pinched his nostrils and made his face all serious again. Damn, damn, damn.

She hadn't noticed. 'I've always dressed differently, always. I mean, even at school I'd do silly things like, oh I don't know… Like one time I sewed wings onto my coat. Gosh, I did, didn't I? I'd completely forgotten about that… And another time I wore odd shoes – one green and one black. I remember, yes… There was always something: a flower in my hair, or lace gloves or… or sometimes I'd wear two ties, with two knots, side by side… I've always been a bit… quirky.'

'Right.' She sat before him, with wings, and a flower in her hair, a peony, he decided was the most appropriate, lacy gloves that tattooed their way up her arms to her elbows, and not much else… The ties spilled over her chest, their pointed tips lapping at her belly button.

'Yes,' she said, nodding. 'Quirky.'

Bugger. He'd drifted. He had to stop bloody drifting. He nodded and stayed silent for a minute. This was useless, but it made the whole 'drifted' silence look intentional. He mentally added a minute to their session and hoped that she would feel pressured into saying something else.

'You think that I have a rebellious streak, don't you? I know where this is going.'

'Do you think that?' he batted back.

'Hmmm.' She narrowed her eyes and looked past him towards the window. Then turned her head ever so slightly, squeezed her lips so they became one plump strawberry, looked right at him and purred. 'Sometimes.' She raised an eyebrow.

It was as if someone had flicked the space between his eyes; thwack! That was foul play. That was for him, that look. She was flirting with him. He knew it. He knew that all this hadn't been one-sided; there was something. He checked himself – he was holding his breath. Breathe! But how could he breathe after a look like that?

She was flirting.

Or…

But…

No…

Actually…

She wasn't. She was continuing with her explanation; the flirty look hadn't been a flirty look, it had only been the trigger for what was coming next. It wasn't meant for him at all. She was telling it now, her story of rebellion; of sucking on helium balloons in the bus shelter… No! That was lame! It was a 'between-professionals' story. It was something she could tell her boss to lift the mood without saying anything compromising. That story didn't warrant such a look. Oh… Disappointment made his ears thud, fading out her voice. She had wanted to give a cheeky, well-wait-until-you-hear-this look; not throw her expression from her face and use it to lick his inner thigh.

'Interesting.' He reeled himself back in. 'What are you not telling me?'

'What?' she half-laughed.

'Do you consider that to be the most rebellious thing you've ever done?'

'No,' she said. 'You know I don't.'

'Mmm-hmm… Go on.'

But she wouldn't. She looked at the space between them. The words were obviously there, just squashed into a ball in her throat.

'This is all in confidence.'

'I know.'

'This is a safe space. This is your safe space.'

'Yes,' she said. Then closed up again, as if she needed time to peel another word from the ball.

'Try starting from the beginning.'

'—'

He allowed a minute to pass before asking another question. 'Do you feel guilty about everything you tell me? Is that, in itself, a rebellious act?'

She replied while he was still saying 'rebellious act'.

'It all started with a notebook that I acquired,' she said. Then: 'Oh sorry, you were saying?' She cocked an ear and waited for him to finish what he was saying.

'No. Please. A notebook?'

'Yes. Well, it was more like a diary, really. It was given to me when I was little – although it was top secret,' she whispered, grinning. 'It inspired me so much that I decided to go into that line of work, only my brother died while I was still studying and… changed how I saw my future profession. Which was probably stupid.'

'Go on.'

'I helped many families,' she had raised her voice without meaning to, 'because of that book.'

Agitation, he thought. He decided to lean forward, narrow the distance; shrink the room for judgement. They were on the same level; they were equal... Two humans having a conversation.

'The bereaved families; tell me about what that means,' he said in a voice that he lilted in all the right places, as if he were asking a baby to smile for him.

'I helped families for my job. But I wasn't meant to. It's something that is considered bad practice, God...' She shook her head, her knees rising as her feet pushed themselves onto wincing tiptoes. 'But I always thought it was right. I think there's no wrong in reuniting people who love each other...' almost panting, '*loved* each other.' She stopped for breath. 'You know, death is the only thing that stands in our way now, isn't it?' Her eyes jumped from the corner of the table to the middle, to the wall and back again. 'There was no harm in it to start with but then it felt like, like... I was playing God. One time a woman approached me in the street with a box of toenail clippings, crying: "Can you bring him back?" and I was frightened that people knew what I did, and she was coming to me with an order. I thought I'd have to go into hiding or something... But she didn't know who I was; she was just another person, crazed by this one thing, you know... that can really take us away. Really.'

Hamish's eyes danced. She wasn't making any sense. 'Talk to me about these families, who are they?'

'I don't know... Me?' She snorted out a laugh, then her eyes wrinkled over and she looked like she was about to cry.

'You?'

'—'

'Emma?'

She cast her eyes down. 'Forget that,' she mumbled, then started again in a new, clear voice. 'I got carried away, I suppose; with being a do-gooder. I read in the news about this tragic man who lost his wife – she died – in a car accident. He was so unhappy that he went, well, a little crazy and had to be taken away… I felt so sad for him.' She paused for a moment. 'Anyway, I sent her to live next door… When he was well enough to come home, of course.'

'You sent who to live next door?' he couldn't help.

'He already had one and there was no reason to target him with a second… But I just thought that if they could be near each other…'

Who? Hamish wanted to ask; two what? Two wives? Instead he swallowed and said: 'Go on.'

She smirked. 'I must have been mad.'

'Why do you think that?' He waited for her to continue but she didn't. Soothing, he thought. He had the urge to soothe and get rid of this agitation. That was a normal urge. Maybe he could try his nice baby voice again, muffle the stimuli a bit… Mustn't let too much through, though; she's a patient like any other, he told himself. Like a child; it was all counter-transference, pressing his paternal buttons. Just imagine she is a child.

'Look,' he said.

She didn't look.

'Look at me!'

She looked up.

He planned to say: 'The only difference is that what is inside will be out, which is what we are working to achieve. Nothing bad is going to happen to you.' Instead he said, in the softest, tiniest, almost-whisper: 'The only difference is that what is inside will be out, which is what we are working to achieve. I'm never going to let anything happen to you.'

She stared at him.

The reflex to scrunch up his face, the hands that wanted to stuff the words back into his mouth, the cry that spiralled up from his belly, the teeth that wanted to clench, the lips that wanted to spit, the shoulders that wanted to hunch – he had to fight all of them; keep them in place because she was looking towards the back of his eyes; and she had read every scrap of meaning in that last sentence. He held the stare. 'Trust me,' he said to her from the inside of his head. 'Trust everything you knew about me up to that point, and let it all swallow up that stupid sentence.'

'Are you ready to go on?' he had to say.

She squinted and blinked a little, and for a moment he thought she would ask him what on Earth he'd meant. He curled his index finger over his top lip and watched for the first word to emerge. She took a deep breath. 'When the cells were taken, I would find the original families. I sought them out; they make out it's impossible but of course it's not! Everything's coded, labelled, recorded – everything has traceability. Except at my level. My level shouldn't have any want or need to be poking into the traceability of a product – that's how I pulled it off. I'd just follow the cell's progression, at the same time targeting the family with whatever techniques I could get away with. It gave me such a buzz. It was as if I were cheating death, like a sheepdog of souls.' She smiled. 'I'd turn herds of them around and guide them home. It was honestly that easy. As long as I got the families through the showroom door, as long as they set eyes on the product, they were always drawn to it… Even when there were several to choose from, they almost always chose the one that… Am I making any sense?'

Hamish started. 'Yes!' he said unconvincingly. She had taken him by surprise. 'I think the important thing here is to just get it all out; then we can attach some sort of narrative.' Bloody hell. That was lame. 'When exactly did you stop?' Good save. An obvious question.

Her eyes wandered over him and suddenly she looked panicked. 'Is that the time?' She consulted the clock projection on the surface of the desk.

'What? Oh, no… Don't worry about that. We can run over a little. It's fine.'

'I can't believe I'm actually telling you about all of this.'

'You're doing well, Emma. It's alright, you can go on.'

She paused for a moment, as if trying to find her place in the story. 'I…' Then: 'Actually. I think I would rather continue this next session.'

Hamish swallowed. He would have given her his entire collection of books if she'd have stayed with him for one more minute. But he had to let her go. 'Right. So… Thank you, Emma. You'll see Sandra to book your next appointment?' He gestured towards the end of the corridor where Sandra's desk was hidden in an alcove.

'Yes.' She got up. 'Thank you.'

He nodded, trying to work out from her face if his error-sentence had been forgotten.

'I'm sure we'll see each other soon.' And she swished out.

Sure we'll see each other soon? Sure. We. Will. See. Each. Other. Soon.

He played these last words on a loop, rubbing at his forehead, willing his brain to work out their meaning.

'Sure we'll see each other soon.'

He touched his desk and it transformed into a screen. 'Sandra?'

'Yes, Hamish.'

'My last patient…'

'Ms Emma Howards?'

'Right… What slot has she taken for next week?'

'She didn't stop to arrange another appointment.'

Oh dear, where was she? Oh dear… Where was she?

Where was she. Where was she. Where was she.

Oh dear.

Oh dear oh dear.

She, she, she… breathed… very… qui-quickly. She, she, she,

what was that? St-still br-breathing qui-qui-quickly her ha-hand felt someth-thing prickly. Like, like… If o-only she could s-see it was s-so dark. Wha-what was th-that prickly th-ing under her… Oh! This was all t-too mu-mu-much!

She covered her eyes with her hands as a funny hot feeling rose all the way up her body from her feet and bottom that were all squished together into a small space on the floor, to her elbows, shoulders, neck, face, it was… It was like getting into her bath. Except she wasn't *getting in* the bath, the bath was crawling up her and if she hadn't already been sitting down she would have had to sit down because her head was full of stuff that seemed to be heavier than her body. It made her feel sick. It made her eyes nudge little floaty white blobs all around the room; the room that she couldn't see.

Room. It wasn't a room. I-it w-was a b-b-box. A box. A *box*! She closed her eyes and breathed slowly… In and out, she thought to herself; in and out.

It was a box. She had seen the outside of it when he had put her in here. Even though she hadn't tried, she was pretty sure that she couldn't stand up. She had seen from the outside that it was too small to stand up in. And the prickly thing she had touched must have been the floor or a wall or something. She'd never touched this kind of floor or wall before, but she occasionally caught a noseful of a familiar smell, something from home, the big brown cupboard in the big She-one's dressing room. Its door smelled of that same smell that was so different from the white shiny table and chairs in the dining room.

Oh. Her eyes felt hot as she thought of the big She-one. Then she thought of Chips's humcoat left to hide under that dirty kitchen cupboard. And his flakes.

She lifted her hand and touched her hair.

And her pink flower had been left under there.

A-and after-ter that a, a, a, b-big h-hand w-was around h-her!

Oh dear. Oh dear. Oh dear. Br-breathe! In and out. In and out. In and out. The bath rose around her again, washed its white shapes through her eyes then sank back down.

And what had he called her? Tilda? Who was Tilda? That wasn't her name. Why would he call her that if it wasn't her name? She'd opened her mouth to tell him 'that's not my name!' but the sound wouldn't come out… Then she had screamed 'Chip! Chips!' but his name couldn't be screamed. She was in biggerer hands, and they were walking through the hallway and he was doing that thing that made Bonbon's ears go red, and he was saying that he was sorry, he was sorry for crying but he thought he'd never see her again! 'I thought I'd never see you again!' He kept saying it and stroking her hair with his finger as he climbed the stairs. 'I'm not Tilda!' she tried to scream again but it was stuck, her mouth could only make the shapes of the words. 'It's alright, Tilda. Nearly there,' he said, putting her onto his shoulder. 'Hop up there instead; I'm frightened that I'll squeeze you,' he said. 'You always told me that I didn't know my own strength.' But 'up there' was quite wobbly. She had to put her hands in his beard to hold on and it smelled of… Well… Not nasty, but *unclean*, and as he went up and up the stairs she looked down and saw the hallway getting smaller and tried one last time to call for Chips.

Nothing.

As they got to the top, she looked towards where they were walking and noticed a tiny picture up on the wall… That was strange. She didn't know why but… but she couldn't stop staring at it, and as they turned onto the landing, her head turned all the way around so that her eyes could still see it and stare at it until they turned into a room and it was gone.

They entered the room and Blankey felt herself calm down; just a tiny bit. Maybe because she'd been busy looking at the picture. Or maybe because the room was lovely. Although it wasn't very *clean*. The air smelled like it had been trapped there for a long time. Pink shiny cushions stood one in front of the other on two low armchairs with curvy white legs. One enormous mirror leaned against the wall between the two chairs, flowers furry with dust peeked over the edge of its frame. Dangly, twisty, white curtains that she could almost see through hung over the bed and one of them was clipped back with a plastic rose. A pair of fluffy slippers, like her own humcoat but made from *pink* cats, stood in front of a white skinny-legged table with a lamp hanging over it. The lamp was made of glass leaves that cupped a dimming light. She would have thought it was lovely, if a bit dusty, had she not been so scared. 'I made it just how you wanted it,' said the beard. Then he told her that he would only put her in the box for a minute, just for a minute – he just didn't want to lose her again, oh no, he couldn't *bear* to lose her again. His Tilda. His lovely Tilda… And the box was shut. Then there were footsteps. Then the door was shut, and as she re-thought these thoughts now, inside the dark and prickly box, the door clicked open.

Oh dear, thought Blankey. Oh dear, oh dear. 'I'm not…' she managed to say, her voice dying as the box was reopened and two hairy eyes blinked in.

'Tilda,' he said, the eyes disappearing behind a reaching hand.

CHAPTER 7

Jinx woke up first. She rolled over and looked at Bonbon, wondering what her first words would be when she opened her eyes. Now that she'd had a good night's sleep, she should be feeling better; she should, well, be back to normal. Jinx thought of the day with the angora cushion and the rose petals… She had been quite nice that day too, because she was poorly. But, she hadn't *cried.* Although she might have cried, if Jinx hadn't found her somewhere nice to sleep. That must've been what had happened last night, she was so poorly and sleepy; she just wanted to sleep.

But she was getting better. That's why she had come home with that thing on the side of her head. It was making her better.

Her lovely Bonbon. Jinx would just look at Bonbon for a moment because she was sure that in no time she'd get up and start giving her orders for the day.

Now what day was it, stone day? String day? Jinx couldn't even remember. Everything had become so mixed up since Bonbon had been away…

Jinx held out her finger; if she poked Bonbon then she might start to wake up, and then she could ask her how she was feeling. But then again, she didn't want her to wake up. She just wanted to watch her. It would have been nice if, today, when Jinx asked her to stay in bed for just a little bit longer, she would stay. And they would have a nice cuddle.

As the word 'cuddle' echoed in her head, two littlers appeared, sinking onto a dirty floor… Chips! She remembered hunting around his kitchen for a humcoat, then lying on the floor, then his big he-one came in and scared her away… His big he-one was much scarier than her big She-one. With his face all hairy like that, and, and so tall that she couldn't see the top of him.

Yes, she thought, all of that hadn't been something that had only happened on the inside of her head.

'A dream,' said the inside of her head.

Yes. It hadn't been a dream.

Oh well, maybe today they'd finally get to have their Big Cuddle, properly. He would come into the yard later and she would go out to see him straight away and then… And then they would talk about his big he-one. And they might even laugh a bit because the same thing had happened to both of them; they'd both been scared away by the other one's big-one. And then she might hold his hand for a while… She liked that. That was nice. And maybe… Bonbon! Bonbon was waking up!

Bonbon sat up straight as she usually did, looked out of the basket at the bowls – as she usually did – saw that they were both empty and started to get out of the basket.

As she usually did.

'It's early, Bonbon, why don't you stay here for a minute?'

Bonbon looked back at Jinx with her face all screwed up and Jinx was sure that she would say 'no', which was nicer than normal; normally she just ignored her and got out anyway.

'Alright,' she said, falling back into the basket, picking up Jinx's arm and flopping it over her as she snuggled into Jinx's side.

Jinx opened her mouth and eyes really wide, wanting to let out a big squeaky sound but instead, so as not to make the cuddle all noisy, she danced her eyes really fast.

That was the first time ever that Bonbon had stayed.

It was like yesterday, in the Outside, when Bonbon had just

walked up to her and thrown her arms around her and... Jinx closed her mouth and let her eyebrows droop.

It was like yesterday.

That meant that she was still weird.

That meant that Bonbon wasn't better.

They lay like that for a while, then: 'Aren't you hungry, Bonbon?'

'The bowls are empty.'

'Oh.' Jinx pursed her lips. 'Should we kick the bowls?'

Bonbon was quiet for a moment. 'Alright,' she said, rolling out of the cuddle and making to leave the basket.

All right? Just like that, everything was all right? This was silly. It wasn't up to Jinx to say things like that; Bonbon should say something like, 'Well, I suppose one of us has to kick the bowls,' or, 'First it's cuddles, then it's flakes. You always change your mind, Jinx. You're such a selfish rat.'

'Why do you always kick the bowls, Bonbon?' she said. Then jammed her eyes shut.

Bonbon stopped, one leg over the side of the basket. 'You can do it if you want to...'

'No!' Jinx opened her eyes. 'I mean, it's not fair on you!'

'Oh,' said Bonbon. 'It doesn't really matter who does it as long as it's done.'

That was a little better. Just a little bit. Jinx thought for a moment. 'Well, let's not do it at all. Let's just wait for one of the biggerers to get up.' Ha! That was really, um, really... That would make her cross.

'Contrary,' said the inside of her head.

Bonbon scratched her jaw. 'We don't usually do things like that.' She glanced at the bowls then back at Jinx.

Yes, that was more like it. 'No, we don't, Bonbon.'

'But, alright.' Bonbon flopped back into the basket.

Jinx puffed out her cheeks with air then slowly blew it out.

Bonbon laughed at her.

Now, that was nice. It was nice to see Bonbon laughing. It was so rarely that Bonbon laughed.

'Why did you do that?' Bonbon nodded towards the bottom half of Jinx's face.

'Don't you think,' she began, 'don't you think that first it's cuddles, then it's flakes? I'm always changing my mind because I'm a selfish rat?'

Bonbon hugged her knees. 'No,' she said. 'I don't think that. I know that I used to think things like that, but I don't today and I don't know why.' She opened her mouth and bit down on one of her knees.

Oh… Jinx understood that. She understood feeling different every day. Sometimes she felt different two or three times in one day. In fact, usually she felt different because Bonbon was nice to her. Or nasty to her. But Bonbon… Bonbon was always the same. Someone must have been nasty to her while she was away. Something must have changed her.

'Has someone been nasty to you?' asked Jinx.

Bonbon was quiet. She didn't really know the answer to that. She didn't think so but, but something in her head answered Jinx's question. 'Yes,' it said. 'Something has been very nasty.'

Jinx had a thought: 'Maybe it's because of that thing?'

Bonbon put her hand to her ear. She'd, sort of, forgotten about the white cushion thing. A picture came together inside her head: she was lying down with the big She-one and the doctor standing over her. 'Does she get grumpy?' asked the doctor. 'That's what's causing it.' Yes! She remembered now, those words had definitely been said.

'You're right, Jinx,' still holding her ear. 'I remember now… This thing is curing my grumpiness.'

'Really?' staring at the thing. Could it really do that? 'Are you sure?'

'Yes, I remember the conversation; the whole thing is on the inside of my head.' As soon as she had said it, another thing appeared. The rows and rows of at least twenty littlers, who were all suffering from grumpiness as well.

Jinx felt pleased.

Or did she…?

Yes, yes, she did because at least they knew why Bonbon had changed. And Bonbon was much nicer now, but… This was a big change. It was as if, as if she were a brand new littler. It meant that the old Bonbon was gone, forever. Did it? Did it mean that?

'Do you have to keep that thing on forever?'

No answer.

Jinx had another thought: 'And, if you take it off, what will… I mean… Will you be grumpy again?'

'I don't know,' Bonbon said, really quietly, before turning her body so that she was in the corner of the basket, still hugging her legs, not looking at Jinx. 'Think yourself lucky, last month it was breast reduction… Then it was rib removal…' The sentence went around and around, like Jinx when she chased her own shadow. That couldn't have been a good thing to say, the breast reduction thing, now that an open breast sprawled inside her head like a pink and yellow flower; where had that picture come from? She had never even seen an open breast. It made her feel sure that something more horrible could have happened to her if… if she had been poorly last month. And she was also sure that she could work all of this out with the inside of her head, as if what happened in there was like, well, another littler, an older littler who could answer Jinx's questions and who knew so much about the outside world, and helped her with it from the inside of her head.

That was exactly what it was like.

She began to suck the top of her knee again.

That's what she would do today. She would spend time with this littler, this littler who lived on the inside of her head, and they would work out everything that had happened to her while she had been away, and then she would decide what she thought about it.

'Are you hungry, Bonbon?' She'd gone all weird again, thought Jinx. 'You're eating your own knee.'

Bonbon looked up. Saliva was running down her leg, but she could only feel it when it got to her shin, when it had had the chance to cool down.

'What day is it today, Bonbon?'

Bonbon looked confused. 'Today.'

'No, I mean, is it paper day, feather day, string day?'

'Oh… I can't remember.' And then: 'I don't really feel like it today…' She closed her mouth, then reopened it to eat her knee.

Jinx climbed out of the basket and headed for the bowls. If this was what that stupid ear-thing was doing to her, then she didn't like it. In fact, it was the most horrible thing ever. She kicked her bowl as she thought the word 'ever' then sat on the side of it and waited.

And waited.

It was so late. The room was really, really bright now. Usually they were given their flakes while it was still a bit grey, and a bit cold; even when it was the day after Saturday.

She kicked the bowl again, this time sitting on the side of the bowl that was facing the kitchen door. It was closed. She was hungry. She'd sent most of her flakes away with Blankey in the blue tube. Stupid Blankey. Oh wait, no, it wasn't properly closed. It was just open; a thick black line stood straight against the length of the door, proving its openness. Jinx jumped up.

'Bonbon, I'm just going…' She stopped. She didn't know where she was going, actually. She walked towards the basket, her mouth stuck in the shape of 'going'. She couldn't go upstairs, they just didn't do that. The inside of her head told her that she was looking for food; but she couldn't go looking for food, because there wasn't any in the rest of the house. 'But that is what you are going to do,' said the inside of her head.

That was silly!

'Yes,' said the inside of her head, 'but you can't just sit here and die.'

She looked down at Bonbon in the bottom of the basket. Feathers and stones and string and AstroTurf and paper and fluff tumbled from the top to the bottom of the inside of her head, like the water tumbled out of that… that thing where the water came from. They were useless, useless, all of those things. The bottom of the basket was much nicer without them…

'Bonbon, I'm going to go and look for something to eat,' said Jinx. 'Even though I won't find anything.' She thought of Bonbon with a cuddle-full of feathers. 'Even though it's useless.'

Bonbon slurped. 'Alright,' she said quietly, still staring straight ahead of her. She understood Jinx, she understood perfectly needing to go and be busy with something; building something, collecting something. She would've done the same, probably. Would have… before…

Once out in the hallway, Jinx stopped. She had heard a rumbling noise. It was long; in fact, it was so long that it didn't stop at all. But there was another funny noise that went with it… Dum dum dum dum dum dum dum dum dum – it was all the time, and very quick like, like clapping hands. Jinx clapped her hands, just to make sure, pulling her mouth into an upside-down grin because that's what her mouth did when she clapped her hands quickly.

It was coming from the big room, and Jinx could see that the living-room door was sort of open. Where there was a black line on the kitchen door, the big-room door had one that was made of grey and sunlight. She went over to the line and put one eye against it. Was that? Was that the She-one? It could have been… She looked like she was running, yes, the noise-that-was-as-fast-as-clapping was the sound of her feet as they touched the floor; but, where was she going? Jinx screwed up her face… She was going nowhere. Why would she run to go nowhere?

'Why would you look for food when there isn't any?' said the inside of her head. That's different, that was totally different. Eating was really important, whereas running nowhere wasn't. The She-one was facing the door; her hair all tied up at the back swung from side to side, side to side. Jinx touched her own hair and thought that she would quite like to make it bounce like that. In fact, maybe that was why she was running nowhere.

Jinx pulled at the door and squeezed through the new, bigger line.

Susan looked up.

'Oh!' she said, then her voice went all breathy. 'Jinx! You haven't had your breakfast, have you?'

Jinx stared at the thing she was running on. That was where the long rumbling noise was coming from. She felt the same feeling that she got whenever she saw that nasty vacuum bot and backed towards the door. She didn't like it. She didn't like it at all.

'Don't be scared, Jinx. It won't hurt you.' The She-one put her hand out and touched something, and the rumbling changed, it seemed to be less angry. Her running slowed down and Jinx noticed that her chest was bouncing in the same way as her hair. She winced and put her hands over her own breasts. That sometimes happened to her when she was running. It wasn't very nice... But, oh! Did that mean that the big She-one had... just like her?

Jinx stared at Susan's chest. She had never thought about it before, yet it was something that she was sure of. In fact, she knew that they were the same. Were they? She looked at Susan's hands. One swung next to her hip and one held a bottle. Then she took her own hands off her breasts and held them up to inspect them. Same. They were the same.

Susan let out a 'Hoo!' as the machine stopped. 'Come on then. Let's see how Bonbon is.' She got off the thing and went walking towards the door.

One leg, two leg, one leg, two leg. Hmmm. They opened and closed in the same way as Jinx's. In fact, she followed Susan across the hall, watching her legs then looking down at her own, just to make sure. Yes. Yes, they did. But… they were funny colours. The big She-one had one blue shiny leg and one black one – not really the same as Jinx's. But then again, Jinx couldn't ever remember seeing the big She-one's legs like that. And she would definitely remember seeing legs that were two different colours. Definitely.

Jinx stopped at the kitchen door. Maybe she could change her legs?

'Oh Miss Bonbon, what's happened to you?'

Bonbon sat with her mouth still over one knee. She looked up at the She-one from the side of her head.

'Are you hungry? Is that why you're all scrunched up in the corner like that? Is that why you're sucking on your knee?'

Bonbon moved her hands, as if to clap a reply but… she couldn't. She couldn't because she *was* hungry, but that *wasn't* the reason why she was, scr… was scran… was in the corner or the reason why she was sucking her knee. That was a bit silly, asking three questions at once when they had different answers.

'Scrunched,' said the old littler.

Susan bent forward, her hands on her knees, waiting for an answer.

Bonbon continued to look back at her from the side of her head.

'Oh, you're not a well bunny, are you?' Susan turned and reached up for the packet of flakes on top of the fridge.

Jinx gazed at the big She-one, angora rabbits tumbling through her head; what a funny thing to say; Bonbon was not a well bunny! She laughed. Bonbon wasn't a bunny!

She heard other laughter; it was Bonbon. They looked at each other. They had laughed at the same time. They had both laughed at Bonbon being an ill bunny! Oh that was lovely… They had never, never laughed at the same time.

Susan turned around. 'Did you just laugh?' she asked. 'You did, didn't you? I'm sure that you both laughed.' She put one hand on her hip. 'Do it again,' she said, tipping her chin.

Bonbon and Jinx opened their mouths to make a laughter noise. Nothing came out.

'You probably need something funny to laugh at…' Susan crossed her eyes and stuck out her tongue. 'Ha aba thith?' she asked through her tongue.

They wrinkled their faces and stared at her. Jinx took a step backwards.

Susan stopped pulling the face and laughed at herself, wiping her bottom lip with her hand. 'That would probably scare me too,' she said, turning back to the worktop. 'I'm sure I heard you laughing…' Picking up the box of flakes again, she bent and filled up both bowls.

Mmm, flakes, thought Jinx, looking at the bowls, then at Susan's feet that were just next to them. She had different feet today, no, different shoes. In fact, she quite often had different shoes. Today they were big and round-looking with funny bits of rope criss-crossing up the front… Jinx hadn't seen these ones before. The shoes usually lived together at the bottom of the stairs in one long line. The He-one's and the She-one's. Maybe that's how she changed her legs? In the same way that she changed her shoes…

Jinx looked at Bonbon. She'd stopped sucking her knee and had one leg over the basket.

Hungry, thought Jinx.

'Come on then, you two, eat up.'

They went to the bowls, got on their hands and knees and started to eat. After a minute or two, the fronts of Jinx's legs got achy. She sat back and started to feed herself with handfuls of flakes instead, crunching them with her mouth open. The She-one stood with her bottom against the fridge. She had a little pot in her hand and was using a spoon to pick up whatever was in the pot and put it in her mouth.

Jinx watched the thing then realized that her legs felt better and she could start eating normally again. Just as she leaned forward, Bonbon came up and started to eat with her hands.

Bonbon stopped and watched Susan. Un-crunched flakes dropped from the roof of her opened mouth to her tongue as she stared at the little shiny thing that sat in the air for a moment, before plunging back into the pot and tok, tok, tok, it scraped the sides, came back up and re-entered the waiting mouth.

What was that thing? thought Bonbon, rubbing her hand against her leg to remove the flake crumbs. She sniffed at her hand and noticed it was yellow. It would smell for ages now, like it always did when she picked the flakes up in her hand.

She looked back up at the shiny thing. And the She-one's clean white hands.

He had a carful of nice things to bring in; what could he have bought? Something expensive. Tactless git. She half-smiled, half-pouted, thinking of the floating kiss he'd sent her just before he went.

In four years, he'd never done that.

And then he'd tapped his cheek as if to say, 'Where's mine?'

She'd loved it when he'd tapped his cheek. He'd looked so cool. She could be cool too.

Wow, he'd really gone to town, that box was enormous! Probably sushi. That was her favourite. And some sort of cake, something French maybe, an Opéra or a Paris Brest – something that she didn't know how to make herself. It would, after all, really piss her off if he'd bought something that she could make, she thought as she ran down the stairs. And she would just eat it, right in front of him. Because she was cool and didn't obsess about things like bellies. She'd munch it down.

She deserved it after an hour of running.

Susan gave her hair another scrunch with a towel before tapping one of the many coloured squares on the glass-top coffee table. The squares merged together and a woman's face appeared: 'Fold away and close AbLab,' said the face. The base of the running machine folded itself back into the opposite wall. The same woman reappeared in a short stretchy pink suit on the screen that covered the length of the underside of the machine. 'Good jahb!' she said. 'How about an upper-body boot camp?'

'No,' said Susan.

The woman made a praying gesture and bobbed. 'Closing AbLab application,' she announced. The screen turned back into the wall.

Susan sniffed the air. He couldn't know that she'd used this thing, she thought, squirting perfume onto her wrist then spinning in a circle with her arm out. 'Suzie, really; don't you think you're being a bit sensitive? Blah, blah, blah…' She stopped spinning. He could think what he liked; she was doing this for Susan not for Hamish.

Of course, had it not been for the floaty kiss, she would have gone back to bed after having to cut herself out of those stupid white jeans.

She ran back to the upstairs window.

Where was he going with that box? What was he… Next door? Oh, there was Mrs Lucas. Mrs Lucas was waving up at the window; bugger, she'd been caught spying… Yes, hello, Mrs Lucas. Waving back… Had better go outside.

'I'm afraid I've been borrowing your husband,' called Mrs Lucas as Susan strolled up the path. She turned to Hamish as he appeared next to her, holding the box. 'Oh you are good,' she said. 'Just stand it on the end of the conveyor belt. It leads right to the kitchen worktop.'

'Are you sure?' strained Hamish, looking over his glasses, being all considerate and, and happy to go the extra mile. Susan smirked.

'Quite sure,' she said, looking into the box, 'wonderful, thank you so much. Such a good old stick, isn't he?'

Susan weighed up the holiday belly and the floating kiss, and now, the fact that he had gone shopping for a little old lady. 'He's not bad.'

'Any sign of the littler?' said Hamish, brushing his hands together having put down the box.

'No.'

'What's happened?' Susan approached the fence.

'Blankey's been missing since last night.'

'Oh no!'

Mrs Lucas nodded. 'I'm afraid so…'

'Have you checked everywhere?' Susan asked. Then felt stupid for asking.

'I've had the house upside down,' nodding. 'It wasn't really necessary. She usually comes when I call her; and she even missed her bath today. She never misses her bath.'

'You bath her?' wincing as soon as she'd said it. Hamish shook his head at her; of all the things to ask, Susan…

'Yes. Twice a week.'

'Mmm,' said Susan, the bat-woman from Batch Mode looming up in her head, wings fully spread.

'I've always said that we should do that.' Hamish, now walking to the other side of the fence, pointed a finger at Susan as if to say: 'Haven't I? Told you so.'

She ignored him. 'I'll check inside the house for her. Sometimes I see her in the yard. Maybe she's hidden away…' She was useless again.

'Oh, would you? Thank you so much. I'm so worried that something might have happened to her.'

Susan remembered seeing Bonbon lying on the angora cushion, covered in rose petals. The same fear filled up her stomach, not my Bonbon, and she thought how horrible it would be if Bonbon got lost… If either of them got lost. 'Of course I'll check,' she said. 'In fact, if you don't mind, I'll call round this evening, to see if she's back.'

Mrs Lucas held her hands together under her chin. 'Oh how kind!' she said. 'Thank you.'

Her hands twisted and rubbed around each other like two lovers.

'You seem worried.'

'You're a psychotherapist.'

He raised his eyebrows. 'Yes, I am.'

'I read something about mental health out patients.'

'Right.' He stretched the word into two tones.

'Is that normal?'

'Erm… Of course. It depends on the illness, and the seriousness of that illness…'

'Yes, but is it normal for people to slip through the net?'

'How do you mean?'

'To go unsupervised, you know, not take their medication and to actually deteriorate once left to their own devices.'

'It would be unwise to leave a serious case unsupervised. With outpatients, a carer, or very often a family member, might make regular visits.'

'How can you know for sure that it's a "serious" case?'

'Erm…'

'I mean… What starts out as "harmless" can degenerate fairly rapidly sometimes, right?'

'Well…'

'Because I was reading about a man who was deemed "well" by the authorities, then cut off his own nose.'

'Ah.' Hamish had read the same story. 'You know why these stories make the headlines, don't you?'

'—'

'Like plane crashes.'

'Because they are rare.'

'I would like to think so.' He sat back in his chair. 'But the problem with mental health is that it's not like a broken arm or…' He searched about her face for an example. She'd let her hair twist around her face like curly fern leaves deadened amber by autumn. 'A haircut, a bad one. No…' He winced. 'Scrap that.'

She laughed. At least he had made her laugh.

'Generally, physical health issues and pain are easier to locate and cure. Mental illness is quite different, it must be sought out and even when you think it's gone, it might just be dormant.' He drew his chin backwards and clasped his hands over his stomach. 'What made you bring this up today?'

'But as long as he takes his medication he should stay "rational", right? Just like you and me?'

'Um…' Were they still talking about the nose-man? 'If he was following his treatment plan then that kind of thing really shouldn't have happened.'

'But how would they know if he was?'

'Well, they would have seen it. They were using equipment that monitored his brain and the reaction of the medication.'

'Then why did he…'

Hamish shrugged. 'Like I say, it's very rare that kind of thing…'

'Where is she now?'

'They're both in the dining room. Look.'

Jinx pressed her nose up against the window. She saw a socked foot with its underside squashed against a chair leg and, for the fourth or fifth time that day, thought about her own body. It wasn't just similar, it was exactly the same. She looked up towards the table; they were eating. Not with those silver things, spoons, but with funny little sticks that opened and closed like a long beak. 'We don't eat the same things as they do, do we?'

Bonbon put her face to the window and watched the funny sticks as they hugged a morsel of something right up into Susan's mouth. She turned to Jinx. 'No, we don't.'

'Maybe we're not the same then.'

Bonbon stepped forward and looked right into Jinx's face. 'We can only eat what they give us, Jinx.' Her eyes darted around the space in front of her as if looking for the being that had got inside her body and made her mouth say what she had just said. Where had that come from? She closed her eyes; spoons grew up through the darkness behind them, and as they got taller, their rounded top bits split into yellow flake-stained fingers. When she opened her eyes, Jinx's face was at the end of her nose, her eyeballs angled at the cushion that was still stuck to Bonbon's ear.

'Oh,' said Jinx, stepping back and tracing a line around her own ear. Then: 'But that's alright because flakes are nice, aren't they?'

Bonbon thought about this. Flakes were nice most of the time. But then, the thing they were poking at with sticks might have been nice. And the thing with the spoon this morning. Maybe that was just as nice as flakes…

'Flakes?' came a voice from behind.

Jinx spun around then launched herself at Chips, kissing him all over his face. 'You're here!' she laughed. 'I've been waiting all day and now you're here!'

Bonbon watched all of this kissing and touching. When had that started? 'Your head's gone all red,' she said to Chips.

Chips thought for a while. 'Why?' he said.

Jinx stood back to look at Chips's head and laughed. 'Doesn't matter!' she said. 'And oh look! You've got your humcoat on!' She leaned forward and sniffed it before opening it up and squirming into it. 'Blankey brought it round for you! I knew she would!'

'Blankey?' Chips looked from Jinx, to the floor, to his own shoulder, and then up at the sky.

'Blankety-Blankey!' sang Jinx.

Ever since he'd been a liar, ever since he'd told that lie yesterday, he had hidden away. Blankey would see him and tell him he wasn't there when she came to his house. 'And why weren't you there?' said a voice inside his head… He squeezed his eyes shut. Because… Because… Because he'd been sp-spying on Jinx and her big she-one.

'Hello?' laughed Jinx. 'Hello? Chips, are you hiding? I can still see you…'

Chips opened his eyes. The last time Jinx had been this close to him was when they were doing The Big Cuddle at his house. He kissed her on the end of her nose, knowing that she would like that. She did. She giggled and started to do up Chips's buttons over her back. He was so skinny that both of them could fit inside his humcoat really easily.

'We've got the same humcoat, me and Blankey,' said Bonbon, holding out one arm, then the other, to look at the way the grey on her coat was darker in some places and lighter in others. 'You'll see when she comes over.' She was sure that it looked nicer than Blankey's. She dropped her arms. 'But I haven't seen her at all today, and today is the day after Saturday. She usually comes the day after Saturday because that's when her biggerers go to the shops.'

Chips coughed and looked at the sky again.

Jinx stopped buttoning the humcoat and gasped at the good idea she was about to have. 'Shall we go to see her in her Outside?'

'No!' shouted Chips.

The other two stared at him.

Chips looked at Bonbon over Jinx's shoulder then lifted some of Jinx's hair to whisper something in her ear. 'What about our Big Cuddle?'

Jinx giggled again. 'Alright!' she said.

Bonbon felt weird about all of this. Really weird. Not in a cross way but… in a way that made her think that she would also quite like to be inside somebody else's humcoat with them. She hugged herself over her own coat. Hmmm, she'd never felt that before. Looking at Chips, she wondered if he'd like to come into her coat. Or she into his. She watched them cuddling each other, like the bin-bag in the kitchen when there were too many things inside. 'I'm just going inside for a minute.' They hadn't noticed that she'd spoken. Their giggles looped through the air, only to be blocked by the flap of the vacuum hatch as Bonbon crept under it.

She knew exactly where she was going… But should she really do that? Really? After all those things that she'd been thinking about… Now, when she tried to bring them up inside her head, her thoughts turned to falling feathers again. Pictures emerged: the big She-one eating with the silver stick and not being allowed to clap 'yes' and 'no'. Trying to speak and, and, and just making her mouth into silent shapes. Not being able to get her own breakfast when she was hungry. What she was about to do now just seemed so… weird.

'Spoon. Silenced. Dependence,' said the inside of her head. That was the other littler. The littler that lived on the inside of her head and helped her to straighten out her thoughts. 'Silenced,' he insisted, then: 'Independence.' She was sure that he was a he, because sometimes she thought that she could see him, this old littler. She was sure that he was old.

Laughter came from the dining room and, at the same time, her feather-thoughts dropped into place. They were stopping her from clapping. They were stopping her from eating morsels with sticks. They were stopping her from using a spoon. So why did she need it from them now? Why did she still need it, knowing everything that she now knew?

'Love,' said the old littler. And as she rounded the doorway and they both looked down at her, she could see that they were happy to see her; especially the big She-one.

'What ya doin' there, kiddo?'

Bonbon unbuttoned her humcoat and let it fall on the floor. Why did she always ask questions that Bonbon couldn't clap out the answer to? She walked under the table that separated the two biggerers; big bowl-shapes hung like dark clouds over her head as she looked up at them through the glass. It was good that the He-one was there. He was always a bit better than she was. He would let her walk about him and wouldn't pick her up, or move her, or try to brush her hair. He preferred just to let her make herself comfortable somewhere on him – a knee, or a thigh, or his tummy – and when she'd found the best place to lie down, she would kick him to remind him of his job in all of this and he would start to stroke her back. Now, as she approached the long sleeping animal that was his shoe, she realized that she had control over him. Not just over him, but over herself when she was with him. She knew that she could leave as easily as she came and he wouldn't try to pick flakes out of her hair or look inside her ears. Control, she thought as she tugged his trouser leg.

'Respect,' corrected the inside of her head.

Hmmm. Respect. That was a nice word… It had 'pecked' in it. It probably meant the opposite to being pecked… Where were these words coming from? A hand landed on the floor next to the sleeping shoe-animal and waited for her to sit in the middle of it. She did.

But how could there really be respecked if he let everything be the way it was? Late breakfasts and no spoons?

The hand travelled upwards so that it was level with a knee and waited for her to step onto a waiting lap. She did. She lay, belly down, on one of the legs, and when she was ready she kicked the waiting hand. A wave of fingers brushed the whole length of her back so that the nail was just grazing the skin and made her feel so shivery that her ears stopped hearing. She closed her eyes. As soon as she felt the littlest finger lift off her right buttock, the first finger landed on her left shoulder blade. Down it travelled, almost not touching her skin, before lifting off her left buttock so that the second finger could start the journey from the base of her neck down to the bit in her back where she was sure she could feel a little tail sometimes. It lifted off. The third finger continued the wave. She rested her head in front of her on her own folded arms and let her skin get tinglier and tinglier and her ears get deafer and deafer.

'She loves that...' said the faraway voice of the She-one. 'Especially when you do it; you must have the "touch".'

'They both love it. Although, Jinx hasn't come to me for a while...'

'Oh!' Susan let her chopstick-free hand flap next to her face. 'I didn't tell you! Jinx has a boyfriend!'

'Oh really?'

'Yes!' mumbled a mouth full of food.

Lucky old Jinx, thought Bonbon, imagining that the fingers on her back were Chips's hands. She imagined rolling over and looking up at his face. She scowled to herself; no, that would be weird. She allowed the face to change, and now it wasn't Chips's hands that brushed her back, but Jinx's hair. She imagined Jinx lying down, so that all of her weight was on Bonbon; fronts of knees against backs of knees, toenails tickling soles of feet, a warm cheek against her own.

Susan's mouth swallowed before continuing. 'That time when I got up in the middle of the night, I found her in her basket with a boy.'

'No!'

'Yes!'

'But where was this one?' Bonbon felt the wave on her back stop for a second, before continuing.

'In hospital,' came the reply through another mouthful.

'Oh, it was that night! She didn't waste any time, did she?'

'Nope.'

'But they can't… You know…'

'I don't think so.'

'It really wouldn't surprise me. After what you said about the clapping and the laughing.'

'Oh, I'm positive that they can do a whole load of stuff that we don't even know about.'

Bonbon's eyes flew open. That was it! That was the problem! The biggerers didn't know. They had no idea that the littlers… Well… That they… She jammed her eyes shut again. It was all so confusing because *she* didn't even know what she had realized… 'That we are human,' said the old littler. Her eyes opened again. Really? Was that it? Were they… Were they exactly the same but little? She blinked. Somehow, she had known this all along and yet… And yet she had only just realized: why was that? She'd never thought about it because… Oh, this was difficult.

'In fact,' the big She-one went on, 'and I know you love a nice conspiracy theory, but after seeing the way the shop assistant reacted yesterday when Bonbon clapped, it was almost like… How can I put it?'

It was all so difficult because… because… Bonbon scrunched her eyes shut. The old littler blew a bubble in her direction with an image of herself inside, sitting on the floor next to her breakfast, gazing up at the biggerer using a spoon.

Susan took a deep breath. 'It was almost like a cover-up; does that make any sense? Like they can't let them progress to a level of verbal communication not just because that doesn't fit the role of "pet" but…'

Pet. Pet? What was 'pet', old littler? The mean grey cat walked to the front of Bonbon's head and swiped its hand at her while hundreds of angora rabbits tumbled behind him. He picked up the Dead Bird in his mouth and stalked away…

'But because, I think that they are worried about what they might say.'

'I'm sure they'd start by asking for some clothes, a normal bed. Maybe a nice entrecôte and a glass of Saint-Émilion.'

And a spoon, thought Bonbon.

'No, silly! I mean about everything they go through before they are adopted.'

The smell of tiles came back to her suddenly. A picture blew up in her head of a small space, filled with sleeping littlers and funny white bits on the floor that stuck to her feet. Chests moved up and down quickly as they breathed and the heat made her skin all sticky.

Hamish smirked. 'It's the same thing, Susan. As soon as they can verbally express facts about their lives, be it past or present—'

'Then they have to be heard, yes, I know that, Hamish.' She pushed her tongue into the pouch that her lip made in front of her lower teeth and slit her eyes at him. 'What I'm saying is that what they know might be more powerful than what we know… Letting them speak could reveal top government secrets about alien landings and, and spies and…'

Hamish let his eyes almost close while lifting his eyebrows. 'Oh dear… We have just reached what I call the Bonkers Point, Susan. The point at which – having listened to a patient present a very reasonable little story – they let slip something that makes me stop and say: "Ah; you are actually bonkers, aren't you?"'

'No, but…' Susan was laughing. 'If you know nothing about something, then how can you actually know anything?'

'Non-bonkers people actually know what to keep inside their heads—'

'You weren't there yesterday! You would've totally… Shit!' She covered her mouth with her hand.

'What?'

'I never called round to see Mrs Lucas.'

'Oh Susan… You'd better do it now. That poor lady.'

'Do you think she's found her?'

'Don't know. I hope so.'

'Maybe she came home. I would have heard otherwise, wouldn't I?'

'—.'

'Could I just phone her… Or?'

'Why not? Good idea.' The fingers stopped waving up and down Bonbon's back. 'I need that hand to finish my dinner now, Bonbon.'

Bonbon lifted her head. This was strange. Normally she could stay as long as she wanted. She got up and stepped onto the waiting hand. But then again, she didn't usually get it in the dining room, and never while they were eating. That had to be the reason.

'Yeah, I think I'll call her. I did check the garden to see if her littler had got trapped somewhere or fallen over or something.'

'Well, you'll have to tell Mrs Lucas that. She's probably too polite to call us and is just sitting at home alone…'

'Oh Hamish, don't!'

The hand travelled down towards the sleeping shoe.

'Waiting for her little… What's her name again?'

'Blankey.'

Still sitting in the middle of the hand, Bonbon looked back through the glass table. Blankey?

'Waiting for her little Blankey to come back. Worried sick about where she could be…'

Blankey was missing? Jumping up so that she was now standing on the hand, Bonbon clapped twice. Four eyes looked through the table towards her.

'That means "no",' said Susan.

Hamish raised his eyebrows. 'Wow! That's actually quite strange when you see it for the first time.'

'Didn't you want to get down?'

No! She didn't! Bonbon clapped twice again. She needed to know what had happened to Blankey!

'She doesn't want to go. Do you think she'd like a piece of brie?'

'No, Hamish! She's not allowed.'

'Why on Earth not?'

Susan thought for a moment. 'I don't know… It would make her ill, wouldn't it?'

'I don't know. I guess, if she's never had it before… Sorry, Bonbon,' said Hamish. 'I want to finish my dinner. And I can't give you any of it.' Bonbon huffed noiselessly, her gaze darting about her. Several wisps of Jinx's hair curled into the far corner of the dining-room doors. She jumped from the hand and ran out of the dining room, across the hall and out through the vacuum hatch.

CHAPTER 8

'Blankey's gone!' Bonbon yelled as she fell running into Outside. Then stopped and screamed. Chips was squashing Jinx up against the edge of the dining-room doors while eating her face. They heard Bonbon scream and pulled away from each other to look at her.

'What were you two doing?'

Chips looked at his feet.

'Kissing,' said Jinx, putting her hands on her hips.

Chips looked back up at Jinx and grinned. He loved it when she put her hands on her hips like that in front of Bonbon. He decided to do the same.

Bonbon wrinkled her face at them for a moment. 'Blankey's gone missing.'

'What?' Jinx dropped her hands. 'Where?'

'Don't know.' Bonbon shrugged.

Chips hugged his arms around himself, ashamed of the little voice in his head that said 'Yes!' as soon as Bonbon had told them about Blankey. That was a horrible thing to think. Horrible, horrible. He was such a horrible lying liar.

'How do you know?' asked Jinx.

'They were talking about it.' Bonbon tipped her head towards the dining-room window.

'Oh.'

Chips's tummy felt weird; how could she go missing? He had only seen her the other day, all wavy and grinny with her new shoes. And now…

'The last time I saw her was when I got back from being poorly and I was in your Outside, with my humcoat on, talking about you. And then you came home: do you remember?'

Chips looked up at Bonbon, his face suddenly very hot. Last night? Last night was when he had found his humcoat in a bag under the kitchen cupboard. Last night was when he had found Blankey's rose. Last night was when he had told Jinx that they should stop looking… that his humcoat wasn't anywhere to be found. Last night was when… was when he had lied.

Jinx looked at Chips. 'Have you seen her?' she asked in a voice that had stopped being all cuddly and kissy. 'Have you seen Blankey?'

'No!' yelled Chips. 'Liar!' yelled the inside of his head. I'm not a liar! I haven't seen her! 'No!' he yelled again out loud, pulling his collar up around his face, squishing his eyes shut. 'I have to go now.' And he turned and ran away.

Jinx's lip started to quiver. Bonbon noticed. She walked towards Jinx and put one arm around her. Jinx looked up, surprised again at the new Bonbon. The old Bonbon stood inside her head, complaining about her ears heating up and she let out a sobby laugh. Bonbon's hand squeezed her shoulder as Jinx wiped her nose on the back of her own arm; her gaze following the faraway black blob of Chips as it disappeared through the tunnel and her eyebrows popping up as she realized something. 'But, he's got his humcoat back, Bonbon,' she said. 'He must have been to Blankey's house; he must've seen her!'

'Where are you going?'

'I'm going after him!'

'But no! We… We can't go through there…'

Jinx turned around. 'Yes we can, Bonbon. I've done it before.' She turned back to run towards the tunnel.

'Wha… What are you going to say to him?'

Jinx stopped. Good point. What was she going to say to him? 'I just…' She turned back around. 'I just want to know how he got his humcoat.'

Bonbon blinked. 'Blankey must've left it in his house.'

'Yes, but…'

'But what?'

'She's gone missing.'

Bonbon gripped a handful of humcoat skirt in each hand. 'Oh,' she said. 'Well, what do you think has happened to her?'

Jinx thought. Blue peacocks strolled through the middle of her head, turning their heads to the side and looking at her through one eye that tapered towards its beak like a colourful fish dipping for food. They all walked swishily, one foot placed right in front of the other, and pink flowers fell from their backs to the ground. 'I think she's been to see Chips.'

'But he said that he hadn't seen…'

'I know. But I think he said something that wasn't…' she wrinkled her eyes, 'true.'

Bonbon shook her head. 'That's silly; why would he do that?'

Jinx took a deep breath. 'Because he's been kissing with Blankey.'

Bonbon opened her mouth only to close it again. Her eyes danced towards the top of the wall where the bars were as she thought about what Jinx had just said. Yes… Yes, she thought she understood. In fact, the whole thing made her feel quite tingly. He shouldn't really be kissing with Blankey; not if he was kissing with Jinx. Not without telling her. She wanted to talk about it more. 'Does that make you feel weird?'

Jinx stepped towards Bonbon. She wanted to talk about it too. 'Yes.'

'Yes,' agreed Bonbon. 'Do you want to go there and see if they are kissing?'

Jinx scrunched up her lips and puffed out her cheeks.

Bonbon laughed.

Jinx grinned. 'Why are you laughing at me?'

'You look funny when you do that!' she giggled again.

Ah… That was something that would really take some getting used to. It was so nice to hear the sound of Bonbon's laugh. She was lovely when she laughed.

Bonbon stopped laughing and they smiled at each other. 'I don't really want to go to Chips's house,' she said, finally.

The peacocks reappeared. They'd gone away when Bonbon was laughing, and now that she had mentioned Chips, they were back. The inside of Jinx's mouth tasted funny: dry and yucky and still a bit like kisses. She blinked down at the new Bonbon, who was still clutching the skirt of her humcoat, hoping that Jinx would say that they could go back inside the house. 'It's alright, Bonbon.' She walked over and took her hand. 'Chips will come back. He always comes to our Outside.' As she said it, questions started to ask themselves: but what if they were kissing? What if Blankey gave him his humcoat and started to cuddle him? What if they'd been doing that for a long time and Jinx hadn't even known about it? 'Blankey doesn't poo!' repeated Chips, inside her head. She frowned.

'Are you sure, Jinx?'

The questions paused. Bonbon never asked her if she was sure; never, ever, ever. Bonbon wasn't better. Bonbon needed looking after.

'Yes, Bonbon. It's alright. Let's go inside.'

'But we can talk about it all inside, Jinx. We can work out what we're going to do.'

'That's right, Bonbon. We can talk about it all inside.'

'Oh! Jesus! Are you alright; why are you staring at me?'

'Were you asleep?'

'Hmm?'

'You were asleep, weren't you?'

'What time is it?' Susan propped herself up on one elbow to look at the clock projection on the opposite wall. 'I was asleep, yes.'

'So who was making that noise?'

03:02. 'What noise?'

'The one that…' Hamish closed his eyes and rubbed the length of his face with one hand. 'The one that woke me up.' Then: 'It was me, wasn't it?'

'Are you kidding me? This is the first time you've woken yourself up snoring?'

'Was that really *me*?'

'Probably, Hamish.'

'How do you know? You were asleep.'

'Because you were snoring when I drifted off.'

'But that was *really* loud!'

Susan baulked then snorted out a smirk. 'It's like that every night.' Using her elbow to pivot onto her belly, she flopped back into her pillow and looked towards the bedside table. An apology would only come if it *wasn't asked for*, and looking right at him just after that last sentence could seem like apology-fishing. After nearly five years of telling her that he never, *ever* snored, this apology could not be buggered up by fishing for it.

She waited, knowing that he was still propped up because the bed hadn't jolted. She knew that he was thinking about his snoring because it had happened to *him*; *he* had been the victim *and* the culprit in this scenario; and so it deserved to be thought about.

'*Every* night,' she couldn't help. She'd said it almost under her breath, *almost* to herself.

'Ye-es…' Stubble scratching noises could be heard. 'There must be some sort of medical reason for it.' The bed jolted and Susan felt a pull on the duvet.

Her eyes danced about in the blue hue of the clock projection as her ears dominated her brain's concentration. The breathing had slowed. The lung-wobble had started. He was asleep! He'd gone to bloody sleep!

Just as the wobble turned into a judder, she swung her legs out of bed and pushed her feet into a pair of flip-flops. Bastard! He'd woken her up to tell her he had woken himself up, and now *he* was… And that meant that *she* was…

'Wha?' he moaned as she got out of bed.

'Toilet!' she almost shouted at him before striding out of the room, yanking a bath towel from the ottoman and pulling it around herself as she left.

Jumping down the stairs, she thought about the fact that her eyebrows turned downwards in the middle when she was angry, and that she must have looked *really* angry but there was no one to see it. That seemed like a bit of a waste. She crossed the hall and remembered the last time she'd been up in the middle of the night, two nights ago. She pressed the kitchen door open. Light oozed over one blonde ball and one brunette ball resting together like chocolates in a box. Her eyebrows went back to normal. Bless them, they were so sweet. Little sleeping chocolates… She pulled the door back until it was almost shut. Mmm… She had watched that documentary two nights ago with a cup of chocolate from the machine. That had been nice. She made her way towards the living room, towards the chocolate sofa bubble. Ha! She had invented a whole scenario about the chocolate sofa bubble; now what had that been about…? There was a sofa involved and Hamish *and* life. That had been quite a happy alone-moment; drinking chocolate and watching TV while the rest of the world was dark and asleep. Pressing the corner of the coffee table, she selected *The Mini Human Phenomenon* and waited for the little glass tongue to deliver her chocolate.

The documentary un-paused a few seconds from where Susan had left off. An interviewer was facing the camera; his interviewee sat in the background, one brown suited leg crossed over the other.

Ah yes. Cloning. *Death.* That was how the sofa-bubble thought had been triggered.

'This brings us back to the initial question: how *did* the scandal of the first batch of pocket-sized people come about?'

Three tags appeared at the bottom of the screen. 'Return to Main Menu'. 'Replay Cloning Interview'. 'Pocket People Scandal Explained'.

Susan swallowed back a sipful of chocolate. 'Tag three,' she sang towards the screen. Might as well follow the order of the narrative.

'In 2063, the company trading under a name that has since been discontinued released a prototype that was to have the world divided: the reason for this controversy? The prototype was a miniature human intended to be marketed as "a family member" in order to breed back into younger generations what the company described as "extinct organic notions of living and loving". Its slogan, "Space and race before interface", set debates buzzing across the globe; but the biggest question on everybody's lips? Just where *did* they come from? At the time, senior geneticist Dr Mark Hector was only *too* happy to give an explanation…'

The screen flicked into footage with a late twenty-first-century look, the colours so bright they blotched and shadowed over in places. Dr Hector grinned into the camera as a shorter journalist held a microphone up to his mouth. 'So, where do they come from?' asked the journalist. Dr Hector repeated the question slowly, as if to help the viewers who might not have understood what was going on.

'Where do they come from?' he grinned. 'Well, as with all brilliant inventions, they come from error! They were a *complete* mistake! We were actually engineering pluripotent cells to see if we could tweak the growth instructions of human DNA to create smaller babies. This… this *demand*, I could say, had been put forward by international environmental officials with the view to create a smaller race in correlation with the massive overpopulation of the planet. Smaller humans require *less.* This idea has been in its planning stages for a while, but because of its overlap into the field of *cloning,* getting the go-ahead wasn't simple.

'Initial research into this area was kick-started in 2016 with Project Isabel, which was terminated several years later due to largely unsuccessful results. In 2029, our team was awarded substantial government funding to continue research. After a few false starts, our cells started to develop into what we have today.' The doctor grinned again, holding his hands together over his chest and tipping his head to one side. Susan realized that her lip was curling. He was a tad smarmy… How *old* was he? His lips puffed over his teeth like shiny hotdog buns. She honestly couldn't tell if his face was that plump and stretched because he was a young person who'd had too much surgery, or an old person who'd… had too much surgery.

'You started to tell us that all of this was an accident?' prompted the interviewer.

'Well, I *started* to answer the question by saying that all of this was an accident.'

The interviewer nodded.

'And indeed it was! The first successful cells are what you see before you today. But, of course, our original mission was fairly *unsuccessful*—' He opened his buns to go on but was cut off by the interviewer.

'Could you tell us why?'

'Let me tell you why. The simple answer was that they were too small. A race of that size would adjust very poorly to our environment, as well as the fact that these miniature people would not be reproductively compatible with the existing human race. It was never our intention to produce a being *that* small.'

'But how did you get permission to market them as a product?'

'So how did we get permission to market them as a product?

What else could we do with them but adopt them out? Their repressed intelligence and lack of instinct meant that they could never live alone. So we adopted them out to families, families that went through – and still go through – rigorous selection processes and follow-up interviews for up to three years after purchase,' shaking his head quickly, 'er… adoption.' He went on: 'Although purchase *does* play a big part in all of this; the adoptive family need to prove their commitment monetarily. At the same time, exhibiting *sustainable* means to be able to provide for the little humans as they, and their families, progress into what will one day be known as the biggest social experiment that the world has ever seen.'

The interviewer took a deep breath to say something but the doctor turned to the camera, filling up the whole of the screen with buns and smarm. Susan stuck her tongue out and made a yuk-face. 'A social experiment that aims to recapture what humanity has lost, after all: the human race needs saving, in more ways than one.'

Oh gross, thought Susan, blowing into the foam on her chocolate. Hamish would *love* this.

The old footage froze and the screen flicked back to the original presenter.

'A very convincing argument,' he began, holding both hands out the way that presenters do, as if holding them after a hand-dryer. Palms, then backs, then one, then both. He went on: 'And what, from the surface, seemed like an effective method of, not only *solving* two problems, but a positive contribution to humanity.' The presenter brought his hands together in front of his chest and smiled. 'A real, happy accident. But…' one hand pointed a figure towards the sky, 'little did Dr Hector know that the truth behind these pocket people was soon to be revealed…'

A different image appeared in the same blotchy twenty-first centuryness as the first. This time, a montage of helmet-haired newsreaders with lip-glossed mouths sailed from one end of the screen to the other; each one tailing off from where the last had begun:

'Leading genetic engineers…'

'Genetic engineers in London…'

'London's leading team of genetic engineers…'

'Entrusted with a mission…'

'The first mission of its kind…'

'Were granted permission to conduct…'

'The creation of several thousand human clones…'

'Has been shut down…'

'Is ceasing to operate…'

'Authorities have disallowed all further developments…'

'Dr Mark Hector…'

'Head of department, Dr Mark Hector…'

'At the centre of this scandal, Dr Mark Hector…'

'Using human embryos…'

'Taking from the "parentless" stock of human embryos…'

'Using embryos from the surplus supply…'

'Experiments have led to the deaths of many human embryos…'

'Clinical assistants speak of deformation…'

'Several members of staff say that some foetuses lived past the legal abortion date before…'

'Before any major physical defects were identified…'

'In an unlikely circumstance, an adoption agency…'

'Brought to light by the refusal to cooperate with adoption agency Billbridge & Minxus…'

'A government request to find parents for dormant embryos…'

'Been kept in a frozen state since the abolition of Embryonic Stem Cell Research…'

'First scandal of its kind since Embryonic Stem Cell Research was banned…'

'Embryonic Stem Cell Research was banned in 2025.'

The presenter returned. 'When initially granted permission

to *go ahead* with studies,' the dryer-hands appeared to cup two oranges and jiggle them with each syllable, 'scientists were specifically informed that a clone was defined as "the propagation of an organism from the cell of a single common ancestor" and quantified as one cell to one ancestor; that's to say, multiple copies could *not* be made of a single ancestor-cell.' He clasped his hands back together. 'The use of human embryos for this research means that, effectively, the mini humans of the Mini Human Phenomenon cannot fall into the category of "clone" but are legitimate human children, with real parents, grandparents and possibly even brothers and sisters. At the time, scientists were divided over this incredible, *illegal*, breakthrough in science.'

The screen flicked to another dated newsreel where a man in a suit stood over three microphones that grew out of the bottom of the screen. His nose was so squashed towards his face that it almost touched his top lip. 'There's no denying that, although illegal, this technique of being able to, effectively, *shrink* a human being while in its embryonic state represents *enormous* progression in genetics and holds invaluable consequences for the future of science.'

A woman with a Scottish accent stood before a conference. 'What we've really got to bring up again is the initial debate that, ultimately, saw the abolition of Embryonic Stem Cell Research: at what stage should a group of cells be governed by the same moral law that protects humanity?'

A young man in a stripy shirt with blue-tinted glasses stood at ease next to a pot plant. 'We mustn't forget, you know, that this is what we wanted. The mission never once stipulated, um… erm… the creation of an entirely new race, because that would be pointless, you know; people would continue to have normal-sized babies while extra humans were being artificially created; no, that would defeat the object entirely. What Dr Hector has done is to immediately implement a technique that would have been adopted in the final stages of the trial, that's to say, altering the DNA of embryos in pregnant women. Of course, using pregnant women at this *early* stage would be out of the question. But working on anything *other* than human embryos, especially when the supply is so… erm… abundant, would have set all research back unnecessarily. In fact, research intended for this mission performed on any other cell other than a human embryo *could* be deemed as largely irrelevant.'

A caped old lady stooped in the street with an owl-like posture; two fabric Tesco shopping bags hung like drooping wings from hidden arms. 'The thing is: they have *parents*… Each and every one of them has a mummy and a daddy who never thought that they'd even *have* these children. Some of them might be eighty or ninety years old by now. I mean, *what* does all of this mean for them? For the parents? Are they going to have any rights over the children?'

Six men and women in suits sat on black chesterfields around a coffee table in a television studio. One sat well forward with his legs apart. 'What we have to put into perspective here is that these embryos were *abandoned*. They were surplus to requirements. In fact, there was a massive surplus. In a society where parents are allowed to produce and freeze potential offspring in such quantities only to abandon them, somebody has to be responsible for the fate of these offspring; *somebody* has to figure out what to do with them. I mean, what is the suggestion here? That keeping them in their frozen embryonic state is the kindest thing to do? Is that really what we mean when we talk of respecting human life? The only reason they're kept in that state is because *nobody* knows what to do with them. They would have been completely forgotten about had Billbridge & Minxus not approached the government about the possibility of adopting them out.'

'It's tricky. This is a tricky one,' said the first lip-nose man. 'It's not that nobody wishes to take responsibility for the embryos; the fact is that nobody *can*. The only person who was granted responsibility for this particular batch was Dr Mark Hector. Forms have been signed by parents claiming that they no longer require the cells, effectively *leaving* them to him. *He* is the closest thing to an adoptive parent, and with that comes such a great sense of responsibility that, just like with a parent/child dynamic, it borders on *ownership*. What he has chosen to do with them in the interests of *science* is ground-breaking, *ground*-breaking! Unfortunately, what he *should* have done was to be straight about his intentions right from the beginning. The fight would have been drawn out, but raising the topic of what to do with these forgotten embryos has long been overdue.'

A pin-striped man with sticky-out grey hair sat at a desk, his hands clasped in front of his mouth; he spoke over his fingers. 'Dr Mark Hector… That name will resonate for centuries. What he did was *crazy*! Think about it: a scientist, in his position, overstepping the lines so dramatically… It would be ridiculous to treat his intentions in the same way as those of a *reasonable* man. His actions were impressive, but completely irresponsible. I would, I would even say *foolish*.'

Susan opened her eyes, inhaled a slurpy breath and woke herself up. 'Stop!' she said, wiping the side of her mouth. Where was she? Oh, still here. Damn! The empty chocolate cup had spilled secret drops onto the white towel that she'd used as a quilt. Susan looked around, shivered and got up. 'Turn off TV.'

'Where were you?'

'Watching,' Susan yawned, 'documentary.'

'—.'

'The *Mini Human Phenomenon* one.'

Hamish was silent, then: 'You never called Mrs Lucas.'

Susan smacked her forehead. 'Oh… It's too late now, isn't it?'

'—.'

Yep. Of course it was… Either too late or too early.

'Why don't you ask them if they've seen her?' His voice was mumbly and slow. Susan knew his eyes were closed.

'Who?'

'Banksy.'

'Blankey?'

'Yes.'

'Ask who if they've seen her?'

Hamish sighed. 'The happy-clappies.'

Susan wrinkled her forehead. 'I have trouble understanding you at the best of times.'

'Tweedledum and Tweedledee.'

She smirked at the darkness. Fuck's sake. Whatever. She swung one leg onto the bed. What the fuck was he going on about? Bonbon and Jinx, probably: Tweedledum and Tweedledee. She was about to swing the second leg up but it froze, sat in that position like a dowsing rod that had just discovered water. Two little people appeared in her mind, sniffing and stroking the grey crinoline coat of a third. Just like Bonbon's coat. They were all friends. Weren't they? She'd seen them! Bonbon, Jinx and Blankey all together in the garden. She looked in the direction of Hamish, her surprised head filling up with this new idea. She could *ask* Bonbon and Jinx if they knew what had happened to Blankey. Why hadn't she thought of that before?

Her legs hesitated.

Two little chocolates snuggled together downstairs; one dark, one white, giving off little zeds as their bellies rose and fell. It wouldn't be fair to wake them up now; her dowsing-rod leg seemed to confirm this as it rose to join the other. We know the water's there, we'll tunnel for it tomorrow, it seemed to say.

'Weren't you here on Saturday? With your littler, you bought the grey, mock rabbit, didn't you?'

'Yes, that's right! Have you had your delivery?'

'We have indeed. If you don't mind, I'm just helping this lady; I'll be with you in a few moments. Is that okay? Do feel free to browse…'

'Yes, righto.' Susan turned to start her task of browsing, as a goose turns on water; all slow and glidey, with its neck straining in different directions. On the other side of the shop she glimpsed the lady who was being served first. A littler sat on her lap with her back to Susan. She had red hair so long that Susan couldn't work out if it stopped where her bottom stopped or if she was sitting on more. A movement beyond the pair drew Susan's eye to another person squatting next to the bargain bin. He watched the sales assistant and her customer, a tiny pair of purple boots swinging from his hands. The customer glanced his way and he lifted the boots to eye-level, turning them this way and that.

'Yes, you're right; the green would complement her hair beautifully,' said the lady who was being served first.

'Let me just see the colour of her eyes.'

'They're blue.'

'Ah yes. Well, *blue* would actually be better. We have royal blue or navy in that model.'

Oh, what a nice assistant! The woman at Batch Mode would *love* all of this matching coat colour and eye colour together. She reached out to stroke a white coat *just* like Bonbon's, but white. Allergens indeed. How could the doctor have recommended Batch Mode? It wasn't a patch on this place. Hmmm… Maybe Jinx would prefer the white? Would she? No… No, Susan would go for the green. Green would look lovely with Jinx's hazel eyes. And anyway, the white one would get all manky and horrible in no time.

Susan heard a clapping noise behind her and turned.

'Now, did you see that?' said the woman who was being served first. 'She said "no", she doesn't want the blue one.'

'What?' said the assistant.

'She doesn't *want* the blue one. Look. Lolly, do you want the blue one?'

Lolly clapped twice.

Susan stepped closer to the clapping scene and peeped out through a gap between two mini mannequins. The shoe-customer stood in front of a little helicopter and flicked his eyes between the sales assistant and the tiny cockpit.

'Twice means "no". Watch again: Lolly, do you want the green one?'

Lolly clapped once.

'You see? Once for "yes". Twice for "no".'

The nice assistant, who was on her knees with a navy blue coat in her hand, leaned backwards and put her hands on her hips. 'I see,' she said. 'Is she from the latest batch?'

'Yes! She is!' said the woman, with a tone that wanted to know why this detail was important.

Yes, thought Susan, why was that detail important?

The nice assistant exhaled a smirk.

Susan started to stride towards them to tell her that she had discovered the *exact* same thing about Bonbon! And Bonbon was from the latest batch! This nice assistant was *much* more helpful than the other stupid bat-lady, and seemed to be better informed. Maybe she could give them *both* some more information.

But the nice assistant closed her eyes and pinched the bridge of her nose with one hand. 'I can't handle this any more.'

Susan ducked back behind a giant display running-wheel.

'What?' said the woman who was being served first.

'This is "communication",' said the nice assistant. 'I now have to call someone to come and evaluate it.' She stood up, produced a remote control that was clipped to the back of her skirt and pressed a button. 'So if you wouldn't mind waiting, they'll be along in just a few minutes.'

The woman pulled her littler closer to her chest. 'But it's bad, isn't it? You said you, you couldn't handle this any more…'

'They will take her away,' said the nice assistant. 'And I'm not sure if you will, erm…' she tailed off.

The woman and the littler looked at each other.

'You'd better… say your goodbyes now,' she whispered, almost mouthing the last part of her sentence.

Susan's mouth fell open. Across the shop, the shoe-customer dropped the boots back into the bargain bin.

'But I'll just leave,' said the woman. 'This never happened. This conversation never happened.'

'You can go,' said the nice assistant in a new, loud voice. 'But they will find you either on your way home or at home.'

'But I'll have more time to, to *think*.' The woman pulled her handbag onto her shoulder, and got up to leave. Striding across the floor, she opened one side of her coat and closed it again so that it covered up her littler. As she got to the doors, they were already opening. Two people walked in. The woman froze.

'Good morning,' sang a tall, grinny woman with glasses.

'I'm not sure that you have the right to just take her like this.'

'I completely understand your concern,' said the woman, tilting her head back and pursing her lips as if she were blowing on a baby. 'But if she is def-ec-tive,' she over-pronounced, 'then it is in the interest of her own race that she be withdrawn from circulation.'

'There's nothing wrong with her. She just claps when she wants something.'

The tall woman smiled and squeezed out a blink to her colleague who stood to her left. He nodded. 'I'm truly sorry but clapping *is* classed as communication,' he said. And he looked like he was truly sorry.

'Littlers are designed so that *developed* communication is impossible. It is the one thing that officially separates them from the human race,' explained the woman, as she took a flat, silver oblong from a pocket on the inside of her jacket.

'But, well, that could be true of many animals!' said the woman who was being served first. 'Dogs bark to be let out, cats meow for food, and, and monkeys, um, monkeys communicate pretty well… I've heard.'

The tall woman answered without even blinking. 'Animals have a "ceiling" when it comes to communicating with humans; we've learned this from sharing several millennia with them. We know that animal communication won't progress into anything sophisticated.' She nudged one arm of her glasses as she said 'sophisticated'.

Her truly-sorry colleague spoke. 'It's too early for us to understand the communication limits of littlers. They're just *too new*, especially this latest batch.'

The woman who was being served first looked at all three of them with wide, angry eyes. 'This is not fair,' she said. 'You designed them to encourage "love in the home", and, and, as soon as we start to love them you want to take them away.'

'Oh dear – don't get upset,' said the tall woman. 'Once you've already been cleared for adoption, the process to adopt again will be so much quicker.'

Susan felt her mouth drop open.

The colleague opened the flap of a carrier basket and held it out to the woman. He was smiling with his mouth but not with his eyes. 'She may well be returned to you as *soon* as we've readjusted a few things.'

The woman dipped her eyebrows. 'Really? I was told that…' She stopped herself, for whatever reason. Maybe to protect the nice assistant. 'Are you expecting me to just hand her over? You could be anyone, couldn't you?'

The tall woman smiled again and retrieved her ID from her inside pocket. The truly-sorry colleague did the same. 'You know,' he said, 'you would have given permission for all of this when you signed your purchase agreement.'

Susan scoffed. What *utter* bullshit. What a load of crap! She puffed out her cheeks and raised her eyebrows.

'Right… So do I have to sign for you to take her away?'

'Yes, of course.'

'But I *didn't* sign for her purchase, so are you allowed to have two different signatures on file?'

The tall woman opened her mouth to say something then closed it again. She signalled to her colleague who produced a barcode reader thingy from behind his back and held it in front of the littler, then her owner.

'She's right,' he said. 'Where is her legal owner?'

'I am.'

'Clearly you are not.'

'She was bought for me. She was a present.'

'Well, where is the buyer?'

She straightened. 'At home, probably.'

'This isn't how we do things,' said the tall woman. 'If she was given to you as a gift, the adoption certificate should have been amended.'

The woman who was being served first looked confused. 'The "gift" is *symbolic.*'

'Well…' The tall woman pressed her lips together and made her eyes really big. 'That would probably be interpreted as abandonment.'

'I can assure you that it isn't.'

'It's a Mr Walter Green,' said the barcode-reader. He blinked up at the woman kindly. 'We *will* have to search him out, I'm afraid.'

'And in the meantime?' she asked.

'You can go home,' said the tall woman, sighing. 'I have to read you a legal blurb,' she said, turning the silver oblong on its side and tapping one end. Glowing words started to roll out from it, disappearing as soon as they were read. 'Please be aware that while we are finding the owner, applications for a littler passport will be refused, and any attempt to hide the littler will be interpreted as abandonment.' The truly-sorry colleague leaned forward and the littler squealed as a stud was clipped into the top of her ear. 'This stud will monitor her movement as well as her company. She will be expected to maintain a period of isolation. She must not mix with other littlers or other people apart from you. Any infringement of these instructions will be interpreted as wilful harm against Billbridge & Minxus. Now please,' said the tall woman, flicking the end of the silver oblong again, 'go and enjoy whatever time you have left together.'

The pair smiled, scrunching their shoulders upwards as they did, turned, and left.

Having stayed very calm up to this point; the woman who was being served first started to shake.

The nice assistant came over to her, raising her eyebrows as if to say, *are you going to be alright?*

The woman nodded back. Yes. She would be fine.

Neither of them spoke, both wary of invisible funnels twisting around the room, waiting to catch careless voices.

With her hand over the back of her littler's head, the woman went through the sliding doors and was gone.

Susan stepped out from behind the display running-wheel, Jinx's green coat still in her hand.

'Gosh, I'd forgotten about you! I'm so sorry!' said the nice assistant.

Her eyes were dim and pink. 'Are you alright?' Susan asked.

'Yes, yes.' The nice assistant sniffed and wiped her cheek with the back of her hand.

Susan dipped her head. 'Sure?'

'Yes.' Sniff. 'Sorry, it was… It's the third time this week that this has happened…'

'It sounds *awful*.' Susan bit her lip. 'What's it all about? Hand clapping was all I could really make out… Is it a sign of aggression?'

The nice assistant looked stunned for a minute. 'Yes,' she said, then: 'No, not aggression. *Communication*.' She flicked her gaze about her. 'If you hear about any cases like this, you really must report it.'

Susan blinked for a moment until she could say: 'Of course.'

'Oh you found it!' the nice assistant seemed to try out a new, bright voice as she nodded towards the humcoat that hung from Susan's hand. 'Would you like to buy it, or…'

'Yes. Yes, please. I'll pay for this now.'

Back in the car, Susan thought about what she'd just seen. She'd told Bonbon that she mustn't clap in Mini-Me's, after what had happened in Batch Mode. Bonbon had obeyed until she had seen the grey coat and she held her hands up excitedly, about to smack them together. Susan had caught both of them in her own, big hand just in time.

What if that had been recorded?

'Home,' she said to the WayToGo.

The car started and reversed out of the bay then stopped with a jolt. Susan looked into her rear-view mirror to see the woman who was being served first standing just in front of the back of the car. 'Park,' she said to the WayToGo, before waiting for the engine to stop and getting out of the car.

'I'm so sorry, are you alright?'

'Yes,' said the woman. 'Well, no, but… That's another story.'

'I know,' said Susan. 'I was in the shop. I heard everything.'

'Oh,' said the woman. They shared a dancey-eyed, twitchy-mouth look; like two teenagers, desperate to kiss each other. 'I had been hiding over there,' the woman almost laughed, pointing to a dark corner of the car park. 'I was waiting for them to go.'

Susan glanced around her. 'Have they gone?'

'Yes. I watched them drive away.'

The little auburn head poked up between the buttons of her coat, the stud glinting from her ear. She smiled at Susan. Susan was stunned for a moment without knowing why. She smiled back. 'She's beautiful.'

'Yes.' The woman looked down at her. 'She's all I have now. Do you have one?'

'I have two, actually,' beaming.

'Two?' The woman gazed up to her right and appeared to be counting to two.

Footsteps fell onto the concrete and they both turned. The shoe-customer had just come out of the shop, a bag swinging from his wrist. Ah, thought Susan, he had bought them after all. The shoe-customer looked over and changed the direction of his feet so that he was walking towards them. 'Hello.' He stopped next to them but his feet continued to shift his weight from one foot to the other. 'I was in the shop, I saw everything,' he said to the woman. 'And you were there too, weren't you?'

Susan made a serious face. 'Yes, I was.'

He glanced at their wrists then checked behind him. 'May I bleep you something?'

The woman who was being served first looked at Susan. 'Yes, alright,' said Susan, holding out her wrist. They bleeped their arms together.

'Alright then,' said the woman who was being served first. She bleeped her wrist against his.

'Do think about it,' he said, nodding towards the glowing patch on Susan's skin. 'Bye-bye for now,' walking away.

Getting back into the car, she said 'home' again to the WayToGo, then 'lock doors'. As the car pulled away for the second time, Susan read the message on her wrist. 'Monday 19 October 2116 LOG Meeting,' she said out loud. LOG? Scrolling down she found a name, an address, a time and, finally, a logo that read *Littlers' Owners Group*. Ah right! That would be worth going to, but… that was tonight. Could she make it? She thought of twenty women sitting in a circle on high-backed chairs in a flowery living room. No, actually, the shoe-customer really didn't look like he would fit that scene. Although it was funny that the woman who was being served first looked *exactly* the type. Ha! There was something about her littler, was it her eyes? They went all sparkly when she smiled – oh, that was it! Her smile. Jinx and Bonbon had *never* smiled, *ever*. It was just too, well, human. But… maybe they had the capacity to smile. Yesterday, she was *sure* that they had laughed…

Monday 19 October 2116 LOG Meeting, she read again. Then pulled her coat around her and watched the road.

It was a little bit rainy today. Not too bad but… She had been fed up with standing outside anyway and now that it was raining… In fact, she was fed up in general today. Oh well, never mind. At least she could see the garden from the dining room. She would be able to see if he was coming or not.

She hadn't seen him since he'd run off. Maybe today, if she could, she would go to his house. Her chest felt funny as she thought about seeing his big he-one again.

Jinx had been the first to get up that morning. It was still dark outside when she had come into the dining room to look out of the window. Her first thought was that Blankey had come to their garden, and was sleeping in front of the dining-room doors. She was so sure that Blankey would be there that when she got to the dining room and couldn't see her, she had been disappointed. Soon she was thinking about Chips and, soon after that, she realized she was waiting for him.

She heard the big He-one get up. Then she heard the front door open and close. Then she heard Bonbon kick her bowl. Then the big She-one got up to feed Bonbon, making all these ooo and ahhh sounds at her, then the She-one went upstairs and Jinx could hear Bonbon making crunching noises as she ate her flakes.

She looked towards the corner of the garden where the entrance to the tunnel was, hoping to see a flap of humcoat reappear just as it had disappeared yesterday.

'Hello.' Bonbon came up to Jinx with crumbs trapped in her humcoat.

'You've got crumbs on your coat,' said Jinx.

'Oh, have I?' Bonbon looked down, picking out the crumbs and putting them into her mouth.

Jinx watched. She really didn't know if it was a good thing or a bad thing, whatever had happened to Bonbon. It was funny how she had always complained that Bonbon had been too nasty, and now all this doing as she was told and being nice and, and listening to Jinx was just, well, not as nice as she thought it would be.

Bonbon sat down in the middle of her coat, looking like an upside-down mushroom. 'You know it's feather day, don't you?'

'Is it?' Jinx turned her whole body away from the window to face Bonbon. 'Is it really?'

'Why are you excited?'

'Are you going to make me search for feathers, Bonbon? Do we have to start now?'

'Well…' Bonbon considered this while looking at the window. 'It might be a good idea. What do you think?'

Jinx screwed up her face. It was no good. Bonbon just wasn't the same, she just wasn't the same. 'Bonbon—' Jinx began.

'I've got—' said Bonbon at the same time.

They stared at each other for a while.

'I've got a nice surprise for you!' said Bonbon.

'Ooo! What is it?'

'The big She-one just told me that she's going to get a humcoat for you today, just like mine!'

Jinx stood up and stared at the wall behind Bonbon as the inside of her head started snowing and she was twirling through the snow in Bonbon's humcoat. No! Not Bonbon's humcoat; her very own! She looked at Bonbon's coat and reached down to stroke it. 'Just like yours,' she said.

'Yes! Except yours will be green.'

'Green?'

'Well,' Bonbon brushed down her coat, making sure that it was fanned in exactly the same way in all directions, 'she asked me if you would like a brown one, and I said no because I remember once you said that brown is a shitty colour. Then she asked me if you would like a grey one and I said yes. Then she had a thought and said that two grey ones might get mixed up... Would Jinx like a green one and I told her yes, but I stood up and did it excitedly so she knew that I thought you should have a green one much more than I thought you should have a grey one. It was a much better idea. She would have asked you but, but, she thought you were outside.'

'A green one,' breathed Jinx, looking at the wall again as she twirled through her snowy head in a green furry coat. Oh yes, that was beautiful. But what green would it be? AstroTurf green or green box green or flake green – even though flakes were almost yellow, so probably not flake green – or plate green like the dirty plates at Chips's house? There were so many different types of green.

'Green is nice, isn't it, Jinx?'

'Yes.'

'I thought so. I think it's better that we have different colours. I was right to think that, wasn't I?'

'Yes,' Jinx nodded at Bonbon, 'you were definitely right.'

'I wonder what type of green it will be.'

'I was just wondering the same thing.' Jinx stopped. 'But Bonbon, how did you tell her that I didn't want brown?'

'I clapped.'

'Oh,' said Jinx. 'Clapping isn't really talking, is it?'

'I don't know. But I can talk to her with claps. Look,' Bonbon clapped once, 'this means "yes",' then twice, 'and this means "no".'

'Oh,' said Jinx, blinking. 'So, how do you say "Jinx doesn't want the brown coat"?'

Bonbon put her hands on her hips. 'No, Jinx. She asked me if you would like a brown coat and I said no.' She clapped twice. 'Like this.'

'Oh!' Jinx tried. 'Like this?'

'Yes!'

Jinx thought for a while, dancing her eyes over the carpet. 'But… that means that we can talk to her, Bonbon! This changes everything.'

'It does, doesn't it?'

An even better thought opened up Jinx's face. 'And we can talk to the He-one, and, and tell them when we want something or when we don't! In fact, we can talk to anyone, can't we, Bonbon? We could even go to the shops on our own! We could—'

'No, Jinx,' Bonbon interrupted, 'we can't talk to anyone. We're not allowed.'

Jinx stared at Bonbon with her mouth still open from where she had been talking. 'Why? Why not? Not allowed? Why not?'

'Because of the lady.'

'What lady?'

'In the shop.'

'What?'

Bonbon sighed. Then explained what had happened, from the moment she had been picked up from the tile-smelling place to the moment she stepped into the garden with Blankey. She had spent the whole of yesterday putting it into order inside her head and now, and now… she could tell it. She told Jinx about the humcoat conversation with Susan, how she hadn't understood at first but then she did, and when they tried to get her the shoe humcoat…

'A humcoat, made out of shoes? And they thought you liked it?' Jinx shook her head in wonder.

Well, that was why she had clapped to say 'no', and then the lady had offered her flakes, but didn't really give her any, instead she told them to wait there, but the big She-one didn't want to, and when they got back in the car, she said: 'We mustn't clap like that in front of other people, okay? It has to be our secret because otherwise, they might take you away.'

'Take you away?' Jinx gasped.

'Or you,' said Bonbon. 'That's why we have to be careful.'

'But why would they take us away?'

Bonbon shrugged. 'We're not allowed to communicate.' She'd found the word at last, the lady in the shop had said it but she couldn't quite remember it. 'We're not allowed to be like them.' She put her legs straight out in front of her and looked at her feet. The big She-one hadn't said this to her, but she had understood. She had understood the lady when she said 'attempted communication', and 'littlers are not animals, but they cannot be called people because they are kept as pets'. As soon as she had said that word, the 'p' word, two cats came running from opposite directions on the inside of Bonbon's head. Grey ones, just like the one that had chased Jinx that time. They flattened their ears a little, sniffed each other, then one lifted its hand and smacked the other on the nose. The other one showed its teeth.

She repeated what the lady had said: not animals, but kept as pets. The big He-one had also talked about pets yesterday morning. She had understood everything. And she didn't know why, but all day yesterday she'd been sad about this. Even though animals were quite nice, some little part of her, like her baby toe, or something, had thought that this was wrong. Now this feeling had spread to her whole foot.

If *they* were kept as pets, then they were kept as animals.

'This is why we have to stick together, Jinx.'

'Why, Bonbon?'

'I don't know,' she replied, all these new thoughts muddled in her head.

'Because we are both the same,' said Jinx.

Bonbon looked at her. That was exactly right! It sounded so simple, but exactly what she wanted to say. 'That's right, Jinx.'

Jinx beamed. 'And Chips. And Blankey.'

'Yes. All of us. And…' she started, consulting her thoughts just to make sure that they matched up with how she felt. Yes. Yes, she was sure that they did. When she thought of everything she had seen in the tile-smelling place, the thing on the side of her head and all the other heads; Champ who was so hurt, yet he asked her if she was all right, and the way, the way that he could talk to the biggerers, and the others could, with their voices; even if it was horrid screaming, it was possible to be heard, she had seen it. And, and thinking about it, now that she had seen more biggerers, and she had seen that they were the same as the big She-one and the big He-one, she was sure that she didn't have a cat face or a bird face, she had the same face as them but, but smaller. She continued: 'And we won't be collecting feathers today. Or ever again…'

Jinx gasped.

'Because that's what animals do, and we are not animals. We are…' Beyond the window two snails crossed the AstroTurf, wobbling under big plops of rain; they both fell over one after the other, their shiny feet sticking out into the air as they just lay like that, letting themselves to be rained on.

'Littlers!' Jinx tried to finish Bonbon's sentence.

'No, Jinx.' Still gazing at the snails, she checked her head one last time. The white and crumpled one stood, nodding at her. Bonbon took a deep breath. 'I'm sure that we are humans.'

Jinx had never heard this word before. But she understood it as soon as Bonbon had said it. It made all of her body go prickly and those prickles filled with air that lifted her off the ground. 'Yes!' she said, jumping up, then: 'You mean little people?'

'Yes, Jinx.'

'The same… as them?' Jinx nodded up at the ceiling where singing and shower noises could be heard.

Bonbon lifted her eyebrows in the middle. 'I think so,' she said.

Jinx looked at Bonbon's legs, covered in coat. Then at her own legs. Then one black and one blue leg walked through the inside of her head. 'Shall we see if we can see?' she said.

'How?' said Bonbon.

'Come on!' and she got up and skipped over to the door, not letting her feet drag even a little bit on the nice carpet.

They ran to the bottom of the stairs and looked up into the stairwell that opened like a mouth with the stairs falling down and curling round like a great big tongue.

'We've never been up there, Jinx.'

'But that's not because we're not allowed.'

'But… I'm not sure if I can pull myself up.'

'Well, I'm going to try.' Jinx put her hand on the first step, which came up to her shoulder, and heaved herself onto it. She put her hand out to Bonbon. 'Come on. It's easy.'

Bonbon shook her head at the hand and managed to pull herself up by clinging onto strands of carpet on the top of the stair and walking her legs up between her arms.

Jinx stared at her, her head on one side. 'Shall we do the next one?' she said.

Bonbon already had her hands buried in the pile and was walking her legs up. Jinx pushed down on the top of the second stair and heaved herself over its edge. They continued like this, each with their own method, the singing and the shower noises getting louder with each step, until they reached the seventh or eighth step. Bonbon climbed onto it then turned herself around to sit with her legs hanging over the edge. Her back swelled and shrank in time to the breathy noises her mouth made. 'Oh!' she said. 'You can,' breathe, 'see really,' breathe, 'far from up,' breathe, 'here.'

Jinx sat next to Bonbon thinking it was funny the way she spoke. 'Look at that,' breathe, 'we have never,' breathe, 'been up,' breathe, 'so high.'

They sat gazing at the hallway that was just about visible after the curve in the staircase. Then Bonbon got up. 'Come on.'

They started to climb again.

By the time they had reached the top, the shower noises and the singing had stopped.

Everything was lovely up here, thought Jinx. There was nice carpet everywhere and it seemed to be really yellow, not a normal yellow but a dancey yellow, as if somebody was turning yellow on and off, really quickly, but whenever she looked straight at the carpet, and the wall, they were both just white.

She felt something nudge up behind her. 'Bonbon, why are you so close to me?' But even as she said it, she could feel Bonbon shaking. 'Don't be frightened. It's lovely here, isn't it?'

Bonbon's eyes were wide and she held her arms over her chest, her wrists limp and her hands curled over.

'But why is it a funny yellow like this?'

Bonbon looked towards the window. It was like the dining-room window but here! Up high! And it glowed so brightly that Jinx had to squint to look at it. It felt like bright yellow, and it sort of was, but it was more shiny than coloured. She stepped backwards to where Bonbon was standing and realized that Bonbon's spot was just out of the brightness, and from here she could look with normal eyes. Her eyes took a moment to get used to the new light, but when they did…

The world rolled out before them in what seemed to be lines of white teeth that started big, then got smaller and smaller, and between them, every so often, a tall skinny thing, much much taller than the teeth, with a turny flower-head, was making the flickers in the yellow. There were many of these flower-head thingies and they faced all different directions. Some were turning really fast and others were being lazy. And way behind the lines of teeth and the skinny flowers, a white wall grew out of the ground; it grew so high that they couldn't see over the top of it. Great big trees, bigger than anything, even bigger than the tall skinny flowers, flicked their green hair along its walls. Bonbon and Jinx ducked as a big bird, like the one that was dead behind the green box, fell down from the trees with its arms stretched out, getting bigger and bigger as it got lower, but it didn't seem to come forward, it just, sort of, stayed on the wall. Then something started to make blue wiggly lines across the wall, over where the bird had just landed. What did that mean? What were those lines?

'EarthSpan,' said Bonbon, squinting at the wall-thing.

'What, Bonbon?'

'Our new salt-powered fleet, taking you to over two thousand destinations.'

'What, Bonbon? What are you…' The last word wouldn't come out of Jinx's mouth. A shadow broke through the flickering yellow, and they ducked back into the door frame that led into another room. It was the She-one.

'Oops,' said the She-one, turning off a light and turning off the shadow. Bonbon clung to Jinx's elbow as Jinx put half of her head around the door, immediately pulling it back again. 'I was right.' But she couldn't say the words. Instead, she pointed into the room, wanting to say: 'Look, Bonbon, look.'

They both looked. Two long legs grew into a bottom that narrowed into a back before widening into hair. The big She-one was fiddling with something. She bent to step on it but put her foot right through it, oh dear! It was broken! But then she put the other foot through it and pulled it upwards, over her knees, and then her bottom. They both stared at the thing with scrunched-up eyebrows. What was it for? It wouldn't really keep her warm, would it? The big She-one turned and reached for something behind her, showing a side view of one breast and a tummy. The thing was long with two ears; she passed it around her middle, turning around as she did so. Two breasts, she had two breasts! Just like them! Then she appeared to be tying both ends together at the front. Mouth open, she looked down at it strangely; another chin growing out from under her real one. 'Shit,' she said. Bonbon and Jinx twitched but didn't move. Then: 'There we go,' as she turned the whole thing around and covered her breasts with its ears.

They eyed it the way they had eyed the broken thing that she had put on her bottom. What on Earth did it do? It didn't matter, thought Bonbon. They had seen enough. She was sure now, absolutely certain. They were exactly the same as her but smaller – exactly the same. Bonbon pinched Jinx, and pointed back towards the stairs.

No. Jinx shook her head; she wanted to stay and watch the big She-one put her legs on.

Bonbon looked at Jinx for a moment then nodded, all right then, she would stay. Jinx smiled. They would leave after the legs, even though she would like to have stayed right to the end. They would leave after the legs because Bonbon wanted to.

'Trousers,' said the inside of her head.

It was worth staying for. Although, they couldn't work out why she had to put the trousers on, take them off again, then put different ones on… Jinx had always wondered how they could change colour like that – it was because she had more than one trousers.

'Pair of trousers,' said the inside of her head.

Pair of trousers, she repeated to herself, thinking that one day, she'd really like to be able to change the colour of her legs.

CHAPTER 9

The Turning of Newspaper Pages. That's what this notebook entry would be called.

One finger slipped up to the top of the page, over the corner, a third of the way down the inside before the whole hand opened up and, swish! The hand pushed it over. Then it rested, palm down, on the middle of the page, just for a moment, as if to say: 'There we are, that wasn't so bad now, was it?' The rest of the paper languished, cradled and trusting across the length of the other arm; like the way Jasper let himself be treated for fleas, or tickled behind the ears.

Drew was so gentle. Even to newspapers. As if separating enormous butterfly wings.

That was a nice description. If Drew had any idea about what went on in Watty's mind, there'd be piss-taking and retching noises right into the afternoon. Watty would write it down later and pretend it was about somebody else if ever it got discovered.

Ah! Already at the back page. One whole arm could be freed, what would it do? The free forearm swung upwards and its beaked hand nibbled at Drew's eyelashes, like a long-necked bird searching for tit-bits.

Birds and butterflies. And golden dogs. Where had he left his notebook? Kitchen, probably; after using that four-berry trifle recipe from it yesterday. Watty frowned at the thought of it; blood-red and slimy yellow, like an operation on a fat person.

'What?' grinned Drew, catching Watty grimace.

Watty's stare travelled up and down Drew's face. 'Have you always done that? Is that why they grow so long?'

Drew's bird hand stopped nibbling. 'Do you want to know the truth?'

Watty sighed. 'Only if it's interesting.'

'I'm picking off my mascara.'

'Oh.'

'Aren't you surprised?'

'Why would I be? You put it on; it has to come off again.'

'Aren't you surprised that I wear mascara?'

'No.' Arms folding. 'I didn't think it belonged to Jasper.'

'What didn't?'

'The little silver tube in the bathroom. And the CC cream.'

'Ha! That's your CC cream and you know it.'

'I hardly use it but I replace it often enough.'

'—.'

'You know, when I go to the shops… in my car.'

Drew folded the newspaper. 'That reminds me, trampolining at five today, Jeeves.'

Watty's pupils rolled upwards, then back towards Drew's eyelashes.

'Where's my egg?'

They both looked up to see Jasper wandering in, tongue hanging out. Isabel sat on his back, her hands lost inside his fur. 'Can I have a whole one today?'

'You can have a quarter of one,' replied Drew with big eyes and spread-out eyebrows.

'I meant to tell you, I got some quails' eggs. Maybe she can have a whole one of them.'

'Did you hear that, Isabel?' said Drew, getting up and going to the fridge. 'Special tiny eggs.'

'What's a quail?' Isabel climbed from Jasper to a kitchen chair.

'A little chicken,' said Watty. 'Here, let me get you your chair.'

'Do animals come in smaller sizes too?'

Drew's eyes came up from behind the fridge door and looked at Watty who helped Isabel into her chair.

'A quail,' began Watty, 'is not really a chicken. It's a small, chubby little thing that can't fly. Like you.'

Isabel laughed. Drew pouted and gave a firm nod and disappeared behind the fridge door.

Isabel wasn't allowed to go outside, or to school, or trampolining with Drew, because she was different. Instead, she read stories from books and stories that Watty would write for her… She also watched a lot of television. From this, she had discovered all kinds of funny things. Giant yellow birds could say the alphabet and fat bears with TV stomachs had somehow bought a talking hoover – of all things – and those two bears and one dog, whose legs were never, ever seen…

She had already worked out the difference between 'flat-colourful' people and 'real' people. Watty had told her that the flat-colourful people were called 'cartoons' – and that they weren't always people.

'Well, what are they then?'

'A mixture of animals and monsters and mythical creatures and…'

'What's a mythical creature?'

'You know, it's like a unicorn or, or Pegasus…'

Isabel screwed up her face. 'You mean Peppa Pig. It's not easy to say. Look, like this.' And she opened her mouth and eyes really wide for the best pronunciation. 'PE-PA-PIG.'

Watty laughed. 'No. PE-GA-SUS is a flying horse.'

'But that's a unicorn.'

'Unicorns have a horn in the middle of their head.'

'And wings.'

'No. No wings.'

Isabel looked shocked. 'Yes they do!'

'No, darling, I'm afraid they don't.'

'Some of them do.'

'Well, maybe, but it doesn't really matter because they are mythical. Which means that they don't exist.'

Isabel looked at Watty from the side of her head. 'I'm not so sure,' she said. 'I think it's just cartoon ones that aren't real.'

'They don't exist at all, not even real ones.' Watty winced. That sentence had come out all wrong. But Isabel nodded. Even real ones didn't exist; she had understood.

'And pigs neither?' she asked.

'Now, that's silly. You know that pigs exist.' Watty held the shape of 'exist' between his teeth. How could she be sure? She'd never actually seen one.

'No. Not like that. Not with two eyes on one side of their face and with clothes on.'

Watty's lips pressed together. Good point.

'And they talk. Pigs don't talk.'

'True, true…'

'So these ones are like people *and* animals *and* unicorns.'

Watty sighed. 'Well, you know that a real person draws them. That means that everything about them has been thought about and decided by somebody and by somebody's imagination. Everything they say, everything they wear, everything they do…'

Isabel listened with her face tilted towards Watty, her eyes looking up to the right.

'Real pigs are real, though. Like you.'

'They are indeed.'

'And they haven't been designed by a person.'

'No,' said Watty, glad that Drew wasn't suffering this particular interrogation, having to ignore a career full of scientific meddling in order to give her a good clean answer.

'No,' repeated Isabel. 'I knew that but I just wanted to check…'

Watty went on. 'So, even though some of them seem like pigs or people, they're just imaginary – just a mixture of things that real people think about. Let's just call them "cartoons", shall we? All of them.'

'Every last one?'

'Every last one.'

'Yes. That's nice. That's nice that they all have the same name.' And she was able to think about something different, happy that she knew everything there was to know about cartoons.

Although it was quite complicated.

Sometimes, real people would hang around with other beings that definitely weren't cartoons. Like Pegasus and unicorns and mermaids… Although mermaids could speak. The horses couldn't. The two bears and one dog fascinated Isabel. They actually spoke to a real man even though they were 'animals'. But they weren't his pets… Or were they? They seemed to all live together and, well, behave like they were the same. And he could understand all of them, even though they all spoke differently. One of them couldn't say anything, nothing at all! He just seemed to whisper into the person's ear. One of them squeaked – the dog one. One of them spoke proper English and she had a bow in her hair, and she wore a dress. The strange thing was that the programme was named after the one that couldn't speak. Isabel had always thought that the nicest and the most important was the girl-one with the bow that could speak. But nobody seemed to mind that the one-that-couldn't-talk was the most important. In fact, they all seemed to be really good friends.

And the best thing of all was their bedroom. It had three little beds, three little wardrobes and lots of tunnels and balconies that covered up their legs when they walked from one bit to another and hiding places, and in one of the little wardrobes there were little dresses – little dresses that would have fitted Isabel perfectly – and it was pink where the girl slept and blue and green where the boys slept and there were little pictures on the wall… Little bedside tables… Little lamps…

After the 'little chicken' question, after Watty had gone off to work and even after lunch, Drew had caught Isabel hammering the remote control buttons with the palm of her hand. 'What's wrong with you, grumpy-guts?' he asked, rubbing the top of Isabel's head with a thumb.

'Where are the other ones like me? I've never seen other ones like me.'

Drew froze. 'What, children?'

'No!' She looked at Drew. 'Little.'

Ah. It had arrived. The conversation had finally arrived. But Watty wasn't there! They needed to speak about this all together, the three of them. They should have explained this morning, over breakfast, when they had the chance… Oh no… Isabel was crying.

'Shall we write Watty a poem for his notebook?'

'No.'

'Come on! How about we practise handstands? Or ice some chocolates?'

Usually Isabel would pout and fold her arms and Drew could coax her into the kitchen. But she cried, and cried, all red and shiny from so many tears that had made a big wet patch along the neckline of her little dress. 'Please!' she said. 'Please, Drew! I'm really sad and I don't know why!'

Drew's heart, inside its chest, detached from its tangle of arteries and fell, plop, to the bottom of Drew's stomach.

The little girl who couldn't go out, who was dependent upon the telly and her dog for company. Who would never play with other children. Who was so sad and didn't know why. Drew knew why. It was time to tell the truth, all of it, today. But Isabel needed to be consoled first.

They had been preparing for this for a while.

Drew took a DVD from its case and popped it into the player before kneeling in front of Isabel. 'Now listen to me.'

Isabel nodded.

'I'm going to show you a programme with little people.'

Isabel gasped.

'But!' Drew held up one finger as if to stopper the little girl's excitement. 'This is not real. They are actors, do you understand that?'

'Yes.'

'And these actors are pretending to be little people.'

'Okay.' She didn't seem to care; she was already looking over Drew's shoulder.

Drew pressed play, then went to call Watty.

Isabel sat and watched *The Borrowers* series all afternoon. When the DVD had come to an end, she pressed play and started the whole thing again, and when she had watched it all over again, she cried because they weren't real.

'I did tell you,' said Drew.

'If they could have spoken to the bigger ones, then they wouldn't have had to live in a mouse hole,' sobbed Isabel. 'Am I going to have to live in a mouse hole?'

Drew sighed. 'Watty's back now. Shall we all sit down and talk about this?'

Isabel's mouth turned from down to up, and she laughed as the yellow bear, the whispery one, as big as her, popped out from behind Drew's thigh.

Watty had thought that buying her a Sooty puppet would help her to understand what was real and what was not. But she screamed when she saw that he didn't have any legs, and spent ages putting his black nose to her ear, squinting, trying to hear what he was saying.

'You listen,' she finally said a few days later, thrusting the bear at Drew. 'He will only talk to people.'

They blinked at her. 'But you're a person.'

'I'm not.' She shook her head. 'I'm not a person.'

* * *

'Gosh! I'm so sorry, I completely forgot to come over last night!' Susan held the phone under her chin and wriggled her way out of one side of her coat at the same time, tossing the bag with Jinx's humcoat onto the sofa. A green light blinked at her from the drinks machine. No more beakers. Already. Susan lifted the edge of her blouse and looked down at the lip of skin that pouted over her jeans.

'Don't worry, dear... I got the impression that your husband was going to prepare something special for you.'

She shook the coat from her other shoulder, wanting to say: 'He's not my husband.' But instead she said: 'Oh, really?'

'I found some of those chocolates among the groceries that he fetched for me, you know; the heart-shaped ones painted with some sort of gold... I don't know what it is... You can eat it.'

Smiling into the handset, Susan strode about the lounge looking for Jinx. 'Perhaps they were for you?'

'Ha! Doubtful,' laughed the old lady.

Susan opened her mouth to say something important but the gold chocolate hearts had pushed out the important thought. Dammit. What had she wanted to say? It was... something about... about Blankey. That was it. She had scoured the garden and looked inside the composting bin... 'I did have a look—'

'I wanted to ask—' said the old lady at the same time. Then: 'Sorry. You go on, dear.'

'Oh. Right, well...' Damn damn damn. It had gone again! 'Have you found Blankey?'

'No,' replied Mrs Lucas. 'I take it you haven't found her either?'

Susan made her lips into the shape of 'no', but the old lady's words had climbed out of the handset and pulled at the corners of her mouth. Her mind drew up an image of the old lady sitting well forward in an armchair, ankles crossed, looking from the phone, to the door, to the littler basket. Gosh; how could she have forgotten to go over there last night? With her free hand, she pushed her hair out of her face and bent to look under the sofa for Jinx. No sign. But her wrist caught her eye. She blinked at it. Instead of saying 'no', Susan's mouth took a deep breath and said: 'I haven't got any news for you…' She stood up and touched the glowing skin with her nose. The LOG meeting flyer illuminated.

'Oh…' climbed out of the handset like a tiny, hungry child.

'But why don't I make us a nice cup of coffee and we'll discuss where to go from here?'

There was a short silence, then: 'I'm sure you've got things to be getting on with.'

'No, seriously. I think I have an idea of who we can ask about all of this. There's definitely something strange going on.'

'Do you really think so?'

'Come over now and I'll tell you all about it. Oh, why don't you bring those chocolates?'

Suddenly the hungry child was a gaggle of happy children, bursting through each hole of the handset as the old lady laughed. 'Well, if we don't know for whom he bought them, we may as well share them.'

'Exactly!' Susan laughed back, goose-bumping at the 'm' in 'whom'.

They said goodbye and hung up. With her free hand, Susan scrolled down through the LOG meeting flyer for the address. The other side of town. She would have to drive them both there. Hopefully Mrs Lucas would be free. 'Jinx!' she called. Nope, not in the kitchen. She turned and scanned the hall before making her way to the dining room. 'Jinx! Bonbon!' She pressed a button next to the dining-room doors and they slid up into the ceiling. 'Jinx!'

she called. 'Bonbon! Jiiiinx! Bonboooon!' Nothing. They hardly ever left the garden. She'd been hoping to ask them about Blankey before Mrs Lucas got there… For coffee and gold hearts. She turned and let her feet swish across the carpet towards the kitchen. Oh well, what did it matter if she asked them later on? Scraping noises came from the vacuum hatch just as she reached into an upper cupboard for beakers. 'Is that you two?' she called without looking over her shoulder. 'Bonbon?'

A clap.

Susan smiled; it was still a bit of a surprise, hearing her clap. But, gosh; they would really have to keep an eye on this. 'Hang on, let me just grab these.' Maybe she should try to explain to them exactly what had happened at the store. She frowned and turned around.

Bonbon stood hugging herself while Jinx sat on the floor, holding her ankle in order to stroke her hair with her foot.

'What are you doing, silly?' Susan squatted in front of Jinx. 'I've got a present for you in the lounge.'

Jinx put her foot down. In half a second she was next to Bonbon and stroking her coat.

'That's right,' Susan laughed. 'Bonbon, did you tell her?'

Clap.

'That was very nice of you! Were you excited about telling Jinx that she had a present?'

Clap.

'Oh, you sweetie.'

Jinx was already pulling one of Susan's fingers towards the lounge.

'Yes, alright. But first…' Susan made a serious face. 'I need your help for something very important; do you understand?' She looked at Bonbon but both of them clapped together. 'Oh! Jinx! You can do it too?'

Jinx blinked.

'Did Bonbon teach you?'

Clap.

Susan's mouth dropped open. That really was quite amazing. The words of the scary technician lady bubbled up in her mind. 'We don't yet know their intellectual limits.' Ha! Too right they didn't. They actually spoke to each other about the new things that were happening in their lives; they imparted knowledge. That was so… human! She felt pressure around her fingertip again and grinned. They obviously still had to learn about patience. 'Yes, alright, Jinx. Now listen, both of you: do you know what's happened to Blankey?'

Bonbon clapped twice. Jinx only once.

Susan stared at them. Maybe she hadn't been clear. She turned to Jinx. 'Jinx, do you know where Blankey is?'

Two claps.

'Oh.' Why did she say yes the first time? 'Did you know that Blankey's gone missing?'

Both of them clapped 'yes'.

'How do you know that?'

They blinked up at her. Bonbon seemed to roll her eyes. Susan laughed again.

'Do you think I'm silly for asking questions that can't be answered with yes or no?'

Bonbon clapped once, slowly and deliberately.

Susan grinned. Bonbon was making fun of her. How wonderful. 'Okay; do you know that Blankey has gone missing because…' Susan searched the ceiling for a reason. 'Because she told you she was leaving?'

Two claps from each.

Ah-ha. That wasn't the reason. 'Because… you saw her go?'

Two claps from each.

'Because… someone told you?'

Two claps from Bonbon. One from Jinx.

'Someone told you, Jinx? Who told you?'

Jinx walked over to Bonbon and held her sleeve.

'Bonbon told you?'

Clap.

'Bonbon, who told you?'

Bonbon rolled her eyes.

'Right, sorry! Erm… Who, no, wait… erm…'

Bonbon walked over to Susan and put her hand on her shoe.

'I told you?'

Clap.

'*I* told you?'

Clap.

'Oh.' Susan wrinkled her eyes. 'Really?'

Clap.

Her finger was being squeezed again. This time Susan let herself be led all the way to the lounge, walking on her knees, wondering when she could have told Bonbon about Blankey. Bonbon followed, and looked on as Susan took the green humcoat from its bag and shook it out for Jinx. Jinx froze for a moment, before scrunching herself up, pulling her arms in, twisting her fingers, wrinkling her toes, jamming her eyes shut and rolling her lips back so fiercely that she was shaking. 'Are you alright, Jinx?' Just as the 'n' in Jinx had left Susan's nose, Jinx jumped into a star and out of her mouth came the highest, tiniest squeal. She straightened and looked around her to see where the noise had come from.

'Did you just squeal, Jinx? Did you just make a little noise?'

Clap-clap.

'Yes, you did! Didn't she, Bonbon?'

Clap.

'Do it again – can you do it again?'

Jinx opened her mouth and stood with it open. Susan watched her with folded lips. Jinx scrunched herself up again, exactly like before, until she was shaking. Doorbells chimed in the hallway. Jinx shut her mouth and looked towards the hall.

'Oh… You look so nice, Jinx.'

Jinx twirled one way, then the other.

'It's so nice in green.'

'I know,' scrunching her face up and gritting her teeth together. 'I'm so happy, Bonbon.'

Bonbon smiled. 'I know you are.'

Jinx tried to look at the back of herself in the dining-room doors, liking her reflection; oh! She just had to show Chips! Chips would really like her in this coat.

'Is this Bonbon and…'

'Jinx. Bonbon and Jinx.'

'Oh how lovely.' Mrs Lucas beamed at them both. 'But that's… that's my Blankey's coat!' She pointed towards Bonbon. 'I mean… That looks like my Blankey's coat.'

'I bought it the other day.' Susan looked at Bonbon. 'Have you got the same coat as Blankey, Bonbon?'

A clap.

'So it is! Little copycat…'

'Is this… Is this the clapping you were talking about?'

'Yes! This is it. Although…' Susan tapped the side of her nose.

'And you really haven't seen my Blankey?' Mrs Lucas looked from Bonbon to Jinx and back again.

Bonbon clapped twice. Jinx watched, wanting to clap but too busy playing with the buttons on her coat.

'That means "no", doesn't it?'

Susan nodded. 'I'm afraid so.'

Jinx stopped playing with her buttons, walked up to the old lady and cuddled her shoe, stroking it like she'd done that day with the Dead Bird.

Mrs Lucas chuckled, then let her stare deaden for a while.

Susan was just about to ask her what was wrong when: 'You're Jinx, aren't you?' she said to her shoe.

Jinx looked up then clapped once.

'Tell me, Jinx, do you know the other one? The one who lives next to me… Skinny little thing, he is.'

A clap.

'You do? Would you be able to ask him for me? You see…' She turned to Susan. 'I'm a bit wary of his owner. If it weren't for him, I'd go round there myself.'

Jinx held a clap between her hands as her eyes were caught by a twinkle that danced along the beaded hemline of Mrs Lucas's skirt.

'Oh really?' Susan shifted her weight to one hip. 'I don't think I've ever seen him… The owner.'

'He's a big, untidy fellow; should really be under specialist care I think. He limps, poor chap, haven't you seen him hobble up the driveway? He won't remember you from one day to the next. Have you seen how skinny his littler is?'

Jinx pictured Chips's biggerer and his big boots chasing her towards the vacuum hatch.

'I've seen him in our back yard once or twice, but he's always had his coat on.'

His humcoat… His humcoat that he hadn't had when Jinx had seen him, but had somehow found afterwards.

'Painfully thin.' She took a deep breath. 'I know it's silly but I have to think of these things at my age. I wouldn't be able to… you know… leave quickly or abruptly or even be particularly assertive.'

'It's not silly at all.'

A dream played out in Jinx's mind; all flickery and soundless. A peacock wandered about a kitchen, yelping meow, meow, like the grey cat. A flower in its hair. Big boots appeared behind it and big hands grabbed its body and pulled it into the air, little twiggy legs wiggled, looking for something to grab on to…

This was silly, how could that have happened? It was like that thought that she'd had this morning, when she was sure that Blankey was sleeping by the dining-room doors. That was such a silly thought. But… they hadn't passed each other in the tunnel after Jinx had run from Chips's vacuum hatch. Maybe she'd come much later, when Chips was asleep? She thought of the day before when Chips had turned and run across her Outside, through his tunnel and away, all red and panicked. And with his humcoat on. She turned and looked at Bonbon.

Bonbon wrinkled her eyes. 'What's wrong?' they seemed to say.

'Would you do that for me, little lady?' Words dropped like feathers from Mrs Lucas's mouth.

Jinx caught every single one and vowed that she would look after them until… Until she could pass them on to Chips. A clap.

'Good girl,' said Mrs Lucas.

Jinx turned and took Bonbon by the hand. The grey and green crinolines disappeared into the hallway.

'I… I didn't mean right this minute. You don't have to go now. Are they going now?'

'I guess so,' Susan replied, wanting to call after them that they should be careful. She bit her lip and watched them disappear into the hallway.

'If someone was potentially in danger and it was your fault, what would you do?'

'There must be more to it than that…'

'What do you mean?'

'Well, the answer is so obvious that… How about this: if someone was in danger and it was my fault, what would stop me from helping them?'

'—'

'Emma?'

'Being unsure of the consequences.'

'Right. Consequences for who?'

She smirked. 'This is all hypothetical, really. It's just one particular incident that plays on my mind…'

His eyes twitched over her. Leave them to rot, he wanted to say; how could anything like that be your fault? He felt his chest rising forward and stopped it, heaving it back as if it were a toddler hurtling, arms open, towards a panther. He opened his mouth.

'It's already time,' she said.

He watched his own feet swinging above the floor and tried to aim each swing so that the line in the tiles below was exactly in the centre. Now his feet were above it… Now they were below it. Now above, and now below. Above. Below. Above. Below. Where could she be? Having come home yesterday afternoon, and having hidden in his cupboard for ages listening to that voice as it called him a liar again and again and trying to rock it away and shake it out of his head; having done all of that, he'd spent most of the night walking around the ground floor, turning over plates and cushions and bags and boxes, shouting Blankey's name. As long as he could hear himself shout, he was alone in the house.

She didn't answer. She was nowhere.

Above. Below. Above. Below. Try. The. First. Floor. Above. Below… Above. The first floor. He stopped swinging. He had to try everywhere. He had to. Because not finding her here would be just as good as finding her here. Well, not just as good… Pushing himself out of the cupboard, he launched himself towards the stairs. But at least they could be sure of one place where she was not. And… and perhaps this voice in his head would stop. Or quieten down a bit. Pulling himself up onto the first stair, he remembered the last time he'd climbed stairs and screwed his eyes up. He remembered liking the feeling of the nice soft stair brushing against his body. He remembered the noises that had pulled him upwards; what he'd found at the top… No. No. He

couldn't think about that now. Certainly not. And anyway, these stairs were horrid; some were sticky, some were rough. Some had carpet, some didn't. All of them smelled bad, so bad that he held his breath each time his face got too close to one. He got to the sixth step and stopped, panting. His stomach made bubbly noises. It was difficult to climb when nothing was pulling him upwards. Bad smells, horrid carpet… And now his foot was stuck to something. His stomach rumbled again. 'If you find Blankey, you can ask her for some flakes,' said the voice. Disgusting, he licked his lips, that thought disgusted him. But he allowed it to pull him up the next few stairs.

She lay in front of the door, arms tangled in the fluffy rug that stretched next to the bed; one giant footprint glowed and faded on the whitish door as her eyes sharpened and dimmed, but never closed. The sound of her own breathing hissed in her ears and sometimes a squelchy pumping noise echoed in her head. She dragged one hand under her armpit and sucked at the fingers. Two tiny droplets dissolved on her tongue. She sucked her tongue, dry like that dusty rug, she thought, before sucking it again then biting it, hard, the pumping beating at her ears. The blood flowed. The pumping calmed. She sucked it all up and bit again. This time it hurt; tears rose in her eyes like bubbles and burst at the surface, spilling over the eye's edge and sliding over her temples. She scooped them up in her fingernails and fed them into her mouth.

That big hairy hand had pushed her to the back of the box, 'I must get you some water, Tilda.' And he'd left, pulling the bedroom door closed behind him. Luckily, he hadn't closed the lid on the box. But that was yesterday. She hadn't had a drop of water since she'd left her own house with Chips's humcoat in her grey bag and a flower in her hair. Why hadn't Chips found the humcoat and the flower? Maybe they were completely out of sight. She thought for a moment: where had she left them? A skinny hand of memory tried to pull itself up behind her eyes, but another fat memory was waiting to stamp on the hand: that big hairy hand curling around her, lifting her up to the face that smelled her, and the breath that surrounded her with the word 'Tiiiildaaaa…' She had shut her eyes. But now she would have given anything in the world to see him, to have that big hairy hand put a nice dish of water next to her and breathe 'Tiiiildaaaa' all over her again.

She tasted her own mouth. Sore patches of tongue remembered where her teeth had bitten. 'Help,' she whispered, then coughed. Then closed her eyes.

A noise broke through the door, weird and echoey as if it had passed through a tunnel in order to get to her. She rolled her head to face the door. Her name… Someone was calling her. 'Ho…' she croaked. Again, the noise tunnelled through the door. 'Blankey!' it called.

Her arms twisted out of the rug and tried to push her body onto its elbows. 'Ho…' she tried again, breathing out as hard as she could. 'Ho!' she sobbed.

'Blankey!' The voice was not calling any more; it was shouting. Had it heard her? 'Blankey!' it shouted again, followed by a thud against the door.

'Chips,' Blankey whispered.

CHAPTER 10

'I have to go through there?'

'That's the only way to get to his house.'

Bonbon looked into the dirty tunnel. 'Are you sure about this, Jinx?'

Jinx nodded. 'Mmm-hmmm.' She watched as Bonbon locked her teeth together and closed her eyes the way she did when she got put in water. 'It's alright, Bonbon, look; take my hand.'

'Alright, Jinx.' The tiny white hand climbed into the air without knowing where it was going as its owner still had her eyes shut. Jinx found it and pulled it towards her.

'You can stay here if you want to.'

'I don't want to be without you.'

'Right.'

Bonbon let herself be led but took the tiniest, slowest steps she had ever, ever taken.

'You know what you found out yesterday? About Blankey?' Jinx said in her kindest voice.

'Yes.'

'If you hadn't have found that out, then we wouldn't have asked Chips if he'd seen her, and so we wouldn't be doing any of this.'

The steps got a little longer. 'Really?'

'Yes, Bonbon. Really. If you hadn't heard what you heard then poor Blankey… Well… Poor Blankey wouldn't be being looked for right now.' The steps were almost normal. 'So if we do find her, she'll have you to thank.'

'And you, Jinx,' Bonbon breathed. 'You're the brave one.'

Jinx smiled in the dark tunnel. 'We're almost there.'

'I'm frightened, Jinx.'

'It's alright. I was too, the first time, but I was all on my own. You've got me.'

Bonbon took a deep breath. 'Right.'

'Now, listen. The inside of Chips's house is very different to ours.'

'Different how?'

'Well… It's not very lovely.'

'Oh.'

'You're not going to like it.'

'—.'

'What I want you to keep thinking about is that if Blankey is in there, then we need to get her out. Alright?'

'I'll try.'

'Good.' Jinx lifted Bonbon's hand and kissed the back of it, then covered up the kiss with a little rub.

'My feet are caught in something.'

'Really?'

Bonbon's hand-squeeze got tighter. 'What is that, Jinx?'

'I'll check, Bonbon. Don't worry,' she replied, bending down to run her fingers along it.

'Don't touch it!'

Jinx recognized the slidiness between her fingers. She'd pulled it out of that blue tube the night that Blankey went missing, but, what was that thing?

'Let's pull it into the light.'

They stepped into Chips's Outside, pulling the thing that curled behind them like that long hairy thing that was stuck to the grey cat's bottom. Bonbon looked around her then ducked back towards the tunnel.

'It's alright. Just hold on to my coat.'

Bonbon reached forward and grabbed at the green fur, arching her gaze from the tunnel behind her, up along the grey wall, higher up to a clouded window, down towards a corner full of dirty shadows and right down over Jinx's shoulder at the little square of she-one held between Jinx's hands. She squished her eyelids almost together and peered closer. It had black hair and a black face and see-through lips but Bonbon was sure it was: 'Blankey,' she almost gasped.

Jinx pulled the long thing through her hands to another square, and another. One smiley, one with the lips all pushed out, one holding a flower. 'They're all Blankey,' she said.

* * *

'We're going to do the candles, Isabel!'

'Alright. I'll be there in a minute,' she said to the photo of a Kayan tribeswoman. Isabel stared at the woman's neck, and for a minute, pictured herself with golden coils around her arms and legs and waist, hyperextending her own body. She gripped her neck with her hands as she read the text that wrapped around the photo. Ah… So the gold coil didn't actually extend the neck, it pushed the collar bones down, giving the illusion of a long neck. Sounded rather painful, actually. She turned the page to the smallest man in the world and skipped right over it. She'd seen him a thousand times in various books and articles. She'd even written to him once or twice. The first time was when she was about ten, she'd written to him to say that she suffered from dwarfism and that he was one of her heroes; was he really as happy as he looked in his photos? A few months later a parcel arrived, inside was a list of societies and associations, as well as a baseball cap signed by the smallest man in the world. He told her that he felt very lucky to have this 'gift' and that Isabel shouldn't say that she 'suffers' from dwarfism as there was no right or wrong way of having a body that works properly. The second time she wrote to him was to thank him for his letter and all of the links and addresses for various societies that he'd forwarded her. And the baseball cap. She told him that although she really liked the baseball cap, it was a bit big as the circumference of her head measured only twelve centimetres; in fact, she thought he should know that the only reason she was writing to him was because she was much smaller than he was, and it made her feel good to know that she was better than someone else at something, and that he should be worried about his job. Drew found the letter before she sent it and went bananas; told her that it was very unkind to say things like that and that she should be ashamed. She was made to rub out the last three lines and replace them with: 'I like the baseball cap because it is blue and my bedroom is blue.'

'Do you want them to come here and see how small you are?'

'Yes!' she had screamed.

Drew had been shocked at this answer. The only really unkind thing in the letter was saying that the man should be worried about his job. The rest of it was worrying… Drew had squatted down in front of her and sighed. 'How about we take you out for a drive – would you like that?'

That was the first time Isabel had ever been out in a car. It was the first time she had seen real cows in real fields and real bunny rabbits in real bushes. She'd gasped so much that she could remember gasping. That was the year when Watty and Drew couldn't believe that they'd never thought of living in the country; the year that Isabel got a new bedroom with a view of the cows, a dwarf hamster and her first book about becoming a vet.

She turned another page. Ah, the Elephant Man, poor guy; she knew his story well and it always triggered one thought: if she turned herself into a curiosity, the world would have to accept her. In fact, she'd be famous! She was much smaller than the smallest man in the world. But this thought was exactly that: a thought. It was what she liked to call her 'chocolate cake thought'. She'd occasionally sit up in bed at night and eat it, thinking about the hotels she'd get to stay in, what she'd say to journalists, what she'd wear to television interviews, conversations with film directors – *The Borrowers* would be made into a film and she would play the lead – maybe she'd release her own perfume…

As soon as she had finished the slice, she was very careful not to take another piece. She would make herself think about something else: just lately it was feline castration, and her online quest to re-house Bonbon and Jinx, the French brown bears living in an impossibly tiny park enclosure. These were important things. Fame was such a superficial thing… Her laptop bleeped. Oh! Two emails pinged into her inbox. The first was entitled 'Still in Captivity'. There was an attachment. She clicked on the link to see two very sad bears chained at the foot. The head of one of them swung droopily from side to side, side to side. She glanced at the message underneath:

'Sign the petition to end their eighteen years of misery.'

Her eyes burned and blurred. She signed the petition under Drew's name, as she'd been told to do with everything, and went back to her inbox.

'Happy Birthday, Izzy, from the Amazon team.'

Isabel smiled and scraped a knuckle under one cheekbone, then the other. She'd made a secret Amazon account earlier in the year, and although she'd never ordered anything (Drew would go nuts) they had sent her a birthday message. Her, Isabel Mahlik, alias 'Izzy'.

'Happy Birthday to you! Happy Birthday to you!'

Isabel closed the window on the screen as Jasper's nose peeked around the door; Drew was shuffling towards her holding a glowing, cow-shaped cake while Jasper danced in circles underneath it. Two other people followed behind: Watty and Watty's brother, Uncle Reg. They were the only people in the world who could be trusted with Isabel's secret. Isabel stood up on her chair; when had Uncle Reg arrived? She would have abandoned her books much sooner had she known.

'Happy Birthday, dear Isabel!'

Isabel laughed as Drew said her name but Watty and Uncle Reg stretched her nickname, 'Quail', over two booming syllables.

Happy Birthday to you!

'Blow them out!' yelled Drew.

She leaned forward, and in eight little puffs, she'd blown out her seventeen candles.

* * *

Chips scratched at the white carpet that he could just about reach through the gap under the door. 'I can hear you, Blankey! I can hear you!' He tried to push his head under but it was much too narrow. 'I'll get you out!' he called. On his belly, he crawled backwards and craned his neck to see the door handle. It hung so high above him that it was all blurry. 'I'll get you!' he shouted up towards the handle. He looked around for something to climb up. A three-legged stool lay on its side in the doorway between the landing and another room. He leapt up, bounded over to it and started to push. The seat rolled, but its legs stayed where they were. Why? Running towards the legs, he pushed them. They moved, but the seat stayed where it was. He ran back to the seat and pushed it a little, then back to the legs, then to the seat. 'I'm coming, Blankey!' he called.

'Chips!'

Chips stopped pushing and cocked an ear. Jinx. That was Jinx's voice! 'Jinx!' he yelled, jumping through the legs of the stool and running to look through the bannisters where he could see the top of Jinx's head. She was halfway up the stairs. A grey shape clung to the side of the second stair – Bonbon! 'I'm up here! Come and help me!'

Jinx looked up and waved, her mouth wide open. 'We heard you shouting. You've found her, haven't you?'

'Yes!' he shouted over his shoulder as he ran back towards the stool. 'Hurry! I don't know when he… I don't know when he…' but he ran out of breath. Instead of finishing his sentence, he pushed at the legs of the stool. Then the seat. Then the legs. Jinx appeared, panting, at the top of the stairs. She shook off her humcoat and ran towards him, tripping on one of her feet. 'Where is she?'

'In there!' Chips nodded towards the closed door.

Jinx looked at the door, then up at the handle, then spun around and eyed the stool. She wrapped her arms around the nearest leg to her and heaved the thing backwards. Chips grasped the seat and did the same. Their feet made quick steps as they managed little bursts of dragging it for a few inches, then stopping.

'Where is she?' Bonbon's voice called from the end of the landing.

'Behind the first door.'

Bonbon staggered up the landing, stopping halfway to put her hands on her knees and catch her breath. Then she ran towards the door and pressed her face up against it. 'Blankey? Blankey? Can you hear me?' Then: 'She's not answering. Are you sure she's in there?'

'I'm sure,' strained Chips as he pulled the stool a little further forward.

'Right,' said Bonbon, running towards them before throwing off her humcoat and running back to put it on top of Jinx's.

With Bonbon now in the middle, the three of them heaved the stool until it was right under the door handle.

'Push your end up,' panted Jinx. 'Help him, Bonbon.'

Bonbon and Chips pushed at their end of the stool while Jinx pulled on the legs. The thing plopped onto its feet and rocked back the other way again before steadying itself.

'You go up, Chips. You're the tallest,' said Jinx.

'I'll give you a push,' said Bonbon, her opened hands hovering around Chips's bottom, ready to push it up or catch it if it fell.

Chips grunted and pulled himself up the leg of the stool, but his foot slipped, once, twice and a third time. 'We're coming, Blankey!' he screamed, so loudly that Bonbon used her outstretched hands to cover her ears.

'Here, let me help.' Jinx ran to Bonbon and, taking one buttock each, they pushed together. The whole thing wobbled and fell backwards.

Chips let out another scream.

'Chips!'

'I'm alright!' He got to his feet. 'Bonbon, you should go up. You're the littlest.'

Bonbon frowned. 'Alright,' she said. 'But I'll go up this side so that I can use the door to help me.'

Jinx pushed Bonbon while Chips held the non-door side of the stool. Bonbon's feet pushed against the leg of the stool while her bottom shimmied up the door. 'I'm up, Jinx. I can pull myself up from here.'

Jinx exhaled through pursed lips. 'Can you reach the handle?' she asked, striding backwards to get a better view.

'Yes.'

'We're coming, Blankey!' yelled Chips.

The door unclicked. Bonbon shoved it and let go of the handle. The other two rushed through the gap in the door towards a white heap of littler tangled up in a dirty rug with red stains around her mouth. Her eyes were open but they looked at nothing.

'Blankey!' Chips ran to her feet, then to her head, then to her feet again, holding his cheeks in his hands. Jinx knelt in front of her head and shook her shoulder. The eyes rolled upwards to look into Jinx's. 'Get up, Blankey, what's wrong with you?'

Bonbon watched Blankey's red mouth from the top of the stool.

Champ and Sweetheart looked up at her from their trolley in the tile-smelling place. 'She's very poorly,' said Bonbon. 'We'll need to carry her back.'

'Carry her?' Jinx's eyebrows spread up into her forehead. How on Earth would they get her down the stairs? And then all the way across the garden.

'No,' Blankey husked and the other three stared at her. 'War…' she said. 'War… ta.'

'Water?'

'She's thirsty,' said Chips. 'We'd better…' His voice disappeared inside his throat.

'We'd better what?' mouthed Jinx as they stopped and listened to the footsteps coming from the stairs. Dum. Dum. Dum…

'Get under the bed,' mouthed Chips, grabbing Blankey's feet.

Jinx looked from Blankey to the bed and took hold of her shoulders. Together they pulled her until she was just under the bed. Bonbon hung by her hands from the edge of the stool, her feet dangling towards the dirty carpet. She let herself drop, then disappeared behind the wall. 'Bonbon!' Jinx mouthed, peeping from under the bedspread.

Fingertips, like dirty half-moons, curled around the edge of the door. An eye, glinting through grey tangles, appeared at the same height as the hand. Jinx yanked the bedspread back down in front of her and closed her eyes. Had he seen her? No… No, he couldn't have seen her. Heavy feet drummed across the floor and stopped just before the bed. She looked at Chips. He watched the shadows of the drumming feet with eyes that twitched and squeezed out blinks. He glanced around at her.

'Bonbon?' she mouthed.

He shook his head and shrugged.

Jinx turned back to Blankey who twisted a strand of Jinx's hair around her fingers and sucked on her own cheeks. Chips shifted position and Jinx looked up as smelly, hot breath surrounded her. 'I think I just found your coat,' said the breath as two pink-liney eyes peeped out at her under grey AstroTurf eyebrows.

Far from the high-backed-chair circle that she had imagined, the meeting took place in the basement of an old house to the west of the city. Rubber skid marks criss-crossed the laminate flooring that spread from one end of the room to the other; a mirror covered the entire wall, a long bar horizoned through its centre. Beanbags made a mountain in one corner and people seemed to be taking them to sit on. Susan fished out a boring khaki one for her and a velour one for her companion. 'Hmm,' she said, frowning between the elderly lady and the beanbag; she was around one hundred and thirty years old, after all.

'It's alright, Susan. I'll manage.'

'Would you like my spare chair?' A voice wafted over Susan's shoulder towards Mrs Lucas. They turned to a smiley lady with a conical mole on her chin that pointed towards her cleavage. She wore a grey paisley-print dress and carried a folding chair under each arm. A long necklace with thick wooden beads lay almost horizontally on her chest and dangled over her belly button like the legs of a sleeping child, its arms clasped about its mother's neck. 'I usually bring a spare just in case mine breaks.'

'Well… That's very kind.'

The paisley lady unfolded her chair and clicked the seat into place with a smack. Beyond her, more elderly people were also unfolding chairs. Susan noticed the shoe-customer blowing up a neck support in the far corner. She waited for a moment for him to turn and recognize her but his eyes were fixed on the swelling cushion. The beanbaggers arranged themselves on the floor in front of the chairs. Susan dropped her beanbag in front of Mrs Lucas and plopped down onto it.

'Wish I could still do that,' Mrs Lucas chuckled, her knuckles rippling as they curled over the head of her walking stick.

'Bet you still can.' Susan winked.

'No… I just like to be comfortable these days.'

'If you could all take your seats, we'll get started,' a voice called over the rumblings of the gathering and the room fell silent. The voice had sounded small and Susan looked behind her to see how many people were absorbing it. Wow! At least fifty, maybe even sixty people. As she looked, her eyes were drawn to another pair of eyes looking back at her. The person, a woman, looked away, reaching behind her to pull her fox tail of hair through a loop she'd made with her finger and thumb. A nervous gesture, Susan thought; the woman had felt awkward about staring.

'Shall we get going then?' said the voice. The audience lowed yeses. 'For those of you who don't know me, my name is Meredith and I am elected president of the LOG. Erm… I think that quite a few of you *don't* know me.' She cupped a hand over her eyes and peered towards the back of the room to emphasize her point. 'Membership seems to have doubled in about a week!' The hand came down and rested on her hip. 'And from what's been going on recently, this is with good reason.' Murmurs rippled across the room. Susan flicked her gaze over one shoulder, then the other. The woman was still looking at her. Again, she looked down as soon as Susan had seen her, then glanced up and smiled. Susan smiled back.

'I think some of you might have some questions regarding recent events, but before we try to answer them, let me just go over the main problems that you, as owners, may be experiencing of late. It seems that the latest batch, Batch Twenty, has demonstrated a capacity for communication. Now, I think you'll all agree that this is rather lovely.' Susan felt the noses around her snort out little smiles. She was smiling too; yes, it was lovely. 'We are obviously very keen to understand just how intelligent these little beings are. Unfortunately, Billbridge & Minxus, as you know, would prefer to keep all of that under wraps. It's been suggested that the centre, where all littlers start their existence, may not be the most desirable of places or, indeed, may have very specific methods for bringing littlers into the world.' Meredith curled her fingers into inverted commas as she said 'specific methods'. 'What is obvious is that the company does not wish, or even allow, for communication to take place. This leads me to a warning, which I will repeat at the end of this session: do *not* under any circumstances let your littler be seen to communicate in public. You should tell your littler this and, of course, explain to them why.' Meredith glanced at a little table to the left of her and Susan realized she was reading prompts from its glass-top screen.

She went on: 'Now; what happens if they are seen communicating in public? From what I've heard, over the last week, a total of thirty littlers have been "recalled" by Billbridge & Minxus. That's to say, that they have been taken away by so-called technicians and their return assured once the problem has been resolved. I have just had news from the very first owners to have encountered such a worrying scenario, two families who had their littlers taken away last Monday… Yes, there's Mrs Osbourne at the back there: thank you for coming.' Mrs Osbourne nodded, her eyes sparkly and mouth quivery. 'Both families have received official word from the company stating that the *product* will *not* be returned to them as the damage is too extensive and therefore considered by them to be irremediable.' She paused to give her audience a moment to gasp. 'I have a copy of the email here – thank you, Mrs Osbourne, for sending this to me today. Let me read their exact words: "Your littler will live out their days peacefully and luxuriously in our retirement centre at the Billbridge & Minxus headquarters. We appreciate the distress that this may cause but, as experts, we ask you to trust us with regard to the severity of this issue." Now, Mrs Osbourne, are you able to tell us what happened to you?'

'Yes.' The lady coughed into the back of her hand. 'Yes. I was buying an exercise ball at LittleKit, and Nanou, my…' She swallowed, her chin dipping as she did so. 'My littler, clapped because she wanted a red one.' Susan craned to see Mrs Osbourne; this was almost exactly what had happened with Bonbon that first time. 'I pointed this out to the assistant, the clapping I mean, and, well, she called a team of people who came and took Nanou away.'

'Tell us what was said, exactly.'

'Well, the assistant was baffled when I first told her that Nanou could clap once for "yes" and twice for "no". She said that was impossible.' Mrs Osbourne paused to fold her lips inwards and flap her hand next to her eyes. Meredith tilted her head to one side and nodded. The woman pinched the bridge of her nose for a moment, then shook her head. 'I'm sorry,' she said. 'I don't think I can…' She looked about her ankles, then ducked down and came back up jamming a sheet of Fibre-Web into the corner of one eye. 'I… I sh-should have just left.' Sniff. 'Nobody was legally *holding* me there.'

'Yes,' Susan felt herself say. She looked around but nobody noticed; other people were nodding and saying 'yes' out loud or 'no' out loud: yes, she could have just left; no, she didn't have to stay.

'You weren't to know what was going to happen.' Meredith shook her head. 'And since these first incidents, the way of dealing with these cases of "communication" has become somewhat slicker, as I'm sure many of you will agree.' A few mmms rumbled around the room. 'I will go into that in just a minute. There is, however, one thing I would like to point out that has to do with the end of Mrs Osbourne's email. That is: "We understand that this will come as a considerable loss to you and wish to offer you a replacement product or a full refund of the purchase price. We are prepared to immediately reimburse all accessory expenses and medical bills subject to receipt of adequate evidence of payment." Obviously, the more statements of this kind we can gather, the more clout we'll have when it comes to our legal battle. It probably goes without saying, but do not accept any "exchange" or "refund" that the company might offer you. Your acceptance will be interpreted as a settlement.' She dipped her chin and let her irises bob to the top of her eyes; 'you have been warned', they said. 'It seems that now the company is aware of this situation, reaction times between reporting an incident and a team arriving to deal with it have shortened considerably. And these incidents are no longer limited to retail outlets such as Batch Mode and Mini-Me's; it seems that the medical centres are also reporting incidents of communication through clapping, finger clicking and blinking.'

'When can we go after them?' someone called from the back of the room.

'Well,' began Meredith, 'timing is critical. As you can imagine, the company has everything legally bulletproof. What we need is people. It's quite easy to silence an individual or even offer them a settlement that they can't refuse, or *even* threaten them. We need to stick together if we are going to take this further. If you come across anyone having similar difficulties, you must bleep them the details of these twice-weekly meetings.'

'If they have everything covered, how are we ever going to beat them?'

'In all honesty, we're not quite sure. At the moment we have retired lawyers combing through the old Billbridge & Minxus advertisements to see if they are in breach of anything. This is quite unlikely, so we either need to wait for the company to slip up, or we cause a big enough row that its top-secret "retirement centre" will be investigated.'

'But it must get inspected all the time.'

'Perhaps. But the worry is that *all* Batch Twenty littlers have the capacity to communicate and as soon as Billbridge & Minxus realizes this, it will recall *all* of them immediately.' A gasp fizzed over the room. 'So we need to do something fast, even if it is only to scare the company.'

'Have there been any reports of littlers being stolen?'

Susan looked behind her to where the voice had come from. Mrs Lucas sat with one hand in the air, the other still on her walking stick.

'Stolen?'

'My Blankey's gone missing. I know it's unlikely but I just thought I'd ask as I'm here.'

'When did she disappear?'

'The day before yesterday… It's most unlike her.'

'We mustn't rule it out entirely. Come and see me at the end so that I can record your case. You never know, more people like you may come forward and this is exactly the kind of slip-up we're looking for. It would be totally illegal… *Totally.*'

Mrs Lucas put her hand back down to its walking stick, her clear eyes twitchy and her mouth all sad. Susan reached up and gave her knee a little pat. The old lady, surprised at the contact, smiled. Susan smiled back, noticing over Mrs Lucas's shoulder the red-haired woman staring at the old lady.

'How do we know that they're not here, spying on us?' someone from the back yelled rather slowly.

Meredith shrugged her shoulders. 'We don't. We can't know that for sure. All I can tell you is that these meetings aren't breaking any laws.'

'But what we're saying is slanderous.'

'It's *speculative.*'

'About the retirement homes and the factory…'

'It's speculative! If they keep their address a secret then how could anyone really *know* what it's like there?' Even though her question was rhetorical, Meredith seemed to spend a moment waiting for an answer, then: 'Mr Willis, would you mind telling us about your experience with Nemo?'

An elderly gentleman with dyed black hair climbed through the camping chairs saying 'excuse me, excuse me,' to every person he passed. When he got to the front, he did up the button on his jacket and nodded at the room. Then he undid the button and stood with his arms behind his back.

'I can say what I like here as Nemo has gone now… Sadly. We were careful not to be seen by the technicians, but our relationship was special. I had a code word that I would use, very silly really as it wasn't overly coded. I would say "silence" whenever we were out in public to remind Nemo not to code anything to me. We were so used to talking to each other; I saw Nemo as an equal. We had his communication techniques so refined that we could have great long conversations about everything.' Mr Willis's gaze oozed over the space in front of his eyes. He jolted himself back to his speech with a sharp breath. 'Sorry, I just… miss him.'

Meredith lowered her eyebrows and nodded.

'Anyway. I would ask him things and he would answer in Morse code. We went on like that for months – it was quite a good little system! Before he got taken away, Nemo told me many things about what it was like to be him. He told me that the time he had spent with me had been like waking up slowly. When he first arrived, he knew nothing of where he'd come from and why he was living with me. In fact, for a long time, he believed that he had always been living in my understairs cupboard. But gradually, his mind started to, well, open up, if you like. He would look at new objects and his brain would give him the word for that object. He would feel new fabrics and know what they were, he would smell new smells and know what they were. One day, I came home from the stables with that synthetic sawdust on my trousers; you know the kind. I brushed it off in the hallway and went about my business and two hours later I found that he had collected up all of the sawdust, put it in his basket and appeared to be smelling it, piece by piece, and stroking it to his cheek. "It smells different," he said to me. "It smells different but this is exactly what we had."

'"What who had?" I asked.

'"Me and the others, at the place I lived before I lived here."

He looked at me with an expression so human that I understood immediately something important had clicked. "I remember it."

'"But… Of course you remember it; you lived there for the first two years of your life!" I said.

'"Two years?" He was shocked. "Was it really two years?"

'"Yes," I said. "That's what I was told."

'"But I'd never even realized I'd lived anywhere but here."

'It was then that I began to suspect that all littlers were given some sort of memory suppressant before leaving the centre. I asked him to tell me exactly what he could remember. He told me about a small glass tank, roughly the size of his basket and tall enough to jump around in. He told me that he remembered feeling hot and looking around him to find that he was lying in a pile of littlers, all of them naked and sleeping. His hair was long and he even had a beard. When he looked through the glass, he couldn't see anything except white walls and a ceiling. There was a door on the left with a round window, and a door straight ahead with nothing. Sometimes, shadows would darken the window and when this happened, he and the others would watch the shadows and even talk to them. He remembered thinking that the shadows were nice, but they never said anything back.

'He told me that another vision kept popping up in his mind: another littler with a huge distorted face was being taken away and Nemo was holding his arms out to her but the lid of the tank was shut. He watched as she screamed, reaching back towards the tank then fell silent, her head looking everywhere around the tank except at them. He banged on the glass, but she didn't notice. The handler did something to her and she flopped, unconscious, in his hand. Then the handler laid her on a trolley and wheeled her through the door on the left with the round window, his shadow filling up the window for a moment before going away. Nemo watched the door for a long time as he realized the truth about the shadows. He and the others never spoke to them again, instead they huddled together every time they saw one. He remembered being taken away himself, screaming and reaching back towards the tank expecting at any second to be injected and taken through the door on the left; but he wasn't. He was carried through the door right in front of his tank and as soon as he was through it, his hair was cut and the hair on his face was taken off with some zappy thing that hurt so that he shouted. The handler injected him in the neck; after that, he couldn't shout any more. He couldn't say anything. Then all he remembered was waking up in a room that wasn't home and seeing me peer into his tank. Now this is the strangest part.'

The man pointed two fingers up towards the ceiling and looked from left to right. 'He told me that he recognized me straight away and was so pleased to be going home. I asked him where he recognized me from, but unfortunately his development hadn't reached that part of his recollection. However, during our time together, we worked on theories and ideas about the elusiveness of his memory and he believed that there had been a stage before the glass tank. A stage where all he could remember was knowing; he had known a phenomenal amount of things about… well… life. He would continually repeat this, backing it up by saying: "Now all I have is someone else's knowledge, there is someone in my head telling me everything that I used to know." He would repeat this so often that, although I listened, it lost its meaning. Until one particular day.

'I had bought a present. A real gardening book for my great-niece. Later, I found Nemo standing in my herbaceous border holding a leaf to his nose. "This is mint," he coded to me, and he seemed extremely pleased about this.

'"Yes," I said, not thinking much of it.

'"But the littler inside my head didn't tell me," he said. "I read about it in the book."

'I was so shocked at what he'd just said that we went back

to the opened book and I made him read the page to me. He did. Word for word he interpreted the paragraphs with his dots and dashes. I was astounded. He asked me where all the books were – why weren't there any other books in the house? Like most people, I sold all of mine during the Paper Boom, so from then on I allowed him to read on the internet. That, unfortunately, was our downfall. As he read, he wrote. As he wrote, he discovered. As he discovered, he grew angry, believing he was human and entitled to the same freedom of communication as other humans.

'Last week, two representatives from that awful company came to my house. They told me they were following up evidence of slanderous behaviour that had been localized to my address. I tried to tell them that it was me but they wouldn't believe it. They turned on their silly apparatus, which located him in the understairs cupboard. They were shocked as they opened the door to see him standing straight and strong, frowning up at them with so much… So much hatred. Again, I tried to reason with them but he had already communicated so much in that one look. "It's no good," he coded to me. "I have described all of my memories online and they are frightened because they know all that I've said is true." As soon as they saw him coding they packed him away in a carry-case and told me that they had to take him back to the centre urgently. I was about to open my mouth, to tell them that this was inhumane and they couldn't gag individuals like this, when I heard the dots and the dashes escape from the carry-case – silence, they said. Ironic really; our warning message being used in that situation. "Will I see him again?" I asked.

'"We'll try our best, Sir," was the answer. And he was gone.

'I searched everywhere online for his blog, but I can only guess it's been erased by the company.' Mr Willis searched the floor then turned his head up to face the audience. He stood fiddling with his own fingertips, his eyes blinking out wettish shines.

Meredith got up and walked over to him. She put a hand on his shoulder. Mr Willis looked at the hand. 'I'm sorry, it's just that… He was my best friend,' he said to her.

She nodded and tipped her head to one side. 'Will you be taking questions at the end?'

'Yes, of course.'

'Thank you, Mr Willis.' She looked back at the group. 'I have recorded other stories of this nature but generally people are too scared to come forward and tell them as Mr Willis has done this evening. I think we owe him a round of applause.'

Clapping and yeses filled the room.

The rip of Tupperware lids released cake-smell into the room. Tupperware, her Nanna had a stack of it. Susan looked around, wanting to put her hands on her hips but changing her mind and pulling down the front of her jacket instead. She was the youngest there, probably. Except for that woman with the hair. She looked for the face that had caught her eye; there it was: a fox tail by the tea urns, just in front of Mrs Lucas. The tail rose into the air as the head it was attached to dipped to watch her hands as they dispensed tea. Susan watched. The woman looked like she was listening to the conversation between Mrs Lucas and Meredith. Meredith nodded as she noted everything onto paper. Onto paper! Ha! Susan thought of all the stories Meredith must have recorded and how much paper that would have taken. Where on Earth had it come from? She stepped forward to watch the pen as it skied a winding path down the paper.

'You must think we're all so old!' laughed the grey-paisley lady.

'Sorry? No… No, not at all.'

A few heads turned to smile.

'We are,' said a gentleman, pushing his glasses up his nose, a red-velvet biscuit between thumb and forefinger.

'Oh… I…' Susan struggled. 'Yes, actually. If I'm honest, I was thinking that I am probably the youngest.'

Another lady nodded seriously, grey ringlets swinging next to her ears. 'You are. The irony is, at one point they – that awful company – were aiming their marketing at elderly people, to give us a bit of companionship. At this rate we'll end up alone again!' she half-laughed. 'That's probably why they think they can win this.'

Susan smiled at the word 'they'. It had long been considered politically incorrect to use it as a term of generalization. She'd always found that ridiculous.

'No,' the others agreed.

'They do what they like. They make out that the surplus older population need company and looking after, but it's all lies. It's a business, that's all.'

'Mmm,' the others agreed.

Susan looked into her cup and thought about her own great-grandmother who had been left in a home until she died. They went to visit her once a month when she was a child. Nanna was always in the same chair, with the window behind her, and would tell them the same things each time. Her mother used to say that she was 'losing her marbles' and how sad that was. Susan remembered thinking that poor Nanna had nothing else to say; she'd heard nothing new, nobody really spoke to her. 'Can we at least turn the chair around so she can look out the window?' she remembered asking, one day.

Susan looked over towards Mrs Lucas. 'Will you all be here for the next meeting?' she asked.

They nodded. 'And you?' two of them asked at the same time. Then apologized to each other for interrupting.

'I should think so, yes.'

'Have you had yours taken away then?' asked the man with the glasses.

'Not yet. Oo yum, thank you.' Susan smiled as the ringlet lady offered her some shortbread. 'But it could happen at any time. We just have to do what Meredith said and try to stick together.'

The circle of people nodded and mmmed.

'No, no, dear. I'm quite sure.' Mrs Lucas's voice came wafting over Susan's shoulder. 'It wouldn't be one of mine, would it? It's blonde!' she laughed. 'I know that so much can be done with DNA these days. Do you really think you can help?'

'Well,' said Meredith, tweezing something into a small tube. 'We are trying to collect as much DNA as possible, for various reasons. Apart from anything, it all counts as evidence of existence. But in your case, it might actually help us to find Blankey.'

'Right.'

Meredith smiled at Mrs Lucas before turning to the room. 'Okay, everyone!' She put the blue tube down next to a tea urn. 'Thursday, same time, same place… And don't forget,' she held one finger in the air, 'no communicating in public.'

It was no good. She had to breathe. She made the tiniest hole in her lips and let the air tiptoe out then in again. Bonbon was pressed up into a corner between the door frame and the wall. She was sure that bits of her were sticking out; but he hadn't seen her. Maybe she had been hidden by the stool. Maybe he had noticed the open door and not noticed anything else. Shit. What now? Ahead of her was the room. Chips had been pushing that three-legged thing from that direction. 'The stool,' said the old littler who stood inside her head. Right. Stool. Thanks, Old Littler. How about something useful like what on Earth was she supposed to do? The doorway to the next room loomed before her again. She turned back to the door where Blankey was and peeked through the gap that its hinges made. A big bottom hovered above the underside of brown clumpy shoes. He was looking under the bed. She breathed down into her belly and ran into the next room, stopping when she was well inside and looking wildly around it. White walls stretched up from orange flowers that were trapped in weird carpet. Her heels fizzed and tingled on it as she skidded and stopped. Bugger. It was empty. Completely empty! Nowhere to hide. She scuttled behind the door and looked through the crack into the hallway.

'Oh, Tilda!' she heard as Chips's he-one came out of the room and disappeared into another at the other end of the hallway. Rushing water could be heard, and continued to rush as the biggerer reappeared with a cup in his hand and padded back into the bedroom. 'Tilda, Tilda, Tilda…' he whispered with each step, looking at the cup to make sure he didn't spill what was inside. He was bringing water to Blankey. That was good; maybe he wasn't so nasty… But what was Tilda? Bonbon watched. Nothing happened. She sat down on the floor and let her legs curl behind her; maybe he would go soon and they could all leave…

Soon her legs were so stiff and achy that all she could think about was moving them. But the silence hung around her as if it were waiting for her to do something noisy; he would hear her, even if she moved just the tiniest little bit. She stayed in that position, eyes glued to the crack in the door. Eventually, her legs seemed to move on their own, fed up with being folded and twisted. Just as the lovely feeling of unscrunching them brushed up her back to her head, she heard a creak. Light from the room illuminated the landing as the door was opened wide enough for him to step outside. 'You two must go back downstairs,' he said. 'Leave Tilda to get better. Poor Tilda… She needs lots of rest.' He stepped out of the room. 'Back downstairs with you.' But he shut the door behind him before anyone could go back downstairs. 'I have to get Tilda some medicine… What's that doing there?' He pushed the stool with his foot so that it fell away from the door; Bonbon watched as it rolled in a circle. 'Where was I?' He turned to go back into the room then turned away again. 'Medicine for Tilda. That's right.' And he thumped down the stairs. Bonbon listened as noises came from below: plates got moved and doors swung open. Feet thudded across the carpet, a bottom sat down on the stairs. A glass of something got gulped down and something else got zipped up. Then, the front door rattled as it was pulled open, slammed shut again and there was silence.

Bonbon turned and ran towards the staircase. Yanking her humcoat from the floor, she pulled it on and swung herself down onto the first step.

CHAPTER 11

She'd wondered if she'd ever see her there, or if she'd already seen her without realizing. But Mrs Lucas had made herself known, she thought, taking the little plastic tube out of her handbag. She'd asked about Blankey in her elderly voice, hoarse with what Emma fancied to be one hundred and thirty years' worth of dust and cobwebs. And the woman she was with could well have been Susan Marley, although maybe she had simply been a great-great-granddaughter; or a carer… Emma had tried not to be so obvious about staring, but apart from anything else, another young person in the room warranted a stare. She shook the tube to see if there really was a hair inside; holding it up to the light; ah yes, there it was. A smile stretched her mouth then disappeared, like a jumping jack. Torn between leaving the hair there and picking it up, Emma had decided that the safest place for it was with her. Not that she'd ever need it. She had all of Blankey's medical files… But she'd panicked and picked it up anyway. It was better off with her. Everything else stayed with her, after all, lurking behind her and tickling her between her shoulder blades. Waking her up in the night. She put the tube back in the bag and let her eyes scrunch shut.

An image of little baby Blankey sharpened into vivid memory; sitting in the corner of her tank, her legs curled around beside her, bluish eyes staring into nothing as her tiny fingers overlapped each toe over the one next to it. She looked lonely, as if she were mourning or pining or… some other fanciful projection of how Emma supposed she *ought* to feel. Emma had chosen her name from the list in the notebook; a floaty, dreamy, childish name; white with soft consonants, billowy likes the curls that covered the littler's ears. Blankey. A pretty way to describe the void that *surely* gaped open inside her tiny tummy, Emma said to herself at the time; like a mother having her newborn taken away, without even knowing she had been pregnant.

Emma touched an icon that hung in the air in front of her, entered a password and opened Blankey's file. The thumbnail of the old photo sat in line with the other documents, two little blue dots beaming out of it – she'd been stunning. The news article striped along the side of the photo like a barcode, under the headline: 'British woman dead in car crash.' She touched the image again and it turned into a 3D head, as big as her own. The two women looked at each other. 'Driver husband loses leg,' read the last sentence.

Emma hid her eyes behind her hands; what on Earth had she been thinking to send her there? She peeped through her fingers at her living room. It wouldn't take them long to question *why* Blankey had been sent to the neighbour's house; then to start digging around the rest of Emma's files. Mrs Lucas had been on the list for well over a year. The fact that she was wealthy, and that her husband wasn't doing too well health-wise, meant that she ticked all the right boxes; a budding A* client; a big, fat Euro sign. Of course, Emma saw her as a lonely old lady, who, like all the other lonely old ladies, would not be able to resist the virtual version of Blankey, a little being animated by 3D pixels and lasers that Emma sent her, that Emma *targeted* her with.

Anyone who thinks that this product is capable of thinking, talking, acting or even looking like their lost loved one is very much under false illusions, Dr Peetzwelt had said during an interview. *Any quest to be reunited with a loved one would be in vain as all of our samples are rendered anonymous as soon as the donor passes on.* This wasn't the case. Otherwise there'd be none of this crap about communication, but the chances were *so small*...

Then Emma came along.

They could quite easily shut her up. She was pretty much alone in London, apart from the lot at the LOG, Hamish, her parents who kept calling her by her brother's name...

Michael clicked his fingers from somewhere down by her ankle and Emma smirked as she bent to pick him up. Not quite alone... Now *he* would care if anything happened to her. She sat him on the desk and he looked at her, swinging his trousered legs.

'Any ideas?' She slouched forward to peer at him.

Two claps. No.

She imagined her Michael kidnapped or locked away somewhere and how frightened he would be; how frightened *she* would be... That's exactly what would happen if ever she were 'dealt with'. Especially if she were taken by surprise. The *obvious* thing to do would be to sit tight and keep quiet about the whole thing. What if he hadn't even taken her? Ha! But then again... Her head whirred this thought around and brought it back to the starting position: what if he had and something happened to her? What if she *died* because he'd done something silly like tread on her or forget to feed her or... Emma breathed deeply and sat up straight. What a ridiculous thought, nobody *died* just like that. She smiled at Michael. Of course they did. She sighed. A big bird swooped down behind her eyes, plucking Blankey out of danger before soaring with her towards Mrs Lucas.

'Family's important, isn't it?'

One clap, yes. Then Michael lifted a finger and aimed it at Emma. She was *his* family.

She snorted out a smile. She *was* his family; but... Was that something he'd remembered or something he'd learned? 'What would happen to you if I got taken away?' said her mouth.

He stopped playing with his buttons and stared at her, his eyebrows rearing upwards at each other, his chin pulling his mouth open.

'No, don't worry,' she said. 'I was just being silly… We won't lose each other again.'

The mouth smiled. The eyebrows lowered. Michael turned to lie on his belly, pushed himself onto his knees, then his feet. He stuck his arms out and wobbled, mouth open in the shape of a giggle, before tapping one foot clumsily on the desk. Swirls of twinkles blew into the air, spiralling in swooping flocks. He turned to her and clapped.

'Not again?'

He clicked his fingers crazily.

'Okay, okay,' she said. 'Playmate!'

The swirls descended and fused together to make the glowing outlines of three faceless virtual littlers; two green, and one blue. They twirled and jumped to the other end of the desk. Michael ran after them.

'You're a lot of help,' she said, letting her chair spin so she was facing a vintage Plexiglas magic eye wall-hanging. A Labrador and a bone would protrude from its zigzaggy configuration whenever the searcher let their eyes glaze over it. Her one book, the notebook her father had told her to look after, was hiding behind it, wrapped in cellophane to trap its smell, and as she thought of it her nostrils filled with the earthy whiff of inky paper, her eyes imagining the sketches of a tiny girl, the recipes for arctic roll and blackcurrant coulis; the changing of handwriting, the sellotaped bunch of golden dog hair, the list of names: Bonbon, Jinx, Blankey, Fola, Mop, Note and Lamb… The book-smell curled through her limbs, into her fingers and the soles of her feet, a whole cabinet fattened with shiny book spines grew in her mind, as 2D as the bookshelf wall-coverings libraries used to decorate their empty corners. *He* turned from his books, his latex gloved hands clasped in his lap and asked her why she was feeling trapped. Surely she had more options.

She rubbed her head, as this new thought rose from its bank and galoshed through all the other thoughts, pulling a little boat behind it.

He told her that nothing could be done about it now; that she should get into the boat.

She told him that it had been too long.

He told her that the boat would protect her as long as it was night-time, and she could think about all of this in the morning.

She pulled herself out of clonings, bereaved families and complete disappearings, and flopped into the boat.

He told her not to worry, that everything she told him was confidential, and that he would never let anything happen to her.

She sat in the boat and let this sentence push her hair back from her face and rub her cheek with a soft thumb. His littler, Jinx, stood on one leg in her glass tank. She put her arms in the air so that her elbows made right angles to her body, then wiggled her bottom. Emma giggled as Jinx swapped legs and did exactly the same wiggle, both she and Jinx forgetting about that past life, read about and cried over through paragraphs snatched angrily from Isabel's thoughts then scratched onto the pre-printed lines. That had been about a week before her heart had gulped at the mention of Blankey's name. 'You remember Mrs Lucas? Well, the couple next door found Blankey…' She thought she would pass out; found Blankey what? '*Utterly* charming. They want to adopt,' the other continued. She breathed out a smile. 'I'll take a look at the file,' she'd said. A young couple, interesting… 'What do they do for a living?' she'd asked, looking them up before the other had time to answer.

'Librarian. Psychologist.'

'A librarian psychologist?'

The sales rep had wrinkled her forehead for a moment before grinning. 'That's not a thing.'

Emma lifted an eyebrow. 'Go and interview them, will you?'

Ten days later, Hamish Wix and Susan Marley had their interview. 'Make sure you push for two,' Emma reminded, 'I don't want them split up.'

'Why not?'

She thought on her feet. 'It would be interesting to see how two progress together.'

'Two littlers means two sales.'

'I'm more interested in product development than sales...'

'It's gonna be tough to sell two.'

'They're both at work all day, play the loneliness card.'

The sales reps, robots that they are, did exactly that. And came back with a full report. Emma read it, recalling the lines of the notebook as she did. She – Susan – liked to bake. He – Hamish – liked to read. They'd wanted a child, but weren't having much luck. They would have liked to move to the country, one day... 'Did they seem to be in love?' she'd asked.

'Of course!' the sales rep gushed. 'Well... She did.'

Hmm, she'd thought, maybe they would fit the bill. But... She'd wanted to meet them, even one of them, just once, just to reassure herself that she'd made the right decision and not messed it up like before. Stupid Emma. No, no, not at *all* like before. And this would definitely be the last time, the very last time she'd target a family. The most important one yet. So three days later, Emma booked her first appointment to see Dr Hamish Wix, to check up on him, to get a *feel* for him, but found herself frowning at the end of their hour. He was a tough cookie to crack. So she bugged his office and booked a follow-up session.

Then another.

And another.

And a few more, after the adoption.

Now, looking back at her desk, she leaned forward in her chair to touch the icon marked 'Ψ' that rotated in the air. She scanned the list of recorded conversations until she got to one of her own that she'd revisited many times. 'Everything that you tell me is confidential… I'm never going to let anything happen to you,' said the recording that she'd played and replayed and re-replayed…

Waking up in her chair, four hours later, that sentence was the first echo of the dream she'd just had, where she lay on her belly in a boat on a lake lapping silver against Hamish's galoshes. *Everything you tell me is confidential*, it began. Sitting up straight, she looked towards where the icons had been floating; Michael and his virtual friends slept in a bundle just next to her handbag. Confidential… Hmmm… Confidential. She looked over her shoulder and husked: 'Coffee.' That's what she would do; she would have a coffee and wait for the morning-time normalness to cage up all of the anxiety bats and lovey-dovey doves that the night had let fly around her brain. Daylight would help her make a sound decision.

She held out her arm and took the coffee from the little glass tongue that zjwoomed out of the machine, closed both hands around it and held it under her nose; wouldn't he be obliged to tell someone? They had rules like that, apparently. Rules that cancelled out the confidentiality clause, like if a patient confessed to murder or something… But she hadn't *murdered* anyone. And anyway, he said that he would never let anything happen to her; surely that meant, well… Did it really, though? Did it *really*? *Just book the appointment and go; who says that you're going to tell him anything?* Emma let go of one side of her coffee and tapped her wrist. 'Number for Hamish Wix,' she said.

* * *

Goggles. No goggles. How on Earth did this concern him? If he were a student, involved in a top government project, and he didn't feel he could do his work because he'd been without goggles for three days, would he really bring it up to the project manager? Dear oh dear, this was a government-funded project – no! A UN-funded project, yet the staff that had been offered to him were *all* students working for a pittance. He didn't care if it looked good on their CVs! He could not give two hoots about their silly CVs! What he needed was someone who would take on this project without tittle-tattling about every little uncrossed 't'. 'It's really unfortunate,' the *student* had said, 'that the lab goggles have to be changed, as they haven't been changed since 1995; did that not get picked up during the audit?' He had replied to the student that upgrading the goggles might be a nice little job for *him*. 'Yes, but what are we supposed to work with in the meantime? I, for one, care about my eyes…' he'd said. 'No eyes, no career!' he'd said. Bloody jobsworth, what on *Earth* had he been working with that could have blinded him – eh? Any substance that was capable of blinding him was unlikely to be sharing a fridgeful of embryos. Was he worried about falling on a test tube at the wrong angle? 'Rules are rules,' he'd said. 'And paying attention to them means that we all stay safe.'

A tubby gentleman joined him as he waited for the lift. A tray of hot drinks wobbled between his hands. They nodded at each other.

But the best bit had been: 'What if I wipe my eyes absent-mindedly? I could contaminate my eye *and* the sample. Ha! If you can't be responsible for your own hand, you're probably in the wrong game. Of course, not all of them were so vocal. Some of them were all wide-eyed and frightened. But then, *obviously*, those ones were *totally* incompetent. They just could *not* work independently. For how long had he put up with this? Three months? Three whole months of spoon-feeding; and every single day of those three months he'd told himself that he was sure, he was *sure* that if he got rid of the lot of them he would have enough money to employ a real scientist. Someone with experience, knowledge and *subtlety*. Someone who could keep their gob shut in the interests of scientific progression. He had known so many people like that before. Aaaahhh, before… Right. Good. The lift. Honestly, if people would just send it back up again then he wouldn't have to wait an eternity for it. He got into the lift with the tubby man and eyed his beaming moon of a head. The man stared out of the side of his eyes while his coffee cups juddered in their cardboard hollows. Everything had become so silly and strict. Pfff… This really was becoming an enormous problem. He would suggest it, he would simply *suggest* it; how could they say no? Maybe he would offer a couple of internships just to butter the spinach a little. Just to show that he *did* give at least *one* hoot about their CVs. After all, there was always room for someone to 'witness' that all *was* indeed cricket. And to make the tea. He needed someone. *Definitely* needed someone. Oh dear. Was he being spoken to? 'Sorry?'

'Are you… You are, aren't you?'

'Yes. Well, I know I *am*.'

'I knew it!'

'Right… Good.'

'I had a feeling you were. In fact, I *knew* you were.'

'Why would you doubt that I *was*? Do I keep flickering in and out of visibility?'

Reg blinked, looked at his coffees then back up to the man. He opened his mouth but the man started to speak again.

'Sorry. I'm a bit grumpy today, I'm afraid.' He smiled. 'Who do you think I am?'

'Dr Mark Hector.' Reg glanced at his tray of two lattes and one cappuccino to make sure that the lift hadn't sloshed any rivulets into his caramel criss-cross nappage or broken the beams on his cinnamon sunshine. It hadn't. Good. It never usually did, but it was always best to make sure.

'In that case, yes, that's definitely me.'

Reg looked up, definitely who? Oh yes! 'Right.'

'Do you know my work?'

'Erm… No…' The lift juddered as it stopped at the ninth floor. Reg checked his coffees again. 'I mean… You've been on the telly but that's not how I know who you are.'

'Oh?'

'Actually, you used to work with one of my friends.'

'Oh, right.'

'Well, when I say work *with*…'

'A scientist?'

'Yes.'

'Interesting. Who is that?'

'Erm… Drew Mahlik.'

The doctor looked up to the right and made a clicking noise with his tongue.

'Do you remember?'

'Just about. Was it a while back?'

'About fifteen years, I think.'

The doors opened again at the fifth floor. 'Hold the door!' someone called from the corridor. Reg went to put his elbow out but that was just impossible. The tray would have tipped up completely. He looked at his other elbow then up at Dr Hector who was still looking to the right and making clicking noises.

'Mahlik. Drew Mahlik.'

The doors closed just as a hand appeared in front of them.

Reg cleared his throat. 'That's right. Drew Mahlik. Tallish. Very blonde. Slim.'

'Going up!' said the elevator lady-voice.

'You know, I've seen so many faces over the years.'

'Of course.'

'—.'

'Weren't we going down just a minute ago?'

'Hmmm?' The doctor put one finger in the air. 'Was it the ex-dancer?'

'Sorry?'

'Drew Mahlik. Trained in classical dance, if I remember rightly.'

'Yes, that's it!'

The doors opened and closed at the sixth floor but nobody entered the lift. 'Going down.'

'Took me a while… Funny the details you remember… But it's all as clear as day now. Drew actually had quite a lot of responsibility.'

'Oh yes, I know.'

'So how do you… Do you work in the building?'

'No, I…'

'I have a feeling I've seen you before.'

'Well, yes, you probably have. I'm the owner of the librette just around the corner.'

'The what?'

'Librette. A library and a launderette.'

'Oh. Innovative.'

'Yes. Flick 'n' Spin. You must have seen it? We do coffee as well.' Reg nodded towards his tray. 'And cakes.'

Dr Hector flipped back the cover of his tablet and was sliding through screens with his thumb, stopping once to lick it then realizing that that wouldn't work and so wiped his thumb on his lapel before continuing.

'I'm quite often here,' Reg went on. 'Your lot have their white coats service-washed. That's how I met Drew. Back in the day when we were just a launderette…'

'I've just pulled up the file; there we go! Ah yes… I know that face. We were working on something similar to what I'm doing now, actually. Probably my first project, now I come to think about it.'

'Oh, really?' The doors opened at the fourth floor. 'This is me, I'm afraid.'

'Me too,' the doctor grinned with his mouth but not with his eyes. 'I'll walk with you.'

'Erm… Okay then.'

'They're not supposed to leave the premises, you know.'

'Sorry?'

'The white overalls. We have a team that wash them *properly* here.'

Reg glided along the corridor. Now he controlled the floor, the floor did *not* control him. Wash them properly. Ha! The word made him suck his teeth. 'Even the students' ones?'

'Ah, no… Now you come to mention it, I don't think we wash student coats; no.'

'Because Drew was a student at the time. That's good to know, though, because if a non-student comes in with their coat I'd probably be wise to refuse them.'

'You would indeed.' The doctor put one finger in the air. 'Erm…'

'Because who knows what they've been working with during the day.' The doctor stopped at his office and held the door open for him. Reg smiled a 'thank you' then wondered why he'd followed him in.

'Nothing too dangerous.' The doctor thought of that prat and his bloody goggles. 'We're not that kind of lab.' He brought the other hand up and steepled his fingers together. 'So…'

'Erm.' Reg looked from the desk to the window then to the door. The old fellow obviously wanted to chat. Maybe he was feeling the pressure of being on the telly. He put his coffees down on the desk. Reg had once heard a story about a celebrity who poured his heart out to a complete stranger. The coffees would stay hot for another two minutes or so. 'Unlikely they'll come to me, though, if they can get it done for free in their own building.'

'You'd think so… Where was I?' The summit of the steeple rested for a moment on the doctor's nose. 'Oh yes! Would you…'

'Reg, by the way.'

'A pleasure.' He took a deep breath and tried again. 'Do you…'

'The brother of Watty. Drew's other half.'

'Oh, I see.' They knew each other *well.* They were family. 'You met Drew through, er, Watty, is it?'

'Yes! Um, no, as it happens. As I said, I met Drew at the librette. As did Watty. Watty and I are business partners.'

They nodded at each other.

The doctor tried again. 'Do you happen to know if Drew's still out of work?'

'Drew went back to dancing.'

'Really?' The doctor squashed his mouth up towards one cheek like a sugar hole at the side of a cappuccino. 'Such a shame. An excellent scientific background. Do you have a phone number for...'

'They started a family, you see.'

'Did they? Good for them! I'm looking to recruit someone with Drew's kind of knowledge. An ex-employee would *sort of* go against company policy but, given the situation, someone who could be integrated straight away with little or no training is exactly what I need right now. You don't happen to know if Drew worked for any other labs?'

'I do, yes. And no. He hasn't done anything but dance.' Wow! Drew would be so excited! To think that it *wasn't company policy* but yet this, this TV doctor would make an exception for little old Drew. 'They had Isabel more or less straight away and decided that something had to give...' God, he was listening! He was drinking in *every* word! Drew would be so *honoured*! 'And then there's Jasper; the dog. Mustn't forget good old Jas.'

'That *is* dedication. The project that we were working on was called Isabel, you know? To name your own daughter after your work, my gosh! I really must get back in touch...'

Well, if there was one thing that Drew *was*! '*Definitely* dedicated. Their own daughter is a scientific breakthrough...' Reg put his hands in his pockets and beamed. Then made a face as if he'd just eaten something bad. Shit. *Shit!* Mustn't talk about Isabel. Had he really just said her name? Shit. Yes, he had. *Twice!* Bollocks! And, and scientific *breakthrough*? Oh Jesus, Reg, where the hell is your head at?

'Oh really? You mean a miracle? Did they have to have IVF?'

'Erm… Well…'

'That's not really a breakthrough, though. Were they testing a new procedure? Seems interesting…'

'I was just referring to the success of the project and how, by *association*, that would also make Isabel a success.'

'The project was unsuccessful.'

'—.'

'Are you sure?'

'Quite sure.'

'Well…' Bugger, bugger, bugger. 'I'm not too sure, actually… Maybe Watty named her after our grandmother, Izzy. *She* was a scientific anomaly. Smoked seventy a day and lived until she was ninety-six.'

'Right…'

'And so by *association*…'

The doctor coughed and looked at his feet.

'To be honest with you, I didn't know her for the first eight years of her life. I didn't want to delve around the details of their fertility problems… I just know they were trying for a while.'

'Eight years? Did they go away?'

Good God. 'No, no…'

'They were in London the whole time?'

'Well… They were, yes.' He really wasn't going to let this one go.

'Yet you didn't meet your own niece for eight years?'

Okay. This was verging on *pushy*. 'Gosh, you really want to know, don't you?'

The doctor breathed in sharply and thought for a moment. 'No.

I'm sorry, it's just that… well… something similar happened to me and…'

Oh no, this was it. The heart-pour. And Reg had batted it back in his *face*. 'Oh dear, I *am* sorry.' Misery needs company. 'What I should have said was… Well… Families are funny really, aren't they? Watty and I didn't really see eye to eye for a while.'

'Ah!' He nodded firmly. 'I understand. Yes, no… Quite right. Strange things, families.'

'All water under the bridge now.' Oh no. There would be no heart-pour. Reg had batted it and the doctor had caught it and put it in his pocket. He'd *totally* closed up.

'Of course! Mustn't dwell.'

'Absolutely.' Reg looked at his feet.

'So you'll give me Drew's number then?'

What? 'What? Oh! Yes, I mean… Should I?'

'Well… Not if…'

'Sorry. Stupid question. Of course. I mean, you're not just *anybody*, are you? Ha! Good heavens, no.'

* * *

She stepped into the office. There he was: all thoughtful, erasing some imaginary thing on his desk with his finger. For want of something to do. Because he had seen her. She saw him seeing her for the tiniest fragment of an instant, before she'd even had time to start a smile. He looked away, towards the thing he was rubbing out on the table; no, no; 'twas not yet time to say hello. Finally he looked up as she stood in the door frame of his office.

'Hello, Emma.'

'Hello.' She blushed; re-hearing that voice that had said those words. Those I'm-not-going-to-let-anything-happen-to-you words. She'd not quite known what to do after that. And now, well, now feelings that she'd not even had the tiniest inkling about seemed to pad around her head as if it had long been their home. It was like discovering kittens that had made their den in her garden, not knowing what to do about them but constantly wanting to play with them. And knowing that they were there meant that she looked out for them, thought about them when she was doing other things, left food out for them. And with every day that passed, it was looking more likely that she would keep them. She drew back her shoulders and took a subtle deep breath, watching as he straightened his glasses so that she could see all of his eyes.

They were a year old now, the kittens.

He smiled. He always allowed himself a smile before they started their sessions.

'It's warm in here,' she said, rubbing her arms as if she were cold.

'Oh… Shall I open the… I'll open the…' But he'd already turned and was fiddling with a button next to the window.

Emma opened her hand, releasing a recording strand that meandered upwards, curving and flexing like spider web. She wiped her hand on her knee and closed it.

He turned from the now-opened window. 'There we go.' He sat down without asking her if that was better, or if it was opened enough or if she'd like a glass of water. She smiled at him and noticed that, as usual, he didn't look at her legs as she crossed one over the other. He was exactly the same, although everything had changed now. 'I'll never let anything happen to you,' he'd said, and now she was looking out for all the tiny signs that would reaffirm this. So far there were none. Just like always.

'It's been a while,' said the voice.

'A year.'

'Oh!' He raised his eyebrows.

He hadn't realized that it had been that long. She smiled again, trying not to look disappointed about that. Maybe he'd pretended not to have noticed the time going by.

They observed each other.

How could he not know that it had been a year? Oh dear, she'd probably got it all wrong… Obviously, there was nothing there. It had all been just a badly worded sentence. 'I'm not going to let anything happen to you.' No: 'I'm never going to let anything happen to you.' The 'never' was key in all of this. Had it been 'not', it would have meant there, in that particular slot of his timetable, while she was in his office, while she was paying him, he wasn't going to let anything happen to her. But it was 'never'. He had said 'never'…

'What's brought you here today?' said the voice.

This time she took a deep breath and closed her eyes. She'd let herself do exactly what she'd warned herself against. It wasn't about them, not in that sense. That's not why she had come today; yet she'd allowed herself to run with it. How stupid. How ridiculous. How unprofessional.

'Emma?'

She opened her eyes. He was leaning forward and looking right at her.

'Is there something in particular that you wanted to talk about?'

'Yes,' she managed.

'Good.'

This was the fork in the session. She could go ahead and launch into everything now, or… Or she could string it out for a while. She felt around for some of her previous issues, were they still there? Of course they were… Where had they left off last time? I'm never going to let anything happen to you. No! Not that. What had she been saying last time? Something about… Something like… His face had changed; in fact, he'd taken off his glasses and his eyebrows hung above his eyes like sad mouths. That was new. Then she realized she'd been staring at him and her face was all wrinkled and scowling because it was really looking at the thoughts inside her head; but he had thought that the face had been for him and now… Gosh, he looked upset, she'd upset him. She straightened out her face.

'Why did you leave it so long?' he said, then: 'Before booking another session.'

'You look… sad,' said her mouth without consulting her brain.

He fought to keep his face neutral, but this time lost. Every expression in the world struggled together under his face, like eels in a bag. He put his glasses back on.

'I meant to say—' Emma started.

'I am sad—' he said at the same time.

She blinked. 'Pardon?'

'I said, I am sad.'

There it was, he'd said it! He'd missed her. He'd missed her! They were on exactly the same page. Her chest thudded so much that she felt like panting. She'd been sure of it. She could tell him everything, she could trust him entirely and then… And then… A woman in a purple jacket sat on a beanbag, twisted her head around to look at her. Emma twisted her mouth to the side to stop it from talking then looked at the walls. They seemed to make her feel better, like everything was contained. Like she could be silly and doe-eyed and unprofessional here, but then she would leave and the world would be as it was.

'Let me explain,' said the voice and she flicked her eyes back to him. He took a deep breath. 'Do you know what counter-transference is?'

She shook her head.

'Okay. In psychotherapy, it's the idea that the therapist… That's to say, me' – he pointed to the centre of his chest – 'might be emotionally entangled with the patient. Now, recognizing the fact that…' – he closed his eyes for a second and scratched his jaw – 'that I have feelings for you is… is critical to understanding the dynamics of this space' – he spread his hands out towards 'this space' – 'and, therefore, ultimately everything that is said and unsaid and, well, why what is said is said and what is unsaid is… unsaid.' He smirked at his own long-windedness and pushed his glasses up his nose. She laughed with him. 'This is in order to make progress with your psychological healing, progress that is relatively… unhindered.' He placed his hands on the table in front of him. In a softer voice he added: 'I am sad because I feel like I might have pushed you away.'

He looked at her.

Her eyes grew hot as she tried to think of something to stop her mouth from wobbling again. She would not cry. She would not cry. She felt herself bite her lip and concentrated on his shoulder.

He cleared his throat and looked at his desk. 'I've put myself out on a bit of a limb here.'

She laughed a sobby, snotty explosive laugh; then sniffed.

He pushed a box of Fibre-Web towards her. She took a sheet and dabbed a tear before it slid down her nose. 'Let me explain what transference is. Unlike counter-transference, transference refers to the feelings that the patient projects onto the psychotherapist.'

She looked back at him. He watched her as if he were waiting for an answer, as if he needed rescuing, as if he would gulp at any moment. The thought made her smile. She bit her lip again.

'Look.' He tapped his desk. 'Dictionary,' he said. 'This might help us. Transference… Ah, there we go.' He rotated his thumb and forefinger on the table so that the screen shifted around to meet her point of view, then seesawed his fingers slowly so that words tilted upwards. 'Read the last definition.'

She read. Transference is often manifested as an erotic attraction towards a therapist, but can be seen in many other forms such as rage, hatred, mistrust, parentification, extreme dependence, or even placing the therapist in a godlike or guru status.

'You see? It sounds quite harmless, doesn't it? I quite like that last bit,' he said. Then winced and pulled his face back into neutral. 'So, it's really not just about having a crush or fancying someone, shall we say? Maybe you see me, as like, a brother or even a parent.'

He waited for a moment, blinking at her. 'Any thoughts about all of this, Emma?'

Emma folded her lips between her teeth and thought for a moment. 'Do you remember one of the last things you said to me?'

He sniffed: 'I think I do but it would probably be best to clarify.'

'That you were never going to let anything happen to me?'

'Yes. I remember that.'

'Did you mean it?'

He sat back in his chair. 'It's good that we've addressed all of this today. The sentence that I'd phrased in my head was very different, it was neutral. What I actually let slip corresponded more truthfully to how I felt, let's say.'

She smiled.

'But, I could never mean that, Emma. I could never protect you *forever.* The feelings that pass between us here have to be acknowledged and, and mourned.'

She felt her stomach wind and twist, wringing out liquid that then seeped from her underarms and over the surface of her eyes. 'Why?' she couldn't help.

'Because, here, we are engaging differently with emotion to, perhaps, how you would do in day-to-day life. On this level, we must identify and understand emotion in order to help you. We mustn't always give in to it. That would be like…' He searched the ceiling for an analogy. 'That would be like looking for an endangered species; locating it, allowing it to breed, feeding it, keeping it warm over a long, long period of time; then going out one day and eating it.' Her face laughed, then she thought of all her kittens and went back to looking sad. He continued. 'But that doesn't mean that you would never think about what it would be like to… erm… eat it. There's nothing we can do about that; we are, after all, only human.' He sat up in his chair and strengthened his voice. 'This is a space where these feelings are allowed to be present without the pressure of anything coming of them. We have to trust each other to maintain certain boundaries. You can trust me. The worst thing I could ever, ever do to you is betray that trust. Imagine the biggest moral law you could ever break and times it by a thousand…' He let his hand flutter into the air to indicate a really big number.

Emma looked at her hands. He felt the same way – it had all come true! But… It had all already ended. She had let herself dream so deeply about this; and now reality was drawing itself over lots of happy dreams that would continue to walk about her apartment like ghosts. If this ghost faded, she'd be so lonely without it. Disappointment made her fingers seek each other out for comfort. She clasped one hand with the other and thought about what it had been like to start and finish a love story in less than twenty minutes. Nothing had really been explained… It would take her so much more time to get over this than the whole thing had taken to… well… be.

Her face felt cross, but she couldn't let that surface. Don't think about it, you're running out of time. Images blew up in her mind of all the little ghosts that were currently padding around houses where owners still watched where they were treading and checked water bowls before going to bed. Mrs Lucas would soon have two ghosts to look after… What time was it? She lifted her head to look at the clock, glimpsing his head incline as she moved her own: like a Labrador waiting for a ball. 10:28 flipped to 10:29 as if in slow motion. This wasn't why she had come here. But at least she was now almost sure of one thing: she could trust him.

She sat and waited for her chest to calm down as 10:29 somehow became 10:33. She let the silence expand like a big, soapy bubble until she felt confident enough to pop it. Straightening her back, she looked right into the eye that was inclined towards her. 'I can trust you, right?'

He shifted. 'Well… Yes.'

She thought quickly; how would be the best way to go about this? 'I know a lot about… my ex-profession.'

'Right,' said Hamish, with a hard blink and a slight jerk of the head.

'And the beings I've been involved with throughout my career.'

'Of course.' The word 'beings' resonated for a second. He didn't ask what it meant.

'I have to keep myself, you know, discreet. But I'm faced with a moral problem now and… and I can't ignore it. I have to interfere; do you know what I mean?'

'Maybe if you explained… Go on.'

'I can only really tell you the absolute minimum.' She swallowed. 'Blankey has gone missing.' She stared at him to see if he recognized the name.

He frowned. 'Blankey?' Then: 'I know that name.'

'Can I go on? Or is it best not to…'

'I think you have to.'

'Yes, but I need you to keep this to yourself.'

He sighed huffily. 'Emma, I can't promise you anything until you tell me what the problem is. If I can keep this between us, then, of course, I will.'

Emma considered this. 'I won't be allowed to come back,' she said.

'Sorry?'

'I won't be allowed to come back if you tell anyone. I'm not playing with you, this is important. I need to be able to trust you entirely or else that's it; I'll have to leave town.'

Hamish took a deep breath through his nose. 'Did you kill someone?'

'What? Good heavens, no!' she scoffed.

'Have you stolen something?'

Her face became serious. 'No. I promise.'

Hamish gave a few deep nods. 'Fine. I won't tell anyone.' He put a finger to his lips but it was shaking so he withdrew it.

Emma's mouth almost smiled. 'Thank you.' She closed her eyes. 'Blankey is Mrs Lucas's littler.' She watched as the realization pushed his eyebrows up with each name. 'She has been missing for two days now.'

'Yes, but how…'

'It is very likely that she has been taken by Terence Bennett: your almost neighbour.'

Hamish's mouth started to open.

'That's all, really. That's what I came to tell you.' She folded her lips inwards.

'But… You know where I live?'

A nod.

'How?'

'I approved your adoption of Bonbon and Jinx.'

He nodded slowly, trying not to look surprised to hear those names come out of this person's mouth as two worlds overlapped. He thought about this as 10:36 flipped to 10:37, staring at her with his neutral face, the only tool he could rely on. She'd known him this whole time. She knew where he lived, his neighbours and… Susan. His eyelids stopped blinking, she blurred in front of him. Stories of stalkings, therapists being followed or phoned or harassed superposed themselves one over the other. 'She is still a patient.' He heard the words in the voice of his lecturer at university. 'You need to help your patient.'

'I realize this is a shock but it's important,' she urged.

'Is this why you booked this appointment with me?'

'Yes.'

Hamish nodded. 'Right then.' He sat up straight in his chair and asked: 'Why would he have taken her?'

She brushed her fringe away from her face and glanced at him from under her hand; had she hurt him? They observed each other for a minute. Her stomach squeezed itself to the size of an acorn. She leaned forward. 'I really think he's taken her.'

His eyebrows rounded back into their sad mouths. 'Right… But, you can't be sure so… how would I go about accusing this, um, Mr Bennett?' Then: 'He has another one; you know that, don't you?'

'Another what?'

'A boy one.'

'Oh! Yes, Chips. Yes, Mr Bennett is the legitimate owner of Chips. I'm not concerned about that.'

He nodded. 'That's strange because Chips, is it?'

'Yes, Chips.'

'He's… well… like a skeleton.'

Her eyes widened. 'How do you mean?'

'Completely undernourished. You can see his ribs, his hip bones; everything. My partner has seen him in our house before.' He winced at the word 'partner'.

Emma didn't seem to notice. She bent forward and rummaged in her bag. 'I had no idea. I had nothing to do with his development…' She unrolled a sheet of plastic and started to type on it with one hand.

'Can't you have someone, you know, look into it?'

'No, but *you* can,' she said while typing. 'This is very good.' Looking straight at him: 'The fact that he is mistreating Chips will detract attention from the Blankey problem, especially as I had nothing to do with placing him there. I need you to call the authorities about Blankey – mention Chips and your neighbour – the company will more than likely investigate him and find her.'

'Really?'

'Yep. When you make the call, say that you're calling on behalf of Mrs Lucas because Blankey has gone missing. Mention your concerns about Chips. Mention that you think she might have been locked in next door. If they do their job properly, they'll investigate your neighbour's house.'

'I still don't understand why you can't do this.'

Emma put the sheet of plastic down on her lap. 'I'm very worried about my previous employers linking me to any of this.'

'Were you sacked?'

'Oh gosh no… I left. I'd have real trouble lying low after being sacked.' She leaned forward. 'I'm really trusting you.'

Hamish curled one finger over his mouth. 'If it's that secret, why say anything?'

She looked panicked. 'Because it's my fault that she's there.'

'Your fault?'

She sighed. 'Remember when I told you that I chose families?'

His eyes took in her fingers as they curled around 'chose'. Then danced over his year-old memories, as clear as the moment they were written. 'She's his late-wife, isn't she?'

She swallowed and said nothing.

He understood. She watched his eyes widen as he thought this over for a minute. 'So, who are Bonbon and Jinx?'

Gosh, she had not been expecting that question. 'I don't want to go into all of that today…'

'My grandmothers? Susan's grandmothers?'

'No, absolutely not.' She waved her hands to reassure him. 'They're in no way related to you, I promise.'

'Then why do we have them?'

She sighed. 'Because you're both young and earning well and I wanted them to stay together.'

'Who are they?'

'Listen, Hamish, you just told me that we have to trust each other.'

'What I was saying is not quite the same—'

She interrupted. 'Trust is the only component of a relationship that we are allowed. You said that I could tell you anything and I trusted that.'

He looked at the desk and pursed his lips. 'You can,' he said after a while. 'You can trust me.'

CHAPTER 12

She would just clap. That was the best way; in fact, it was really the only way to get her attention. Eventually she would figure it out, even if she did ask loads of stupid questions beforehand. She must have been worried about them. They had been gone ages! It was still daylight when Bonbon had come through the tunnel. And now she was wobbling back the other way on her own, her arms stretched out so that she didn't bump into the sides; she saw an opening up ahead, yes! Home! And ran through it. Gosh! Where on Earth was she? Two funny balls rushed up to her and bounced into her legs. She screamed then covered her mouth before bending to pick one up. The smell of it made her eyes close and flick through pictures on the other side of her head. She pushed its pointy folds into her nostrils. A man at a table, looking at a sheet with funny markings on it, it had the same smell as the thing she was holding now. She opened it up – what were these funny markings? 'Darling Helena…' It read. Bonbon felt her skin go bumpy at the word 'darling'. Her ears went hot as she heard the word whispered into them. Her eyes closed as they searched the pictures for the face that owned the whisper. 'Darling,' she said to herself, breathing air right to the bottom of her belly. 'Geraniums,' said the inside of her head. She opened her eyes. Black shadows of flowers bent down and sprang back up as the wind danced them in front of a light that seemed to be inside spurts of musical water that sang with a plip-ploppy voice rather than a horrid rushing sound that she made when she went for a wee or when Chips's he-one had left the taps on. The water curved into a big bowl that had fish mouths all around its edges singing out the water. Bits of flower tumbled from their mouths, and sometimes, when the wind licked the top of the bowl, they would spill right over its edge with a whole gush of water.

Bonbon stepped closer; this was Blankey's house. The dining-room doors were different, with curly black shadows for handles and a long brown spidery thing that hung down in front of them making tok-tok noises in the wind. This was where Blankey's she-one lived. The lady that had asked them to go to Chips's house. There was no light behind the shadowy handle-curls and the legs of the spider. There was no light coming from any window, only the fountain. Maybe Blankey's she-one was still at their house, with Bonbon's She-one? Bonbon ran her hand over 'Darling' before re-scrunching up the paper. Jinx was waiting. With Blankey… Turning towards the tunnel, she made herself go back inside, holding her breath and filling up her cheeks with geranium air; telling herself that she wouldn't take another breath until she'd gone through her own vacuum hatch.

And she didn't.

Running back into the kitchen, she gasped, looking around her for the She-one. She opened her mouth and screamed: 'She-one!' Then strode towards the kitchen door before realizing that if her voice could be screamed, there was nobody there. She went to the dining room and did the same. And the big room. She left her ball of paper and coat at the bottom of the stairs and climbed to the middle step to scream again. Nobody heard. 'Not even the He-one,' she said to herself, picking the paper back up and dragging her coat to the basket. She would just wait until somebody got home, and if nobody did get home, she would just have to go back again.

* * *

Drew looked up from the newspaper and reached into the fruit bowl for a yellow apple. The little person who sat just across the table, on her booster seat, had been silent for a while, and looking up now Drew realized that she wasn't reading the book that lay closed between her elbows, but holding her cheeks up with open hands and pouting at its cover. 'What's the matter, misery guts?'

'Jinx is dead.'

Drew, mid-bite, let the apple hand fall back on the table to reveal a circle of glinting teeth-marks. The tale of the brown bears had been a constant source of excitement and anguish ever since Isabel had started reading a blog about them. She had begged Drew to let her write to the blogger, to let her show her support. 'Why don't you let me write to them for you? Or at least use my name…' Watty had accused Drew of being over-paranoid, and Isabel had always got too cross for them to work out a solution. Now it was too late. The acid from the apple fizzed in Drew's stomach. 'What happened?'

'Don't know. Apparently she was found dead in her enclosure.'

'Oh Isabel, I'm so sorry.'

'I just keep thinking about Bonbon. He'll be all alone now.'

Drew sighed and cut a slice off the apple, peeled it and handed it to Isabel.

She took the apple and half-smiled. It looked like a piece of watermelon in her tiny hands.

'I'm so frustrated. Imagine what I could have done if I'd have been allowed on a train or a plane or something. With all my medical knowledge…'

Drew's gaze crawled across the table. 'I know, darling. We're very proud of you.'

'Don't patronise me.'

'I'm not! I'm so disappointed for you and… And I don't know what to say to make you feel better.'

Isabel rubbed the edge of the apple with her thumb. 'I didn't mean to snap.'

'I know, it's okay.' Drew sighed, wondering what could be said to cheer her up. Poor little Isabel. Drew imagined the bear that had been left alone, prodding at his dead mate, trying to revive her, then feeling suddenly very sleepy and waking up to find that she was gone. 'Animals cope with death a lot better than we do.'

Isabel snorted.

'I mean, things like this happen all the time, Isabel. The truth is that, even if you were out in the world, being a vet, you'd soon find it impossible to protect *everything*.'

Isabel looked horrified. 'Even if I *were* out there? You've just said it, haven't you? My studies are completely pointless. I'll never be able to help *anything*.'

Drew swallowed. 'Of course you will!'

Isabel shook her head and stared at nothing. A thought unravelled that she had had many times. A picture, of the world covered in teeny-tiny flames that were snuffing out so quickly that the few people who were trying to keep them burning couldn't work fast enough. All she could do was watch. Her fists clenched and she rubbed at her cheeks so hard that she made red lines with her knuckles. There, somewhere in a park enclosure in France, two tiny flames had been flickering together and now one barely glowed alone. 'Poh!' she whispered with her mouth as if blowing out a candle. 'I'll be forever useless.'

'Don't say that.' Oh dear. Surely there was something that could lighten the mood? Ah yes! Remembering the heavy satchel that had been dumped on the kitchen floor, Drew got up and glided towards the kitchen. 'Hey, I brought you more books from the library!'

Isabel's eyebrows spread upwards but her mouth stayed sad. 'Really?'

'Yes, really.'

'Hello!' called Watty as the front door shut.

'Good evening, Watson,' Drew grinned, rising from the ground where the satchel lay, now empty on the floor.

Head, body, arms and legs rose up into the air as if that was where they belonged, as if they were birds flying from the ground to a tree. No! As if they were made of the lightest porcelain that had been smashed on the chair and the whole scene had been replayed backwards in slow motion. Yes, that was a better description. That was one that Watty would jot down later. 'Got some more books for Quail?'

'Yep,' said Drew. 'Good ones. *Cytology and Haematology*, *Emergency Medicine*, and this one is more for Jasper, I think.'

Isabel read aloud. '*Physical Therapy and Massage for the Dog.*'

'Oh excellent.' Watty took a grape from the fruit bowl. 'Did you hear that, Jasper?'

Jasper lay in his basket, his greying muzzle resting on crossed paws. On hearing his name, his pupils floated to the top of their eye sockets and his tail beat slowly against the floor.

'Wait, you forgot one, Drew.'

Drew turned quickly. 'Yes, I know, that one has to go back.' But Watty was already reading the title.

'*Zoo and Wild Animal Medicine.*' Watty turned the book around to reveal a brown bear standing upright in long green grass.

Isabel blinked and stroked the cover of *Emergency Medicine.*

Drew throat-cleared. 'Erm, we have a bit of sad news, Watty: Jinx died today.'

Watty put the book down and strode over to Isabel. 'Oh darling, I am sorry.'

'It happened this morning.'

'Poor old Jinx; you must be devastated.'

'I am. Because at least they had each other.' She sat back in her chair and sighed. Then smiled at Watty who had made sad eyes and an upside-down mouth.

'You know, as sad as this is, it should make you even more motivated to support other causes. The majority of them can only move forward because of their following, even if you don't send any money,' Watty shrugged. 'Just knowing that there are like-minded people in the world can really fuel projects like this.'

'Yes,' said Isabel with a jerk of her head. 'I do hope so.'

Drew watched as Watty kissed the top of Isabel's head and ruffled her hair. She was almost smiling now. Watty could *always* get her out of one of her moods.

'And you know what?' Watty asked, walking away. 'If you happen to have any of Jinx's DNA, Drew will bring her back to life.'

Drew winced. That would not go down well. All the shadows and dimples in Isabel's face seemed to scuttle out of the way as if running from a rain cloud.

'She is dead!' she shouted as her little fist hit the table top. '*Dead!* There are so many more alive things that need to be taken care of, why did you waste your time creating new *freaks* of nature like me with your *stupid* experiments?' she yelled, gesturing towards her chest. 'I'm such a mutant that I can't even *help* anything.' She sat back sobbing as Watty bent down to hold her. 'Real life should be put first,' she cried. 'This isn't a life.'

Drew looked at the strands of Isabel's hair that were stuck to Watty's jawline, before turning and walking back to the kitchen. With palms flat on the work surface, Drew tried to breathe as silently as crying would allow.

'You are mistaken, darling. Drew's entire career has been *devoted* to protecting real life. You *are* real life, you come from a real egg that your real mother donated to the hospital; do you know how many embryos died before we were lucky enough to find our Quail?'

'But *why* did you kill them?'

A loud sob echoed in the kitchen. Isabel looked surprised.

'Nobody was killing them, Drew was trying to *save* them.'

'By making them *smaller*?'

'You have to understand, Quail…'

'I could have been a normal size, couldn't I?'

Watty looked at the table, lips pursed.

'You were supposed to die,' came the answer from the kitchen. 'None of you were supposed to live. If I had respected the law you would be dead like the others.'

Isabel looked towards the kitchen where Drew reappeared, burst mascara tears glistening.

'Why did you keep me?'

'It was my job to kill children.' Drew's voice quivered at the word 'kill'. 'I had to make *something* good come of it. You were the only one in a batch of twelve that survived. I was supposed to observe your development for another two weeks before terminating the experiment. But after two weeks, I couldn't do it.' Drew plopped into a chair and looked towards the window. 'I remember sneaking into the lab at night to sing to you and talk to you and arriving every morning before anybody else, praying that the monitor would still be beeping. I would go home at night and think of nothing else until the next morning, and so obviously, when the day came… Well… By that point you were my baby, I had to bring you home, and now…' Drew's voice broke. 'You're so unhappy, I'm so sorry, Isabel. I just couldn't kill you…'

They all looked up as the handle of the kitchen door creaked. Uncle Reg poked his head around the door and noted each miserable face one after the other. 'A bad time?' he asked.

'Erm…' Watty got up from kneeling on the floor, Isabel's hair unsticking from his face, strand by strand like spaghetti falling from a colander. 'Actually, Jinx is dead.'

Drew looked at the floor and nodded slowly. Yes, that was the best answer.

'Ah.' Uncle Reg crept around the door and closed it behind him. 'I'm afraid I haven't come here to cheer you up. The thing is… It looks like I've committed a bit of a boo-boo.'

* * *

It was Tuesday. First day back to work after almost two weeks off. Oh God, she had to wash her hair this morning; what time was it? Quarter to nine? Oh no… Thirty minutes to get dressed and go. Maybe she could just shove a headband on. Or a hat.

She rolled over. Hamish had gone. She had been sleeping on his side of the bed and the mug of coffee that he'd left for her stood on her bedside table. She leaned over and dipped her finger in it; tepid. Yuk. Cold coffee. Still, she would drink it. If he ever found out that she tipped his coffee away, he'd definitely stop making it. She sat up and took a swig from the coffee. Oh, it was gross. *Freezing* cold, how long ago had he left? Maybe she'd just tip this one down the toilet then vow to get up earlier and drink all the others; just like she'd vowed to get up earlier and run for forty minutes… Oh well. She swung her legs out of bed and looked in the mirror. Not *too* bad. It was just the bits above the ears that caught her out. She'd been hoping to come back to work looking all glowing and, and radiant. Like someone who'd just been on holiday. She'd just wear it loose, then come back at lunchtime and wash it. After her run.

Mug in hand, she went into the bathroom and asked for a shower at thirty-nine degrees. Dear oh dear, tipping coffee away; runs at lunchtime. When would the lies stop? She giggled as the shower radio reminded her that it was 08:54. Shit. She still had *everything* to do and she hadn't even had a good cup of coffee.

She frowned and bit her thumbnail as shower-drops scattered along her shoulders. Oh dear, a bad feeling – what was that? Was it Hamish? No… No, it wasn't Hamish. Was it work? Well, yes… But that wasn't *it.* Ah! That was it! Mrs Lucas. She mustn't forget to call round today. And before that, she'd have to ask Bonbon and Jinx if they'd had any news from Chips. But that wasn't the bad feeling, was it? Why would that make her feel bad? Because she'd forgotten to call her the last time, that was probably it… No! Because she'd forgotten to check on Bonbon and Jinx last night after the meeting. *That* was the reason.

Susan finished showering, got dressed, stamped on her eyeliner and sprayed her cheeks with blusher. Damn. She had really hoped to look nicer today. Oh well. She ran down the stairs, smacked the glass coffee table and yelled 'Coffee!' at it, before rifling through the understairs cupboard for presents that she'd bought for her colleagues… Fuck, Hamish! He'd stacked all these bloody boxes in front of her presents. 'Hamish, you *arse*!' She'd have to get them at lunchtime as well. So much for her Big Return.

She ran into the kitchen, grabbed a yogurt from the fridge, and flicked her eyes over the bowls. Excellent, they were full. At least he'd managed to do that. She went back into the lounge, snatched the coffee from the glass tongue and remembered that she'd been meaning to do *something.* Ah yes! Check on the chilly-billies. Popping her head around the kitchen door, she saw Bonbon sleeping on her humcoat with her arms over another lump that didn't look like it could've been Jinx…

Susan squinted; maybe it was.

Maybe Jinx was out with her boyfriend.

09:13, bugger. She would look for her at lunchtime.

Right.

Shoes.

Keys.

Phone? She looked at her wrist and flicked it onto 'silent' mode.

Coffee.

And we're off.

Awake.

Bonbon's eyes opened as the front door closed. Like a kiss, she thought, it always sounded like a kiss. She looked at the ceiling for a moment before flipping herself over. Jinx wasn't there.

Shit!

Her humcoat lay on its back, arms outstretched; an invisible head inclined towards her, gasping for water. Blankey. Oh no, poor Blankey! She jumped up and ran towards the hall, screaming with a voice that was dry in her mouth and soft in her ears. She coughed and tried again. It was a little better, she could definitely hear herself: maybe one of them was still upstairs? She climbed to the middle stair and stood there shouting. Yesterday's screaming had made her voice all poorly, but she could still be heard. She climbed back down, listening for shower sounds or footsteps or spoons chiming inside cups.

Nothing.

She got to the kitchen. Both bowls were filled with flakes. A mug stood next to the thing where the water came from as well as two fallen yogurt pots, one spoon hung over the edge of the worktop, the other… She looked down to the ground. There it was, resting against the cupboard on its side, its silver bottom pointing towards her like the back of a sleeping Jinx. Oh dear… They were both out. She walked towards the spoon, her upside-down reflection growing in its bowl, before picking it up with both hands, running to the basket and snatching up her humcoat. The ball of paper that had been underneath crisped as if it were waking up.

Bonbon threw on her coat and spooned up a pile of flakes. How could she have slept all this time? A layer of flakes shivered from the spoon to the ground where they melted in water splashes that glittered next to the water bowl. She looked between the spoon and the water bowl and plunged the pile of flakes inside. The spoon came back up as a clump of yellow; at least they weren't falling off now, she thought, and Jinx would be able to suck the water out if she needed it. 'U' she read as she turned to leave. Or a 'C'. She stopped and turned back. The flaky water on the floor had made a letter. The Darling letter squiggled its way across the inside of her head. She put the spoon down and plunged her hand into the yellow gunge.

Five minutes later, she was running with the spoon, across the tiles and towards the vacuum hatch.

She imagined them, all together underneath the bed; very thirsty and hungry. Maybe Blankey would be, she would be… Bonbon swallowed. The Dead Bird lay in her mind, a bald patch in its side from where she'd yanked all its feathers out.

She crossed Chips's Outside and made for the dirty, blackened hole that was his vacuum hatch. Shit. What if Chips's he-one had come home? The thought made her rise up onto her tiptoes and leap forward silently from foot to foot, listening for big boots and crackly breathing. She walked across the kitchen and went into the hall. Boots came out of the living room. She stood still and closed her eyes.

Had he seen her?

'It's morning time. Shall we go and give Tilda some water?' he said.

Bonbon opened her eyes to see him bending down towards her with one opened hand, its creases so deep that it looked as if it had brown stripes.

She swung the spoon as far back as it would go before smacking the hand over and over. Yellow sludge splattered up the wrist as the hand got closer. The air from his mouth was hot and horrible on her face as he laughed. 'You've got a bit of a temper, haven't you?' Fingers closed around her as she hit out at his wrist, and even when the spoon was tugged from her hands and she heard it plop onto the carpet, her empty hands smacked against his fist.

'Come on.' He stood for a moment. She opened her eyes to see that he'd covered his own with his other hand and was making a funny, straining noise. 'It's no good… I can't remember,' he said. She peered at him; he'd been trying to find something that was lost inside his head. 'That's it!' He pointed up into the air and she jumped. 'We were on our way to get some water,' he said, stepping up to the first stair and waiting for his other foot to be on the same step before stepping up to the next one. 'For Tilda. Then you started hitting me with that spo-spoon.' He laughed again and the fingers loosened. She buried her hands in his beard and held on, looking wildly around her; she'd never been in the air on the stairs like this. Her eyes flitted over a tiny square that hung so high up on the wall that she wouldn't have seen it from the stairs. She focused on it, it was a picture of… Of Blankey! She screwed up her face. Blankey was dressed all weird, with a different colour on her lips and a long skinny thing that poked out from between her fingers. Was it really her? Yes, yes, it must have been. She had the same eyes, the same cloud-like hair.

The sound of rushing water reached her ears, and suddenly she had been turned around and was looking into a bathroom. Thick green spots grew up the walls and became black stains in the corners that licked at the ceiling. Three brown hand prints climbed up the wall just next to the toilet, which was open, shit streaking up the outside and sitting inside, like wet rocks, at the bottom of the bowl. The skin-coloured bath had a thick, flake-sludgy line around it and specks of black covered its bottom. The taps in the sink were still running from yesterday. Bonbon tried not to breathe and looked behind her, back across the landing towards the bedroom. The door to the room that the others were trapped in was still shut.

'The tap's on,' mumbled the beard. She looked at the tap as

he tried to turn it but it was stuck. 'Just you stand there,' he said, putting her down into the bath, its edge growing over her as she was lowered inside. She tried clapping twice, No! No! But he just stood up and put his hand over his eyes again. He stood like that for a while before poking the air. 'Tap!' He turned and forced it shut, then looked at it for a moment before turning around and leaving the bathroom.

Bonbon clapped and thumped the side of the bath until he came back, *good*, and looked down at her, his eyebrows as thick as Jinx's hair and his eyes all blue and liney. She opened her mouth and rubbed her throat, pointing towards the bedroom and the closed door. They were in there, and they were thirsty.

He looked around the bathroom then behind him to where she was pointing. 'What?' he said, squinting at her. He rubbed his eyes again and made groany noises, just as he had done in the hallway. 'I can't remember...' he moaned; then 'Tilda!' he said before turning in a circle and picking up a dish from the windowsill. Its slimy contents dropped into the sink as he tipped it this way and that, trying to turn the tap back on while holding the dish in his massive hand. 'Why is it off?'

Bonbon watched as he sighed at it and thumped it with his fist before bending down and turning the bath tap on. Water rushed out and beat the bottom of the bath making her legs shake and her hands reach for her ears. She watched as he filled up the dish, turned and left. 'No!' she shouted, and her voice let itself be used, as nobody could hear her when the taps were on. She looked down as the water covered her feet and threw herself at the side of the bath, outstretched fingers trying to cling onto anything that they could dig their nails into, but she bounced straight back with both hands full of sludge. She wiped them on her humcoat and tried again, this time falling against the side and sliding down. The water was up to her knees and sucking at the soles of her feet when she tried to jump. She took off her humcoat and let it float off to where the water was pushing it. Slumping against the side of the bath, she thumped it until her fists wouldn't open and the black bits from the bottom were floating around her waist and getting stuck to her elbows. She screamed and held her arms above her head, darting her eyes over the ceiling. Dangly items hung over the bath, a shower, the tap, a hand towel, a long thing with a brush on the end of it, all way out of her reach, as if they were pointing and laughing at her while she… while she… 'Drowned,' said the inside of her head. 'They are laughing at you while you drown.' She tilted her head right back as the water reached her ears and underwater swirls nudged at her legs. This was it. The old littler had told her that she would drown; any minute now, she would go under. The ceiling speckled into almost blackness as her gaze followed it towards the door. She imagined it was night again and she was reading 'Darling' over and over in the geranium-smelling garden, where black shadowy flowers swayed and the fishes used water for voices while the wind licked petals over their heads. 'Darling,' said Jinx into her ear, with the voice of a man, as the water butted at her feet so that they rose and her head jerked backwards and disappeared under the surface.

CHAPTER 13

'Oh dear, Reg, you didn't?'

'I'm so sorry.'

'Did you give him my real number?'

'I'm afraid so.'

'It's not that drastic, is it?'

Reg and Watty looked at Drew. 'The thing is, if Mark Hector wants something, he can be pretty pushy.'

Reg shoved his hands in his pockets and rocked on his heels. 'Yes,' he said. 'I got that impression.'

'And he wants me by the sounds of it…'

Watty leaned forward in his chair and scratched at the exposed skin between the top of his sock and the bottom of his trousers. 'You're not going to accept the job, are you?'

'Even if I'd wanted to, I can't. It's a bit too risky… for my liking.'

'Fine. Don't accept the job.'

'I won't.'

'And that'll be the end of it.'

'Well…'

'Short of coming to the house, what could he do to discover Isabel?'

'It's fine, we'll just…' One hand grew up through the air, turning in circles as it did; a blooming flower on fast-play, like on one of those BBC documentaries, thought Watty. The hand bloomed. 'We'll just move.'

'Pfff.' Watty got up, grabbed the fruit bowl from the table and walked to the kitchen with it before turning his back to the sink and leaning against it. 'Did you actually say that we had a daughter?'

'Yes. Called Isabel.'

'Right.'

Reg held both palms out to them. 'Look,' they looked at him, 'if he calls, he calls. If he doesn't, then great.'

'He'll call,' scoffed Drew, eyes resting on the middle of the table where the fruit bowl no longer was, then turned to a jacket that hung over the back of the chair and started rifling through the pockets.

'Sorry to be a burden.' Isabel stuck out her bottom lip and folded her arms.

'Oh shut up, Isabel.'

Isabel's face dropped. Watty strode over from the kitchen and put his arm around her chair.

Drew rummaged for a while then came back up from the jacket with a mobile phone. 'I don't know why I didn't think of it before; I'll just change the number.'

'Drew…' Watty's head tipped towards Isabel. Drew's brows rose in the middle like a lifting bridge, allowing Isabel's expression to pass under. 'I'm so sorry, darling.'

'S'alright.' Isabel sniffed.

'Of course you're not a burden. It's just that silly doctor, he's stressing me out.'

'I know.'

Drew put the phone, screen down, on the table.

'Do you think he'd come and badger me for your new number?' asked Reg. 'He knows where Flick 'n' Spin is.'

'I don't know where it is—' said Isabel.

'I won't bother to change it,' interrupted Drew. 'He'd probably turn up on the doorstep. It's best that he calls me.'

Reg looked at his hands. 'I am sorry, Drew.'

'In fact, it's weird that I've never been there,' insisted Isabel.

Watty got up. 'Let's change the subject, shall we? How about some tea, Reg?'

'Are you listening to me?'

Reg looked at Isabel. 'What is it, Quail?'

'Can I come and stay with you this evening?'

Watty and Drew turned and gaped. 'Out of the question,' said Drew, finally.

'Why?' Isabel signalled that she wanted to get down from her chair. Reg got up to help her. 'In fact, there is no question… I'm going with Reg.'

Oh bloody thing. So slippery. Really must get a cover for it. Ah, that's it, gotcha. 'Hello?'

'Drew Mahlik?'

Oh God. He hadn't wasted any time. 'Yes?' Drew swallowed. 'Who's speaking, please?'

'Oh, well, I feel like a bit of a blast from the past, actually. It's Mark Hector.'

Drew winced at the ceiling. Stay strong. Must refuse him. 'Dr Mark Hector?'

'Yes. That's the one.'

'Wow! This is a surprise.'

'How are you?'

'Erm… I'm good, thank you. Doing very well.'

'Jolly good.'

'Yes.'

'Well, I must say!'

'Huh!'

'Right.'

'Mmm.'

'Funny eh?'

'Ha! Yes.'

'Good.'

'Ahem.'

'—.'

Drew's eyes scrunched shut. 'And you? How are you?'

'Well… I don't know if you've been keeping up to date, have you?'

'Erm… No. Not one bit actually. To tell you the truth, I've somewhat abandoned that… that interest.'

'Oh really?'

'Yes.'

'Oh… Oh dear. That is a shame. Any particular reason?'

'Well, ha!' Think, Drew, think. 'God, actually. I've found, erm, religion.'

At the other end of the phone, Dr Hector took a loud breath then didn't seem to exhale. Silence stopped the air as if it were freezing it. Drew smiled a non-smile. The kind of smile that is necessary when one's teeth are clenching. Suddenly, Dr Hector started to laugh.

'Brilliant!' he boomed. 'If you only knew the week I've had… That's just topped it off. Ha! God! So simple.'

Arrogant bastard. He'd always been an arrogant bastard. Drew laughed with him anyway but couldn't help adding: 'I might, um… I might not have been joking, you know.'

'What?'

The 'what' was a short bark, transporting Drew back to the lab, into a white coat, placing a clipboard in one latex-covered hand and making the floor underfoot grey and chemical-smelling. 'Every one of the last batch died before reaching term,' Drew explained. 'What?' came the response, with a glinting pair of eyes that stared and stared like toothy piranhas about to swim out of their caves and eat Drew's face.

Drew shuddered and swapped the phone to the other ear. 'If I'm honest, I have been keeping up to date with your study. It sounds like you're making progress.'

'Oh really? Good! Well… Not as much progress as I'd like and, actually… um… funnily enough this is the reason for my call.'

'Is it?' Drew husked, then throat-cleared. 'Is it?' he repeated.

'Yes.' He was quiet for a second. Drew imagined his piranha eyes snapping open and shut as his brain put together his next sentence. He began. 'The thing is, I have some fantastic scientists and some, let's say, not so fantastic. I'm in a bit of a spot and… well… your record caught my eye and, in short, I could really do with someone like you… Someone with experience.'

Someone who doesn't mind being bullied and, and someone who knows how to keep their mouth shut – ha! How dare he? How dare he phone up like this and expect Drew to drop everything and go back to those horrid experiments; killing children and keeping it a secret. Drew's lips opened and mouthed angry shapes into the phone before they could calm down and let through a small but solid 'No'.

'Sorry?'

Drew blew slowly through pursed lips. 'Yes, well, I'm turning the situation over in my mind but… But I really don't see how it would be possible.'

'Very simple. Just say yes.'

'Well… In an ideal world…'

'Blow your ideal world! Just make it happen.'

Drew's heart clawed at its chest, like a lab-rat scratches at the walls of its tank.

'I… um… It's just impossible.' The words were louder than intended. Drew winced before adding: 'I'm afraid.'

A deep inhalation hissed at the other end. 'Do you know how much of a privilege this is?'

Oh God. Drew's eyes closed. 'I do.'

'Do you know how many scientists would tumble over themselves for this opportunity?'

'—.'

'Well?'

'I'm in no doubt.'

'I don't think you realize that at this very moment my secretary is drafting five letters to dismiss five student researchers, kids whose interests are rooted in advancing science for the good of our planet and the future generations with whom said planet must be shared, as well as our translation of its mechanisms that we are chipping our way into, day by day, so that our children have major building blocks to cement together; all of this, all of this they realize because they are scientists, but I would get rid of the lot of them in an eye-blink in order to hire you.'

Drew's head shook slowly. 'Why me? I'm not that good. We had at least twelve excellent scientists on our team if I remember correctly.'

A pause pulsed at the other end of the line. Drew listened with one eye shut until the sound of a breath intake confirmed that his tantrum was over. 'You're right. You're absolutely right. And we've had many more since.' Then a long sigh. 'I'm sorry, I just… I'm just in a bit of a spot. I'll find someone. I'm sorry if I got all shouty.'

The voice went muffled at the word 'shouty', as if a hand had been rubbed down the length of its face. Huh! He'd never apologized before… Perhaps he'd mellowed in his old age.

'You'll find someone.'

'Yeah… It's just I can't believe the government has landed me with a load of students.' A chuckle echoed at the other end. 'Useless bunch don't know their arses from their elbows.'

Drew pursed his lips; he'd always had it in for them. It wasn't like they were undergrads… They were probably third-year doctoral students; some might even have been doing postdocs… He was frightened, that was the problem, because they were attached to universities and universities valued standards and *good* practice. Jesus, this man was so wrong. Mustn't say anything else, though; he was nearly gone; he was nearly out of their lives for good. 'You'll find someone,' Drew repeated.

'Oh, I'm sure I will…'

'You will.'

A pause, then: 'You're still dancing, are you?'

'Erm…' Why not? If that would make him go away. 'Yes, actually. Although I'm getting a bit long in the tooth now.'

'Ha! Long in the tooth? I've got grandchildren now; up in Scotland.'

'Oh… That's nice.'

'Yes. Far enough away. I've done my share of babies.'

'Yes, they're hard work, aren't they?'

'And you've got Isabel, is that right?'

Drew froze. The heart lab-rat seemed to rise up on its hind legs and twitch its whiskers. That name, coming from that mouth; that mouth had uttered that name so many times in an entirely different context. The rat bolted around its cage, looking for a way out; sending up loud, frightened breaths that forced Drew to face away from the handset so Mark Hector wouldn't hear them. 'You know about Isabel?'

'Sorry, yes! Your friend told me that you had a child.'

Drew exhaled… Phew! It was Reg. Reg wouldn't have said anything compromising. Not more so than he already had, silly bugger. 'Yes, she's just turned eighteen.'

'Eighteen? Was it really over eighteen years ago that you left? My gosh.'

'Yes! Funny, isn't it…'

'Something I could never do; give up on my whole career because of a child. Your wife must have felt supported, though.'

'My wife?'

'Yes! Watty, do they call her?'

'They do but… He's definitely a "he".'

'I'm sorry?'

'Watty's my husband.'

'No!'

'Sorry?'

'Really?'

'Yes.'

'Well, who'd have thought it?'

'I think the name's a bit of a giveaway…'

'Ha! You've foxed me there…' He paused for a while. The piranha eyes were probably darting this way and that, trying to make sense of the territory outside their caves. 'You know, if there's one thing I've never understood it's this trend for being gay.'

Oh dear. Drew pulled his shoulders back and folded his lips inwards.

'At what point does it start? That's the million-dollar question… Ha ha! If I had the answer to that I'd be the most successful doctor on the planet.'

Don't do it. Don't bite, Drew. Just clench your teeth and, and… 'You're an expert in genetics. You should have a very good idea of the point at which "it" starts,' Drew's mouth seemed to say all by itself.

'Oh, don't give me all that clap-trap. Why did you never see it back in the day, eh? And now all of a sudden they're everywhere.'

Drew sighed and flopped against the sofa back. 'I blame Roundup.'

'Ha! Quite. You're alright, you see, you've got a sense of humour. You know what? If this project does go completely belly up, I'll just figure out a way to turn everyone gay – that'll solve the population crisis.'

'You know, you should probably be more careful about what you say… Given your position.'

'Oh goodness, we're only mucking about. And anyway, it was you who suggested that it could be manipulated genetically.'

'Um… Not quite.'

'But in all honesty, all it would really take is for you people to realize that we are here to procreate. And giving into your whims is… is totally anti-family. I should have guessed, actually, you being a dancer an' all.'

'I should have had it tattooed on the back of my neck. Then you wouldn't have had to guess.'

'I'll tell you one thing: as good a scientist as I am, I haven't managed to make one baby with two sperm cells.'

'—.'

'Have I?'

'—.'

'Or has anyone, for that matter?'

'—.'

'True, isn't it?'

'I bet you've tried, though.'

'What?'

That was it; the camel's back had positively dissolved. Drew sat forward, holding one hand high in the air. 'How can you say that I'm anti-family, Doctor I-could-never-give-up-on-my-career-because-of-a-child, when you've spent your lifetime killing children?' Drew scrunched his eyes shut and listened to the silence that hummed through the handset. Not a breath, not a sigh, not a gasp; nothing. Just as he was about to hoarse 'hello?' Dr Hector piped up again.

'And so what does that make you? You spent most of your scientific career terminating embryos without a hope in hell of going on to procreate. You're a veritable dark angel, Drew Mahlik.'

A veritable dark angel. A veritable dark angel. Drew's eyes grew hot. His thumb hovered over the red hang-up button as his top eyelids sought the bottom ones so that they could hold each other while they cried; droplets squeezed between them and burst on his knees, the wet stain marking the end of one short existence before another would fall, and another; his eyelids continuing to hug each other to save them. 'I have a child.'

'Well, so does every other normal person on this planet, Drew. Did you adopt her? Buy her?'

'I'm not like you. I wanted to make something good come of all of this,' he sobbed.

'Did you grow her? Ha! There's a thought.'

'I tried to save them! I wanted to make Project Isabel work. I knew that as soon as they were babies they'd be safe from you. They'd be protected by the law...'

'You grew her, didn't you? Are you telling me that you grew her?'

'No,' he whimpered. 'I. Just. Wanted. Them. To. Live.' The sobs pulled his head downwards and it rested on his knees.

'Well, they didn't. And you're just as responsible as I am.'

'I used to sing to them. I used to read them stories...'

The front door clicked behind Drew. 'Drew, we found the biggest blackberry bush ever!' But he didn't notice. He sat, curved over his knees, his feet hoisted onto their toes, feeling each little wet globe as it splashed and evaporated on his thigh, imagining each evaporation as a tiny white soul... 'Drew, who are you speaking to?' Watty set Isabel down on the floor and strode across the room.

'*They* were just bunches of cells, Drew. The day you took on Isabel was the day you destroyed a real child's life.'

'Hang up the phone, Drew. Hang it up!'

There was a click and the line was dead. Dr Hector listened for a moment, then redialled the number on the scrap of paper. Answerphone. He leaned back in his chair and curled his index finger over his top lip. No wonder he'd left; mentally unstable queer. And all this business about him bringing up a child... The doctor shook his head; that was incredibly wrong. The world had completely turned on its head the day that gays were allowed to adopt. That's if he did adopt her… He had plenty of opportunity to grow her. Ha! *Ha!* No… Impossible. Not on his nelly. The problem with Drew Mahlik was that he had a sappy conscience that had obviously broken him, over the years. He'd seen it happen to one other person, maybe two… The man just broke down in tears! 'I wanted to make something good come of all of this!' he'd cried. Well, didn't we all, Drew Mahlik? Didn't we all…

Ha! Growing his own child indeed…

But had he actually said 'no'? Yes, yes, he had said it but… Just 'no'. Not: 'No, you're bloody crazy!' or, or: 'No! How on Earth would you expect me to do that?'

Just 'no'.

But then again, such a silly question would only really require a 'no', wouldn't it?

Mark Hector found himself typing 'Isabel Mahlik' into his tablet… But would it be Mahlik or… Bugger. He didn't know the other one's name. He clicked the tablet off and drummed his fingers on it.

Just wanted to make something good come of all of this. Just wanted them to live.

Oh dear. The seed had been planted; this would niggle at him now; what if? What if? His whole life's work had been building up to creating something like this and, well, what if it already existed? He picked up a coaster on his desk, turned it over and put it back down again before getting up and striding to the window. And anyway, even if he had grown his own baby, which was highly unlikely, there wasn't much that they could do about it now. No, no… That would be too much trouble, too time-consuming. Who had the time to go around breaking up families for no particular reason? Plus, it would drum up bad press, not what he needed at the moment. The real problem was, if Drew had grown Isabel, which he probably hadn't, then where had he got the embryo? The lab was the most obvious answer. Theft, ha! And if he had stolen the embryo to make Isabel, the chances of which were very slim, then the lab embryos at the time had been specifically modified... The question was if he'd made his own baby, which he probably hadn't, and if he'd stolen a lab embryo to do it, which in itself would be in breach of too many regulations to even consider, but if he had, had he stolen it before or after modification? That was the question.

Dr Mark Hector shook his head and chuckled. Drew Mahlik hadn't done any of these things. 'Your shortfall, Hector, has always been that bothersome dose of fantasy.' He walked back to his desk and sat back down. Right, this wasn't going to get him another scientist anytime soon! He clicked on his tablet and slid through the second-choice profiles. Drew had most certainly been among the best; among the top three, he would say. That's probably why he'd ended up in such a mess, ha! Might even have turned him... 'Follow the three-day rule, Hector,' he said aloud to himself. 'If you're still thinking about this in three days, then you may do something about it.'

* * *

Hang on... She could see. But she wasn't breathing; her mouth wouldn't let her breathe. Was that possible? She'd never put her head underwater before and now it was there her mouth and nose had closed up. The black speckled ceiling blurred and wobbled. She pushed her face towards the surface and broke through, her mouth opening up and filling with air. She was breathing... and floating. Like a geranium petal or, or the shit inside the toilet bowl. She could see across the bath to the edge and even over the side. The edge wasn't as high up any more. It was like the fountain when it had been licked by the wind; the water could fall over the side at any minute. If only she could get to the side and fall over with it. Little domes of air formed and popped on the surface. Her humcoat drifted, tummy down, towards the edge. She wriggled after it, wincing as her hair caught in her armpits. The water was right at the top now; one lick and it would slosh over the edge. She pushed out with her forearms and a small wave spilled over, dragging her slightly nearer. Reaching and kicking and twisting her shoulders, her fingers rubbed the edge of the bath until she was able to put her hand over it and pull herself towards it. She hauled herself onto her belly and gazed across the water at her poor humcoat. 'I'm alive,' she exhaled. 'You told me I would drown.'

'We told *us* we would drown,' said the old littler.

Water oozed over her. Bonbon held on to the edge of the bath and let her feet dangle down as far as they would go, the way she had done with the three-legged stool, and dropped onto the carpet, spongy and bitty between her toes. Her feet gripped at it while she picked hair out of her eyes before running to the door to look through its line. The landing was clear and… and the door was open. She ran across the landing, squelching in the bouncy-wet carpet; Chips's he-one must have dropped most of the water from the dish. When she got to the door frame she peeped around it. Checking left and right she darted forward and swept back the bedspread. Jinx held the soap dish out in front of her, its edge against her belly.

'Is that… Bonbon! Bonbon, where have you been?'

'Mrs Lucas?'

'Yes?'

'We're maintenance technicians from Billbridge & Minxus. Your littler has been reported missing.'

Mrs Lucas opened her mouth and stood there with it open. What were these people doing here? The very day after she'd been to that meeting. She let the edge of the door slide closer into her cheek and temple. There were two of them, both dressed in black T-shirts and combat pants. One had a great long rubber cord wrapped over his right shoulder and down and around the opposite side of his waist. An enormous plastic suitcase hung from his left hand. He looked young, very young, with a slim head that would have had crumb-coloured curls if he'd let his hair grow out. He didn't say anything. The talky one looked more formal, well, he was *older* to start with; and wasn't made to carry anything except his ScreenJotta. He also wore glasses. Nobody really wore glasses these days. Maybe he was trying to disguise himself. Hmmm… She didn't like that one. The other one seemed all right but *this* one… No; not one bit.

'Can we come in?'

'You're not here to take her away, are you?'

The technicians pinged a look at each other. 'Why would you think that?'

'It's just… I'm very mistrusting at the moment; you'll have to excuse me.' Mrs Lucas put one hand on her hip and the back of the other against her forehead, a sheet of Fibre-Web squeezing through the gaps in its fingers. The door slid back to the edge of her hip-arm's elbow. 'But who reported her as missing?'

'Your neighbour, Hamish Wix?'

The old lady's face opened up. 'Oh heavens! The thought never even occurred to me.'

'Yes, he reported her as missing at…' The talky one looked at his wrist. '12:52. About ten minutes ago.'

'I'm starting to think that she may have been *stolen*.' She plucked another ball of Fibre-Web from her sleeve, unscrunched it and pulled at her nose. 'Hence the distrust. Did he mention that she might have been stolen?'

'We don't want to jump to any conclusions. Our equipment can track as far as twenty metres away and we would like to do the tour of your premises with it; would that be okay with you?'

Mrs Lucas hesitated for a moment. They seemed nice enough… And if it would help to get Blankey back then…'Yes. Alright. Do you need to come inside?'

'If you wouldn't mind.'

Oh, how she wished that Jerry were there! She let the door slide back and stepped aside. 'Come on through.'

'We'll start inside then work around your back yard.'

'Right.' Mrs Lucas clasped her hands, her thin skin shining like her rings and fingernails. She looked about the room. 'Erm… Might I ask…'

'Yes?'

'Is this part of the service, or…'

'There will be no fee, Madam.'

'No. I didn't mean that. I'm just surprised at how seriously you're taking the situation.'

'A missing littler *is* a very serious situation.' Talky folded his arms and nodded at the old lady with wide-opened eyes.

'Oh, of course… I…'

Crumb-curls started to talk as he unravelled the rubber cord. 'And the fact that you allowed her to go missing while she was in your care.' His voice was happy and sing-songy, as if he were explaining something that wasn't about her. 'And I'm not being funny but you are, like…' He stopped unravelling to roll his hands, one around the other, as he searched for the best way of saying what he was going to say. Talky looked at him over his glasses. 'Not getting-on-a-bit, but, like, *elderly*, that's the proper word. Maybe you just can't look after her any more, like, it's a bit too much for you now.'

'Bradley!' said Talky.

Bradley looked at Talky then at Mrs Lucas. 'Sorry about me, I shouldn't be saying things like that.' He dipped his head. Red patches footstepped up is neck and over his cheeks.

'That's quite alright.' She smiled at him. 'You're training, are you?'

'Yeah! This is only my third week. Still got a lot to learn.'

'Bradley, you can just attach that bit to the scanner. There's no need for the extension, we'll take it all upstairs when the time comes.'

They worked in silence for a moment.

'Should I just leave you to it?'

'As you wish,' said Talky without looking up.

'I'll make some tea, shall I?'

Talky looked up and jerked a nod without smiling. Bradley started to open his large black suitcase.

'Right then.' She turned and went to the kitchen, picking up a telephone handset on the way through.

Bonbon held her nose and looked around her. Blankey lay stretched out on the floor; her lips smacking together and her hands twisting about weirdly. Chips sat holding his feet and rocking, groaning to himself. Bonbon glanced down to where his hands were; his toes had become ten bloody stumps. A little mound of shit sank slowly into itself just under his twitching elbow. He dug his fingers further into his toes and yowled.

'What's wrong with him?'

'Your hair's all wet, Bonbon. Squeeze it into Blankey's mouth.'

Bonbon leaned over Blankey and twisted her hair over the opened mouth. A tongue patched with white gunge slapped against crusty lips. 'What about you, Jinx?'

'I'm alright. He just brought us water.' She nodded towards the soap dish. 'There wasn't much of it, though.'

Bonbon looked at Chips. 'Why is he doing that?'

'He spent most of the night trying to climb up the door. His fingers are the same.' She nodded at the poo. 'He can't walk. I had to hold him up while he did that.'

Dried blood crusted its way up Chips's legs. '*Oh* Chips, it's all my fault…'

'I'm alright, Bonbon. I'm alright. Just waiting for your she-one.' He yelped again as he pinched his big toe.

'Stop squeezing them, Chips. You'll make it…' But as she said this, Chips shoved his fingers in his mouth and sucked on them hard, his eyes twitching over his feet for blood.

'He's hungry, Bonbon,' said Jinx. 'Where is the She-one? Is she downstairs?'

'I…' said Bonbon. 'I couldn't find her.'

'What?'

'She wasn't at home.'

'Oh no, Bonbon! What are we going to do?'

Jinx's face, which had been so happy to see her; which had looked at her so seriously when she'd asked if the She-one was downstairs, which had stood close to her ear and whispered 'Darling' in a man's voice, now drooped its mouth and eyebrows at the same time. Bonbon's ears burned, all the way to her neck. She took both of Jinx's hands in her own. 'Listen, Jinx. The door's open, let's just go, shall we? You and me. We don't have to stay here. The door *is* open.'

'What?' Jinx's eyes dimmed like the red lights on the vacuum bot when it was being switched off. 'No, Bonbon! No! I can't leave them, I *won't*.'

Bonbon looked at the floor. She'd made Jinx's eyes go out; Jinx's eyes that had been all glowy for her even though she'd fallen asleep last night, even though she hadn't brought food and even though she hadn't talked to the She-one. She twisted her hair over Blankey's mouth again; then did the same with Chips. 'Stop that, Chips.' She took one of his bloody hands and repeated the words that the old littler was saying inside her head. 'You need your blood to survive.' Lying on the floor next to him and the pile of shit, she smoothed her hair into one flat strip and wrapped it around his feet.

'What will we do then, Bonbon?'

Bonbon wiped away a water-drop that was climbing down her eyebrow. 'I've left a note,' she said.

'A what?' Jinx's eyes swivelled up to the left as the inside of her head translated. 'But how did you do that?'

'With wet flakes,' said Bonbon. 'I think I can write. I think the She-one will find it and come to save us.'

'Really, Bonbon?'

'Yes,' Bonbon nodded. Then winced as her hair pulled at her head. 'I wrote it on the tiles in the kitchen.'

Jinx spun around in a circle. 'She's coming!' she sang. 'Did you hear that, Chips? The She-one is coming!'

'But…' said Bonbon. 'We have to wait for her to find the note. She might not find it until tonight. She might not come until much, much later.'

Jinx put the dish down and crouched in front of Bonbon. 'It's alright, Bonbon. I know she'll see it and she'll come straight away.'

Bonbon took a shivery breath. 'I think we should go and get more water.' She sniffed then wiped her nose on the back of her hand. 'There's loads of water coming out of the bath.'

Jinx nodded. 'I'll go,' she said.

Bonbon tried to sing until she got back, listening for any cracks in her voice, her palms feeling the ground for rumbles from biggerer footsteps. 'Are you alright, Jinx?' she called after a while. Chips wiggled his toes and sucked a big puff of air through his teeth. 'Don't they feel better at all?' she asked him.

'It's really heavy, Bonbon!' shouted Jinx.

'Um… Bonbon?' said Chips.

'Go slowly, Jinx! Try not to spill any!'

'Bonbon?' said Chips again.

'I'm going slow but my arms are getting tired.'

'Put it down for a moment if you have to.'

'Bonbon?'

'Yes, Chips?'

'You know you said that this was all your fault?'

'Yes.'

'It's not.'

Bonbon looked up towards the top of her head where she could see Chips leaning over her, all upside down and weird. 'What do you mean?'

'It's mine.' His upside-down eyebrows curved into one long smile and he started to cry.

'Why?'

He sniffed wetly then swallowed. 'I told a… I told a lie.'

The old littler translated 'lie' and Bonbon's eyes widened. 'What kind of lie?'

'I *knew* B-Blankey had c-come that night. I found her things underneath the cupboard.'

'Is Chips crying?'

'Don't tell Jinx,' he whispered. 'I *love* Jinx.'

Bonbon's mouth made a short, straight line. 'Alright,' she said, not knowing if she should think that he was bad or… or something else. She started to unravel his feet. Pictures popped out of each uncovered toe. Chips in the garden with his humcoat. His face when they'd asked him if he'd seen Blankey. Chips kissing Jinx. Chips kissing Blankey. Bonbon kissing Jinx. 'I love Jinx,' he'd said. 'I *love* Jinx.' The word whispered itself. She let it form and pop on her lips like the bubbles on the surface of the bath. Bonbon loved her too. Yet she hadn't saved her… Bonbon turned to Chips: 'Maybe we've both been bad,' she said, 'I don't think it means that we're bad, though.' She pulled herself to her feet and went over to Blankey who lay on her back, letting out little snores.

Chips stopped rocking and wiped his eyes with bloody thumbs. 'I never thought I'd hear her snore.'

'She's hungry,' said Bonbon, holding the bottom of the bedspread up and looking out for Jinx.

'Hungry, who's hungry?' Chips looked up and started to nibble the brown blood under his fingernails.

Jinx appeared at the door, her top half bent right back to allow the dish to rest against her belly.

'I'm coming to help!' Bonbon shouted, letting her voice bounce around the room. Where was he? Running up to Jinx, she took the other side of the dish.

Jinx blinked and stuck out her tongue as she concentrated on walking very quickly without spilling the water. Bonbon looked at her, 'love' and 'darling' floating as words around her head in flake-coloured letters.

'Why was Chips crying?'

'He wasn't crying,' Bonbon strained as they lowered the dish to the floor. 'Just pretending to be someone that was.'

They heard the front door slam below, sucking the bedroom door shut with a fwuuumf. Bonbon turned and looked at up at it. Browny red lines smeared up and down the back of it from where Chips had tried to get out during the night.

'Do you think it's the She-one, already?' said Jinx.

Bonbon shrugged. 'I don't know.'

'Mr Wix?'

'Yes?'

'I'm sorry to bother you; it's Mrs Lucas here.'

'Mrs Lucas?' said Hamish at the same time that she'd said 'Mrs Lucas'. 'Oh no… Are they there already?'

'The technicians? Yes, they are.'

'Really? Oh dear, I was just about to call you.'

'Well, they don't hang around, I can tell you.'

'I'm so sorry, I should have called you first. I don't know why I didn't. The idea just occurred to me and I…'

'Don't get me wrong, I'm very grateful for your concern.'

Hamish took a deep breath. 'I just thought that if she'd been locked in somewhere, this would be the quickest way of finding her. I called as soon as I thought of it because… Well… If she hasn't had any water then she'll probably be very dehydrated by now.'

'Yes, you're right. Thank you for calling them for me; that's such a kind thing to do.'

'Would you like me to come over? Are they a bit daunting?'

'Would you mind?'

'I'll be two minutes.'

'Thank you *so* much.'

'What are *you* up to?'

Hamish jumped and turned around. His own body had been hiding Susan. And Susan's ears. She stood there with one hand over a white towel that swirled upwards on her head like chantilly cream. When did she get back? 'Nothing. When did you get back?'

'About forty minutes ago. I… um… didn't have time to shower this morning. What are you doing back?'

'I don't have another appointment until four.'

Susan nodded. 'Who was that on the phone?'

'Mrs Lucas.'

'Oh right.' Then: 'Is she okay?'

'Yes, yes…'

'Has she found Blankey?'

'Erm… No… But…'

'You're all guilty.' Her gaze flicked down and poked him in the stomach.

'Pah!' Hamish sat on the second stair. 'Says she who's home at lunchtime wrapped in nothing but a towel.' He saw her skin pale and her mouth grin the tiniest bit before trying to be serious.

'Don't change the subject.'

'Who's guilty now?'

She touched her right hand to her left shoulder; a protective chest-covering gesture, also employed to detract attention from the grin that was trying to break out again. He grinned at her exaggeratedly while pulling on his shoe. She forced her mouth into a pout, then laughed at the front door, the tip of her tongue held between her teeth.

'You're a pain in my arse.'

'You should know not to pick a fight with me.'

'You're so clever, Hamish. If only everyone could be as clever as you. Where are you going?'

'To Mrs Lucas's house. She wants me to, to reach something down for her.'

'To reach something *down* for her?'

Hamish stopped and sighed. 'Yes, Susan; to reach something *down* for her.'

'Alright. Don't get stroppy.' Susan walked towards Hamish as he did up the lace on his second shoe. 'I'm allowed to be interested if my other half's being all heroic.'

'Ha! Hardly.'

'Would you like me to come?'

'What? No!'

'Are you sure? It's just that I'd like to see her. I said that I'd give her a call today anyway, it would be just as easy to… I'll just throw my clothes back on.'

'For pity's sake, Susan, why do you have to push it all the time? I just said "no".'

Susan stepped back, her mouth a little twitchy. Oh bugger. He'd upset her.

'I mean that… It's been a long morning. I just want to relax, if I'm honest, Suzie. I'll only be about five minutes, then I can come back and we can get on with our meeting.'

'Meeting?'

'Meal. I meant to say meal. Sorry… I'm a bit tired. I bought some wine from Shepherd's. Why don't you open it while I'm gone?'

'Wine? Hamish, I have to go back to work.'

'Oh, yes… I got you some ice cream. The Smurf one. You know that all those e-numbers make you feel like dancing.' Hamish bounced his shoulders up and down to indicate dancing.

Susan slit her eyes. 'You're being weird.'

'Fine! I'm being weird.'

'Weirdo.'

'I have to go. Open the wine.'

'No!'

'Ice cream. I mean, ice cream.'

She watched as the door buzzed open and he disappeared through it, sun beams jumping into his hair and lighting up the growing patches of skin between each follicle on the crown of his head. She covered a smirk with her hand. It would take him two lunch breaks to treat that hair-loss. But as long as he hadn't noticed, she wasn't going to tell him. Right, she had five minutes. Holding her towel she ran into the living room, tapped one of the many coloured squares on the glass-top coffee table. 'Fold away and close AbLab,' said the table as the running machine folded up into the wall. 'Good jahb!' the pink lycra woman gushed, then: 'How aboud a boody builder burn-out?'

'No thank you.' Right. Coffee. Clothes. She turned and walked to the kitchen – oh dear, what was that on the floor? One of them had an accident, probably… She got closer, her knees bending and her brow denting to make out… letters. She squatted, letting go of the towel, her finger tracing out a sentence…

Sheewun jinks iz in trubbal at chips hous.

CHAPTER 14

'I just can't believe I've never been here before.'

'Well, Quail, it's not the safest place in the world for you to be.'

'It has the best cakes, though.'

'I don't need you to tell me that.'

'And anyway, they wouldn't have let me come here if it was that bad.'

Reg rested his chin on his hand and gazed into his teacup.

'Would they?'

He pushed his chin forwards and scratched at it. 'Knowing my sibling as I do, Watty would have said to himself that you were better off staying here than running out into the wild with all the bears and tigers.'

'Don't be silly,' Isabel said through a mouthful of coffee and walnut. 'I wouldn't have run away.'

'You would have vented all that crossness somehow.'

'Not true!'

'I saw those flashy eyes.' He caught a brown crumb from her chin with the hollow of his fingernail before looking behind him at the door.

She saw him looking over his shoulder. 'Whose idea was it then, this place? Yours or Watty's?'

'Well. Watty wanted to sell cakes in the morning, then slouch in an armchair all afternoon, reading and writing. I thought that a launderette would be much less hassle than cake-baking.'

Isabel nodded. 'Fewer rules?'

'There is that. But also, a launderette can run itself; you don't have to be on the premises. "But I need things to write about, I need to see people!" Watty used to say. "I want them to come here because it's a nice place to write and draw and be lazy..." Every day I'd get shown a notebook page with drawings of cupcake mountains and menu plans... We eventually reached a compromise: a launderette/coffee shop with a few books thrown in.'

'And then Watty ran off with Drew!'

'And then Watty ran off with Drew, leaving me to make cakes and "see people"...' Reg twisted his shoulders around and looked at the door again.

'I'd like you to take me back tomorrow,' said Isabel.

'The cake can't be that good then.'

'You can't keep pretending to me that the shop's open. Don't you think I can see the closed sign through the blinds?'

'Oh; did I forget to turn it around?'

'No, you didn't.' She broke off another crumb. 'Your customers will go elsewhere.'

'Quail, honestly. You can stay as long as you like.'

'Thanks, Reg.' Then: 'I just wanted to have a think. Just for one night.'

'—'

'Why do you think that Drew kept me?'

'Honestly?'

'—'

'Because you were the only one that stayed alive. Even before Drew and Watty were together, Drew would come in here two or three times a week and talk about how awful it was to work in that lab.' Reg tilted his head in the direction of the lab.

'Discreetly of course. I didn't really know what was going on. It was Watty who became Drew's little confidant. Would dish out free cake and coffee, and wash Drew's lab coat. Didn't bother me. It took me a while to work out that they were smitten. But I've never been tuned into that kind of thing… "I'll never have children," Drew used to say, "not when I've killed so many. I don't deserve them." Killed him inside; he became obsessed with them.' Reg steepled his hands in front of him. 'I think you were very unexpected, Isabel; and Drew was in a position where a big decision had to be made quickly without entertaining the consequences. Knowing how much heartache Drew endured, precisely because none of these children would stay alive… You can understand why it was an easy decision to make.' He twirled a spoon in his empty coffee cup. 'Think about it, Quail, what would you have done?'

Isabel stared at Reg. 'Do you really want to know?'

'—.'

'I would have brought the baby, me, to term and then made it public.'

Reg wrinkled his brow. 'That would mean prison; and the baby, you, would have been taken away.'

'That would mean that I would be taking responsibility for my actions to give my baby, me, a normal life.'

Reg was quiet.

'Don't you think that would have been the right thing to do?'

He took a deep breath. 'Isabel, I can't even begin to understand what eighteen years of complete confinement can do to someone, but my knee-jerk reaction to what you've just said is that you shouldn't repeat it in front of your parents.'

'I don't know my parents.' Isabel looked at the table and flicked a crumb from just in front of her.

'Oh Quail!' Reg sat back in his chair.

'—.'

'Drew adores you. They both do.'

'I know,' she mumbled. 'I should never have said all of that… It's just that—'

Isabel ducked under the table and Reg spun around as they heard banging on the window.

Two men stood there, noses pressed up against the glass, white coats hanging from the crook of each elbow.

'We're closed!' called Reg, getting up and tugging at his collar, pulling the cord at the edge of the window so that the blinds gushed shut.

'I think they saw me,' said Isabel from under the table. 'What should we do?'

'No, no…' muttered Reg, eyes fixed on the window. 'They didn't.'

'They did!'

'Don't worry about it, Quail. Finish your cake.'

* * *

Susan arrived at a front door that seemed to be exactly the same as hers, maybe a bit dirtier. She put her hand out to knock, oh, it was already open. She knocked anyway. Hamish stood on the other side, his look changing from scowl to surprise. Afterwards, she thought to herself that she must have given him the same look. Reaching something down, indeed. Mrs Lucas must have been tipped off somehow… Maybe it was the skinny one, Chips, who had gone to her house while Jinx stayed with Blankey.

She stood on tiptoes to peer past Hamish's shoulder, about to open her mouth but he nodded her inside without saying a word. More important conversations were happening at the bottom of the stairs. A very large man sat on the last but one step. His head bent forward to show a bald patch, the collar of his grey tee-shirt was yellowy. He looked like he was talking to a man with a digital clipboard who squatted in front of him, until the yellow-collar man let out a loud sob. Susan twitched. The man slowly lifted his head, a sob trapped in his open mouth. He looked at her, a string of saliva hanging between his top and bottom teeth. One clear rivulet ran out of his nose. His eyelashes were clumped together from being wet and his cheeks were all shiny.

'That's the man who took Blankey,' was whispered into her ear. Susan looked at the whisperer; it was Hamish; he had his work-face on, but Susan noticed a slight nose-wrinkle as he looked around the room.

'Where is Blankey?'

Hamish flicked her a glance as if he hadn't heard what she'd said but then nodded towards the living room. Another man, a young man, dressed in black paced backwards and forwards in front of the living-room door, speaking into his wrist. 'Best get here straight away, really. What's that? I'm not sure how that would work, you're more likely to know than me. I mean, he seems…' He dropped his voice. 'He seems like… not a crack-pot but the proper expression. Mentally unstable, that's it. Well, she's not dead so it's your call whether or not you tell them to bring the police. Alright then.' He stepped out of the way to let Susan pass. 'What's that? Say that again…'

The room was empty except for one armchair that faced away from the living-room door and towards the window. Lumpy and patchy and blonde – camel-like. Susan could see one of Mrs Lucas's elbows sticking out from its side. 'It's Susan; I don't want to make you jump.'

The shadows around the chair changed as the occupant tried to turn to see Susan, but failed. The camel chair was too big. Susan walked around its edge. 'Hello. Oh goodness!'

'Hello, dear.'

'Is she alright?'

Mrs Lucas cradled Blankey. Her cheekbones jutted and purple stains underlined her eyes.

'She's very weak,' whispered the old lady. 'She's eaten a little bit. I'm just waiting for the doctor to come.'

Susan nodded. 'You must be *so* relieved.'

'I am.'

Susan glanced around her ankles. 'Apparently Jinx is here too, have you seen her?'

'No.' The old lady looked concerned. 'Are you sure she's here?'

Susan glanced behind her, then nodded.

'Oh dear, maybe she's still upstairs.' Mrs Lucas tried to get up.

'No, no… Don't get up. Stay with Blankey.'

A cry came from the hallway and Susan spun her head towards the door.

She looked back at Mrs Lucas; they raised their eyebrows at each other.

'They're trying to get him outside,' Mrs Lucas mouthed.

'Oh,' Susan mouthed back. 'Do you think I can go upstairs?'

The old lady looked towards the hallway then blinked at Susan.

Susan gave a firm nod. 'I'm going to see if I can go upstairs.'

'Alright.'

Four new faces had appeared in the hall, two of which looked like security guards. Hamish was trying to be heard above the man who roared and sobbed intermittently. 'Look, he's obviously not well; I really think we should call the psychiatric unit.'

'We'll call them once we get him into the van.'

'Yes, but, they would give him a sedative to calm him down.'

'We'll get him into the van, don't you worry about that. There's enough of us.'

'But he's *stressed*!'

The two guards continued to pull on the still-sobbing man's arms.

'No!' said Hamish. 'This is inhumane; I'm going to have to intervene. I'm calling the psychiatric unit.'

'Sir, we have the situation under control.'

But Hamish was already talking into his wrist.

'Sir, this man is a criminal,' smiled a tall woman with glasses. Susan eyed the black uniform and the strange remote control device she was shaking at Hamish. Perhaps it was the woman she'd seen in Mini-Me's. Difficult to be sure… 'The officer just told you the situation was under control. He's used to dealing with situations like this.'

'Hamish is a professional, too.' But no one seemed to hear Susan. Except for Hamish.

'It's alright, Susan. Leave it.' Hamish made his hand into an open beak and closed it gently, signalling her to be quiet.

Susan looked away before he could finish the gesture. Prick. He deserved to be told off by the glasses-lady. She hovered at the living-room door moving from one foot to the other, every so often looking behind her towards the old lady to avoid staring at all the pulling and crying. Mrs Lucas had leaned right around her chair to see if she'd managed to get upstairs; go on! She nodded towards Susan. Right, it was no good; she'd have to go up there. 'Erm, could I just…'

The doctor arrived at the door and Susan stepped aside so that he could go straight to Blankey. She bit her lip, oh dear, now she'd get caught up in having to listen to the doctor and be all concerned. She tried to catch Hamish's eye, but he stood staring at the guards as they pulled the man. He screwed up his lips, walked in a little circle, and stared again. Susan swallowed and went over to the stairs. 'Excuse me, could I just squeeze past, please?'

The security guards stopped trying to calm the man and looked at her. One of them blinked and shook his head as if what she'd asked had been so stupid that it hurt his eyes. 'Why?' asked the glasses-woman, eventually.

'Because there are two more littlers up there.'

The woman turned to the two men dressed in black jump suits. 'Did you pick up two others?'

They looked at each other and shook their heads; then the young one with the combat trousers spoke: 'But we was only scouting *her* chip. And that skinny one.' He pointed towards the living room. 'There might be others up there. We wouldn't know because we only put one set of chip data on the radar.'

'Well, could we please go and look?' said Susan. 'I'm pretty sure that there are two of them.'

* * *

'I don't know what I'd do if I didn't have you, do you know that?' Drew sat on the arm of the sofa and looked down at Watty who was tossing cashews into an opened mouth. Every other throw was missed entirely and he giggled to himself as his hand went delving for the tiny white moons between legs or under cardigan buttons.

'Oh, not this again…' Watty crunched, brushing his hands on his trousers before looping both arms around Drew's waist. He pulled the dressing-gowned bundle down to the sofa.

'What?'

'Another sad little moment.'

'But she was seen, Watty.'

'I know,' Watty sighed. 'I know.'

Drew picked at a frayed corner of the dressing-gown belt and looked over towards Jasper. 'He was your gift to me.'

Watty laughed a surprised laugh. 'Yes. Funny that over the years he's become Isabel's.'

'Watty?'

'Yes.'

'He's not anyone's. He's his own dog with his own personality.'

'Well, yes, but… Good heavens, you are emotional, aren't you?'

'We can't own him.'

'Well, no. Parents can't own their children, but they are responsible for them.'

'He's too old and dog-like to be a child.'

'He's a friend. We let him hang out with us and we give him food. He even sleeps in our bed.'

'He does not.'

Watty scoffed. 'He does.'

'I don't let him because you don't like that.'

'I hear him jump off the bed as soon as I open the front door.'

'I have to help him down now…'

'Ah… The accomplice.' Watty clicked his tongue at Jasper, who heaved the front of himself up from the floor and pricked up his ears. 'You know, Drew, you can only let someone be free if they actually want it. I don't think he'd go.'

Drew was quiet for a moment; then: 'Do you think Isabel would go?'

Watty's lips folded themselves inwards. 'Apart from anything else, she'd be too frightened.'

'I think she's been more of a pet than Jasper.'

'Don't be daft.'

'At least Jasper wants to be here.'

'Of course she wants to be here. But Isabel is an exceptional case, darling. You'd rather have her existing and protected than never born…'

'Yes, I would.'

'Well then.'

'I just think that…if anything happens to me…'

'Nothing is going to happen to you.'

'I know, I know. But just say that it all came out – then she wouldn't have to hide any more, would she?'

Watty frowned at the smartphone that lay at an angle to the coffee table's edge. One silly moment, one little guilt-haemorrhage and the house would be full of press and, and scientists and Isabel would be international news. 'Come on, face-ache,' said Watty. 'It's a lovely day and you're ruining it. Let's go for a picnic.'

'I don't really feel like it.'

'Well, Isabel, Jasper and I think that we are overdue a family outing. Let's set up down by the stream where the cows are.'

Drew's eyebrows arched. 'Are there cows down there?'

'There are.'

'She'd love that.'

'She was the one who sniffed them out while we were blackberrying.'

'—'

'Drew, it's been at least three days. Stop worrying. Did you really expect to get through the whole of Isabel's life without any near misses?'

Drew's eyes closed as the words looped themselves out of one ear and back into the other. The whole of Isabel's life. The whole of Isabel's life. Isabel was eighteen. She had at least another sixty years of her life to get through; would they all be lived out inside this house? That was only an existence, that wasn't a life. And then what would she do when they were both… Well… And Jasper? Drew's eyes opened and rested on Jasper's white whiskers. She'd be all alone.

Watty prodded Drew in the hip. 'Get up, then. My stomach needs quiche.'

'That's a good idea, is there any left?' Drew mumbled.

'I hope so! Mmm… And cottage cheese with some of that blackberry jam.'

'You mean the soup?'

'No. I mean the jam.'

'If it were anything nameable it would be soup.'

'Coulis. That's my final offer.'

'Ha! A fruit sauce!'

'It's delicious and you're jealous.' Watty leaned forward on the sofa and strained as Drew almost fell from his lap. 'Time to move. Quail!' he called. 'We're going for a picnic!'

* * *

The man and the glasses-woman looked towards the stairwell, then pushed past the wrestling bundle in front of the stairs and jogged up. Susan followed close behind, rounding the landing and following the flaps of a black coat as they disappeared into a room on the left. Susan stopped in the doorway to see one bottom sticking out from under the bed. The woman with the glasses gazed down at it with her hands on her hips.

'Come on, my lovely,' strained the bottom.

'Is she under there?' Susan strode over to the bed and crouched down beside it. 'She's scared! Jinx, Jinx, it's me, sweetie.' Two other little hands grabbed hold of her ankle just as the bottom was backing out. 'I've got her! Oh, and Bonbon, have you been here all this time?' She sat back on her heels with the two littlers sitting on her forearm, watching the bottom. Jinx reached towards it.

The head that belonged to the bottom emerged, then an arm, then a hand. Inside the hand flopped a little being with skin so grey he was almost transparent and contrasted horribly with whatever that brown crusty stuff was on the tips of his fingers and toes. Purple smudged across his under-eye and sooty shadows had painted themselves from his ears to his nose. 'This one doesn't look so good,' said the man.

Jinx fought in Susan's grasp. Susan helped her onto the floor.

The woman with the glasses bleeped a gun-shaped object over Chips, then appeared to read the screen that she held in her other hand. 'He belongs to this address,' she said. 'I'll take him down to the doctor; he'll probably have to come back to the centre with the other one.'

'What other one?' said Susan, tightening her grip on Bonbon and plucking Jinx back up from the floor.

'Mrs Lucas's.' The woman scrolled down her screen with her finger.

'Blankey?'

'Yes.' She looked at Susan before turning to her colleague. 'Apparently he was a gift from the gentleman's daughter, after he lost his wife.'

'Ah. Companionship,' the man mumbled, upright on his knees, holding Chips in front of his eyes and turning him this way and that. 'There's a surprise.'

The woman's mouth travelled around to her left cheek. Susan guessed that this was a smile. She caught Susan watching her and fanned half of her mouth out towards the right cheek.

'But why would you want to take Blankey?' Again, Jinx managed to scramble down Susan's leg and was re-plucked from the floor. This time Susan stood up.

'To check for psychological damage,' she gushed.

'Tilda!' the man yelled from below.

The woman winced, then resumed her smile.

'In that case, I'll drive Mrs Lucas so that she can stay with her.'

'You can't do that.' The woman turned towards the door. 'But she'll have her back within the week.' Susan stood in front of her.

'But that poor lady has been so panicked these last few days. She's very elderly.'

'Yes, but I have to do what's best for the littler. This kind of thing is detailed in the contract Mrs Lucas signed when she purchased her.' The woman lifted her shoulders and sighed them back down again with a smile.

'But what if she doesn't come back?'

'What makes you think that she won't?'

'Because she might *communicate* something that she shouldn't.' The words came out before Susan could stop them.

The woman looked across at her colleague before slitting her eyes at Susan. He stood swaying slightly, as he filled out some sort of report on his tablet. Chips's face stuck out of a tiny, hooded sleeping bag that nestled in a pouch attached to his chest. The man stopped typing to raise one eyebrow at the glasses-woman. 'Right,' she said. Her gaze flicked to Bonbon and Jinx. 'Batch Twenty are they?'

'Erm…' Susan panicked. 'I don't know.'

The woman took out her gun-thing again and flashed it at the two littlers who then stood squinting their eyes and shaking their heads. She flipped the cover back from her screen and read it again. 'Well, for your information, they are Batch Twenty.' She flicked the screen off and looked straight at Susan. 'How did you know that these two were hidden upstairs?' Her question sing-songed upwards.

Susan took a deep breath and made herself taller. 'My husband told me Blankey had been found upstairs,' she lied.

The woman flipped back the cover on her screen again and verified something before saying: 'But you're not actually married.'

Susan baulked. 'You are on *such* a power trip.'

'Not at all. I just don't get why you'd call him your "husband" when he's not.'

'Am I allowed to ask *you* about your husband or wife?'

'I'm not discussing that with you…'

'Because I certainly feel *extremely* bloody sorry for them.'

'Language,' mumbled the woman's colleague, still typing.

'I'm sorry, I just don't see why you have to take Blankey away.'

'And Chips,' said the woman, glancing at Jinx then back at Susan. 'We'll most certainly have to take Chips away… And the chances are he *won't* be coming back.'

Bonbon realized what was going on and held on to one of Jinx's hands tightly. Wet streaks shined their way down to Jinx's mouth, which had turned into an upside-down kidney shape. That other she-one, with those silly circles on her face, was trying to make Jinx clap, how silly. Jinx had only been clapping for one evening out of her entire life; she wouldn't know how to do it just like that… She'd probably try to shout something or wave her arms about. Or even dance. But she wouldn't clap her hands…

'Right, well…' Susan huffed. 'All of this is just…' Then stood nodding and dancing her eyes.

The woman looked Jinx and Bonbon up and down for another couple of seconds before turning and leaving. 'I think they've got him into the van,' she called to her colleague from the bannisters then walked back and stood in the doorway.

'I'm going down to the doctor.' He looked at Jinx and pointed at her with his pen. 'Do you think she'll need a session too?'

The glasses-woman shook her head. 'She's in good hands; we'll check on her in a week or so. Just bring the boy.'

The man strode towards the door. Jinx wriggled and scratched but Susan held on to her. The woman turned from the bannisters and followed the man to the top of the stairs.

'No!' shouted Jinx, in a voice so high and so well aimed into Susan's ear that she jammed a finger into it, trying to loosen and pierce the bubble that formed over her hearing. When she looked up, the two technicians stood in front of her, staring at Jinx.

The woman looked startled for a moment before resettling her eyebrows and letting her mouth say: 'I'm afraid that…'

Susan rubbed at her deaf ear. 'What?' She turned her head the other way to try to listen with the other ear.

'We're going to have to take her away.'

A vision filled up Bonbon's head; a table made of something that smelled like it felt, old and strong, was covered in big squares of paper like the one she'd found in Blankey's garden. It all made her feel as if as if this had already happened, as if she'd worried about being separated from Jinx before… Suddenly, she wanted to cry. The hand that belonged to these eyes inside her head, the eyes that looked at the table, wielded a thing that had made all those funny markings; the exact thing that she'd been looking for earlier in the kitchen. Panic grew out from her like two enormous wings that protruded from her back and dragged over her shoulders so heavily that she thought she would never get up again. They were going to take Jinx away… They were going to take her away. Bonbon sat forward in Susan's arms. No way were they going to take her. No way were they going to separate her from her Jinx. She raised her hands and smacked them together twice.

'I'm sorry?' said the woman.

Clap-clap!

'Do you want me to take Jinx away?'

Clap-clap!

'Do you want to come too?'

Clap!

The woman looked at Susan who watched silently, still squeezing her ear.

'We'll have them back to you within the week,' she said.

* * *

The long grass buzzed and tickled; feet stuck out into it from a spotty blanket island that Watty had tried to cover in a feast-like spread, but quickly realized there wasn't enough room for all of them and the picnic. 'I can't believe you brought a vase of geraniums,' laughed Isabel. They ate quiche and drank cider and Jasper took turns between trotting after cows and sleeping. Watty almost ate a wasp that decided to drink his blackberry jam. 'He was eating it; you can't drink jam.' Afterwards, they paddled in the stream, seeing who could throw the furthest and trying to catch fish with their hands. Isabel was the only one to catch one. A minnow that looked more like a salmon writhing between her fingers. They got home as it was getting dark, lugging clanking bottles and cutlery, Watty and Drew with crowns of dandelions and daisy bracelets, Isabel with one huge dandelion upturned on her head. They unpacked the remains of the picnic and decided to have a glass of single malt in the garden where they watched the sunset with next door's cat who made herself a den between Jasper's front paws. 'This is nice,' whispered Isabel, wrapped in a tea-towel. 'We should do it again tomorrow.'

That night, Drew dreamed of those words as dogs and gunmen stormed the house, dragging them from their beds and throwing them into the stream, which grew into a river, the cows watching and wading into its depths before turning into hippos that jostled for a piece of human or dog. Only Isabel continued to sleep in her bed; so small that nobody had found her. She would wake up alone, thought Drew.

A smartphone blinked away to itself on the coffee table, a little telephone symbol glowing in the bottom left-hand corner.

* * *

They'd arranged to meet here. How weird to be here looking for her and knowing for sure that he was going to see her because she'd agreed to come here.

He'd have to hurry up, though, poor little Suzie. He'd left her lying on the sofa with her eyes sometimes closed, sometimes staring towards the floor. 'I'm so angry, Hamish!' she kept saying. 'Why do the people always get beaten? It's not even the government or, or a dictator or something… It's these companies that have become so big and so powerful that they behave as if they're the law.' She'd looked up at Hamish who was stroking her hair. 'Did you hear the way that woman spoke to you?'

'I'm not a psychiatric nurse, Suzie…'

'Yes, but even so, you knew that the man needed professional help because of… because of what you do.'

'I knew that he needed professional help because I am human, Suzie. Didn't you think the same thing?'

Susan looked at her thumb and chewed on its nail for a moment while she thought about this. 'I wasn't really thinking about the man, I just wanted to get upstairs.'

Hamish nodded. 'I have to go,' he said, shifting position so that he was more ready to stand up.

'Really?'

He nodded again.

'Did you call Mrs Lucas's daughter?'

He nodded a third time, not wanting to open his mouth and set off another round of questions. Clock hands ticked in his ears; he was going to be late.

'Is she coming?'

He kissed her on the head and stood up, answering as his head got further away from hers. 'She's at the hospital with Mrs Lucas's husband; apparently he's decided to opt for the euthanasia.' He put his hands in his pockets and looked down at her. 'She'll be along afterwards.'

'Oh no… No, that's awful… Does Mrs Lucas know?'

A nod.

'She must be in the depths of despair… Do you think that—'

Hamish interrupted her by bending forward and stroking her cheek. 'I'm going to be late, darling. But I promise we'll talk about this later. If I were you I'd go round there… Take the ice cream.' He called the last bit from the hall as he pulled on his shoes.

Susan repeated the word 'darling' in her head as she got to her feet. That had sounded weird coming from his mouth. He could be so gentle when she was upset. Her feet found their slippers and she ran into the hall just as keys were jangled then silenced by a pocket. He was going to work. Such a hard worker, and then he'd go to Shepherd's and fill his basket with things that would make her happy, so that they could spend the evening together, munching all kinds of goodies. Together. Together was good. What would she do if anyone took him away from her? She grabbed his arm as the front door opened, stood on tiptoes and kissed him under his jaw. He kissed an eyebrow and dashed off. She watched for a minute to see if he would turn around.

He didn't.

He was in a hurry.

There was no meeting in his office. The meeting was at Shepherd's.

Now, as he drove slowly past all the parked cars, looking out for hers, he remembered that he shouldn't know what kind of car she drove, bugger! He sped up a little, searching for a parking space instead of her parked car. From the edge of his eye, he saw a fox tail bobbing out of an old white hatchback. His fingers drummed the steering wheel once, heavily, shaking out whatever it was that had started to pump around his body, making it all rigid and wanting to run as soon as he had seen her hair. 'Park,' he said aloud. Maybe that's why Spanish dancers had castanets, or, or clapped their hands, so they could constantly let out a bit of that chemical that made fingers go all rigid. The car obeyed and as it reversed, she walked past, upright, her tiered skirt skipping about in the wind like a child around its mother's sensible legs. He tapped the steering wheel again before smirking at himself and opening the side door. Mustn't say 'Spanish dancer', he thought as he got out of the car. Flamenco dancer. A dancing style could not use nationality to define itself. He locked the car and followed her. Sometimes nationality couldn't even use nationality to define itself. His feet and hands felt strange as this chemical reached his extremities and couldn't go any further, so it swirled in little circles. He held his hands out to the sides and shook them; then cupped them over his mouth and blew. This was ridiculous, why was he following her? He gulped a mouthful of air then spluttered, 'Emma?' He tried again. 'Emma!'

She turned around.

He was sure that if he moved, he would fall over. Why was it all so different to seeing her in his office? She looked to the right then walked towards him.

'Because every time you come here you fantasize about what would happen if you saw her,' said his own voice inside his head. 'What you would say if you saw her, what you would be doing when she saw you. You would be saving a child from getting run over or helping an old lady load up her car... You have conversations in your head with her during which you make witty comments that have taken you ages to plan. She laughs so much that you rewind the conversation and say the comment all over again. She finds you attractive. She doesn't say anything when you grab her hand and run with her to your car. She finds you noble. She looks at you respectfully, *yearningly*, when you tell her that you can't... That it wouldn't be professional. She kisses you and you enjoy it, until you tell her that you can't see each other again, that this has gone too far; that she must take her own personal development more seriously if she wants to help herself. Then you ask her to get out of the car and you leave and you hope that she will book another session, and in your fantasy she does...'

She was in front of him.

'That's what's so different about here,' said his own voice inside his head, before flicking through every single sordid image that he'd ever dreamed up about her.

'Hi,' she said.

'Hello.'

'What's wrong, why are you standing there like that?'

He couldn't move, he'd wanted to say. Instead he said: 'It didn't go too well. I was… I was just working out how I would tell you that it didn't go too well.'

'You didn't do it?'

'Yes! No, I did do it.'

She nodded, folding her lips between her teeth before looking around her.

He followed her state. 'We can't talk here.' Taking his keys from his pocket and turning away he said, 'I'm parked just over there.'

She followed.

* * *

Drew stumbled out of the bedroom, found the phone and swiped the alarm off. The blue missed-call box flashed up on the screen with a number that hadn't been saved to contacts. Drew looked at it twice then blinked and looked again. Yep, it was him; he'd called three times and left two messages. Drew dialled his message inbox and listened.

'First new message. Message received yesterday at seven fourteen p.m.'

'Hi, Mark Hector here, um, Drew, I can't stop thinking about our conversation the other day and, well, it ended rather abruptly. Perhaps you wouldn't mind giving me a call back so that we can talk about this. I'm at home now, so… I'll be in all evening.'

'To return the call press three. Second new message.' There was a knock at the front door. 'Message received yesterday at nine seventeen p.m.' Drew made his way into the kitchen as the second new message played.

'Look, I really am a man who gets a bee in his bonnet. I would have liked to talk to you this evening but it's getting a bit late now.' Drew grasped the door handle and pushed it down. 'I really feel like I owe you an apology. No need to call me back tonight, I'll try again tomorrow. Or maybe I could come to the house? Well, anyway… We'll talk tomorrow. Bye!' Drew hung up and pulled the door open.

'Hello, Drew.'

Hector stood in the doorway. His lips looked weird, swelling across his face as if they'd been pinned to his nose and chin. His forehead stretched open those same piranha-teeth eyes that Drew had looked into every day for the best part of ten years.

'Gosh… What are you doing here?' Drew managed, puffing out his face with a twitchy smile.

'These are for you.' Mark Hector held a pot of roses into the space that separated him from Drew. 'Won't you take them?'

'It's really unnecessary… I… It's been ages!' Drew glanced past the doctor to the end of the drive. A navy blue car waited.

Mark Hector followed Drew's glance. 'I'm alone. Won't you invite me in?'

Drew stepped outside, pulling the door so it was almost closed. 'Of course, but… Is something wrong?'

'Are you really wondering what I'm doing here?'

'Actually…'

'Because, with the best will in the world, I don't think you are.'

Drew snorted his eyebrows upwards.

'You know my motivations, don't you? If I could realize my lifelong dream, then coming to someone's house with roses wouldn't seem crazy at all, would it?'

'I really don't know what you're talking about.'

Mark Hector observed the gestures of this pyjama'd being; the way he tightened the cord on his dressing gown; folded his arms across his chest; scratched the end of his nose.

'Just answer me one question and I'll leave you in peace.' He pointed one finger to the sky. 'And it may be hypothetical.'

'Right.'

'Do you know how much trouble someone could get into for growing their own baby?'

Drew cocked his ear. 'I'm sorry?'

'I'd just like to meet her, that's all.'

'Who?'

'Come on, Drew… What if she's ill? She has no birth certificate, she's not registered in any of the schools around here…'

'Who?'

'She has no passport.'

'Okay, I think you should go home now.'

'She has no passport.'

'Because she doesn't exist.'

The doctor looked at his shoes and rubbed his cheeks with both hands, stretching his lips inside out. The pink flap that joined his teeth to his gums leered taut and shadowy. 'She was seen, Drew.' Then: 'Don't you think I can't tell when someone's lying to me? Do you know how red you've gone? Have you seen your pupils?'

Drew swallowed. 'I'd like to be able to help you but this is making me feel uncomfortable.'

'I'm not going to give up on this. You're lucky that this time I've come alone. If I'd have pressed charges for theft…'

'Theft?'

'Of an embryo.'

'You have no proof!'

'It doesn't matter. I could have been much more underhand than I'm being now.'

'So this is nice harassment, is it?'

'It is this time, yes!'

'Are you threatening me?'

'Call the police.' He shrugged his shoulders and bared the gum-flap again. 'Call the police and let's see which one of us gets taken away. Because if it's you, you'll be gone for years and years and years. Wouldn't you prefer that we work something out between us?'

'Yes, he would!' a voice came from just inside the door frame.

Drew's gaze flicked to the bottom corner of the barely open door. 'Isabel, no!' Drew hissed.

'I don't want you to be taken away…'

Drew pulled the door to close it. Mark Hector slid his foot forward, wincing as the door slammed hard against it. He elbowed it open into the kitchen, eyes falling on another man tying up his dressing gown as he strode towards the scene.

Mark Hector dropped his gaze. His mouth gaped. His body crumpled to its knees. 'I don't believe it,' he whispered.

Isabel peeped up at him between fuzzy strands of mousy curls, her arms wrapped around Drew's ankle. As she spoke, the doctor sank lower until his elbows were resting on the parquet. 'Please don't take Drew away,' she said as Watty crept up behind her and scooped her into the crook of his arm.

'Don't worry, Quail,' he whispered.

'Who are you, anyway?' From Watty's arm Isabel scowled down at the greying man in his pin-striped suit.

'Ha!' exploded the doctor. 'It's perfect, it really is just… And intelligent! Drew, it's simply a… How did you…' His voice closed up as his brain concentrated on what it was seeing. He felt his knees carry him forward to get a closer look. 'How did you…' She inched away as his hand floated down towards her. He caught it in time and shook out the fingers as if trying to get rid of whatever had made them do that. 'I'm sorry,' he said.

'Hello,' said Drew at the same time. All three faces looked up. Drew stood with a mobile to his ear. 'Yes, police please.'

'Drew, hang on…' Dr Hector rose onto his knees. 'What are you doing?'

He pushed his free ear closed with a fingertip and turned away. 'Yes, hello? I'm frightened for the safety of my daughter.'

Watty closed his eyes and covered them with his free hand.

Mark Hector pulled himself back onto his feet. 'Don't do that, Drew. I'll just go.'

Drew squinted as a faraway telephone voice demanded his attention.

'What, and that's it?' he replied.

Dr Hector shrugged. 'We've got each other by the balls.'

The telephone voice persisted. 'It's okay, erm… We've found her,' Drew said before hanging up the phone. 'You're frightened of being investigated.'

'No… I'm frightened of losing this opportunity, completely.' He let his eyes rest on Isabel. 'Do you know how many years I've spent trying to make a being like you?'

Isabel pulled herself into Watty as the doctor's gaze landed on and took off from different parts of her body. He blinked and reached into his inside pocket.

'If you'd ever be interested in helping me…'

'No. I don't think so.' Drew strode towards him.

The doctor held his palms in the air.

'Why not?' Isabel snapped and they all looked towards her. 'Do you mean that I could work for you?'

Dr Hector's face opened up. 'Yes, yes! I mean, we could certainly come to some sort of arrangement.'

'Isabel—' Drew started.

'And would I see other scientists?'

'Ab-absolutely,' he stuttered. 'Although only a select few.'

'Give me your card,' she said, ignoring Drew's scowl. 'I'll think about it.'

CHAPTER 15

Bonbon watched Jinx as she looked through the bars on the little cage they'd been put in. 'How did you do that?' she said.

Jinx looked at her. 'What?'

'How did you say "no" like that?'

Jinx shrugged and craned her neck again towards the opened door of the van. 'He's going to be alright, Jinx.'

Jinx's mouth wobbled.

'We'll see him soon.'

Her head flicked back around so she could look straight at Bonbon. 'Do you really think so?'

Bonbon pulled herself closer to Jinx and put her arms around her. 'I think they're just going to make him better. That's a good thing, isn't it?'

Jinx thought about this for a long time before she said: 'It *is* a good thing. I don't think he was very well at all.' She sat fiddling with her toes for a few minutes, still thinking about Chips getting better, then asked: 'Where do you think we're going, Bonbon?'

Bonbon shivered, then thought how awful it would have been if Jinx had gone to wherever they were going all on her own. 'Let's not think about that until we get there.'

* * *

Isabel perched on the edge of the worktop with a cake-mixture-smeared ramekin on her lap. Watty vibrated next to her, gritting his teeth as he whisked buttercream and peered over his glasses at the recipe in his notebook. She'd been dragging her finger around the ramekin and plunging it into her mouth, gazing down at Jasper as she sucked on her tongue, and ignoring Watty. 'I've definitely given you too much cake mixture,' he panted. You probably shouldn't eat it all.' Drew had shuffled in from the study and told them over his glasses that he'd probably be looking at ten years if he turned himself in.

'But ten years is for cloning! You didn't clone me.'

'No. I didn't. But my toes were in cloning territory when I modified your nucleus. We had very serious regulations to abide by. All the modified embryos were intended to be destroyed and I took one home and grew it into a baby. They'd see it as… as growing a mutant. Sorry, Quail. But that's why these regulations are in place, to prevent that kind of thing. They may even have been more lenient with me if I'd have replanted you into a real uterus, but the fact that you were grown in a fake womb has added to the, um, Frankensteinesque quality in all of this.'

Isabel stared into the ramekin and thought for a moment. 'He'll keep quiet, won't he?'

Drew took his glasses off. 'It's not him I'm worried about, Quail.'

'What *are* you worried about?'

'Ten years isn't that long, you know.'

They jumped as Watty slammed the bowl down on the table and turned to face Drew, communicating a warning look that brimmed with words of past conversations. If Drew were to do this, two years would be reasonable; five would be the absolute cut-off point, but ten? Watty stared for a moment, then let his face go blank. 'This is separating,' he said. 'I'm going to take it outside.' And he went.

'Why did Watty go?'

'Quail, you know what he's like about his buttercream.'

'I'm not ten years old any more.'

Drew looked at his socks.

'It doesn't matter; even if I didn't have to take Watty's feelings into consideration, there's no way I'd let you go to prison.'

Drew smiled. 'Don't let's decide anything now…'

'What's to think about?'

'Isabel; ten years of being a prisoner, compared to a whole lifetime, is really no big deal. Think of everything you could do! You could go to vet school, you could make friends…

'—.'

'And you'd become more independent, you know? Watty and I aren't going to be around forever…'

'Stop!' Isabel interrupted. 'You're not going anywhere. And that's final.' She put the ramekin next to her and lined her feet up over Jasper's back. 'I don't think Jas can take me jumping on him any more. Get me down, please, so I can stomp off.'

* * *

A clattering noise woke Bonbon. She sat up and rubbed her eyes, feeling her whole body rise and fall in time to clicking footsteps striking the ground. She looked at Jinx who was still sleeping next to her. The footsteps stopped and they were put on the ground.

'Hey, Carol,' said a she-one's voice.

'Hello, Rosy,' said a different voice that she recognized.

'Got another one?'

'Another *two*.'

'Communication?'

'Yes.'

'Got their records?'

'It's all in there.'

'Thanks. Do you need it back tonight or are you clocking off now?'

'You can keep it until the morning, I don't need it.'

'Great. Take them down to Waiting, Len'll come an' see to them after his break.'

'Buzz me in?'

'Yep.'

Bonbon felt the cage swinging again and watched through the bars as the ground disappeared.

'Thanks.'

'See you.'

They stood swinging in front of what looked like a wall. There was a loud buzz, the wall split in two and they walked right through it. Bonbon felt the cage being lifted higher before it was set down again onto a surface. The clicky footsteps walked away, the zjwooom noise of the door closed them outside and there was silence. Bonbon looked down at Jinx; should she wake her up? No, no… Better let her sleep through this.

Bonbon hugged her knees with shaky hands. Her eyes rested on a stripe in the wall that was probably the edge of a door, although she couldn't see the other edge because the wall of the cage blocked it out. She thought about moving right up close to the bars to get a better look but her arms would not stop hugging her knees. Oh, please wake up, Jinx; please wake up.

After a while, the stripe in the wall opened up in the same way that the first door had. She had been right. A shadow slid across the wall then fell away when there was no more wall to slide on, as if it were crawling across the floor and transforming itself into the head that now appeared at the bars of the cage. Bonbon tried to squeal but instead only felt herself breathe in quickly. The head was completely white apart from a black glass window that covered the eyes, and grey lines, like the bars of her own cage, which criss-crossed over the mouth.

'Hmmm,' said the mouth through the criss-crossed lines. 'You're a bit frightened, aren't you?'

Bonbon jammed her eyes shut.

'Well, at least you've got your friend with you. Most littlers come here alone.'

Bonbon thought that this was very true; if she'd had to come alone, after everything that had happened at the doctor's, she would be dying by now, she was *sure.* She opened her eyes. The head was still there, waiting for her to… to do *something.* 'That's better,' it said, then seemed to go off to a different part of the room. It had only wanted her to open her eyes, phew… She heard things making clanking noises as they were picked up and put down again and banged against each other before the head reappeared, just as suddenly as the first time.

'Right,' it said. 'There are two ways of testing what I'd like to test now. I need you to demonstrate your level of communication. You can forget everything your owner told you about not communicating in public because none of that matters any more. Do you understand?'

Bonbon looked at the floor.

'You see, that's the part where you tell me if you've understood or not, and this is the first way of testing you. The second way is rather nasty, I'm afraid.'

Her eyes snapped upwards. The cage door opened and a white hand came inside holding a tube thing that looked like the tube Jinx had used to carry flakes in. The hand held the tube over the sole of Jinx's sleeping foot, put its thumb over the end and pressed down. The thing clicked and Jinx woke up, her mouth trying to scream but nothing coming out, she scrambled to the back far corner of the cage and squashed herself into it, holding her foot and rubbing at it. Bonbon looked at the thing. It glistened with little sharp points that had jumped out of it when the hand had pressed the button. One of her feet crossed itself over the other one, protectively.

'I'm sorry, I really don't like doing that, it's just I need to leave in half an hour and it's much quicker this way…'

Bonbon looked over at Jinx who sat in the corner shaking. She turned back to the head, her lips wobbling.

'I really am sorry.'

'—.'

'It won't do her any harm, I promise.' The head tilted so it could see towards the back of the cage. 'It won't do you any harm,' it said again. 'Trembling lips; interesting. Can you cry in front of your owner?'

Bonbon stared.

The head stared back, then repeated: 'Can you *cry* in front of your *owner*?'

Bonbon didn't know what 'owner' meant but she knew he wanted her to clap. She clapped twice. The only person she could really cry in front of was Jinx.

'We have established communication. Thank you.' The man appeared to be tapping at something that was too far below the cage for Bonbon to see. 'Let us communicate with one clap for "yes" and two for "no". Is that the system that you are used to? If it is, clap once now.'

Bonbon clapped.

'And you, erm…' He looked down at the thing he was tapping then looked back. 'Jinx?'

Jinx's eyes rolled upwards, in one glistening movement like wet snails falling over. Her mouth closed so she could swallow, then opened again and hung like that until he had to re-ask his question. Nothing. With her legs curled round to one side, she rubbed her foot slowly and stared.

'Can she communicate?' he asked Bonbon.

Bonbon held both hands in the air to clap, then hesitated.

'*Can* she?'

Again, she hesitated.

The mask sighed and up came the hand with the horrid pricky thing. Both of them jumped; Bonbon flung herself to the back of the cage over Jinx, clapping her hands together, clap, clap, clap, clap, as the thing came towards them.

'Is that a "yes" or a "no"?' he asked, retracting the pricky thing.

Two claps.

'Now listen; there is a reason why you are *both* here.' The body seemed to slide backwards and then stand up so that all they could see was a stomach. 'I'm going to leave the room for a moment so that you can talk about that reason; when I come back I will ask you the question again.'

They watched as the stomach turned and left the room, the door swooshing open and then shut again. Bonbon hummed in her throat to check her voice. It worked; he had gone.

'Jinx, listen; you have to clap.'

'Where are we? What was that horrible thing?' Jinx's voice was all shaky, her eyes fixed on the cage door.

'Jinx, look at me! Look at me, Jinx?'

Jinx's eyes turned towards Bonbon.

'You have to clap, Jinx. If you clap then he won't hurt you with that thing.'

'But we're not supposed to clap…' She looked away again.

'We're not supposed to clap because otherwise we'll get taken away. We've *been* taken away, Jinx. That's *why* we're here!'

'But that means if I *don't* clap, I might get to go home.'

Bonbon stared at Jinx. 'No, Jinx. They already heard you *speak*…'

'I don't want to clap, Bonbon.'

'But *I* have. I've clapped! Even if they *did* send you home, they'd keep me.'

Jinx's eyes snapped back. 'No, they won't, Bonbon. Don't say that.'

'Yes, they would! And they'll poke you with that thing again and again…'

'If they let me go, I can come back and save you.'

Achy clouds formed behind Bonbon's eyes. She scrunched them shut and thought of the moment in Chips's he-one's house when Jinx had cried out and Bonbon had clapped just to be with her.

'Bonbon?' Jinx put one of her hands over Bonbon's.

Bonbon looked up. 'Yes?'

'I'm not going to…' but her voice disappeared inside her throat.

The door swooshed open again and the head appeared at the cage. 'Have you had time to talk?'

Bonbon looked at Jinx, then back at the head. She clapped once.

'Good. Jinx, I'm going to ask you again. Can you communicate?'

Jinx stared back at the head and pressed her lips together.

'Jinx?'

Jinx's arms wove around her knees.

A hand appeared next to the head with the pricky thing again. Jinx watched as it approached her shin. 'I'm sorry. I just need you to co-operate, Jinx.' He pressed the thing and it struck her leg with a click. She tipped backwards then onto her side, cradling her leg to her chest.

The head sighed loudly again through its metal mesh as it looked back down towards the thing it was tapping. A buzzing sound could be heard. Then another voice.

'Hey, Len.'

'Hi, Jeff,' said the head. 'I was wondering, I've got a bit of a case down here; has stubbornness been a characteristic of any Batch Twentys so far?'

'It's not a characteristic of Batch Twenty, Len.'

The head sighed again. 'I *know* that, but have you had any cases reported of refusal to communicate?'

'A few. Yes.'

'Even after the pins?'

'It's rare but it *does* happen. You got a non-co-operator there?'

'I'm not sure if I have or if she genuinely cannot communicate.'

'I'd be wary...'

'Thing is, she was brought in with another. They live together.'

'Really? That's unusual.'

'Yeah... So I just wanted to know, am I allowed to strike the other one to get her to talk?'

'Um... I'm gonna look that up for you, Len. I'm pretty sure it's not allowed, though. Hang on a second.'

Len's white head turned back to the cage as muttering and tapping could be heard at the end of the line. Bonbon could just make out a nice smile through the grey criss-crosses. It made her heart slow down a little, for some reason... Why was he wearing such scary clothes? She was sure that everything would be nicer if she could see his face properly. He looked at his own hands as he twizzled the horrid pricky thing around and around in his fingers.

'Nope, Len. Not allowed.'

Len nodded once. 'Can't inflict pain upon a co-operating party, right?'

'You got it.'

'Does that mean I can't separate them?'

'Um... It says nothing about emotional pain so, yes; you can.'

'Right.'

'I'll leave that up to you.'

'Right. Thanks, Jeff.'

There was a click and the conversation ended.

'I have to leave soon. Jinx, I'm gonna see you tomorrow, and I *really* need you to co-operate, okay?'

Jinx said nothing. She was now sitting upright and had both her arms tight around Bonbon. There was no way that nasty white head wouldn't separate them.

The head seemed to contemplate them, then it looked to the left and thought for a moment. 'Bonbon?' it said finally, looking back.

Bonbon clapped once immediately.

'I won't separate you this evening. However, you have to talk some sense into her, okay?'

Bonbon held her hands up but didn't clap. Yes, she'd understood but, no, it probably wasn't going to be okay.

'And Jinx? If you want to stay in the same cage as Bonbon, you really have to step it up. Don't think for one minute that we'll let you go home if you don't show any signs of communication.' He snapped off his gloves in time to 'signs' and 'communication'. 'Hasn't happened to *anyone* so far; usually, once you're here, it's for keeps, I'm afraid.' He got up from his chair, picked up the thing he'd been tapping and bleeped it against the wall.

'Good job, Len Eight!' said the wall. 'See you at eight thirty-seven tomorrow in room R.'

'Room R,' Len repeated to himself. 'Bye, you two.' He fanned his fingers at them then left through the swooshy door.

Jinx's cuddle relaxed and she let her head flop onto Bonbon's shoulder. Bonbon opened her mouth to speak but another swoosh followed by footsteps interrupted her. She felt Jinx's head lifting from her shoulder just as the cage was swung up into the air, turned and travelled to an opening in the wall. Once inside, they were set down again on the floor. 'Going down,' said a voice as the whole room seemed to move.

'They said they'd let me know in a week; do you think they'll give her back to me?'

Susan bit her lip and looked towards the window. It seemed like now was a good time to put her arm around the old lady's shoulders. 'I'm really not sure,' she said. 'They said the same thing to me.'

'But that would be…' Mrs Lucas's eyes darted around the room, searching for what 'that' would be. 'Monstrous!' she said eventually. 'After calling them out to find her they'd just take her away again?'

She clapped her hands together underneath her chin, shaking her head so slightly it was as if it were trembling.

'I'm going to call them every day; don't you worry. I've already had the president of the LOG on the phone…'

Mrs Lucas's eyes flicked up. 'Really? And what did she say?'

'She's noted everything that happened. She said that they were perfectly entitled to take Chips away… And as far as their "communication rule" goes, they were "entitled" to take Bonbon and Jinx away.' Susan winced at herself for curling her fingers into quotation marks. 'But, anyway… Where was I? Oh yes! As long as Blankey hasn't shown any signs of communication they can't simply take her away because you are elderly. Not just like that, anyway.'

'So… There's some hope then?' Mrs Lucas held her own cheeks with the fingertips of each hand.

'I'll call them every day, twice a day, to see how things are progressing.' Susan held crossed fingers up to her face and gave them a little shake. Then winced at herself for that too. 'When is your daughter getting here?'

'Anytime now.' The old lady looked up the driveway to where her daughter's car would surely appear. 'She's only coming from the hospital… Do you know about Jerry?'

Susan scrunched her lips together and nodded. She'd been wondering how to bring that up.

'I won't have it. He can't go without me.'

'He's probably feeling a bit low… Do you go and see him very often?'

'Well, yes… We're going now, actually. I've been trying to go every other day, but what with Little Madam going missing and, well, I had no idea what he had in mind and then when I got the letter…'

Susan wanted to ask 'What letter?' but tilted her head to one side and nodded instead.

'He wrote me a letter; telling me goodbye and…' she chuckled, 'reminiscing about old times… I won't have it, you know; I scrunched it into a ball and threw it up the garden.'

'Do you think you can talk him out of it?'

'I have to try!' She shrugged her shoulders and kept them up around her ears while she went on, her eyes wide open. 'What I find surprising is that he's in better shape than I am!'

The driveway crunched under car tyres. 'That's your daughter.'

'Yes! And my granddaughter. Won't you stay to meet them?'

Susan hesitated. 'No, if you don't mind. Another time when…' she thought for a moment, 'when Mr Lucas is back.'

Mrs Lucas smiled. 'I'll tell him that. Maybe that will motivate him a bit.'

Susan felt herself blush. She was hardly motivation for someone to stay alive. Mrs Lucas squeezed her hand. 'You're a lovely girl.'

'So are you.'

The two women smiled at each other.

'I'll see you soon,' said Susan, giving the cold hand one last goodbye squeeze.

'Alright, dear.'

Susan turned to walk back to the house, nodding at the carful of grey heads as she hoisted one leg over the fence, wondering who they could be. She realized that she'd imagined Mrs Lucas's daughter to look, well, a bit like a daughter. In reality, Susan could have been her great-great-granddaughter. Gosh… She'd never get her head around such an age difference. She thought about the part of the conversation with Meredith that she didn't pass on to Mrs Lucas: Meredith suggested that they may have taken Blankey because of Mrs Lucas's age. 'Do they have a right to do that?' Susan had asked. 'Not unless negligence can be proved,' said Meredith. 'And letting your littler be kidnapped by a neighbour is something they will surely use against her.'

'Letting her be kidnapped?'

'I'm afraid they're very good at twisting things. We'll try our best not to go down that road. We suspect that they are on a mission to collect up all the Batch Twentys indiscriminately, which they have no right to do. It's just a matter of collecting enough evidence together; like the story you told me today.' She paused. 'We're very determined.'

Susan had put the phone down imagining a tableful of retired lawyers typing up reports, squinting at their screens, calling up younger colleagues for advice, only to be told they were busy... She puffed out her cheeks, the picture of what was most likely to happen engulfing the picture of what should happen like a snake eating a vole... In six days she'd receive an email telling her that her littlers would not be returned to her.

As she walked back into the house, she realized she'd bitten her thumbnail so much that it was bleeding. Heading for the kitchen, she noticed one of Hamish's legs growing out of the sofa and wondered if he had Jinx on his lap as he often did in the evenings.

Oh no, of course he didn't.

She crept around the kitchen door so as not to bang it into anyone who might be standing behind it and shuffled her feet along the floor so as not to crush a little hand or foot.

But no... She didn't have to do that now.

She glanced at the flake bowls as she rinsed her thumb, looking for the box of flakes up on the fridge and telling herself not to forget to top their bowls up.

Oh dear, Susan, get a grip.

Hamish found her twenty minutes later sitting on the tiles. He stood with an empty wine glass in his hand and watched her for a minute to see if she was crying.

'Do you think they're frightened?' asked Susan.

Hamish topped up his glass, gave it to her, then sat down on the floor.

'No. It'll probably seem strange but… they won't be frightened as long as they're together.'

Susan put her head on his shoulder as he took the glass out of her hand, sipped from it and put it back again. 'Where have you been?'

'To see Mrs Lucas.'

He nodded. 'She gone?'

'Just leaving.'

'Did you… Did you phone the company?'

'No. I phoned the LOG.'

'The?'

'Littlers' Owners Group.'

'And what did they say?'

His cheek was inclined towards her forehead as she rested on his shoulder. He was really talking to her; not just at the space in front of his face; he wasn't just making conversation, he wanted to know what was going on. But then… But then he had been quite involved with the situation today. Susan studied his cheek; she should really stop thinking that he didn't give a shit.

'Suzie?' he prompted.

'Did Mrs Lucas fill you in on everything that happened before I arrived?'

'No. She couldn't really talk…'

'Shall we go in the living room? I'll start right from the beginning.' Hamish jumped up then turned and held out his hand to her. 'Yes, let's do that. Hold on… I'll get my Jotta.'

Susan pulled herself up and smiled after him as he dashed into the hall. Why was it necessary for something bad to happen for her to see the real Hamish? She took a sip from the wine glass he'd left in her hand and dragged her feet across the hallway to the living room. Maybe they would get through this. They were young enough to be taken seriously – as horrible as that sounded – and clever enough and outspoken enough to kick up the right kind of fuss. She sat on the sofa and shivered, sure that she would feel cold until he came and sat next to her.

'Right,' said Hamish, striding back from the hall and unravelling the clear sheet of plastic. 'Tell me everything.'

CHAPTER 16

'Level minus twelve. Doors opening.'

Bonbon covered her face with her hand. She looked at Jinx; Jinx had done the same thing.

'Jeez it stinks,' said the person who was carrying the box. They were taken towards a wall where, again, they heard the soft tap-tap of fingers on a screen. 'Last cleaned eight a.m.? That's too long.' The box turned and travelled the length of a very narrow corridor. 'I'm gonna have to say something.'

With her hand still over her mouth and nose, Bonbon sat right at the back of the cage, squashed against Jinx. Through the bars at the end she noticed a face; but not a nasty face; not even a *big* face. Her mouth dropped open. Was that… a littler? Wriggling out of Jinx's arms and onto her hands and knees she crawled to the front of the cage. Yes! Yes, it was and… Wow! As she looked from left to right at the many-more-than twenty cages that filled the walls of the corridor, *loads* of littlers came forward, cage by cage, to press their faces up against their bars and look at Bonbon. She strained her head to get a better view of the ones on her left. Some of them smiled… Bonbon tried to smile back but couldn't. How could they smile with a biggerer in the room? Bonbon looked to the right. Jinx stared with spread open nostrils at the littlers on that side. She turned and grinned at Bonbon.

'How do you…' Her mouth made the shapes but her voice was switched off inside her throat.

The cage swooped into the air past more cages, more faces, more smiles and waves. They were slotted into a space between a blonde, curly littler who reminded Bonbon of Blankey and what looked like an empty cage. Bonbon strained to see the Blankey-one as the box was turned and backed into a slot. The biggerer unclipped a flat black square from a strap of many black squares that hung over his shoulder and clipped it to the door of their cage, before turning and walking away.

'Hey, Rosy? Yeah, it's Lewis. Hi there. I've just dropped the last two off for the day. Do you know if any of the cleaners are still knocking around? No? It's just it stinks so badly down here… I don't know how many times a day this place gets cleaned but it's *definitely* not five.'

The lift doors swooshed open then closed again, trapping the biggerer and his voice inside before humming back up to where it had come from.

Bonbon and Jinx looked at each other, then at the black clippy thing that had started to beep before two glowy red stripes came shooting out of it. Jinx ran towards the back of the cage and Bonbon fell stomach-down on the floor; but the stripes chased them, beaming along the walls and across the floor until one found Jinx's stomach. She squashed her side up against the wall of the cage as skinnier beams reached out of the main one, making a net over her body before disappearing back into the clippy thing.

'It's alright, Bonbon, it doesn't hurt; look, it's doing it to you!'

Bonbon covered her eyes. 'Is it gone? Is it gone?' She felt Jinx's hand on her back.

'Yes, Bonbon. It's gone.'

'It does that twice a day.' A voice came from the cage on the left; the cage that Bonbon had thought was empty. 'It's checking to see if you are hungry or thirsty. Or if you're ill. Sometimes it thinks you're ill and the biggerers come down to check on you.'

'Who's talking?' said Jinx.

'Oh! Well, there's a curious question. *You* must be a Batch Twenty to ask such a question.'

There was a clunking noise and a hatch in the back of the cage opened. Yellow hissed out of it and made a neat pile. The hatch closed again.

Bonbon squinted. 'Jinx, they're flakes!'

'I'm not hungry,' said Jinx.

'The machine thinks you are,' said the voice. 'Your body is even though your mind isn't.'

Bonbon sat up and put her face to the bars of the cage. 'You mean… the littler inside my head?'

There was silence for a moment.

'Hello?' asked Bonbon.

'You could call it that, yes.'

'Where are we?' Jinx appeared next to Bonbon, holding a bar in each hand and pushing her cheeks between them. A row of littlers looked back at her from the fronts of their cages.

'You're inside the centre,' called one of them.

'They told us that we couldn't go home… That's not true, is it?' Bonbon called back.

'Yes; when can we go home?' added Jinx.

A voice boomed from far away, at least ten cages along the corridor. 'You won't want to!' it cried. 'Not when you know everything…'

'But… We can't stay in here forever!' shouted Jinx.

'Ha! Neither can we!' said the voice from next door. 'And we're not going to… Is it five o'clock yet?'

Someone called up from down below: 'Yes. Four minutes past.'

'Well, come up then, what are you waiting for?'

'Not tonight, Ed, it's Tuesday.'

'It's not Tuesday, it's Monday. And anyway, Moira's not back from Athens until *Friday*. I don't know if you've noticed, but that's why the place stinks like shit…'

'Moira came back *last* Friday, Ed. And today is definitely Tuesday.'

'It's Tuesday, Ed.'

'One hundred per cent sure.'

'It really is, Ed.'

'No doubt about it.'

Bonbon and Jinx sat at the cage door, moving their heads in the direction of each voice as if watching a fly landing on furniture.

'Oh,' said Ed. 'Then why does it stink so much?'

There was silence for a few seconds. Bonbon noticed that the faces opposite, which had been all excited, were now looking sadly up towards Ed's cage.

'Because Valentine and Tony have gone away to Bruges,' called a squeaky, faraway voice. 'Which means that Karin, Lee and Michael are the only ones here at the weekend.'

'And if each one comes once a day… that's not enough.'

'No! That's not enough.'

'I think *Lewis* should do it.'

'Lewis isn't a cleaner!'

'Yeah, but he complains so much about the smell, why doesn't he just do something about it?'

Bonbon and Jinx continued to watch the furniture-fly. It was weird, thought Bonbon, everyone had something to say but it was never said all at once. It was like, like, everyone had their *turn*… The deep voice called out to Ed again. Once, twice then…

'What *is* it, Mop?'

'Ed, are you listening to what we are saying?'

'Of course.'

'Then tell us what we have just said!'

Silence blanketed the corridor.

Ed sighed. 'Today is Tuesday. Moira *is* coming to clean because she got back from her holiday in Athens on Friday—'

'Which Friday?' interrupted Mop.

'*Last* Friday!' Ed sighed again. 'The smell is due to the fact that Valentine and Tony are in Bruges, *together*, which means that Karin, Lee and Michael have been the only cleaners here this weekend.'

'And Lewis?'

'Lewis is *not* a cleaner.'

'But?'

'But maybe he should stop complaining and start cleaning.'

The faces opposite tilted towards Mop's voice, waiting for him to answer. Finally he said: 'Excellent. I will test you again tomorrow.' Then: 'Be strong, Ed.'

'Be strong!' chanted the others, making Bonbon and Jinx flinch at the same time, then look at each other with big eyes. The others started to clap. Jinx stood with a clap between her hands, her mouth stuck in the shape of a bite. 'Jinx?' said Bonbon. 'Why have you got that face on?'

The clapping stopped and everyone listened to Bonbon. The faces opposite turned to Jinx. 'Jinx? Is that your name?' said a pale littler with short black hair.

'Yes,' said Jinx.

'Why did you have that face on?' said another.

'I was going…' Jinx's voice was all dry. She coughed and started again. 'I was going to say something.'

'She doesn't understand,' said Ed. 'She's only just arrived, how can she understand what's going on? Can't you *remember*?' He said the word 'remember' in a weird voice as if it were a stone and he was trying to see how far he could throw it. 'Can't you *remember* what it was like on your first day?'

The others started to mumble, this time all at once. Could they remember? Could they think back that far? Yes, yes, they could. But, hang on… Were they sure?

'Scared!' shouted one.

'Scared!' shouted at least five others.

'Sick!' shouted another.

'Funny in my belly!'

'Worried!'

'Sad!'

'Unhappy!'

'Unsure!'

'*Angry!*'

'They can remember!' said Mop, and everyone was silent. 'But Ed is right. We must work to preserve our memories. We should, all of us, talk about how we felt when we first came here. We will begin when Moira is gone.'

'Jinx,' said Ed, 'and Jinx's friend; soon you will understand everything.'

More clapping. It seemed that everyone agreed with this idea.

Another voice, which sounded like it was full of bubbles, suggested that they ask Piddle, Loop and Osmo why they had been taken away for two whole hours during the afternoon.

'It is very serious,' said Loop. 'They have started to give us *two* pills.'

A gasp fizzed across the corridor.

'And did they tell you why?' asked the bubbles.

Loop sucked air hissily through his nostrils. 'The result from the most recent clinical trial has shown that two pills will *not* be toxic for our bodies, but will be doubly effective.'

'Did you keep them under your tongue?'

'I couldn't! They checked inside my mouth! But luckily for me, they checked Piddle and Osmo's mouth first. I had time to snort one of the pills into my nose. And good job too because Piddle and Osmo have been sleeping ever since we were brought back down.'

The corridor simmered.

'This is a terrible, terrible…' started Mop, before his voice died inside his throat.

The lift door rumbled open, and almost straight away a whirring noise started up, along with the voice of a she-one. The whirr quickened into a hissy scream.

'Yeah, so anyway; I told him that I should be entitled to take the Friday as well but he said he couldn't approve that because Tony and Valentine booked the Friday off months ago to go to Bruges, which meant that I had to re-book my flight to get me back here a day early. Yeah, Carol knows about this but she's a *bitch* too. Ha! Don't worry, I'm underground now. There's no recording device underground. Yeah, there is *one* room that's been set up like that on purpose; it's the one they go into after this one… Poor loves. They're *so*… What's that word? You know, that word that you use to describe someone whose whole body seems to, well, *flop*, because they are so miserable… Haven't you noticed that I call you at the same time every day? It's because I can only do it in this room; I think it was set up in a bit of a hurry to cope with all the stuff that's been going on… I can call Carol a bitch and Len a wanker as much as I like! Dejected… Maybe. No! Forlorn! Forlorn is the word I was looking for… Yeah, they're all so forlorn.'

The hissy scream got closer; Bonbon and Jinx peered through the bars again to see where it was coming from. Jinx opened her mouth to yelp and Bonbon smacked her hands to her face and looked through her fingers. The biggest vacuum bot Bonbon had ever, ever seen crawled across the floor between the two walls of cages. It swayed from side to side, side to side as it made its long, shiny path and searched with its mean red eye, sending out funny tubes and brushes every now and again to reach the bits it couldn't get into. Bonbon stared as it touched the end of the corridor then, making a different breathy noise, turned itself around and blew on the shiny path all the way to the other end.

'Oh, I forgot to tell you; Benjie has decided that he wants to be an accountant when he grows up. Yes! Funny, hey? I thought you'd like that. I said to him, you must talk to Auntie Lyon about this; I'm sure she can tell you how to go about it. What's that? Yes; although his reading age is below average, but his guide told me it's normal for that development phase. And thinking about it, *I* was the same right up until I was about eleven, and then I just got it! Some kids are like that, aren't they?'

Bonbon was sure she could hear the cages opening and closing one by one. She strained her eyes to get a better look and managed to glimpse a red shape. It seemed to be getting bigger and closer. A movement in the cage opposite caught her eye. One of the littlers was waving at her to do something.

Bonbon shrugged; what was she trying to say?

Jinx had noticed as well; she pulled on Bonbon's arm and signalled for her to go to the back of the cage. Ah… That was what the waving littler wanted them to do. But the noise was getting nearer and Bonbon wanted to see exactly what that she-one was doing.

'I know! The problem with yellow is, even if you have the *tiniest* hint of red in your skin, it makes you look like a strawberry. I'd stay well clear; or you could take a pigment pill? What? Who cares if it's not summer, you could take one that just gives you a slight *glow*, you don't have to go orange.'

Suddenly, two black shutters cut off the end of their cage so only a line of light could get through. They blinked; the shutters hmmmmed towards them. They turned and ran to the back of the cage. 'No!' Bonbon yelped, pressing herself into the wall. Just as she felt the wobbly hmmm tickle up her belly the shutters opened and were sucked back into the walls. The floor in front of them was wet and smelled like clean tiles. A face appeared at the end of the cage. Big brown curls tied up in a red scarf. The eyes seemed to be covered in blue paint. 'Eye-shadow,' said the old littler, inside Bonbon's head. They couldn't see the mouth.

'Newbies!' Short lines jumped from the corner of each eye. A finger tapped their square clippy thing. 'Lyon! I've got two new ones,' she said. The eyes flicked at the screen then back again. 'Bonbon and Jinx! Hi! I'm Moira. You'll be seeing me *a lot*.' Both eyes squeezed together for a second as if each one were giving a quick smile, and the mouthless head turned and opened the next cage. 'Gosh, there have been so many during these last few days! Well… Apparently, they're not supposed to communicate, but they've found out a way of doing just that. No, I mean communicating with their owners; they're allowed to communicate with each other. Um… Well… They'll go through some memory thing… Some kind of treatment I think, then they'll be put into the room I told you about, you know the one where they can't speak? And then… I'm not exactly sure… What? When I'm speaking now, you mean? Yeah, they understand most of it, I think…'

Moira appeared at the cage opposite; she pointed a remote control at it and the black shutters travelled to the back. She opened the door and squirted something on the cage floor before scraping up bits of flake and shit and toenails that made a little ridge just in front of the door. She vacuumed up the ridge with a sucky tube attached to a bright red box on her back. She closed the door, hit the clippy square and moved on to the next cage just as the shutters were reopening.

Bonbon turned to see if Jinx was watching but she lay on her tummy, her head rested on her arms and her eyes closed. She looked around her feet; the floor was already dry. Strange. The tiles at home took much longer to dry. Jinx would often slide about on them. But that was before that one time when some of the liquid got into her mouth and she stayed in the basket for three days all shaky and sweaty. After that she would hide in the plant or the toilet box whenever the floor was wet. Bonbon crawled next to Jinx and watched her for a minute or two, dabbing at the floor with her fingers to be sure it was dry, before lying down beside her. She'd get up and listen to what the others would have to say once Moira was gone.

* * *

That awful day came… They had known it was coming.

At least he went in his sleep, Isabel thought to herself. He was, after all, almost twenty years old. Isabel knew that cases like this were extremely rare, for… well… 'that particular race' to live to such an old age; but that was no comfort. She couldn't form the words, even inside her head… Dog, Labrador, Jasper… That horrid vision of him lying on his own paws, tongue out and eyes closed, always seemed to envelop those words. She knew as soon as she saw him in the living room that morning; he didn't look peaceful and asleep as dead things are supposed to. He looked dead.

None of them could make the words to talk to each other without their faces crumpling, without the vision of the dead thing filling the spaces where the words were supposed to be; even the pen that scratched across Watty's notebook made horrid words like 'putrefying', 'decompose', 'rotten'… So they all skirted around the subject, ignoring the empty cushion and the missing tap-tap-tapping of clawed paws on the parquet every time the fridge was opened. There was an echo in the house where a song used to be; a draught where there was warmth. Three brains would trick their owners into thinking that a head popped up from behind the sofa when they came in through the front door, that skinny feet lolloped across their beds in the night and that the pressure of a solid, dog-smelling object brushed against their legs as they sat at the kitchen table reading the paper. They were amputees, scratching at their missing itchy limbs.

'I should have loved him more,' Isabel whispered to herself as she lay alone in her room; knowing there was no cure for old age, but more cuddles and games might have, at least, made him feel younger.

* * *

Susan lay on the sofa, her knees hooked over the arm and her feet dangling into nothing. One slipper had fallen onto the floor, the other clung to her toes. Every so often, she'd draw her feet up towards the ceiling as she asked herself what would happen if some sort of sharp-toothed animal was loose in the house and had caught sight of her feet. Inevitably, thoughts like this would jump to something else, then something else, her feet lowering back to their original position and the back of her mind would again be focused on the bowl of chocolate raisins that balanced on her belly.

She squinted at the TV as the picture seemed dimmer than it had done the last few times. It must have been because it was daylight, just about; and the late afternoon sun fought with the TV to claim the living room. She could have raised her hands and clapped them three times; that would have brought down the shutters, but that kind of movement would have made the bowl of raisins wobble dangerously. For the past fifteen minutes, she'd been telling herself that the TV would eventually win its battle against the sun; it would start to get dark soon enough.

Two men in brown suits sat opposite each other, a pot plant and a glass table between them. They leaned back in their chairs, their legs crossed the same way and their elbows following the angle of the chair arm, like two people who'd just eaten a big lunch. As they took turns to speak, their hands wiggled and waved, limp at the wrists; their arms too lazy to punctuate what they had to say.

'I suppose many people are wondering why Billbridge & Minxus was allowed to take over after Dr Hector's rapid, erm, decline.' He paused for a moment, then: 'Tell us about Isabel.'

'Well,' the other replied, 'Isabel was the first successful case story of the Mini Human Phenomenon. She agreed to collaborate with Dr Hector.'

'Wait… How did she agree? Did she use sign language, or—'

'No, no,' the other interrupted, smiling. 'Together they drew up a contract, which she signed with her own hand. She had full-human capacities, you see. She could speak and write.'

'Really?'

'Mmm-hmm.'

The interviewer leaned on one elbow and traced the outline of his mouth with his index finger as he thought about this. 'But the new race was designed to be limited with regard to communication and, um, ability?'

'Ah! Well, this is the greatest mystery. Nobody knows the exact procedures that were used to bring her into the world. That, in itself, is another story…'

'Apparently, it was a great scandal.'

'No.' The interviewee coughed and crossed his ankles. 'I prefer to use the word "story".'

A nod. 'Of course.'

'Anyway, given the circumstances, the fact that she even came to *be* was miraculous. The obvious conclusion is that her egg hadn't been manipulated before the point of implantation; a theory that was backed up by Dr Mark Hector, given that he'd been working for years to produce a being like her and hadn't been able to. He was so inclined to believe that Isabel was the unlikely result of nature that he plunged into a thorough investigation and found that her embryo had been taken before the manipulation of the nucleus.'

'So she was really a, er, a natural miracle?'

'Nobody really knows the truth… But the fact that he believed she was put her in a very dangerous situation.'

'Why was that?'

'Well, because Dr Hector, who'd always been fascinated by how she came to be, made several clones of her.'

'What did he plan to do with them?'

'We think he was trying to harbour egg cells from the clones to continue his quest to make a smaller human race; he wanted to find out what would happen if he combined the cells from Isabel with cells taken from a full-human; would he get the result he'd been looking for all these years? We can only assume that he failed as, shortly after Isabel died, he shifted his attention back to full-human embryos. By that time, the original problem of overpopulation seemed to have, somewhat, come off the boil.' The speaker's eyeballs rolled downwards and gazed at the pot plant for a moment. 'When the embryo scandal did come to light, it was made public. But the Isabel scandal, um, *story* was kept rather hush-hush...'

'Are the clones still with us today?'

He shook his head. 'No. The Isabel clones were, unfortunately, not destined to live for very much longer. Many didn't make it past their fifth or sixth year out of the lab.'

'And so, after a while, the company decided to pick up from where Dr Hector had left off?'

'Well... The same but different, some might say. Still adopting, without having to search very far for the adoptees.'

'Many would find it surprising that you were allowed to do this.'

'If we hadn't, we would surely have gone out of business. You see, a lack of unwanted children in the world is something that we were, of course, very happy to be presented with. But a lack of children full stop: that was certainly something that Billbridge & Minxus couldn't foresee. When scientists started to perfect the skills that had, ironically enough, been suggested by Dr Hector in order to cover up his embryo scandal, we approached the authorities about a potential collaboration.'

'Yes! This was a phenomenon in itself, people just weren't having children.'

'When we released our first model ten years ago, the average age for new mothers was forty-five, the *average* age if I might clarify; and seventy-eight per cent of all offspring had only-child status. That's to say that those who were not strictly only-children had at least twenty years between their own age and that of their nearest sibling. Our "Little Love" scheme is primarily in place to give children something to love so that the next generation of adults will be less individualist and more *open* to procreating.'

'Wouldn't you agree that it's ironic how many elderly people have been attracted to the scheme? Given the principal intentions of "Little Love".'

'No.' The other uncrossed and re-crossed his legs. 'This was all foreseen. It's only natural that older people should want, and be entitled to, something to love. Especially those who live alone.'

'And are littlers ever removed from families or elderly owners if they fail to look after them properly?'

The other leaned his head so far to the side that it was almost on his shoulder. He searched the ceiling for his answer. 'It's rare because… Well… You have to remember that choosing families has long been our main occupation at Billbridge & Minxus, so, I guess what I'm trying to say is that we're rather good at it.'

'Stop!' shouted Susan. 'Rewind! Play!'

'And are littlers ever removed from families or elderly owners if they fail to look after them properly?'

'It's rare because… Well… You have to remember that choosing families has long been our main occupation at Billbridge & Minxus, so, I guess what I'm trying to say is that we're rather good at it.'

Hmmm. Could Susan interpret that to mean that if an owner had been chosen by the company, it was because that owner was believed to be fit and capable? Maybe. She would hold on to that thought and tell Hamish about it when he got home. It could add to Mrs Lucas's case… But it wouldn't help Bonbon and Jinx. 'Play,' she said.

'And how are the new beings made? Can you assure us that there's no cloning or embryo manipulation going on here?' the interviewer chuckled.

'I'm afraid, in the nicest possible way, I'm going to have to ask you not to associate those words with the processes at Billbridge & Minxus.'

'Ah!' said the other, holding both his palms up and bowing his head. 'Of course, forgive me. Let me ask that question again so that there can be no misunderstanding: unlike the cloning techniques and embryo manipulation used by the-previous-company-whose-name-has-since-been-discontinued, Billbridge & Minxus collaborated with scientists who'd come across a new way of creating human cells; would you care to elaborate?'

Oh God, thought Susan as she plunged her hand into the bowlful of raisins; Hamish would love this.

'Of course.' He coughed and leaned forward ever so slightly. His lunch was obviously only just going down, greedy bastard, thought Susan. 'The cells are taken from the donors and coaxed into an embryonic state. However, before they reach that state, scientists are able to manipulate the cell structure so that it is different to that of the donor. The result cannot, therefore, be classed as a clone.'

The interviewer wrinkled his nose for a fraction of a second. Then smiled and went on.

'Some people might ask why Batch Eight, the first model, were all exactly the same if they were not… I mean… After the worrying techniques used by the-company-whose-name-has-since-been-discontinued you can understand what sort of *completely* wrong conclusions some people would jump to.'

The other slit his eyes. 'Quite.' He leaned back in his chair again. 'I must be clear here, they would naturally have grown to look very different from each other; it was Billbridge & Minxus that manipulated their appearance so that they would all look the same. Giving them the same sex and aesthetic was simply due to the fact that we were trying to limit the variables that could potentially affect behaviour over time…'

Susan heard the front door slide back and looked up. 'Hi,' she said.

A Hamish-shaped lump sat on the stairs and started to untie its shoes with sharp yanks.

Oh dear; they'd changed mood again. But fuck it; she'd really had enough of being such a misery guts when *he* was down in the dumps. Last night he'd been *lovely* to her when he'd found her crying in the kitchen. He'd even got his ScreenJotta out. Maybe she should take a leaf out of his book. 'What's wrong, babe?'

Hamish put his hands over his face and exhaled into them loudly, hoping that the heavy breath would drag his thoughts of Emma out with it. It did. But as soon as he had no more breath left to breathe out, the air in his head regathered into shapes of her. This was shit. This was terrible. He'd tried staying at work until well after his last client. He'd tried going to Shepherd's on the way home. He'd tried sitting on the driveway for twenty minutes, and now he was back in the house. With Susan. When all his brain would let him do was think about Emma.

'Is anybody in?'

He pressed his fingers into his ears. He should never have phoned her, he knew he should never have phoned her; in fact, that was the last thing he'd said to himself before leaving the house: 'You know, Hamish, it would be against your better judgement to phone her.' He'd obviously totally lost the plot… And now he'd gone and stirred everything up and there would be no putting it right again. He'd arrived at the office extra early, which meant lying to Susan. He'd acquired the phone number from Sandra, making her suspicious, and then he'd told Sandra that Emma was coming to the office and shouldn't be charged – making her doubly suspicious – and then he'd fucked everything up with Emma. 'You are a reasonable man, Hamish!' he heard himself saying out loud although his voice sounded all muffled and underwatery because his fingers were still stuck in his ears.

Susan's hand waved in front of his eyes. He unblocked his ears.

'Did you just stick your fingers in your ears so you didn't have to listen to me?'

'To hear you, not listen to you. I mean… I'm sorry, Suzie, I've had a funny old day. I, um…' He scratched his cheek and followed his hand with his eyes back to its hanging position between his legs.

Susan nodded; pictures of yesterday evening with the cuddle and the ScreenJotta and all that complicity, seemed less bright and lovely. No, no. She wouldn't cave. She would let him be sad for a change. 'That's okay. Everyone has bad days.' She nodded, tilting her head to the side, waiting for the rewards for her patience to trip from of his mouth. Oh Suzie, I don't mean to be gruff with you. Then he'd stroke her cheek or say something like: I'm sorry, let's go and enjoy an evening together. Or most probably: How are you feeling today? Any word of Tweedledum and Tweedledee?

Hamish sighed and smiled. 'I'm going for a shower,' he said, getting up and climbing up the stairs.

Susan watched after him, her mouth open wanting to call him back and tell him that, well… Was that all he had to say to her? Surely he would turn around… He didn't. She closed her mouth and let her eyes dance up the stairs. She knew it! She knew that she was setting herself up for disappointment. She sat down where he had been sitting, thinking that if he saw that she was still there after his shower, he would realize that something was wrong and that it was largely down to him. She leaned forward and closed her eyes against her knees looking at the inside of her eyelids; at whatever it was that made a gazillion little coloured stars whenever she put pressure on closed eyes. Was it only she that could do that or could everyone? If it was everyone, how come she'd never heard anybody talk about it? Maybe nobody had ever bothered looking. In that respect, she was special. She didn't need much when all she had to do was close her eyes to see the stars. It would just be nice if other people realized that she was the type of person who could see stars like that.

Below the stars, wet roofs pitched over empty houses with windows dark and still, like dead eyes. Mud splattered over mud as tethered dogs struggled to get out of the rain, or barked to be let into their houses by people who no longer lived there. Susan thought about taking the dogs and running with them to the wall, but today she found herself kicking through puddles. She imagined the town and the rain suspended in a kind of snow globe, where above was covered in stars, and the stars curved right around the top until they touched the pink flowers, and the pink flowers mattressed right across the underside until they found the stars again, and every direction would lead to somewhere better, yet she was loitering at the centre of the housing estate. She saw a dog barking in a nearby garden and thought that it would seem a lot fatter if its fur wasn't so wet. She clicked her teeth at it and it walked to its fence. Its ears pricked up slowly under the weight of wet fur. It wasn't tethered; it was just hoping for something to change.

The shower hissed in her ears. She really should stop losing herself in shitty fantasies. Stop it, Susan! This was the tip of the downward spiral; the bit where she should collect her mat to sit on and slide down, but at the bottom there was nothing except one thoroughly miserable evening. And her eyes were starting to hurt. Turning her head to the side, she thought about that poor little dog that had cocked its head at her as if it already loved her; its tail all bedraggled. Maybe she would get a little dog like that. She could go to the dog shelter during the week and get a dog. But no, she couldn't. It would scare the littlers…

One flat hand slid under her cheek as she thought again about all the phone calls she'd made that day. She'd called Mini-Me's to see if they would give her the company's geographical address. They weren't at liberty to give that information. She called Batch Mode; they couldn't either. She called the doctor. The doctor was much nicer to her, even seemed to sympathize with her, but also, regrettably, could not give her the company's geographical address. 'I am desperate,' Susan had said.

'I know, I understand,' the doctor replied. 'But you can't just go there. If you turn up at the front door, they're going to wonder how you found the geographical address and they'll have us all under interrogation. It's already happened. It wasn't pretty. People lost their jobs over it.'

Eventually she found herself standing on tiptoes, reaching the box of flakes down from the fridge. She scanned the back for a phone number and dialled it straight away. The call was answered by the receptionist at Billbridge & Minxus. Shit! They made the fucking flakes too?

'Hi. I'd like to speak to someone about visiting my littlers who were taken earlier in the week.'

'I'm afraid that visiting is not permitted.'

'That's what I've been led to believe. Would you mind telling me why this is?'

'We are under no obligation to give you our geographical address.'

'But you have something that's mine.'

'Your product has been recalled, Madam. If you read your terms of purchase you will see that product recall is one of the exceptional circumstances where we revoke ownership.'

'Well, I have read my terms of agreement and this "recall" hasn't been formally confirmed to me, which, as is clearly stated, it should be.'

'You will receive an email in seven days.'

'Why? Why seven days? How can it take you seven days to write an email?'

'Your littler needs seven days for the treatment to become effective. We'll be able to tell you if it's worked in seven days.'

'But you can't send me an email to tell me all of this?'

'You would have been told when the product was recalled that you would receive an email in seven days.'

'Could you at least tell me how they are?'

'All littlers in our care are in a stable situation.'

'Are they together?'

'—.'

'Are they together?'

'At this stage, they will most certainly be in the same holding corridor.'

Susan swallowed, not wanting to think that there would be a stage after this stage. 'But one of them didn't even communicate. She just made a, kind of, squeaky noise.'

'We observe protocol very seriously. Your littler wouldn't have been taken without a valid reason.'

'And if I want to dispute this?'

'How do you mean?'

'Legally?'

'You are fully entitled to take your purchase agreement to a lawyer.'

Susan had curled her lip. Maybe she should just call their bluff. Surely any lawyer could see that what they were doing was completely out of line.

'Listen. Based on your experience within the company, could you please just tell me if some of them do make it home?'

The speaker paused for a moment. 'I'm not at liberty to speak about individual cases.'

Susan rubbed her hand down the side of her face so slowly that her cheek ached. It was as if this woman were reading from a script. Maybe the only way she could deal with having to do such awful things was to read everything she had to say and her body would become some sort of… some sort of reading machine, and she could hide in another part of it while it sat and read horrible things all day. That was quite a deep thought. How many people thought thoughts like that? Wouldn't the world be nicer if everyone who didn't want to do something would just say: fuck it! I'm not doing that.

She'd tried this line of reasoning. 'I don't get it,' she'd said. 'It's not as if I'm dealing with the managing director. You're a human like everyone else, how can you bear to act so inhumanely?'

There had been a short silence. 'I would ask you to refrain from making personal attacks.'

'But then we're not equal,' she'd said. 'I'm calling you from my sofa with a towel wrapped around my head. I'm calling you because I have a personal problem. I personally am very sad, in fact I've not been to work today because I'm so sad; I've been crying all day because I'm so sad; how can you ask me not to be personal with you?'

Another silence. Then: 'Yes, but that's not my fault personally, Madam.'

'Do you have children?'

'Please don't talk about my children.'

'You do have children.'

'I asked you not to talk about my children.'

'You see, I don't have children but I tell anyone who asks me that I do have littlers. Two of them. And they are the closest thing I can imagine to having children. Now… Someone came and took them away from me, for reasons that I don't really get, and now

I have no idea where they are and if I'm ever going to see them again. Do you see what I'm trying to say here?'

'—.'

'Do you think that's fair?'

'I'm going to have to put you on to my supervisor.'

'Do you know what a pyramid is? Well, you, like me, are currently somewhere near the bottom with lots of other people just like you. If you gathered all of them up to tell your supervisor to "fuck off", then maybe that would—'

The line beeped and another voice cut in. 'I'm the supervisor in charge, good afternoon.'

'Oh hello. I was just talking about you to your—'

'I know, I heard. I had to take over the call. Can I help you?'

'Yes. I would just like to know when I can visit Bonbon and Jinx.'

'And they are… your littlers?'

'Yes.'

'I'm afraid visiting is not allowed. We are under no obligation to give you our geographical address.'

'Yes. That's what your colleague told me. Could you give me an idea of when I'm likely to see them again?'

'Certainly.'

Susan sat up straight on the sofa as screen pixels fizzed and whirred on the line. This was an answer she hadn't yet had.

The pixel fizzes stopped.

'You'll receive an email in six days.'

She flopped back again. Bitch! Fucking bitch! How could they get away with this! They really were all reading from the same script. Well, two could play at that game. 'Can I ask you, do you have children?' she asked.

'Excuse me, can I get by?' Hamish asked as he stomped down the stairs with no shirt on.

Susan stood up and looked at him. At the top of the downward spiral that led to the miserable evening, the mat-man told her to give this one last shot before sliding down.

'Hamish, I'd really like to talk to you.' She put her hands on her hips.

He blinked. 'Can I just get down, please?' he said. 'The shirt I want to put on is in the dryer.'

Fuck. Of course she had to let him get his shirt. She stood aside to let him pass. He was always so bloody logical about everything. He was topless and needed to cover up, that was reasonable. How could she tell him that he couldn't get his shirt? Especially when he'd said 'please'. Yet she felt like she wanted to thump her fists on his belly; how uncalled for would that be? The headline flashed through her mind as she bit the nail on her little finger: 'Man attacked by partner for asking to get shirt.'

She looked towards the kitchen. Hamish's shadow was doing up shirt buttons. 'Hamish, please talk to me. I'm allowed to worry about you, aren't I?'

The shadow stepped aside to let the man fill the doorway. 'You know I go quiet when I've got a problem.'

Ah yes, she thought; of course he did. The woman needs comforting, the man needs space. She'd read that in a very old book a long time ago. He could still say hello to her; that wouldn't make his problems any worse… No, Susan! Stop! Don't take the mat yet; don't sit on the slide. The man needs space, said the mat-man.

She strode up to him, stood on tiptoes and put her hands over his eyes, slowly so he could let her do it. 'Hamish? Can you see stars?'

'Not really,' he said. 'What are you doing?'

'Giving you some space,' she replied.

He smiled. Just a little bit.

'Can you really not see them?' she said.

'No,' he replied, taking hold of her wrists and moving her hands. 'Oh! Now I can see one.'

She grinned. That was probably the nicest thing he'd ever said to her, ever. The mat-man winked at her, then covered his pile of mats up with tarpaulin. The miserable evening was now closed.

Hamish looked at her and breathed out slowly from his nose. Susan was sure there was an 'I'm sorry for not saying hello' hidden somewhere in that breath. She smiled back as if to say 'It's okay.'

'How was your day? You seem brighter.' The 'brighter' got deformed in the beginning of a yawn.

'Okaaay,' she said. 'I was a bit teary this morning. Then I called everyone I could think of to try and get hold of a geographical address…'

'Well, that was a lost cause.'

'I know, Hamish, but I couldn't just sit and do nothing. Anyway, I eventually got hold of the company this afternoon and…'

Hamish's long yawn seemed to get sucked out of him and his mouth snapped shut. 'And what did they say?'

'Well… I was a bit rude actually. But they just make me so—'

'Hang on!' Hamish held his hands up to her. 'I'll go and get my ScreenJotta.'

* * *

'How does it feel? To be little.'

She'd seen this look a thousand billion trillion bejillion times. The way they said 'little' then scrunched up their noses and almost twitched them like rodents.

'It feels like I'm easily patronized.'

The woman flicked her shiny, shit-coloured hair forward to cover up a largely uncovered boob, and grinned at Isabel; a little diamanté glinted from the bottom of one front tooth. 'You're actually very intelligent, aren't you? I mean, you've been holding your own for quite a while now, behind the scenes. What is it you're qualifying for? Vet-er-in-ary science?'

'We're all intelligent,' replied Isabel.

'Yeah but… You're the first of your kind, everyone's so curious about you, how does that feel?'

'I just want my dad back now.'

The woman turned her mouth upside down. 'That's upsetting… Do you visit him?'

'Every other Tuesday. And I write to him daily. I feel it's unfair that he should be punished for creating me when you all seem so pleased to have me around. I feel that punishing him for creating me is as good as saying I should never have been born. I feel that punishing him for creating me is total hypocrisy when hundreds of embryos just like mine were destroyed legally. I feel that punishing him for creating me has been done to use him as an example to everyone that you can be unethical as long as it's legal. I feel that—'

The woman pressed her ear with two different-coloured fake nails, before nodding and interrupting Isabel. 'You're so right,' she gushed. 'Tell me, is it true that you wear Barbie dresses?'

'I feel it's unfair that he should be punished for creating me when the government has funded a project to create a whole race like me.'

'It's sad about your daddy, Isabel.' The woman nodded seriously then flicked the hair back off her boob. 'That's why today, at Teen-V, we wanted to focus more on you so that other young adults, who are also different, can be inspired by your courage.'

Isabel resettled herself in her chair. 'Alright then.'

'So, what would you say to kids today who might have hang-ups about their bodies?'

'As long as it works and doesn't cause you pain, then you are in possession of a gift.'

'Wow… Deep. Is that how you feel about your body?'

'I try to.' Isabel focused on the woman's boobs. 'Is that how you feel about yours?'

'Yeah!' The woman tittered. 'Do you feel happier now that you're out of hiding?'

'Erm…' Isabel thought for a moment. 'If I could give it all up and have my dad back, then I'd do it without hesitating.'

'Of course you would.' The woman nodded seriously again before turning the corners of her mouth back up. 'So where do you get your shoes?'

Isabel rolled her eyes. 'I have them made.'

'Adorable! Every girl's dream.' Then: 'And your teeth?'

Isabel frowned. 'They're my own teeth,' she replied as something hard fell onto her tongue.

'But one's just fallen into your lap.'

'Don't be ridiculous,' said Isabel, as bits of teeth fell into the space between her bottom lip and bottom teeth. 'But they're mine!' she said, trying to pick them out and gather them up. 'They're my teeth!'

The woman stared at her and curled her lip.

Isabel jolted awake and looked towards the end of her bed for Jasper. Oh no, he wouldn't be there any more, would he? She lay on her side, tears spilling from one eye into the other as she tested each tooth with her thumb and forefinger.

CHAPTER 17

They woke up to the sound of metal being flicked. Jinx peered at the door; what was that? It couldn't have been… It was!

'How did you get up there?' she asked, squinting as the cage door swung open; a skinny littler with short brown hair hung on to it.

'Most of us know how to pick locks.' One hand drifted outwards, gesturing for them to come outside. 'I take it you two were never locked in?'

'No.' Chips waved at her from the hole in his dirty cupboard. She stopped crawling towards the door for a moment to watch him and think about him. Where was he? Was he there too?

'We're lucky that they keep us in old-fashioned boxes like this. If they were anything like the ones you get at the vet's then we'd be well and truly stuck. The doors are made of glass and don't have any locks on them. They lock automatically.' He started to pick at the lock on Ed's cage while he talked. Jinx noticed that he had a shadow on his face where his cheekbone was, just like Chips. 'Have you ever been to the vet's?' he asked.

'What is "vets"?' asked Jinx. Although she was pretty sure she'd never been there.

'The doctor's… Or the hospital if you like.'

'Oh… I haven't, but Bonbon has.'

He glanced at Bonbon as the other door clicked open in his hand. 'You know the doors I'm talking about?'

Bonbon nodded. 'A vet is an animal doctor,' she said.

'They think we're animals, Bonbon. They don't say it, but that's what they think,' he said, shaking his head as he swung away. 'You'll learn a lot here.'

'She already knows deep down,' said another littler as he clambered onto their door.

'Ed,' Jinx said to herself, knowing that he'd come from the next cage. There was something wonky about his face that made his whole body look a bit broken… 'Are you Ed?'

'I am,' Ed smiled. His teeth were yellow with tiny brown lines. 'I'll guide you both down. It's a bit daunting the first day.'

'Thank you,' said Jinx, wondering what 'daunting' meant. She watched as Bonbon started to climb down first; her face all opened up and frightened, her head bobbing lower and lower slowly, carefully… That's what daunting meant, probably, she thought as Bonbon's head disappeared, it meant *scary*. Jinx started down. All those heads at the bottom made Jinx think of their basket on stone day. Bonbon was already climbing down the last box, two boxes below theirs. Jinx looked up. Another two boxes were stacked above their own and a line of legs and bottoms was quickly getting bigger. She sped up, wincing as the wire pressed into the circle of holes on her foot.

She got to the ground and looked around for Bonbon. A crowd had formed just next to the opposite wall and words rose out of it and wove their way into her ears; hello, welcome, hi there, pleased to meet you, good to have you here… As well as: we're going to help you, you'll see, you'll realize, you'll understand, we must work together, we're a team, Bonbon…

Bonbon! Jinx made her way over to these words. The crowd turned towards her, opening up and re-forming around her like the arms of a cuddle. 'Jinx! We'll help you, you'll remember, you'll know the secret, you'll pass it on…' Touches, strokes, a few kisses, grins, squeezes… Jinx smiled so much that it became hard to see through the tiny slits that her eyelids made. They laughed when she rose onto tiptoes and spun on one leg. They copied when she reached her hands so far into the air that her shoulders squashed her cheeks and her heels came off the ground.

'Welcome!' said one deep voice and the crowd grew quieter and quieter until it was silent. The voice's body appeared next to them. It had thick red hair, spiky like AstroTurf. His body was also thick, Jinx thought, especially in the places where Chips's was thin, and also very hairy in the places where Chips's was shadowy.

'I am Mop,' he said. 'I am not a leader; I've just got the biggest mouth.'

The others laughed. He opened his mouth to continue but another voice sang out from behind the heads of the crowd. 'He's the best at keeping his memory.'

Mop bowed towards the direction of the voice, pleased that someone had said this about him. 'The first thing you will notice here is that when one person has something to say, everybody listens.'

The word 'leader' translated in Jinx's head, but was too difficult to understand. How could one person be in charge of a group of people? Why would they all do what one person said? What if they felt like doing something else, like sleeping or jumping or… spinning in a circle?

'The first thing that I noticed is that you use lots of words we don't know,' said Bonbon. Jinx stared at her, blinking.

'Don't know straight *away*,' she added.

'You have not been stimulated enough by your biggerer,' said another voice. 'You have only relied on your internal guide.'

'In two days,' said Mop, 'you will see how listening and speaking and sharing new words will have you talking like us.'

'Yes,' said another voice. 'It's all about exchange. We have much to learn from you *too*.'

The others clapped; they agreed with this. Then they started to sit down on the floor, crossing their legs in front of them. 'It's time to tell you about our battle,' said Mop. He bowed to the group, then tiptoed his way through the heads and sank into a space.

Jinx sat down. So did Bonbon. And one at a time, the littlers spoke. No one said 'quiet' or 'it's my turn'; they spoke one at a time while everybody else sat and listened. This meant that the conversation would wind in different directions as each one waited for their turn to speak. 'Erm, with regards to what Osmo said when we were talking about "two orange pills" half an hour ago…' Jinx and Bonbon didn't know how long they sat there that first evening, listening as they told stories of what had been happening that week. 'One of the pills was definitely off-white, Osmo. That's what you told us when you came back from the lab. And Mop said the same thing.'

'Yes, Osmo. One off-white and one orange,' said Mop. 'Tell us the story again, correctly.'

'It's like they're trying to practise their memories,' Jinx whispered to Bonbon.

'They're weird,' replied Bonbon. 'What does "off-white" mean?'

They did this every evening, Mop explained. It always had to happen after five, except on a Tuesday when Moira arrived late. They had to be back in their cages before eleven, as this was when a ribbon of light would scan them to see if they were hungry or thirsty or ill. The big black panel on the wall by the lift displayed the clock time and they would take turns to sit in front of it and make sure they didn't forget to go back to their cages.

'We can *read* now,' said one of them. 'After you've been here for a few days, you realize you can read everything that is stored inside the black clippy square.'

The inside of Jinx's head translated 'read'. 'Bonbon can read,' she said.

'I didn't know I could, but I can,' added Bonbon.

'You must have been stimulated. Your brain must have grown,' said one.

'When something *difficult* happens to you, you find that you start to think differently.'

'Everything suddenly becomes clearer,' said another.

'Your guide becomes your friend,' said Ed.

The others clapped.

'Who is the guide? Is it the littler in my head?' asked Bonbon.

They told Bonbon that they didn't know *who* it was, but they all agreed it definitely felt like *another* littler; it couldn't have been their own thoughts because they were thinking things that they didn't even know about.

'Soon you will be seeing pictures,' said one of the littlers. 'Soon you'll be so close to your guide that he'll show you his world.'

'She'll show you where she lives.'

'You'll see everything he does, and you'll feel everything he feels.'

'Sometimes it's very challenging,' said Ed. 'It's as if you are feeling your own sadness or your own love.'

'But it's a great thing! We must work together so that we don't lose it,' said Mop.

'Why would we lose it?' asked Jinx. 'Why would we forget when we've just started to remember?'

Bonbon and Jinx would be taken up in the morning, they said. They would be interviewed, separately, to see what they already knew, they said. They must *pretend* not to know very much at all, they said.

'But we don't know *that* much,' said Jinx.

'And anyway, isn't that *lying*?' asked Bonbon.

But, it was necessary, they explained, because these people wanted to steal their memories, and without memories, how could they know the truth, and without the *truth* the whole *world* would be lies!

'Tomorrow, you must do what I did if they give you two pills,' said Loop. 'You must snort the second into your nose.'

'You must!' called Piddle. 'I have had to learn everything all over again this evening. I feel like I'm hearing all of this for the first time… The memories are so faint.' He shook his head. '*So* faint… Like shadows.'

There was silence as everyone seemed to think about how horrible this was.

'But if we lose our memories, we can go home,' said Jinx.

'Nobody goes home,' said another. 'Home is a lie.' Maybe *their* home was all nice and clean and full of flakes but many of them had horrible homes… Jinx thought of Chips, dropped her chin to her shoulder and kissed it.

And anyway, they went on, even if they *did* have nice homes, were they allowed to walk up and down the street and talk to people in shops? No, they weren't.

'*And* we can't use spoons,' yelled Bonbon. 'Even though we have the same bodies, we are forced to eat with our hands!'

Everybody clapped.

'We are a bit like pets, but it shouldn't be like that,' Jinx joined in.

'Because we're the same. Because we are *human*.'

More clapping. They agreed. They *were* human, but a different species of human, maybe. A few of them believed that they had been designed specifically to live with humans and fulfil the role of pets. On hearing this, some of them covered their ears. The thought of being designed as entertainment for a higher being was too horrible, they said, they still had to think about it some more before they could *believe* it.

'Bonbon says we used to live in a shop,' said Jinx.

They discussed shops for a while. It was quite a common memory to have after 'brain-growth'. This was why the being-designed-for-entertainment theory was so popular.

'There is one littler who knows everything about where we came from,' explained another. 'We were brought here on the same day; his name is Nemo. He told me that he *knew* we were born in shops and designed for entertainment.' As the littler explained this, a few of the others put their hands over their ears. 'He was treated as an equal by his biggerer. They had a whole sign-language system worked out between them, they could talk about anything. His biggerer even explained to him that he'd been bought in a shop. He knew so much that they isolated him completely a few days ago.'

'But why couldn't his biggerer get him back?'

'Because…' More littlers put their hands over their ears. 'Because when we are bought, our biggerers have to promise to give us back in case of a *design* fault.'

Jinx and Bonbon thought for a moment about what that could mean, before letting their mouths drop open and covering their ears.

'You only have to hear some things once to remember them,' said Ed.

'But what will happen to us?'

'We have one week here, maximum. Then we'll be taken to the silence-room.'

'Two more got taken away this morning. They just couldn't fight the memory drug any more.'

'That's why we have to fight. Our memory is the only chance of…'

'Time!' a voice called out over the room. It was the clock-watcher. The crowd got to its feet.

'We must go back to our cages now,' said the blonde, curly littler who reminded Bonbon of Blankey.

Bonbon nodded and climbed back up to the cage, thinking carefully about which one was theirs as they all looked the same.

'Where do you think they are?' Jinx asked as she climbed in behind Bonbon.

'I don't know, Jinx.'

'Will we ever see them again?'

Jinx had said 'them' but Bonbon knew that she meant Chips. 'Yes,' she said. 'We'll see them as soon as they are better.'

* * *

'Final time before I buzz.'

Isabel rolled her eyes. 'Drew, I'm sure.'

'*Sure* sure, or just sure?'

'Sure, positive, certain. Can we please go in?'

Drew pressed the buzzer. Isabel passed her hands over and around each other, then up her wrists towards her elbows. Her hands did that fairly often, now that they didn't have a dog to stroke… One quarter of her little world had dissolved that night. Afterwards, she'd followed Drew around for hours, clinging to the back of his jeans like she used to when she was a child. She shouted and spat when they suggested she get another pet; and clenched her fists until her shoulders shook when Drew said he was having second thoughts about turning himself in to the authorities. 'Do you still have his card?' he asked, one day.

'Yes,' Isabel had said, without asking whose card he was talking about.

'Now might be a good time to see if he still wants to take you on, you know, on to pastures new an' all that.'

The door clicked open and they walked along a corridor towards Dr Hector's office. Scenes of memories superimposed themselves over the floors and the walls. Shadows of former colleagues ghosted through the swing-doors. He kept his eyes on the little being who marched along in front of him. 'Shall I carry you?' he'd offered. She glanced up at him, and for a moment he was sure that she'd say yes. But she shook her head.

'Isabel!' Dr Hector stood up from behind his desk, his face

looking at her the way it had when he'd first seen her: as if he were starving and she were a nice fat sandwich. 'And… Drew. This is pleasant.'

'Good evening,' they murmured, one after the other.

Dr Hector sat down. 'Thank you for coming,' he said, mostly to Isabel but flicking his eyes over Drew as he did. They sat down. Hector mopped his head with a handkerchief. The silence pulsated like the pressure in his fake lips. 'You said there was something you wanted to discuss.'

'Yes.' Her fingers creased her skirt into pleats. 'I'd like to work for you.'

Dr Hector's eyes twinkled. 'Well, that's…very good news.'

Drew snapped forwards. 'But we need to know what exactly you're going to do with her.'

'Oh… Well. You know.'

'Not really.'

'My intention was to use her… erm… use her help answer several questions I've had regarding my project.' He leaned forward and rested his forearms on the desk.

Drew glowered. Isabel trembled.

Dr Hector scratched the bag under one eye with a craggy nail and continued. 'That's to say, just how she came to be. Was she a lucky miracle?' His hand fanned out as he said 'miracle'. 'Did she even come from my laboratory?' He dipped his chin and stared over his glasses at Drew.

Drew said nothing.

'In which case, is she even human? She could be, you know, an extra-terrestrial.'

'Don't be absurd,' said Drew.

'If it's not impossible then what must it be?'

They both blinked at him.

'A possibility. Exactly. I want to explore every possibility that could have led to the making of this unique young woman,' he straightened his shoulders, 'before I consider the most ludicrous of them all; that I, the leading expert in this area, after all my years of lab work, have been beaten to the post by some ballet dancer beavering away in his own front room.'

The doctor leaned back in his chair and narrowed his eyes. 'How many embryos did you take home before you got this result?'

'One.'

Mark Hector sniffed. 'Impossible.'

'I thought you had "carefully detailed records".'

'Yes. That *you* made, Drew Mahlik.'

'The buck didn't start or stop with me.'

Dr Hector shrugged then let his eyes stagger across the desk. 'I know. I'm just so eager to find out the truth that—'

'You want to explore every possibility,' repeated Drew.

'How long would you need me for?' Isabel's face rippled with twitches. Drew watched her as she tried to control her lips by folding them into her mouth.

'I have no idea!' Dr Hector laughed. 'Until I stop breathing!' Isabel's eyes widened. He coughed and tried out a gentler voice. 'I'd monitor your development, your deterioration, your brain function – everything. Everything that could possibly change over the course of your lifetime. And even after your death.'

'But I'll outlive you,' she scoffed.

'I hope so, my dear, but death is also an aspect of your existence that could be influenced by your physical state.'

Isabel's top lip twitched.

'I'm sorry but it's the truth.'

'I know,' she managed to wobble out of her throat. 'I like the truth. I'm studying medicine, you know.'

'Ah, well, there you go.'

She nodded once and rearranged her hands in her lap.

Dr Hector scratched his forehead with the nail of his little finger and blinked hard. 'I'd like to employ you to take part in various studies. There'd be no invasive procedures and nothing would be done without your permission.'

'Right.' Isabel paused for a very long time, gazing up and out of the window. From the corner of her eye she saw him scratch the middle of his forehead twice more while she hoped that Drew would step in and say something.

'We have some conditions,' said Drew.

'Now don't think you can start calling the shots.' Two red scratch-lines glowed in the centre of his head. 'I can't help thinking that this is between Isabel and myself.'

Drew carried on: 'She will agree to participate in these clinical studies as long as she is paid like every other employee. As you have just mentioned, there will be no invasive or harmful procedures – that is the second condition. Thirdly, she will be chaperoned at all times by me or Watty.' The doctor opened his mouth but Isabel held up her hand. 'Fourthly, the chaperone will be paid too.'

The doctor rubbed at his chin. 'You grew a baby at home, Drew. What you did was massively illegal. She has biological parents somewhere in the world who would have had to sign consent forms in order for that to take place and…'

'The sperm and egg cells were donated anonymously, surely?'

'Well…'

'Surely?'

'In most cases, yes…'

'And, in fact, as of 2025 the law would side with my decision not to terminate development.'

'I think you're clutching at straws.'

'I'd get ten years,' said Drew. 'I've looked into it. And what is more, if anything untoward were to happen to Isabel, I'd out myself immediately.'

Isabel's heart thudded so far up her chest that her throat vibrated. Maybe she wouldn't cry, or she'd probably just pass out.

She held out her hand, indicating that she wanted to get down. Drew took her in his hands and lowered her to the floor.

'Think about it, will you?' Dr Hector said as he followed her descent, still looking like he wanted to eat her.

Drew stood up straight and gave a firm nod.

'Bye then,' she quavered, as she walked back towards the door.

'Wait!' called Dr Hector. 'You'll need me to let you out!' And he shuffled along the corridor after them.

* * *

She woke up just as Hamish put a mug down on her bedside table. He sat down on the bed and looked at her.

'What time is it?'

'Seven thirty. Are you going into work today?'

She hoisted herself onto her elbows. 'Yes. I don't think I should have any more time off.'

'What about hassling the company?'

Susan balanced on one elbow while she rubbed her eyes. 'You know, part of me thinks it would be better just to wait for the email.'

'Really?' He screwed up his face.

She stopped rubbing her eyes and squinted up at him. The night before he'd seemed disappointed with the lack of information she had for him. He did ask some pretty good questions like: did you ask if they'd had any demonstration of communication since taking the two littlers? Did they realize that Jinx hadn't actually communicated? It was only a *squeak*, really… Are you sure that the first woman was not a machine? Yes, Hamish; she was sure. But did they say anything else, Susan? Did they say *anything* else? Did you ask to speak to someone else?

'You can't speak to someone else, Hamish. They don't let you.'

'Right.' He switched his ScreenJotta off and sat with it on

his knees. 'Best see what they say tomorrow. They might have someone different tomorrow.'

Susan shrugged. 'It probably won't help.' Then: she looked at him from the side of her head. He stared at nothing, then flipped his stare back into her one eye that was looking at him. She shivered, thinking of how often she must do that and he knew he was being watched.

'I'm tired, Suzie, I'm going to have to head up.'

And he did. And that was the end of their team spirit. At eight fifty-one in the evening.

They hadn't even had dinner.

'I should be finished early today, why don't I try and give them a call?'

Susan shrugged. 'If you want. I don't see how that would make any difference.'

'As I said, someone else might pick up. We might get a different answer.' He stood up and bent to kiss her on the head. 'Bye then.'

'Bye.'

Susan got up and took her coffee down to the kitchen, glancing at the bowls; they were empty, best fill them up. She turned to the fridge. Oh no. That's right, there was no point. She'd come down to get a yogurt but didn't really fancy it any more. She glanced at the basket as she headed for the door. They'd been sleeping in it so peacefully two nights ago, and now… She'd had this conversation with herself yesterday and it had ended with her taking the mat from the mat-man, and *that* had all been triggered by the fact that she'd come to get a yogurt. She'd got as far as sticking her head out of the front door, all dressed and ready for work, but the snap in the air had made her think of snow and how last winter Jinx had run outside while it was snowing, completely naked, with her arms stretched up towards the sky and her mouth wide open to catch the flakes on her tongue. Bonbon had rolled it into balls and managed to bring it into the house. That was during the days when she couldn't work out how they brought things in from outside; clever things. *Independent* things. They'd never see snow again, she thought, then shut her head back into the house and phoned her boss, snivelling into the phone.

Bloody morning yogurt; she couldn't let it trip her up again. 'They are gone!' she said to herself. 'Look in the bowls,' said the mat-man. She did, and as she did, she told herself that they would be empty from now on. 'Look in the toilet box,' he said. She did that too. Empty. No Jinx hiding because Bonbon had been nasty to her. 'Look in the basket,' he said. This was the most difficult bit. This was the bit she'd tried to avoid. They were at their cutest when they were in the basket. She would miss seeing them cuddled up to each other. She looked in. Empty except for a few blades of AstroTurf and… What was that? Was that… She picked it up, flattened it out and started to read. *Darling Helena…*

CHAPTER 18

Bonbon was the first to wake up. She sat up and looked for the edge of the basket – oh but… There was no basket. The smell of Jinx's hair had made her think that she was at home. 'You won't ever want to go home again,' Mop's voice said inside her head. Hmmm. She wasn't too sure about that.

What time would that funny ribbon thing jump onto her stomach? She crawled to the end of the cage. Soon, hopefully. And she could do with a bowl of water. She scratched her armpit and looked at the cages opposite. A head ducked down and reappeared, its mouth full and munching. Hang on… Bonbon's stare zipped along the cages either side. 'When did you get flakes?' she yelled.

A littler sat back on his knees, his cheeks full of flakes. He concentrated on her while he finished his mouthful before answering her question. 'Just now. Haven't you got any?'

'No!'

The littler rocked back on his heels and stood up. 'Bonbon and Jinx haven't had breakfast!' he called. Fingernails clinked against bars and bulging faces stood chewing at the wire doors.

'It means you'll be taken this morning,' said the littler opposite. 'Just remember everything we told you. And don't tell them too much.'

'Act stupid!' called Ed.

'Try to co-operate *while* acting stupid,' called another.

'Be strong!' called a third.

'Be strong!' they chanted all at once. Bonbon wondered why they were allowed to say that particular phrase all at the same time, then wondered how she knew how to think of words like 'particular phrase'.

The black shutters snapped together in front of her nose. She yelped and scrambled to the back. The cage started to slide, then rise so quickly that Bonbon's tummy seemed to fall into her bottom. She squinted through the black air. 'Jinx!' she called.

'I'm here, Bonbon!' Jinx called back just as the movement stopped.

Bonbon stumbled forward two or three steps. The shutters reopened. She held up one hand to break the path of the light that beamed into her eyes.

'Good morning!' A head appeared. The same white head that they had seen the day before with the criss-crosses where there should have been a mouth. Bonbon looked closely to see if she could see the smile. She could. 'How are we feeling today; good?'

'—'

'Hungry?'

Bonbon clapped once then held her hands behind her back. Was that giving too much away? She would have to ask the others later.

'Hungry, Jinx?'

Jinx pushed out her bottom lip and blinked.

'Now, Jinx, what did we say yesterday? If you don't communicate with me now, you'll be sent to a different room. Away from Bonbon.'

Jinx lifted her hand into the air and started tracing circles on the wall.

Len made a noise that sounded like a laugh. 'I've had the time to read your file properly. It seems that your arrest was due to a *vocal* outburst.'

Jinx's circles turned into one long, curly line that travelled up the wall of the cage and over her head.

'This puts me in a bit of a predicament,' said Len. 'I'm inclined to believe that you don't know how to clap, and the fact that you managed to scream "no" could have been triggered by intense emotion. Huh? What do you think, Bonbon? Am I right? Was Jinx so sad that she shouted "no"?'

A clap.

'Are you sure? Because if you're sure she can't clap then I will almost certainly have to put her into a different room. Right now, in fact. We won't waste any more time here.' He folded his white arms across his chest. 'Are you *sure*, Bonbon, that Jinx can't clap?'

Bonbon looked at Jinx. She'd stopped drawing lines and was now staring back at Bonbon.

Two claps. No, she *wasn't* sure. But the claps hadn't come from her…

Jinx stood with her hands held out in front of her as if she'd thrown a bundle of feathers into the air. Bonbon's eyes grew hot. The skin on the Jinx-side of her body felt tingly and happy as if all the little hairs were trying to touch her. She wanted to call her 'darling' and kiss her and say the word 'love' into her ear. But… 'Don't let them know too much,' said Mop's voice. Her stomach fell into her bottom. Jinx had refused to clap *then* clapped, letting them know something that even Bonbon didn't know about her: she could keep secrets.

'You've surprised me,' said Len. 'Both of you.' He tapped the thing that was next to him, like he had done the night before. 'There's obviously a lot to learn about *two* littlers that have spent a substantial amount of time together. You *lied* for her, Bonbon; do you realize that?'

Jinx clapped twice; it wasn't a *lie*!

'Oh yes she did!' he said. 'It seems like you *do* have something to say, Jinx. Well…' Len opened the cage and plucked her out.

Jinx opened her mouth to scream but couldn't. She reached back for Bonbon who ran forward to grab her hand. The cage door closed, rattling as Jinx kicked it. Her toes curled and disappeared up into the air with the rest of her leg. 'You will be interviewed by my colleague today. Now, I don't want you to worry. You'll be in the same cage again tonight; I promise.' Bonbon pushed her face between the bars and watched Jinx wiggling in Len's hand, her hair flicking and her hands pulling at his plastic finger. 'Jinx, calm down. Calm down. We're not going to separate you, I promise.' She stopped pulling and put both hands over her eyes. Hiding, thought Bonbon. She often did that when Bonbon shouted at her or asked her to go and collect AstroTurf when she just wanted to lie in the basket. Her shoulders shook as she pressed her palms into her chin. 'It'll be alright, Jinx. You'll see Bonbon again tonight; look, wave goodbye to her... Bye-bye, Bonbon.'

Another white stomach passed in front of the cage, a clapping box pressed against it. Jinx... Bonbon held her cheeks in both hands. Oh Jinx, you'll be in so much trouble.

'Now Bonbon, I have to tell you exactly what I'm going to do with you today. Let's start with this.' He held up a silver square. 'This little baby will monitor your brain activity while I ask you questions, so I'm going to stick it to your head in just a moment. It won't hurt, I promise.'

Bonbon sat and stared at the line in the wall that had opened up and closed again, trapping Jinx inside it. He stuck the silver thing to her head. It didn't hurt. He'd promised that it wouldn't hurt and it hadn't. He'd promised that she would see Jinx again; maybe she would. He closed the door of the cage and looked down at his tablet.

'What are you thinking about, there?'

Bonbon shook her head then reached behind it.

'No. Don't touch it. I'll take it off at the end. What were you thinking about just after I put it on? Were you happy that I touched you?'

Two claps.

He looked at his tablet. 'Yep, I can see that. Were you thinking about Jinx?'

Bonbon held her hands out to clap but Len went on: 'Wow, yeah; you were definitely thinking about Jinx. This is fascinating.' He rubbed the top of his white head with his white hand and looked at her. 'We really need to investigate littlers who live in pairs.' He looked down again. 'I've never, ever seen so much love in one brain! Not even a full-human brain!'

Bonbon scowled, wondering what a 'full-human' could be.

Was she happy at home, Len asked, did she talk to her owner at home through clapping? Was she thirsty? Had she ever used the internet? Had she ever been in a car? Had she ever been to the vet's? Did she have a humcoat? As she answered, Bonbon wondered how she could answer in such a way that she wouldn't show how much she knew. That was really difficult when there were only two ways she could answer: yes or no. Except for the internet… She didn't really know if she'd used that… If she didn't know, it was probably because she'd never used it… In any case, she'd decided that telling the truth was the best way to answer his questions. At least he would think that she didn't know how to lie.

'There's a lot of noise here, Bonbon… Are you thinking about other things while I'm asking you these questions?'

Shit. Could he really see all that other stuff she'd been thinking about how she should answer?

'Not to worry. It's a big day for you today, I know.' He started another round of questions. Bonbon tried to concentrate on what he was saying and not think about how she was answering; although, that wasn't too difficult because the questions seemed much harder this time. Had she ever been angry, had she ever been in love, had she ever wanted to kill something, had she ever been scared, had she ever wanted to touch herself between her legs, had she ever been anxious, had she ever been sad, had she ever felt shy… She didn't know what most of the words meant; they tumbled over her, one after the other like a, a *feeling*.

'Angry and sad, eh? Have you ever been happy?'

A clap.

'Well, that's a relief!' Len looked at her. 'Never been in love?'

Bonbon thought about this then clapped twice.

'But you love Jinx? Hmmm… Maybe you're a bit confused with the words. It's normal but… but you did strike me as *more* intuitive than the others.'

How could she have ever *been* in love when she was *still* in love?

'What did you just think?'

Bonbon gazed at Len and put her hands on her hips. Why did these biggerers ask questions that she couldn't answer?

'And there… What did you think just then?'

Idiot.

'Okay. Let me ask you again about love.'

Bonbon straightened and puffed out her chest. This time she would answer yes, she *did* love Jinx; even though he would ask her if she'd ever been in love.

'Have you ever been in love?'

Yes. A clap. She *did* love Jinx.

'Right.' He peered at her for a moment, then continued with his questions.

Had she ever driven an Aston Martin, had she ever dined at The Ritz, had she ever read Shakespeare, had she ever played the cello, had she ever written poetry, had she ever been fishing, had she ever baked a cake, had she ever been to Scotland, had she ever been on an aeroplane, had she ever lived in the country, had she ever swum in the sea, had she ever written a story, had she ever ridden a bike, had she ever stroked a cat…

What the hell? What on Earth was Shakespeare? What did

'driven' mean? What was an Aston Martin? No, no, no, no, she answered two claps after two claps. The only word she had understood was 'cat', but 'stroked'? Nope… Not a clue. Then again, all she'd ever done to a cat was throw things at it. She answered no; she'd never stroked a cat.

'Good,' said Len. 'But… are you frightened of cats?'

Two claps. She thought about the day she'd thrown stones at the grey cat's head. If she ever saw that cat again, she'd kick it on the nose.

'Be honest, Bonbon. Are you scared of cats?'

Two claps. No, she bloody wasn't!

Len laughed. 'I get the impression that you really believe you're not.' He looked back at the screen. 'So what about all this writing and cake-baking?'

Bonbon wrinkled her head. What?

'Living in the country?'

Len kept his eyes on his tablet. 'Yeah, I thought not. Don't worry; we'll get rid of all of that before it has the chance to surface.' He looked at her. 'Now, let's see what *has* reached the surface.'

Bonbon scowled at him. Reach the surface. Like she did in the bath. Was he going to ask her about that? How did he know about that?

Had she ever woken up with lots of other littlers? Had she known any full-humans before she knew her owner? Had she ever lived anywhere else before she'd lived with her owner? Had she ever been in a glass box before she'd been with her owner? Had she ever been to a shop before she'd been to one with her owner? Could she remember anything before being with her owner?

Memories fuzzed in Bonbon's head. A memory of a thought sharpened. She woke up in a glass tank, curled up in a pile of littlers whose tummies rose and fell so quickly that they looked as if the rest of their bodies should have been running. She remembered thinking a thought about being too hot and little white bits sticking to sweaty feet. She remembered telling Jinx: 'Don't be silly, we *came* from a shop!' Then she remembered not thinking about all these memories of thoughts again. Until now. They were probably just funny thoughts that her brain had made up. It did sometimes. 'Don't let them know too much!' echoed Mop's voice. No, she answered. No, no, no, no. And it wasn't a *lie.* The truth was that she *couldn't* remember. She couldn't remember if they were memories or thoughts. It wasn't a lie, no, no, no; it wasn't a lie.

'More noise, Bonbon. I'm not sure about all this, I'm really not sure.' Len's single black eye turned back towards the cage.

What are you not sure about, Len? she wanted to say. Why don't you believe me? Are you trying to tell me that those thoughts were memories of memories? Are you trying to *make* me remember things? I thought the whole point was to steal my memories!

Len looked back at the screen. 'Lots of noise, indeed.' He started to type something. 'My guess is that *these* ones are just starting to surface, but you can't quite work them out. Am I right?'

Bonbon narrowed one eye and gnawed on the inside of her cheek, her palms held around a clap as if they were clutching a ball.

'Am I right?'

Two claps. She scratched her head. One clap. She held on to her shoulders with opposite arms and squatted so that her buttocks were almost touching her heels. What did he want her to say?

'You're not sure.' The long, black eye stared at her for a while before turning all the way around to a cupboard up on the wall behind him. 'Fine. Okay. I have to keep things moving, and I'm sure you could do with some breakfast. Your brain has been flashing "hungry" ever since I clipped that thing on your head.' He opened the door of the cage. 'I'm gonna start you off with one today.' He put an orange stone in front of her.

Bonbon eyed the stone. That must have been the memory pill. Loop had told her to snort the second pill into her nose, but there wasn't a second one. Len had said that he would give her one today and two tomorrow. Tomorrow she would definitely have to snort one into her nose. Maybe she should practise today.

'Eat it,' he said. 'Crunch it down! It's yummy.'

She picked the pill up and put it on her tongue. A taste filled her mouth that she didn't recognize. It wasn't the same as flakes; flakes were *completely* different; so different that she wasn't hungry for flakes any more; all she wanted was more of these pills. She sucked, hard. The orangeness bounced over her tongue, down each side of her neck, over her shoulders, her back, her breasts, her tummy; like putting on her humcoat on a cold day. She shuddered. Mmm. It tasted like the best thing she would ever *ever* eat… But wait. She wasn't supposed to eat it. It had to come out again, and *quickly*. She thought about the kind of cough she'd have to do in order to get the thing into her nose. Gosh, that would hurt. Maybe she could eat this one, then definitely snort the second pill tomorrow. Surely one wouldn't be so bad?

'I can see that you're enjoying that!' Len laughed.

The sound of his voice stopped her tongue from sucking; the orange rock was getting smaller. No. They would not win this fight with a yummy tasting piece of stone! The back of her throat sucked the pill upwards and at the same time she coughed through her nose, putting her hand over her face as the pill came shooting towards the end of her nostril. Her eyes watered and she held her breath as another cough fluttered at the back of her throat.

Len flicked his eye back at her. 'What did you do? Show me your hand.'

Bonbon opened both hands. They were empty.

Len looked back at the screen. 'Why are you experiencing pain?'

More flutters. Bonbon's head jerked as she held back the cough.

'Are you choking?' Len frowned and poked a tube through the bars. Bonbon's eyes widened; it was that mean metal insect! She turned to run towards the back of the cage just as the end of the tube lit up. Oh… it was just a light. She stopped and watched it as it searched this way and that.

'It's not on the floor. Open your mouth.'

Bonbon opened her mouth as Len shone the light inside.

'Must have gone down the wrong hole.' Len flicked off the light. 'Drink some water when you get back. I keep telling them that we should use injections to avoid all of this choking business; but there's some law…' he tailed off. 'I'm going to send you back now. Tomorrow I'll remind you to chew it, just like you do with your flakes.' He reached behind her head and unclipped the metal square, closed her cage door and waved goodbye. 'Jinx'll be up with you shortly.'

The shutters came down again and the cage swerved and lifted. Bonbon hung on to the side with one hand and snorted the pill into the other hand. She folded her fingers into her sticky palm until the cage reached its slot back in the corridor; mmm, maybe she would lick her hand… Just one tiny lick.

The shutter disappeared into the roof of the cage and Bonbon looked into her hand. Hmmm… What would she do with it now? She glanced up to see the faces opposite watching her; cheeks pulled backwards by the metal bars.

'I coughed the pill into my…' she tried to say, holding up the pill between her thumb and finger so they could see. But her mouth was making shapes. The shutter on her cage slammed back down again and pushed her towards the back wall. Was it Moira already? Was the cage being cleaned? She scrunched her hand shut and covered it up with the other one. Surely they couldn't know about *that*? The shutter was sucked back into the walls. Brightness filled the cage again. The sound of biggerer footsteps tap-tapped their way back along the corridor. Jinx lay at the front of the cage. Her eyes closed and her hands curled over her chest in a weird way. Spit bubbles formed and popped on her lips and the marks of a metal-legged insect speckled her shins and thighs.

Jinx! Bonbon tried to scream, skidding to her side and falling to the floor. 'Jinx!' she managed to whimper as the lift door at the far end of the corridor opened and closed. 'What have they done to you, Jinx? My poor, poor Jinx. What have they done?'

Jinx's eyes rolled towards Bonbon's and her mouth made noises that didn't sound like words, but more like noises that Bonbon made when she was lifting something really heavy or when she was just getting up in the morning.

'Help!' Bonbon called. 'Help me! Jinx is ill!'

'What's wrong with her?' called someone.

'Can she speak?'

'Is she awake?'

'She's awake but she's really hurt. I don't think she can walk…'

As she answered, the two ribbons appeared from the black box. 'Go AWAY!' she shouted. But the ribbon landed on Jinx, sending out all its legs to walk over her body, being careful to feel the weirdness in her wrists and the insect footprints on her legs. 'She's ill, you horrid, *stupid*, thing!' screamed Bonbon as a dose of flakes gushed into a pile behind her. The thing folded its legs into its body and was sucked back inside the clippy square. Bonbon fell to Jinx's side, holding her weird hands together and stroking her face with the edge of her fist, the pill still melting inside it, then gasped as her hair froze to her cheeks. Water had fallen on them like a cold blanket. A whole bowlful. Bonbon jumped up and smacked the ceiling with the knuckles of her pill-holding hand. 'What was that for?' she shouted at it. Her feet slipped on the floor as she jumped; the floor, the soaking wet floor – how on Earth would they sleep on that? she thought as she looked behind her, then in front… Oh! Jinx had propped herself onto one elbow and with her other hand was wiping water out of her eyes.

'Oh Jinx!' Bonbon fell to the floor next to her again. 'Are you better? Can you talk?'

Jinx blinked hard. 'I think so.' She looked around. 'Where am I?'

'You're back in your cage, Jinx. With me, Bonbon.'

Jinx was quiet for a moment as she looked around. 'But where, Bonbon? Where are we?'

Bonbon stared, her mouth open ready to tell Jinx where they were, but Jinx *knew* where they were; she *knew.* Why should she have to tell her again? She already knew the answer. The door of the cage rattled as Mop and Loop unpicked the lock. 'This is serious,' said Loop as he climbed inside. 'How much do you reckon they've given her?'

Mop crouched down in front of Jinx. 'What happened to you, Jinx? Can you remember?'

Jinx rolled onto her side and rested her head on her forearm. 'Will you stroke my hair for me, Bonbon?' she asked. 'I'm sleepy.'

'Of course I will,' replied Bonbon, already picking wet strands out of Jinx's face. 'Do you want to eat some flakes?'

'No. Just want sleep.'

'She's been drugged,' said Ed as he swung into their cage. 'She must have refused to clap.'

Loop put his hands on his hips and shook his head. 'Silly girl,' he muttered. 'Silly *brave* girl.'

'No!' said Bonbon. 'No! She definitely clapped! I was with her. They told us that we would be separated if she didn't clap, and she finally gave in.'

'Well, why is she like this then?' asked Mop.

'They keep changing the rules.' Loop crouched down and looked at the air just in front of his face. 'How are we supposed to fight if they keep on changing the rules?'

'They make 'em they can change 'em,' said Piddle as he heaved himself in.

On the inside of Bonbon's head, she stood in the arms of the She-one, watching as Jinx tried to struggle out of her grip to go to Chips; an enormous arm swooping over her on its way to an ear. An ear that had just been screamed into. 'It isn't because she wouldn't clap,' said Bonbon. 'It's because she wouldn't *talk*.'

The others stared at her.

'What?'s popped up all along the corridor until Mop silenced them by asking: 'She knows how to speak in front of them?'

'No,' said Bonbon. 'I've only seen it…' She stopped to remember: the laughter, the green humcoat, in the She-one's arms. 'I've only seen it three times. And it was just noises not *words*. One time it was just laughter and even *I* managed to laugh with her.'

Loop got to his feet. All four littlers stared first at Bonbon, then at Jinx who slept in Bonbon's lap.

'She had too much emotion,' came a voice that Bonbon had not yet heard. 'Emotion is the link between body and mind, you know. The body that is the human race is linked by communication, it needs to speak and be *heard*; emotions *communicate*…' The voice took a scratchy breath. 'I heard about a bear who was so sad that his body died. Emotions need to be communicated or else the body goes bad.' The voice breathed again.

There was a pause. Nobody clapped or even *moved*. The four littlers in front of Bonbon stood frowning, each holding a finger over his lips. The voice continued. 'And one might make that mistake if he has only his *own* body to think about; but not when he feels responsible for so many others.'

Bonbon stared towards the front of the cage, then at Loop and Piddle until enough silence passed in front of them that she was sure the scratchy voice had stopped talking. When their eyeballs rolled back to Jinx again, Bonbon asked: 'Who was that?' A little girl wandered into her mind, put her hands above her head, turned in a circle and laughed. The littler inside Bonbon's head also laughed with a voice that Bonbon didn't recognize, then turned towards Bonbon; his body sprouted white hair, paled and wrinkled, and changed from a body like Chips's to a body like hers. Her hand lifted and reached out towards the voice.

The others stood, holding their heads and muttering words to themselves, their lips making sounds that had just been spoken; their mouths bending into shapes of different words... Bear, emotion, sad... They were memorizing what had just been said. Maybe she should be doing the same thing? But she'd said something about Jinx. She'd said that Jinx could talk because she had too much emotion. What had she meant? Bonbon's eyes flicked towards the front of the cage again. 'Can I see you?' she called through the open cage door.

'Yes!' the voice answered after a while, sounding happy. 'But it's five to eleven.'

'Time!' called the clock-watcher.

'Come and see me when Moira has gone.'

Mop, Loop and Piddle looked at each other. 'What does she mean?' said one. 'I don't know,' said another as they walked back to the door and climbed down the cages, jumping the wire squares two at a time.

'I'll lock them in!' called Ed.

'Who was that speaking, just then?' asked Bonbon.

'That's Windy,' Ed replied. 'She's the only Batch Eight that I've ever met.'

'Batch Eight?'

'Mmm-hmm,' he nodded as he locked the cage door. 'She knows a lot of things but she doesn't like to talk,' he said through the wire bars. 'She keeps telling us that there's no point.' He leaned closer and dropped his voice. 'Do you know what? I think she's right.' Smiling, he ducked back into his cage.

Bonbon looked down at Jinx and stroked both of her cheeks before moving her head from her lap to the floor. 'Windy,' she repeated, lying down in front of Jinx so that the shutters wouldn't bash into her and wake her up.

An enormous brown thing that was too big to be a cat, and had too many legs to be a bird, wandered into the centre of her head.

White points peeked out of either side of its mouth. It wiggled its nose and butted it against another brown, fluffy tummy… A bear, said her littler, her *guide.* With her name, she thought; the bear's name was Bonbon, and as she thought it, her eyes blurred and spilled over. Inside her head, a hand picked up a pen and started to write a letter. A letter, a *letter*… Hadn't Len asked her something about a letter? She was sure that he had. She was sure that it was one of those stupid questions he'd asked her earlier. And she had no idea how to answer it although he even asked her *twice* just to make sure. 'They haven't surfaced yet,' he said. 'I'll only give you one pill today.' And then… Shit! Bonbon opened her hand. The pill had almost gone. She scraped what was left of it onto the floor of the cage. Moira's sucky machine could have that, she thought, wondering if her hand was orange as the black shutters came down.

Moira talked her way up the corridor, and back down it again, laughing as the lift doors closed behind her. As soon as she had gone, cages clicked open and legs and bottoms shimmied down to the floor.

'I should stay here with Jinx,' said Bonbon as she leaned out of her cage and looked down. 'She's still sleeping.'

'Why don't you leave her to sleep? called the girl who reminded her of Blankey.

'I left Piddle last night,' said Osmo.

'We have things to talk about,' said Mop.

'Are you still coming to see me?' said the funny scratchy voice.

Windy! thought Bonbon. Windy's voice pulled her to the edge of her cage, as if there was something outside that she really wanted, like flakes when she was hungry or a pile of string on string day; why was that? Maybe because the voice was so strange. Maybe because Bonbon wanted to see the face that went with it, this strange scratchy voice. Or could it be because… She thought of the white and wrinkled one again. Because they'd seen each other before.

'I'm coming, Windy.' Bonbon bent over Jinx's ear to whisper that she would be back later. Jinx slept with her mouth squashed open by her own arm. Bonbon kissed her on the nose and started to climb down the cages, her tummy pulling her back upwards until the back of her throat started to burn. 'I'll go back to her later, I'll go back to her later…' She inhaled and exhaled the words as her body worked hard to keep her hanging on to the wire doors.

At the bottom she tried to pant quietly. The conversation had already started. This time, the blonde one, who reminded Bonbon of Blankey, stood in the middle to introduce the subjects with another littler who had short black hair and tile-white skin. The tile-white one noticed Bonbon and watched her while the other spoke.

'Firstly, we have to go through everything we have ever known up until now in order to preserve our memories,' said the-one-who-looked-like-Blankey. Everybody clapped to show that they agreed. 'Then we will move on to new things. When Bonbon and Jinx are ready, we shall discuss what has happened to them today, as well as the fact that Jinx can talk.'

The crowd clapped again.

'Bonbon doesn't know where to go, Fola, shall I take her?' said the tile-white one.

The-one-who-looked-like-Blankey, *Fola*, turned her head towards Bonbon and nodded. 'Yes, and I'll finish here.'

The tile-white one stepped around shoulders and over legs, bringing her knees up high as she made her way towards Bonbon. When she was really close, Bonbon noticed that her ears turned into a point at the top.

'I'm Lamb,' she said, smiling and holding out her hand. 'Windy's cage is right at the end.'

Bonbon looked at the hand before deciding to squeeze it with her own. 'I'm Bonbon,' not taking her eyes off Lamb's ears.

'I know you are,' smiled Lamb.

'You've… I mean… It's only because your hair is short, um…'

'My ears?' Lamb took Bonbon's hand and led her along the corridor.

'Yes, I didn't mean… I think they're really *lovely.*'

'My She-one picked out this design when I was being grown.'

Bonbon thought for a minute then wrinkled her head. 'What?'

Lamb giggled. 'Sounds horrible, doesn't it?'

'But can they… do that?'

'The rich ones can.' Lamb jumped over a gap in the tiles, the way that Jinx did when they were in the kitchen at home. 'I mean, the very rich ones. But soon they'll all be able to.'

Being grown. The words repeated themselves inside Bonbon's head. Being grown, being grown. The only time she'd heard the word 'grow' was when the She-one told the He-one to grow up, or when the She-one would tell them to be careful when they jumped inside the plant-pot. 'It won't grow!' she'd say. It wasn't true; the plant *had* got bigger since it arrived. That was because it was always growing, even though the She-one was worried that it wasn't. Bonbon couldn't reach its leaves any more, not even if she stood on tiptoes. If she'd been grown too, did that mean that she'd been even *smaller* than she was now?

Lamb looked at her. 'Nearly there.'

Bonbon started to ask a question then stopped. Then decided to all the same. 'Was I grown, then?'

'Well,' said Lamb, 'it's one of the theories. I only believe that I was grown because my She-one used to talk about how she'd chosen my lovely ears.' She said this as if she really believed that her ears were lovely. 'Maybe you should ask Windy about things like this; she has lots of opinions about how we all came to be here.' Lamb lowered her voice. 'But she has to be in the mood to talk about them.' She put her normal voice back on. 'Here we are...' They stopped and turned towards a cage that was at ground level. 'Hello, Windy!' called Lamb.

'Hello, Lamb,' came the scratchy voice as Windy emerged from the black at the far end of her cage. Her eyes fell on Bonbon and she stopped to squint at her for a minute.

Lamb started to pick the lock on Windy's door.

Bonbon squinted back at the figure who stood on the other side of the metal door and reached out to hold on to it. Her chest was so jumpy that her mouth wouldn't let her talk and air hissed loudly from her nose.

Peering back at her with one green eye and one brown eye, through a face of brown lines that made Bonbon think of her own basket, was the white and crumpled one. 'It's you!' said Bonbon. 'I've been... I've been *thinking* about you!'

Lamb turned to look at Bonbon, her head all wrinkled and her mouth upside down.

Windy put her head on one side and smiled. 'Have you?'

'You were at the doctor's!'

The scratchy voice laughed. 'I haven't seen a doctor for years.'

Bonbon's smile fell. 'Yes you have! It was definitely you!'

'It was surely one of my sisters,' she said. 'We all look exactly the same.'

The door swung open and Lamb stepped back. 'I'll go back now,' she said. 'You should come out this evening.' She tipped her chin at Windy. 'Good for your memory.'

Windy waved Lamb's invite away and chuckled. 'How can I forget? I can't ever forget.' She fanned her hands out in front of her. 'I *am* the memory.'

Lamb took hold of Windy's hand and squeezed it, turning to Bonbon. 'See? She always says these things, about memory, emotion, *bears*, but she *won't* tell us what she means.'

'I keep telling you, there's no point, Lamb.' Windy reached

out and tucked a piece of Lamb's short black hair behind her ear. 'They're so pretty,' she said. 'Just like a fairy, or a pixie… Or some other legendary thing.'

Lamb beamed. 'I don't know what any of that means. And if you're not going to tell me then I'd better go back. I'm helping Fola with the subjects for this afternoon.'

Windy rubbed Lamb's hand. 'Off you go then.'

Lamb grinned and walked back towards the crowd of littlers.

Bonbon turned to say goodbye, but by the time she'd looked back towards Lamb, the little black head was bobbing far along the corridor. Had she been staring at Windy the whole time? She turned back to the old littler who had sat on the edge of her cage and let her legs dangle towards the floor.

'Why did you say that you *are* the memory?'

Windy patted the space next to her. 'Because I am.'

'But can't you remember being at the doctor's?' asked Bonbon as she sat down.

'It wasn't me, dear. It was probably my sister. I'm a Batch Eight, you know. We all look exactly the same.'

The word 'dear' crept up behind Bonbon and rubbed her shoulders. 'Exactly the same?'

'Yes.'

Bonbon wondered what it would be like to have a sister. The image of sleeping Jinx flicked on and off again in her mind; as if it were a television screen. Where had her mind found the words 'television screen'? she thought, as she saw a very little girl with almost-brown hair crying in front of a square picture, a television, telling of how she wanted to see people just like her… Except she wasn't really telling of that at all! The words she said didn't match the feeling that Bonbon took on as she watched her. Fingers rubbed over the eyes that watched from the inside of her head and Bonbon realized that the eyes were not hers, the sadness was not hers. It was like the others had said; she was feeling what her littler was feeling. She closed her eyes and tried to turn them inwards to watch, but the image was gone. 'I just saw something.'

Windy nodded. 'Memories,' she said as if it were the most boring word in the world.

'I'm so confused about all these pictures in my head,' said Bonbon, wanting to hold Windy's hand and put her head on her knee. Instead, she crossed her ankles and swung her legs, letting her heels tap against the cage. She shook her head. 'I'm sure it was you I saw. I remember really well because seeing you made me not want to leave the doctor's. And hearing your voice just now made me want to run to your cage.'

'Hmmm,' said Windy, nodding her head, the same way she did with the others when they wouldn't stop telling her to practise her memories; when they wouldn't believe her that there was no *point.* 'It's nice of you to want to come and see me, dear,' she said.

'Darling,' said Bonbon, as 'dear' gave her another hug from behind.

Windy straightened and blinked at Bonbon. 'Where did you hear that word?'

'I read it,' she said. 'It's my favourite word.'

'Oh.' Windy's back curved into a slouch again. 'It's good to read.'

'Can you read?' asked Bonbon.

'Yes,' replied Windy.

'It's funny because I read that word and it made me feel so… um… I don't know really. It was a *big* feeling, though.' She swung her legs up high and looked at her toenails. 'Jinx can't read but she can make noises in front of the biggerers.'

'She must be a very emotional littler.' Windy rested her head on her hand.

Bonbon noticed that her hand was full of bumpy green lines. She looked at the back of her own hand before her eyes were drawn back to Windy. The sound of breathing hissed in her ears; but not the ears on the outside of her head… She breathed in and out quickly and realized that the breathing in her ears continued on its own; slowly in and slowly out. In and out. They weren't her breaths; they belonged to the littler inside her head. He was watching Windy and concentrating on her. Sadness pulled at Bonbon's eyelids. 'The bear was called Bonbon,' said Bonbon. 'Like me.'

Windy narrowed her eyes as her head cocked to re-hear what it had just heard. 'Sorry?'

'Bonbon,' she repeated. 'The bear was called Bonbon.'

Windy's eyebrows crushed her eyes into slits and her nostrils opened wide as she breathed deeply. 'How do you know that?'

'I don't know,' said Bonbon. 'I'm right, though, aren't I?'

'—.'

'Tell me, Windy; his name was Bonbon, wasn't it? And the other bear… The other bear had Jinx's name, didn't she? The bear who died and left Bonbon all alone.'

'—.'

'Why won't you help me? Why won't you tell me what it all means?'

Windy shrugged her shoulders right up to her ears. 'Because there's no point, Bonbon.'

'But why?'

'You'll never beat them.' Windy's eyes darted over all the cages in front of her as if what she was saying was so obvious that bits of it were lying around everywhere. 'I've been here for six days and in the beginning, I told them *everything* I could. It didn't help. One by one they've been taken off to the next room, and the next day another littler appears in their cage with *so much hope*.' She looked straight at Bonbon. 'Do you know what the next room is like? The one after this one? My sisters do. They've been there and stared at the walls until their brains rotted.' As she said this, one of her arms crept down towards the floor and pointed at it. 'They tell me when I close my eyes; they show me what it's like when I sleep; they beg for me to talk to them every night until they've forgotten how to talk. The memories of Batch Eight are powerful memories, Bonbon, but they are managing to disperse them like flakes in water.' She turned to face Bonbon; her mouth straight and liney like a comb. 'It's painful to forget. Especially when you can *feel* it happening. You, Batch Twenty, you don't stand a chance. Why are you working so hard to preserve something that *will* be taken from you? You should just let yourself go, Bonbon. All of you should let yourselves go.' She gestured towards the other end of the corridor, towards those who should have been letting themselves go instead of repeating everything that had happened to them since they'd been there, the same way they did every afternoon and evening. 'They are right, those biggerers. We shouldn't communicate. We *shouldn't* stimulate our brains. We should live *without* always trying to discover the truth…' She shrugged. 'There's no point,' she repeated.

As Bonbon listened, the breathing in her ears became so loud that she had to lean closer in order to hear. The heart that wasn't hers beat so fast that it had to take over her own one, for help, or else it might have exploded. The sadness that tugged at her eyelids pushed up her eyebrows and pulled back her lips. Her fingers shook with an energy that hadn't come from her and drummed the side of the cage in a way hers never would. *There's no point!* played over and over again as pictures flicked one after the other of biggerers she'd never seen before, laughing on a spotty blanket and shouting around a table, a bowl of green rocks at its centre. In every picture was the little, almost-brown-haired girl; an animal, like a cat but bigger and yellower, stood next to her or behind her or under her; Bonbon felt the top part of her head being pulled back as words that weren't her own bubbled out of her mouth and into the air. 'There's always a point, Isabel!' she shouted.

Windy gasped. 'What did you call me?'

'Isabel,' said Bonbon. 'I called you Isabel because *that* is your name.'

'How do you know that?'

Bonbon's chest pumped so much that she thought she would be sick. She thought of the littlers in the glass tank who looked like they should have been running. Her eyes started to ache and tears formed and tumbled over her nose. 'I don't know!' she said. 'Help me, Windy! Help me to remember!'

Windy stood up as quickly as she could, her feet searching for the ground, her back bending forward; she gripped the side of the cage with shaky, green-striped hands and puffed out her cheeks as her weight fell onto her ankles. She hobbled over to Bonbon and put her arms around her. 'It's alright, I'll tell you,' she said as Bonbon sobbed. 'The bear was called Bonbon. And his mate was called Jinx.' She rocked Bonbon's body inside her skinny hug. 'I am called Isabel,' she said. 'My sisters and I *are* called Isabel.'

Like dirty moons, he thought, turning his hand out and gazing at their black nail tips. His gaze tumbled down to the lump that stuck out just underneath his chest. Like a buttock, he thought. Like a large, hard buttock, but on the front of him, blocking out his feet. He belched and laid his head back down. Those black fingernails had come from scratching at his feet when he was under the bed with Blankey and Jinx. The baby ones weren't black. He never scratched anything with the baby ones. They just weren't strong enough. He brought his hand to his eyes. This time yesterday, had he properly thought about it, he might have eaten those useless baby ones. He definitely would have pushed his bottom tooth under each fingernail, and eaten up the black stuff. A ribbon of light swooped out of the black clippy thing that was stuck to the front of his cage. Oh no… He let his head roll to the side. Not again. No more… The ribbon travelled up his body. He lifted his hand to cover his mouth, but the light caught it and held it. 'Please, no more, no m—' A tube of light held his mouth in the shape of 'more'. A thinner tube buzzed its way through the centre of the light and into his mouth. Chips wriggled and writhed, trying to arch his back or tip his head to the side. The light on his body strengthened its hold. He gagged as the tube continued over his tongue and into his throat. The noise started. Like a low hum heard through pinched closed ears. He'd often hum with his fingers in his ears. It would stop him from feeling hungry. But now… He let his eyes water, maybe that was his belly making them water; his hard buttock-belly getting bigger and bigger and pushing all the water out to make more room for whatever was buzzing out of that tube. He spluttered but the thing continued. He moaned but the thing continued. He breathed a long breath through his nose and watched his belly rise above his chin line.

The thing continued.

CHAPTER 19

Oh gosh, who were all these people waiting for? Surely not him? They were definitely shouting in his direction. Look away. Just look away.

'This way. Hold it on your head, Drew. Cover your face. But careful on the steps; here, take my hand.'

'Okay.' Just follow Tim. Tim won't let them tear you to bits. Tim just got you out of prison.

'Baby grower! Baby grower!'

'You're GAY, not God!'

Drew would have laughed at that had it not been yelled at him by about twenty people. Oh dear, where were Watty and Quail? Concentrate, Drew, just think about them; they'll be so pleased to see you. Then they would all go home together and have a lovely meal.

'Shut the fuck up, you lot! Didn't you get that he's not right in the head?'

Respect to the man who just told twenty people to shut up, but was this really how that part had been translated? Tim's way of putting it had been more… elegant. 'Mental anguish' would for evermore be known as 'not right in the head'. Watty would laugh, he would most certainly laugh. Good Lord, how many steps were there?

'Nearly down, Drew, just watch your step.'

The jacket slipped from his head and a camera flashed in his face. Three microphones appeared with three journalists attached. One of the journalists screamed as she got crushed by the other two. 'How does it feel to be free, Drew? Do you think what you did was right?' But Drew didn't answer; he gazed at the row of men and women dressed as ballet dancers, all of them with red lipsticked smiles painted right up towards their ears. They stuck their middle fingers up at Drew.

Drew let his eyes close. He'd never dance again. What a horrible thing to do.

'Baby grower! Baby grower!'

'Do you think that gay couples should have the right to grow their own babies?'

'Do you think that we'll ever see baby-grow kits sold in high street stores to assist gay parenthood?'

Tim pulled the coat back over Drew's head as Drew laughed. Baby-grow kits! How did they dream up these ideas? He thought about what Tim had said in court: 'What we should really be asking ourselves is why a drug-addicted teenager with an unwanted pregnancy would be allowed to keep her baby yet a geneticist, capable of producing a human child in, perhaps, safer conditions than a natural womb, should have terminated his? He wanted to save a life, may I remind you. Would it have been more acceptable if he were a woman who couldn't have children naturally? Surely we cannot hold the fact that he is not a woman against him?' Clever Tim. Clever Watty for going to the same university as clever Tim.

'Justice has been done, Drew! We love Isabel!'

'Thank you for Isabel, Drew!'

Drew pulled a buttonhole over his eye and peeked out. A group of round ladies with smiles like thumbnail dents in potatoes stood with their children sat on their hips. The children made heart shapes with their thumbs and forefingers. They wore tee-shirts with pictures of Isabel at the centre, all done up like a little Barbie doll. Ha! Quail has been working hard. A placard appeared next to them. 'Drew Mahlik crushes gay parenthood acceptance.' Drew looked the other way. Dear oh dear, was that what people really thought?

On his left-hand side, men and women stood in a line with their hands in a praying gesture. One after the other, they bowed as Drew passed. 'Our pro-life brother,' they said. 'Thank you.' Then a flower was poked underneath the coat. Drew lifted the edge of the fabric to see the face that had offered it to him. 'She's a miracle,' said a very smart lady with a grey bob and a black shirt-dress. 'Well done for saving a miracle.' He took the flower, his eyeballs tingled and blurred. The lady reached out to put a hand on him but was pushed away by more journalists sweeping around him, snapping photos and trying to poke their microphones under the coat. 'Why are you crying, Mr Mahlik? Do you have any regrets? Do you have any regrets about what you've done? Do you? Do you regret anything, Mr Mahlik? Why won't you answer the question, Mr Mahlik?' Suddenly, a pressure on Drew's head pushed him down and forward into a car. Tim scrambled in behind him, pulled the door shut, and there was silence.

Drew pulled the coat from his head. Tears beaded his jawline. He rubbed his eyes and looked towards the front seat.

'Hello, darling.' Watty's pupils glittered. Drew's nose snorted, his mouth screwed up into a wiggly line, he bent his blonde head forward and, as if he were a reflection, Watty did the same. Foreheads touching, Watty held Drew's cheek with his hand. Drew put his own hand over Watty's and started to kiss his face until both wiggly lines touched and they sat in that position and sobbed. Outside, cameras flashed and the crowd knocked and smacked at the windows.

'Where's Isabel?' Drew asked, dragging his eyelid towards the edge of his face with the heel of his hand.

'Who?'

'Isabel, where is she?'

'What?'

The earth moved underneath him, bouncing his horizontal body up then back down again – wait – horizontal? Darkness billowed about his eyes before curtains started to glow beyond the far-right bed post that stood black and straight like a muscle farm column in calm sea.

'In bed, one would hope.' A pause. 'Were you dreaming? You're panting.'

Drew pressed two fingers to his jugular. 'It was one of those vivid ones.'

Watty rolled over and curled an arm around Drew's waist. 'A bad one?'

'It's alright,' Drew said through a yawn. 'It's over now.'

* * *

They walked back to the crowd together, slowly as Windy couldn't walk as well. She reminded Bonbon of Blankey's she-one, and as she thought of her, she wondered again where Blankey could be. Heads turned to stare at Windy as she took her place at the back of the crowd. The speaker was remembering Hester and Note, two littlers who had been moved to the next room just that morning. Bonbon left them and climbed back up to her cage. 'Jinx!' she hissed as her head poked over the edge. The space where Jinx had been lying was empty. Bonbon looked towards the back to see her bent over her flakes, her face pushed into them, her teeth and breath making greedy noises. 'Jinx!' she called again. 'We're having a meeting. It's an important one.'

Jinx sat back and watched Bonbon until her mouth was empty. 'They were so horrible to me, Bonbon.'

'I know,' Bonbon nodded. 'I saw the marks on your legs.' She climbed into the cage and walked towards Jinx, her arms already in the shape of a hug. 'We need to discuss this with everyone else. They want to know what happened.'

Jinx nodded and stood up, brushing her hands on her thighs even though she hadn't needed them to eat her flakes. 'Let's go down.'

When they reached the crowd, Bonbon whispered that they had to sit with Windy. 'Who's Windy?' Jinx hissed.

Bonbon felt the jumpy and shaky feeling come back as she looked in her direction. 'My littler knows her.'

Jinx screwed up her face. What was that all about? Bonbon didn't have a littler, did she? If anyone was Bonbon's littler it was her, *Jinx*; is that what she had meant? That was a bit of a weird way to say 'Jinx'. But then she did have quite a few new words recently, like… darling.

Jinx stopped. She stared so hard at the other littler who now sat next to Bonbon that the white head turned, and one hand like a bird's foot rose into the air to beckon her over. Jinx walked towards her as if she were being pushed from behind. She stared down at Windy for a minute, then crossed her ankles and lowered her bottom to the floor. Windy eyed her from the side of her head as, rather than facing the middle of the crowd and the speaker, Jinx had sat herself down so that she was facing Windy. She continued to stare.

Bonbon's eyes widened and she thought of something that she hadn't thought in a long time. Fuck, she could be weird. Why did she have to be so *weird*? 'Jinx,' she mouthed. Jinx didn't notice. She leaned forward and put her arms around Windy, who let out a 'huh!' and a smile, before leaning her head against Jinx's and closing her eyes. Bonbon looked away. How embarrassing, she thought. But then Bonbon had felt like doing that. She hadn't dared to do it, though. Funny old Jinx, never frightened to give cuddles or kisses; Bonbon looked back at them and saw that Jinx was crying, her head still tucked under Windy's, big silent sobs making her body jump. Windy's hand had made its way up to Jinx's hair so that she could stroke it while Jinx cried.

'Were you given the memory pill, Bonbon?' Shit, they had asked her a question! Bonbon flicked her head around towards the speaker, but there was no speaker; Fola had taken her place among the crowd.

'Erm… Yes!' replied Bonbon. 'And I snorted it into my nose, like Loop.'

'What questions did they ask you?'

She told them about the clippy thing and the questions. Some of them were quite weird and she didn't know *why* she'd been asked them, but she answered as honestly as she could. In fact, she was sure that Len could see when her brain was trying to lie, so she tried not to think about anything except for the answers to the questions. 'Did I give too much away?'

'No,' called Loop. 'In my opinion, you can't remember as much as we can.'

'I agree,' called someone else. 'I don't know *why* I have those memories, but I definitely have them.'

'Oh.' Bonbon dropped her head and fingered the arch of her foot.

A hand rested on her arm.

'It won't take much for you to remember,' whispered Windy. 'I'll help you.'

'Jinx!' called Fola. 'Tell us what happened to you today.'

Jinx lifted her head from Windy's shoulder. Glistening lines joined the corners of her eyes, her nostrils and her top lip. She sniffed loudly and opened her mouth to speak, but Mop's voice cut in.

'Did they give you any memory pills?'

'Yes,' croaked Jinx. 'Three pills.' The crowd gasped. 'They tried three times to make me swallow a pill. I tried to snort them into my nose, but that hurt so much I spat each pill onto the floor.'

'You spat them onto the floor?'

'Yes.'

'Weren't you punished?'

Jinx told of how she'd been bitten by the metal insect so many times that it almost made her sick. It wasn't just because she wouldn't swallow the pills that they had punished her, but also because she wouldn't speak. What they didn't seem to understand was she couldn't *speak*, she could only make noises, and she didn't really know how she did that. They had made her so *angry*! She didn't want to answer their stupid questions…

'Why do you keep saying "they"?'

There were two of them. There had only been one to start with, but when he asked the first question three times and she wouldn't answer, even *after* he'd stabbed her with the metal insect, he called another he-one. 'Do you think she understands?' he said. 'I've never met one like this before, she looks kinda stupid.' The new one replied that she'd clapped for Len eventually; they just had to be patient and try everything they could to make her talk.

'Weren't you frightened of what they would do to you?'

As the two biggerers talked together, it became obvious that they thought she couldn't understand. 'Is faking stupidity a characteristic of Batch Twenty?' one had laughed.

'I'm pretty sure it's not,' the other replied.

Jinx quickly learned that the metal insect was the *only* form of punishment that they were allowed to give her. And even *that* was limited. The second biggerer counted the amount of times she was stabbed, each time saying: 'You only have six punches left. You only have five punches left.' As soon as she realized he was talking about the insect bites, she let them stab her until there were none left. By the end, the first biggerer was so cross with her that he had wanted to stab her again, but the second stopped him. 'Can you imagine?' he had said. 'Can you imagine stabbing a full-human with a six-needle gun in order to make them talk? In my book that's called "torture". Yet we are using these techniques every day on beings who are protected by the same laws.'

'So, what do we do with her?' asked the first.

They stared at her for a while as they thought about this. Jinx lay on the floor, hugging her legs to her; her eyes were crying but inside her head she felt good about herself, about how *strong* she'd been. Until, that was, the first one spoke again.

'We'll just have to separate her from the group,' he said.

The other shook his head. 'No,' he said. 'Once the rest of them see her legs, they'll abandon any ideas they might have had about not co-operating.'

The other had smirked. 'I do feel sorry for her, though. I'm pretty sure she's stupid.'

'Her brain patterns would suggest that there's a light on somewhere.'

'Her brain patterns would suggest that she's in pain.'

'Give her a sedative,' said the second. 'Go heavy on the dose. In fact, make it a tranquillizer. She can sleep it off.'

'Are you sure?' said the first.

'Absolutely… Just be sure to move her session to lunchtime tomorrow. It should be out of her system by then.'

The others listened, mouths open. Was that all? How much did the metal insect hurt? Could they be as brave as Jinx and take all that pain? And they really didn't *force* her to take the pills? How would they kill her memory if they couldn't force her to take the pills? They could all do this! They could all behave the way that Jinx had behaved and then they'd get to keep their memories! And then, as their brains got stronger, they'd figure out a way to leave!

Jinx pressed her lips together and scratched at a gap in the tiles.

'Tell us how much it really hurt, Jinx. Would we be able to stand the pain?' asked Mop.

'The thing is,' Jinx replied, 'before they gave me the drug to make me sleep, they told me that, as of tomorrow, I'll be living in the next room.' She looked at the tile crack again. 'They're going to take me away to punish me for not speaking.'

Silence. Eyes darkened and rolled their gaze towards the floor.

Bonbon's mouth stretched and shrunk into shapes that couldn't turn into words. Jinx was going to the next room? To the *next room?* Her head slumped onto Jinx's thigh, silently squeezing all the tears out of it before taking a long, shuddery breath.

'Don't worry, Bonbon,' said Jinx. 'We will either see each other in a few days or…'

Her voice sounded like it was coming from the kitchen, while Bonbon was buried under the cushions in the big room. Bonbon stared up at Windy from Jinx's lap. They'd only *just* found each other, and now they would all be separated again.

'You're looking better, fella!'

A wire mouth. How could it speak if it couldn't make shapes? Chips pushed himself onto his knees and shuffled towards the front of the cage. Flake shapes swelled and shrivelled inside a cloudy frame that curled around his eyes. Flakes… Not more flakes. He stopped to lean forward and let out a puddle of yellow vomit.

'Oh dear, buddy. I guess you're not used to this, huh?'

He looked up at the wire mouth and dragged the back of his hand across his face. The clippy thing buzzed and his gaze leapt on it. The ribbon shot out and started to dance over his belly. Not again, please… He held his hand over his mouth.

'Okay, enough of that.'

A large, white finger touched the clippy thing and the ribbon disappeared.

'He's had enough.'

Chips gazed at the wire mouth, his knees shuffling forward through the vomit towards it. He would kiss it. He would hold on to it and cuddle it. He was safe now, it would keep him safe…

He stopped. Something bit his buttock and the flake shapes started to dance about again in front of him.

'We need you to sleep for a little while, fella. Just so we can show you off to your lady friend.' The wire mouth laughed. 'We'll clean you up first, don't worry.'

Moira came again at five. Everyone squatted at the edge of their cages, straining their eyes to see her. She would be the only person to come in and out of the room tomorrow. Tomorrow, the day that Jinx would leave… They watched to see if she really looked in the cages. They listened to the conversation she was having about her son who didn't want to be an accountant any more; he wanted to be a baker. They fell on their cage floors after she'd cleaned them, smelling the slippery chemical that was left, dabbing it up and rubbing their fingertips together. The ones at ground level eyed the huge vacuum bot, and its long nose that could easily suck up a littler or two and carry them back to Outside. They shuddered at its great, red belly and wondered why it screamed and wheezed as much as it did.

Once Moira had gone, Lewis came. Lewis! Of course! His head didn't even come as high as the fourth cage… He was *much* smaller than Moira. And thinner. Stares glinted over him, then back towards the opened lift. Smiles started to stretch out under noses.

Lewis slotted in a cage where Note and Hester's cage had been. A new littler peered out through the bars. As his cage swung into Jinx's view, she noticed that he had brown hair that curled over his eyebrows.

That night they welcomed the new littler, Tuff, and Jinx loved watching his eyes swell as everyone hugged him and kissed him the same way that they had been hugged and kissed on their first day. They sat him down and explained everything to him, going through their exercises, then adding everything that had been added since. They started to talk about a plan; scratching heads, puffing out cheeks and flopping chins onto hands.

'We're just too small,' said one.

'But nothing will work,' said Piddle. 'There's just no point.'

'There's always a point!' said a scratchy voice at the back of the crowd. 'Could I take my turn to talk now?' Windy asked. 'Because I'm sure that when I've told you everything, you'll all be ready to think up another plan,' she said, winking at Bonbon. 'A *better* plan.'

* * *

Thirty candles glowed on the arctic roll that leaked its milky innards onto a long Madras-print platter.

'It's too hot for arctic roll,' said Watty. 'It's going all runny. Quick, Isabel, blow out your candles.'

'Hang on. I'm thinking of a wish.'

Watty let the tart-slice flop with his hand and sighed.

Isabel blew out her candles and the two men clapped.

'Honestly,' said Watty, picking out the pink plastic holders, 'it's gone to *mush*.'

They sat out in their garden, as they always did when it was a nice evening; each holding champagne in a shallow glass, the kind that 1940s movie stars, dressed in long silky dressing gowns, would hold while swishing around their bedrooms. They toasted old Jasper, as they always did, who was buried under wild flowers in one of his favourite spots in the garden.

'Poor old Jas,' Drew sighed.

'He was just a very old boy,' said Watty. Isabel gazed at him, remembering that Watty had locked himself in his room for hours after they'd found Jas. *He was just a very old boy*, she'd tried to tell him at the time.

'One of the best-loved dogs in the world, ever.'

'I'll drink to that.' Watty clinked his glass against Drew's.

'I don't know how you two can be so relaxed about something like that.'

'He was our dog too, Quail,' said Watty, hoarsely, as champagne bubbles stuck in his throat.

'One of Watty's first presents to me.'

'Really?'

'Mmm-hmm,' Drew nodded.

'I'd rather drink to the year ahead and… well… say a little prayer for Jasper. After all, he wasn't a great drinker, was he?'

Drew and Watty took a minute to think about this.

'Quail's probably right,' said Watty. 'To the year ahead!'

'To the year ahead!' chimed the other two.

'Let's hope I won't get called into the lab too often. I've been rather lucky so far.'

Drew and Watty looked at each other over their champagne glasses.

* * *

Windy got up early in the morning. Way before the first clean was due. As she prepared to wake the others, she noticed that a few were already awake, waiting beside the black clippy boxes for the ribbon of light to weave out and find their hungry bellies. Yesterday evening, they had gone back to their cages and eaten every single flake, much earlier than they normally would. They wanted to be sure that the ribbon would find their bellies empty, and that each littler would have the maximum amount of flakes for the task that followed. Then they had returned to the floor and talked about the plan over and over and over… The ones who were due to be taken to the next room, including Loop and Osmo, pushed the others to repeat the plan long after it had been learned; everyone had their part and each part had to be synchronized.

'We are lucky that there are so many of us,' Windy had said. 'Or the plan would never have worked.'

The others clapped. They *were* lucky that there were so many of them. The plan *would* work.

Windy looked up at the clock. 07:28. The ribbons would come in two minutes. Moira would arrive in twelve minutes. She always came while they were eating as they were already at the backs of their cages and the black shutter wouldn't ram into them. They'd heard her explain this to whoever she talked to while she was cleaning. Windy got the feeling that everybody quite liked Moira; although nobody had said it.

Nobody liked Lewis.

As she thought this, the ribbon came out of its clippy box and snaked its way towards her. She never got many flakes. She understood that her old body didn't need as much food as the younger ones who spent their time climbing up and down cages. The only time she'd received a proper pile of flakes was on the first day when the others had helped her move from her cage up on the fifth row down to the ground where she would be able to go in and out more easily. Afterwards, she sat panting in her new cage while they swapped over the clippy squares.

'Are you sure nobody will notice?'

'Of course not,' they'd said. 'Don't you remember, we did exactly the same with you last week?'

They'd confused her with one of her sisters who'd been moved on to the next room. The flakes tumbled into the back of the cage. Her belly felt empty, but she couldn't manage a single mouthful.

Now, she waited as the ribbon zipped back into the black box, listening for the flakes to fall onto the floor of her cage. One at a time the cages were given their dose of flakes, but instead of the munching and rustling sounds that would usually fill the corridor, the air became still enough to hear the lift stopping at each floor above them. Moira was on her way.

The air hung still for the next nine minutes; not being pushed around by breath and movement, it wove around bellies, pressing them in, and bored into cheek hollows to open the mouths and dry them out. It refused to swoop under armpits, letting the drops of sweat build up, and it jumped into ears, bouncing off eardrums, making them thump inside the rows of waiting heads, all squashed between cage bars. New hands held on to the bars, new eyes looked towards the lift-end of the corridor, and new energy filled up the space inside the heads that had once been doubtful about carrying out plans. This plan would work! This plan would work because they were no longer littlers battling the biggerers, but, as Windy had told them last night, they were humans battling humans.

'Ready?' called Windy as she heard the lift rumbling downwards.

Feet swished and slid to the backs of cages where flakes were scooped into handfuls as the shutters came down and Moira started on the first cage, letting her vacuum bot scoot ahead of her like an owner lets his dog off its lead in the park.

As the first shutter came up, Windy heard the scattering of flakes being thrown on the floor, then scratched back up again. They would then be rolled into soft, damp balls that were hurried back to the other end of the cage so that Moira wouldn't notice what a mess they had made on her clean floors. Not that Moira would have noticed.

'It's seven thirty here, what time is it over there? I know, I know I ask you every time. You should stop answering, by the way. You're supposed to be taking a break from this place. How is Valentine, is she gonna bring you up some breakfast? Still asleep? Alright for some! I started at six. Yeah, six. I'm on split shifts now that *certain* people have abandoned me. Oh she heard that, did she? Pass her over so I can say good morning. Lazybones.'

Windy knew that her cage would be one of the last, as Moira's habit was to start on the opposite side and come back along hers. Thank goodness she was on the other side; Moira would have already left the corridor by the time she was scrabbling about on the floor then struggling to get up again.

Not that Moira *would* have caught her.

Windy stood waiting with her two small handfuls. As the shutter came back up, she lowered herself to the floor and rolled her handfuls into balls. By the time she got up again, the rest of the chemical had dried up.

'I could only manage two,' she called, long after Moira and her vacuum bot had gone back up in the lift.

'It's alright, Windy,' called Fola. 'Do you think they'll work?'

'We should taste one!' called Osmo.

'No! It's poison!'

But Osmo had already bitten into one of the sticky balls and replied through a mouthful: 'Yuk! They're horrible!'

Clapping crackled along the corridor then faded out as everyone repeated the next part of the plan, over and over, while they waited for Lewis.

CHAPTER 20

Jinx and Bonbon had gone to bed early the night before. While the others discussed the plan, the two of them wished that it would stop getting later so they could enjoy cuddles without feeling sleepy.

Now Jinx climbed from cage to cage, climbing inside of some to give cuddles and stopping only to wave into others. Bonbon lay at the back of their cage in silence, getting up to curl herself around Jinx whenever she came back to check on her.

'It's alright, Bonbon. We'll see each other this afternoon and then we'll be together forever!'

Bonbon frowned, her lips pressed into ridges and shadows as her gaze tumbled over Jinx. When the shutter came down, Bonbon flopped against her, folding her arms over her shoulders and losing her hands in her hair.

'Make this work, Bonbon. Make this plan work,' Jinx said as she hugged her back. 'Then you can come and rescue me.'

'I will!' sobbed Bonbon, telling herself that when the shutter went back up, she would refuse to let go of Jinx. If the worst they could do was stab her with the metal insect then they could do that as often as they wanted, as long she could stay with Jinx… The shutter started to lift. A purple light-ribbon came into the cage and held Bonbon so that she couldn't move. Two fingers entered the cage, unhooking Bonbon's arms as easily as if they'd been brushing dust from Jinx's shoulders. Bonbon's head was fixed at an angle. She stared at Jinx from the side of her face. She too was locked into a purple ribbon of light and pulled from the cage, her arms stuck, outstretched towards Bonbon. The cage door was shut and the ribbon deactivated. Bonbon ran to the front of the cage where she fell onto her bottom, her mouth trying to scream Jinx's name.

* * *

'Pick up, pick up!' she whispered to herself. The lab had called her in *again* and there was no one at home to take her… Again. After a couple of minutes, she hung up. They hadn't even left a *note* today; 'Just got up and went,' she said to herself, stabbing at a number on her keypad with each syllable.

They *knew* she worried. That's why they *always* left a note. Or picked up.

Maybe they were at the cinema? She took her earpiece out for a moment. Watty had had her phone designed by an anti-smartphone company. Isabel had been a fan of their cause: smartphones alienated people from, well, *people.* She was thrilled to bits when they managed to get her a mini handset, *custom*-made. It was about the size of a full-human thumb. This was still an enormous thing to put against her ear, but she couldn't ask Watty to send it back… Especially as Drew thought he'd taken a bit of a risk in having it made. 'Things like that can be traced,' he'd said. Watty had gone a bit quiet after that, eyeing the thing uneasily every time Isabel jabbed out a text message. Most of the time, she wore it in a bum-bag, preferring to use the teeny-tiny hands-free kit that was way less clompy. Now, she frowned at the glossy black handset lying in her bum-bag, still and lazy like a mini hippo. They knew she worried… Why did they do this to her? She pressed the 'call' button again and waited, tapping her foot as she stared through the window at the sky. At this rate she'd never get there. Not that she even cared about ranting any more. All she wanted was to know that…

'Hello?'

'Drew?'

'Hello, lazybones; finally out of your pit, are you?'

'Where the hell *are* you?'

'Oh Quail… You were fast asleep. Did you not see the note?'

'*No!* Where are you?'

'We're at that pick-your-own organic we told you about.'

'What about your mobiles?'

'Mine's in the car. I've just found Watty's in the grass.'

'What's the point in having them if you're never…'

'I'm sorry, darling.'

Isabel pouted into the phone.

'Did you want something, Quail? Do you want Watty to pick you up?'

'No… Actually I'd almost forgotten what I was calling for; I've been called into the lab.'

'Again?'

'Yes. Apparently they want to start a new round of tests.'

Drew paused, then: 'What for?'

'I don't know. Some new product they'd like me to "work with".'

Drew scrunched his face right up and skipped his gaze across the rows of strawberry plants towards Watty. 'You're not going on your own, are you?'

'Well, yes… They called me at short notice.'

'I'm on my way.'

'No, Drew… It's too late. They're sending a car.'

'Not on your own, Quail. Please.'

'I'll be fine. I'm not frightened. Honestly.'

'Well… I'm coming anyway.'

'No!'

'Yes, young lady. I mean it.'

Isabel was quiet for a moment, then: 'Fine. But only if Watty comes in with me. I don't think it's a good idea for you to see Hector.'

'I'm not worried about him. He must be getting on for seventy now—'

'I have to go,' she interrupted. 'I haven't had a shower yet. Promise me you'll wait outside?'

The line went dead. Drew tapped his mobile against his chin; what on Earth did Hector want with her? He heaved himself up from his row of strawberries and watched as Watty reached into the depths of a sprawling tomato plant, his face screwing up as he felt around for the fleshy globes. Neither of them was getting any younger. He wondered if Watty would look across and notice that something was up. 'What does he want with her?' he said to the tip of the phone, now resting on his lips, his unblinking eyes idled over the rows of berries and bent-over backsides.

'I've told you a gazillion times not to put the phone in your mouth.' Watty stood in front of him with gardening gloves in one hand and a basket of tomatoes in the other. 'What's going on in there?' he nodded towards Drew's forehead.

'Isabel's been called in to the lab.'

Watty tutted. 'Always at such short notice.'

Drew shrugged. 'Will you drive us there?'

'Absolutely,' Watty nodded, pulling off his gardening gloves.

* * *

Them again. What were they planning on doing to her today? The metal insect, probably. Well, fine… The worst thing they could do would be to put her into the Next Room. And that was exactly what they were going to do…

Jinx felt her stomach dent as if someone had poked it. Planning the plan had helped her to take her mind off, well, the rest of her *life*, and in fact, that was the problem. If the plan went well then the rest of her life would be as lovely as the first part. They would come to rescue her, then they would all take the lift to the top floor and run away from the building. She blew out her cheeks and held them like that; there were a few problems with the plan. None of them knew how to work a lift; in fact, most of them didn't know what one was until they'd arrived here. And even if they did manage to make it move, they didn't know how to find the Next Room, or the way out; how silly was that? And Lewis probably carried something on him, just like Moira's talky thing, so he could call someone in an emergency. Jinx felt her shoulders curl over and realized that her cheeks were still puffed out.

'Are you going to answer us today or not?'

'Did you hear the first question?'

Jinx let her pupils float towards their gaze and started to chew her finger.

A hand came in and clipped something to the back of her head. 'Let's see what's going on in there, shall we?'

'Do you remember where you lived before you lived with your owner?'

'—.'

'Okay. Have you ever communicated vocally with your owner?'

Jinx sat on the floor and started to squeeze one of her feet with both hands. This was very easy; the worst thing that could happen to her was going to happen; what did they expect her to do?

'Do you have a friend called Chips?'

Her eyes snapped upwards.

'Ah! Did you see that?' said one.

'That's nothing. You should see her brain activity!'

'Love?'

'Oh yeah. *Big* time.'

'Are you in love with Chips?'

Jinx glared as the one who was looking at the screen whooped at what he could see. 'I think we've got her!' he cried.

'Would you like to see Chips?'

Jinx folded her arms and scowled, hardly realizing that she'd jumped up, and strode to the front of the cage.

'Well, would you? All you have to do is say so.'

Maybe she should just clap. They would just keep hassling her until she *did*; and this wasn't for nothing, this could be the last time she'd ever see her Chips. Surely she should just clap. Her future would be the same whether she clapped or not, but if she *did* clap, at least she'd get to see her Chips.

'Maybe she doesn't believe us. You'd better show her.'

A square of wall illuminated behind the two white heads. They stood aside to let her see. It was like a, sort of, black window partly filled with orange light. It reminded Jinx of the thing that the She-one used to make things hot. In the middle, a littler slept on a ledge. Jinx squinted. It seemed a little fatter than Chips. Its closed eyes slept above white skin instead of purple smudges; and it lay still and peaceful, not twitchy or panicky. But she knew even before she'd noticed all these different things, it was her Chips. As the hairs on her body rose towards him, lifting her arms upwards with them, her eyes seemed to rub out the lines of the cage that blocked her view, then make a hole in the window with the funny light and hover over her Chips.

'Would you like to touch him? Would you like to give him a cuddle?'

Jinx's eyes felt squeezed as they hovered over her sleeping Chips. Tears plopped from her nose and her own arms wrapped themselves around her own shoulders. A hot feeling started at her toes, like when she accidentally pissed on her own feet, yet rather than hammering down on them, it seemed to be filling up her ankles and legs, getting angrier as she wouldn't move them, as she wouldn't let it run her legs from the cage, through the air and to her Chips. Instead she let it fill up her tummy, and chest, and arms; maybe she would use them to fly herself to Chips. She didn't. The feeling got angrier, rising to her throat, and as her mouth opened, she lifted her hands and bashed them together once.

'Right,' said one of the men as he turned to switch off the window. Chips disappeared. Jinx gazed up at the men. What would they do? Would they get him out? Or would they take her to him?

The cage door opened and a hand came in holding a tube. The hand pressed the end of it and the insect bit her belly. As she tried to scramble away it was pressed again on her thigh, and one last time on her shoulder blade.

'That's what you get for holding out on us,' said one.

'What was the point? We knew you could clap! Just like we know you can speak,' said the other.

'I've never known *any* of them to refuse like that.'

'But even from her brain signals!'

'Oh, I could tell that there was more to her from the brain signals.'

'Yeah, but she's obviously a bit of an actress.'

Jinx heard them talking but didn't listen, not knowing which part of her to try and make better first. The skin on her tummy was so soft, she was sure that the insect had bitten her right the way to her insides; and it had bitten her leg in the same place as yesterday. She covered her mouth with one hand and tried not to be sick on the floor. The pain from her stomach pulled both her arms back around it and she dropped down onto her side and cried. The two technicians talked about how they weren't paid to resolve this kind of behaviour and they'd almost certainly make a 'special services' claim. Why weren't the mentally ill ones weeded out from the beginning by Len? They had never, ever seen anything like that before. She was obviously defective… Jinx imagined herself pulling her arms from her arms as if they were coat sleeves, her head from the hat that was her own head, and pulling her legs up and out of her own legs as if they were trousers.

'Why did you get her on the stomach?'

'I don't know… She was struggling and… I just had to get her where I could.'

'And on the shoulder? Jeez! Never above the legs!'

'I'm sorry, like I say she was… she was trying to get away.' He paused for a moment. 'What do we do now?'

'We're going to give her a warm bath then send her to the silent room.'

'No more questions?'

'No more questions.' He shook his head and turned away. 'If she's only clapped twice in seventy-two hours, she's not going to speak.'

Jinx imagined herself curling up under the bones in her chest, away from her ears, her eyes and the bite in her stomach. She thought about the plan. Pulling it over her like a curved, green leaf.

'Um… Did you take him out?'

'No, why?'

'The box is empty.'

* * *

One, two, three, four and… one, two. Four up, two across. When Isabel was only an embryo, Drew would run from the bus stop every morning to see her. For some reason, his legs were never fast enough. He would count the windows on the lab building; one, two, three, four up; one, two across; letting his mind do something while it waited for his slow legs to take him to the other side of Isabel's window.

Now, in the car, he counted again, the same feeling blowing out his chest, as if someone had stuck a foot pump in his heart.

So many seconds would tick by between shifts; had he missed the very one, because it only took *one*, for death to scurry in and snatch his little egg while nobody was around to shoo it away. He felt the sweat under his arms from where his body remembered itself running; the smell of morning London, exhaust fumes, fried breakfasts, perfume and bad breath, swirled around his nostrils. One, two, three, four and... one, two.

Watty's legs walked towards the car. Were they Watty's legs? Drew looked up the body; they were indeed. And, he was holding Isabel! That was unusual. He didn't often pick her up these days... He got out of the car and waved. Neither of them waved back. Watty's face was serious.

'What's happened?'

Isabel was crying. He ran towards her. 'What's happened, Quail?'

'It's alright,' said Watty. 'Let's just get into the car.'

'Tell me. What's happened?'

'In the car, Drew.'

'Why? I'll bloody knock him out, Watty! What's he done?'

'That's precisely why you're going to get into the car.' Watty put Isabel in the front passenger seat, then pushed Drew into the back seat of the car. 'Mind fingers,' he said, before shutting the door.

* * *

At one o'clock they were ready for him. It was just a case of waiting, as he could come at any time. Every cage door rested against its lock not *quite* closed. Every ball of flakes had been moved to the twelve central cages at ground level; six on one side, six on the other. Lips moved quickly, shaping words that remembered the role of each person; over and over again. Every now and then someone would shout a question: 'Do I stand on Lamb's shoulders or will Lamb stand on mine?' and the answer would come back immediately: 'You, then Lamb, then Fola, then Bonbon because Bonbon's the littlest.'

'Me, then Lamb, then Fola, then Bonbon. Because Bonbon is the littlest…' would echo back in a whisper.

At three o'clock, Windy heard the lift and knew from the sound of its approach that it had skipped the room above, where it would occasionally stop, and come straight to their floor. 'I think it's Lewis,' she said. 'But hold fire; it might just be Moira.'

The lift doors opened. The first sign that it could be Moira, the vacuum bot, did not come scooting out as it usually did. This was it. This was Lewis.

Lewis walked out of the lift, checking that it had stayed open as it was supposed to. These underground corridors were creepy. He liked to be sure that the lift hadn't malfunctioned and buzzed away to another floor while he was busy installing the littlers. For a successful company, the technology in the underground corridors was very ropey. Almost primitive. He didn't trust it one bit. He always programmed the lift to take him to the floors that he absolutely had to stop at; the less time spent down here, the better. He checked the number on the cage to see where this new littler, Video, would be placed for the next week or so. She was actually quite cute, he thought as he took his first steps into the corridor; *hot* even. He would probably have a little think about her later; obviously the life-size version. Why was it so quiet down here? Jeez they could be weird sometimes. All standing at their doors, looking at him like that. Yuk! So *creepy*. At least it smelled better in here now.

He heard a noise; a cage door opening. Such a simple, *normal* noise that he didn't realize he shouldn't have been hearing it until all of the cage doors were opening and littlers were on his shoulders and his head and pulling at his legs trying to knock him over. He lifted his arms; littlers hung from them, wrapping themselves around his wrist as he tried to lift it to his mouth to shout for help: what the hell was happening? His eyes were pulled shut and his nose pinched closed; he gasped and something was thrown inside his mouth. Sweat and cheese and strong vinegar dissolved into his tongue. He opened his mouth again to spit it out but more was thrown inside, this time burning the tip and sides of his tongue. Tiny hands pulled at his trousers and sleeves. Several littlers now hung from his wrist as he tried again to raise it into the air and across to his mouth; his toes were pushed upwards and he rocked on his heels. He opened his mouth to shout and more of whatever that stuff was landed inside. He tried to spit again to make room for air, more stuff was thrown in and pushed to the back of his tongue. The hands pinched at his nostrils, tightly, forcing Lewis to swallow. Tiny bodies threw themselves against his shins; he toppled and fell on his back. Winded, he shook his head to free his pinched nose, it worked, he breathed one deep breath before his nose was stuffed with the vinegar-smelling cheese. He spluttered, his throat contracted; his mouth tried to gag. His eyes still held tightly shut by sharp little fingernails.

After twenty minutes, each littler was sure that Lewis would not get up again right away. In fact, they had felt that way after ten minutes but couldn't tell each other, so they stood on his belly or his chest or his thighs with their hands on their hips, waiting for everyone to finish. Two of them went to let Video out of her cage and gestured that she should go with them.

Loop jumped into the centre of the corridor and put his hand in the air. The others followed him right into the lift where they looked for where the button should have been. Hmmm… There was one on the outside, where was the one on the inside? Fola realized that they had to press the outside one in order to close the doors. She waved to Lamb and Bonbon and they followed her. They staggered and wobbled and toenails dug into hips and backs; Fola kept slipping so Piddle took her place then Bonbon climbed up the whole swaying tower. Bonbon stretched and pushed in the button with the very tips of her fingers before being launched forward into the lift where she was caught by the waiting crowd.

Piddle and Lamb zipped through the line in the closing lift doors. 'We…,' breathe, 'did it…' gasped Piddle. The others cheered then were silenced by a recorded voice that told them they were going down.

'Is that the right way?' asked one.

'Don't know,' said another.

'Are we going to the Next Room?'

'No. No, we can't be because the Next Room is *above* our corridor.'

'Is it?'

'I'm sure it's below. Didn't Moira say it was below?'

'We *must* be going there.'

'There was only one button,' said Bonbon. 'And it didn't say where it went to.'

'Maybe we have to go all the way down in order to go back up again?' said another.

'Well, then we're bound to come across the Next Room at some point.'

Yes, they agreed, they would find the Next Room at some point… In the meantime they planned who would get out at the next floor to press the button.

'If it is the Next Room, we have to rescue the others,' said Windy.

'I'm sure it's not,' said another.

'But what if it is?'

'What if Jinx isn't there yet?' said Bonbon. 'We'll have to come back for her.'

'We can't rescue the others now anyway; what if Moira is trying to call the lift back up? The lift would go without us,' said Mop. 'Our priority is to get out of here.'

'It's the best thing to do for the others as well…'

'We'll be no use to them if the plan fails and we all end up trapped.'

'If we are free, we can help them.'

'But… we have to get Jinx!' Bonbon's gaze jumped from face to face. Each pair of eyes looked at the ground, or the walls, or the ceiling. Lamb put an arm around her.

'Think about it, Bonbon. We're no use to them if we're trapped.'

Bonbon thought. If she made them stop and search the room, then the lift went away and left them there, it would be her fault; the plan would have failed… She had *sworn* to Jinx that she would make the plan work. She held a hand out to steady herself on Lamb, her breathing so fast that her chest felt hot. 'We will come back, won't we?' said Bonbon. 'It's a long way down but we *have* to come back.'

'The doors will be opening soon; I will go out and press the button,' said Mop. 'Fola, Lamb, Bonbon; will you get onto my shoulders?'

They nodded, then climbed onto Mop.

They waited, eyes angled towards the door.

'Doors opening,' said the lift.

Hands covered cheeks and teeth bit lips as the doors ssshhhed open, the silence on the outside so thick that it seemed to push the three littlers back into the lift.

They wobbled out into a dim corridor. Bonbon let out a noise as she felt herself swaying too far one way. That was funny; how could she make a noise in the Next Room? Obviously this wasn't the Next Room. That meant that Jinx wasn't there! Thank goodness… It felt so horrible and dark in here; it would have been awful to get back into the lift knowing she was stuck in this horrible and dark place.

'Gloomy,' said the old littler. Yes, she agreed; gloomy. Hopefully nothing had to live down here at all.

She reached for the button. A face watched her from the nearest cage. One side of the face was much larger than the other and the cheeks and forehead were covered with dark hair. It lifted an arm to wave at Bonbon but there was no hand at the end of it. Bonbon stared.

'Hurry, Bonbon,' called Fola.

Bonbon pressed the button and was thrown back into the lift. The others caught her and placed her feet on the floor. She turned to glimpse the handless being but the doors had already closed it behind them.

'Going up,' said the lift.

'So, that was the Next Room, where we would have been doomed to spend the next few months,' said Mop.

'That wasn't the Next Room,' said Bonbon. 'Didn't you notice when Fola spoke? The Next Room is supposed to be silent.'

The others wrinkled their heads. 'So where was it then?'

Bonbon shrugged. 'I don't know,' then: 'What if we don't stop at the Next Room? How will we know where it is?'

'It must be above our corridor,' said one.

'It must be!' said another.

Bonbon shook her head. 'I really think we should rescue them as soon as we stop there.'

'But our priority is to get out!'

'We won't stop there,' said Windy. 'Lewis didn't stop there on the way down.'

Bonbon scrunched up her eyes. 'But then how are we going to get back in to rescue the others?'

'We'll hide somewhere. Just like we said in the plan.'

'But…' Bonbon scratched inside her hair. 'Don't you think someone will notice we're gone?'

'Don't start getting panicky, Bonbon,' said Osmo. 'We just have to hope that Moira doesn't look in the cages, that's all.'

'Shit, this is risky.'

'She never looks in the cages.'

'But what about Video?'

'She never looks in the cages!'

'But Video's cage is on the floor,' said Bonbon.

The lift went silent.

'Lewis is on the floor!' shouted Bonbon. 'This whole plan is complete shit!'

Loop came forward and put his arm on Bonbon's shoulders while Lamb slipped hers around her waist. 'Bonbon,' said Loop, 'we can't come back for the others.'

'What?'

'You said it yourself, Bonbon. If we hide somewhere and try to get back in, the plan won't work.'

'The biggerers will be looking for us,' said Lamb.

Bonbon watched the space just in front of her eyes. 'A lie,' said the littler inside her head. 'They told you a lie.' Her gaze focused on Windy, who looked around at all the faces trying to figure out if everyone knew about this. Tired from the meeting, she had gone to bed even before Bonbon and Jinx.

'The plan won't work *anyway*!' she shouted in her scratchy voice. 'Where do you think we're going to go when the lift stops? Do you think they're going to let us leave the building?'

'The best chance of us getting out is if we are quick,' Loop replied. 'Before anyone realizes that we're gone...'

'But we *promised* her!' shouted Bonbon; her fists clenched and the edges of her mouth pulling downwards.

The others blinked at her. 'It would never have worked,' said Fola, stroking Bonbon's forearm.

'Doors opening,' said the lift.

'But she's waiting...' sobbed Bonbon. 'She'll be all on her own; she'll be...'

Bonbon closed her mouth as daylight filled up the lift. A hallway opened out in front of them. It was white and empty. Not ten metres away, glass doors closed the grey sky outside. A window in the far wall darkened slightly as whatever was behind it shifted position.

Mop tried his voice. It worked. There was nobody to hear them.

They had no choice, thought Bonbon, trying to step forward but not being able to move her legs; as if Jinx was holding on to one of her ankles as she used to do at home. 'Come back to bed for a while, Bonbon,' she would say. Bonbon closed her eyes; as soon as she found the She-one they would come back and get her. Together.

Loop and Mop beckoned them out of the lift. Bonbon felt for Windy's hand.

Awake. Orange lights striped across the ceiling. Something pinched at his belly.

'Good trick that. I'm surprised she even recognized him.'

Chips sat up. Two biggerer backs gleamed white through the black glass. He leaned closer but, ouch… What was that on his belly? And ouch! Again on his thigh.

Movement drew his eye back to the window. The backs separated. An elbow stuck out from long hair and a hand covered a tiny tummy. Jinx! He leapt towards the window. His Jinx! He waved, but she was all hidden in hair. He called out to her, 'Jinx!' but his voice wouldn't work. He lifted his hand to smack on the window but, ouch! His belly. He glanced down towards it, then back at her. She had pushed her hair back and he could see the up-and-down of her top lip. It wobbled and glittered with snot. He felt his ears get hot as his eyes reached the hand on her stomach and then the circle of holes on her thigh. His own thigh throbbed in exactly the same place. He looked down at it; there was nothing. An arm was raised and a metal tube swooped to the back of Jinx's shoulder. Her wobbly mouth opened and she flopped forward. His own shoulder stung; he turned to see who had bitten it – no one, there was no one there! The heat from his ears rolled through his neck and along his arms. He pressed at the glass, his gaze flicking between his hands and Jinx. That wobbly, soundless cry. He would never forget that wobbly, soundless cry. A bumping in his chest knocked down into his stomach. He turned and strode to the other side of the cage, pressing at the bottom of the wall, then at the top, then screwing up his face and letting his whole body fall against it.

A white line opened along the bottom. Chips stopped and followed it with his eyes, along the bottom, up the corner and across the top. He pushed harder. The line grew fatter. Glancing back through the black window, he ran to the corner, held his belly in and slipped through the white line.

* * *

The tiny teacup wobbled in its saucer as Reg set it down on the table.

'Here you go, Quail.'

'Thanks, Reg,' she sniffed.

'Poor Quail. How about I get you some chocolate cake? Freshly made this morning.'

Isabel shook her head. 'No thanks.'

'Everything alright?' Reg took in the sagging mouths, one by one.

'Tickety boo, Reg,' Watty answered. 'Nothing we can't handle.'

Reg winked at Watty. Understood. He hoisted up the waistband on his trousers and went back over to the counter.

Isabel took a deep breath and sat back. 'She was just so perfect. You know, exactly the same as, as *me*.' She smirked. 'I never realized I looked like that until I saw… myself. I suppose you could say.'

'It's an outrage.' Drew uttered the words without intonation. He stared at nothing.

'Where do you suggest we go from here?'

'We'll expose him.'

Damp patches bloomed under Watty's arms. Bringing Hector down would also expose Drew. 'Now listen, Quail. Are you absolutely *sure* about what you saw?'

Isabel's irises tripped in their whites, red patches trotted up her neck and across her face.

'Alright, darling. Of course you did. I'm sorry…'

'She was right there, on the other side of the glass. Like a reflection. And then she grinned at me just as someone scooped her up and took her away.'

'Who took her away?' asked Drew.

Isabel shrugged.

'Did they see you?'

'I *think* so.'

'Was anything else said to you about all of this?' interjected Watty.

'No. Just… No, nothing.'

'Mmm,' said Drew. 'I just don't understand what he wants it for… And what if he makes more than one? He has to be stopped before he makes more.'

Isabel smacked her palms on the table. 'You two do what you like. *I'm* going to try and talk to her.'

Drew's eyes flicked towards her. 'Who?'

'The clone. I want to see her again.'

Watty opened his mouth but Drew spoke. 'You can't really, Quail…'

'Why not?'

'Because… Do you think they'd let you?'

'If I say that I've already seen her, they might.'

'Isabel, I understand exactly what you're feeling…' Watty began.

'How can you?'

'Because I brought you up!'

'—.'

'The fact is that, whatever you're expecting… *she* will never be your friend.'

'So, what will happen to her? He can't tell anyone about her. She'll just sit in a cage and rot.' She shuffled in her seat. 'That's not a life.'

'Someone else in the lab will take care of her.'

'But I can help her!'

Watty shook his head. 'I really don't think you should get involved.'

'Anything could go wrong with her, Isabel. She's not human, not *properly* human.' Drew sat back in his chair, watching his hand as it twitched on the table like a dying rodent. 'She's some poor hash-together of bits of your cells. She'll be dead in months, Isabel. Maybe a couple of years… I won't let you see that, I just won't.' He glanced up from his hand.

'Isabel!' Drew stood up and looked about him. 'Did you see where she went?'

'No,' said Watty, already hanging on to the table and peering under it. 'I was listening to you.'

'Isabel!' said Drew again. 'Isabel! Isabel!'

'What's happened?' called Reg.

The three of them searched the launderette, leaning over washing units and peeping into gaps between books.

'Do you think she went outside?' said Reg.

'I don't see how… She's probably just really well hidden,' said Watty, checking behind a pyramid of cheese scones.

Drew got up from his hands and knees. 'I bet I know exactly where she's gone.'

Watty read his mind. 'Isabel, if you are here, Drew's just about to trawl the streets for you. Do you really want him to do that?'

The three men bent down and cocked their ears. Drew stood up and shook his head. Three seconds later, he was gone.

CHAPTER 21

Jinx had never had a bath before. The only water she'd ever played in was the tile water and that had made her sick once. But this water smelled of heat and made lumpy clouds around and above her. She opened her mouth to bite one. Nothing. It tasted of nothing.

The biggerers had left her for at least ten minutes. She thought about this, as she made noises with the water by flicking her toes; they were only being nice to her because they had hurt her. And as they couldn't hurt her again, they wouldn't have to be nice any more… She leaned forward and fluttered her eyelashes on the surface of the water, making plopping and tinkle noises. This would probably be the last time she would have a bath. And it was *only* the first. She didn't want to never have another bath…

'Jinx.'

Jinx spun her head to the side. 'What?'

'Come here!'

Chips! 'Chips, is that you, Chips?'

'Yes.'

She stood up in the bath and turned all the way around. 'I can't see you.'

'Why?' he said.

She screwed up her eyes. A head popped out from behind a white brick-thing. Jinx sloshed out of the bath and splatted over to it.

'Quickly, Jinx!' he hissed as she threw her arms around his belly. 'We have to go.'

'Is it really you?' Her eyes blinked at his belly. He put his hands on his hips and stuck it out.

'And your *arms*...' she said, squeezing the top part of his arm. 'I can't make my fingers touch.'

'And my cheeks, look how fat my cheeks are.'

She laughed. 'You're all crusty around your mouth!'

Frowning, he folded his lips in.

'Doesn't matter.' She stood on her toes and kissed him.

He took her hand. 'Let's climb down to the floor and wait for the door to open.'

He turned to run, but Jinx pressed back on her heels. He stopped. 'Come on, Jinx!'

'It won't work, Chips, they'll be back soon...'

He wrinkled his eyebrows. 'We have to *try*...'

'There's no *point*.'

'But, what else are we going to do?'

Jinx understood that; doing things that didn't mean anything. Like collecting stones or... searching for food when there was no food. She breathed a breath all the way to the bottom of her belly and nodded. 'Okay.'

Chips went first. 'Put your feet on the sticky-out bits. That's where I put mine when I climbed up.'

'I can't believe you're really here, Chips!'

'You'll have to jump at the bottom, but I'll catch you.'

'Okay.'

At the bottom, Chips lifted her down. Easy-peasy, she thought, with his new arms. She looked about her and pulled him into a gap between the thing they'd climbed down and a tall basket. 'We'll just,' breathe, 'wait here,' breathe.

He put his nose against hers and looped his arms around her shoulders. 'Let's stay together for always.'

Jinx's cheeks squeezed wet twinkles from her eyes. 'But they'll catch us…'

'No… Don't say it.' Chips spread his eyes. 'We can just pretend. Just while we're here… Like a lie, but a *good* lie…'

Jinx thought for a moment. 'A wish,' she sniffed.

'We'll have a nice basket,' he said, pulling her wet hair out to the sides to make two long ears.

'And it'll smell nice,' said Jinx.

'And we'll have nice humcoats.'

She looked down and put her hands on his stomach. 'And we'll fill your belly every day with as many flakes as you want.'

She felt her cage being slotted into its place. 'Chips.' She made the shape with her lips as she leaned over her knees and pulled her hair around her face. She would not look to see where she was. It would all be new, and newness meant that time had pushed her forward, into a new bit of life. She didn't want it. She wanted to go backwards, just a little way, and stay there. In that gap between the basket and the thing they'd climbed down, she and Chips, and then go forward again, but to the nice-smelling basket, the humcoats and the flakes…

They'd waited in that gap for a line to open up in the door. It did. The two white biggerers walked through it.

'They've gone behind the laundry basket. I *knew* he'd come out.'

Chips looked at Jinx and made his eyes big. He jerked his head towards the door.

'We should have come back straight away.'

Jinx took Chips's hand and peered out from behind the basket.

'Come on… No harm in letting them have a little cuddle.'

'Just because you stabbed her three times.'

Chips tapped Jinx on the shoulder and pointed for her to go. She held his cheek in her free hand and kissed him. Then they turned and ran, their hands breaking hold as they neared the door.

'There they are!'

'Shut the door.'

The doors drew together. Jinx ran ahead, glancing back at Chips. 'Go,' he mouthed.

'She's going to get through.'

'She won't get far.'

'I just hope nobody else sees her…'

She slid through the gap and headed for a plant with branches that curled down towards the floor. Good, maybe they could climb one and hide in the leaves. It would look after them, like the one at home whenever that bot was swooshing about. She turned back.

She stopped running.

Her knees wobbled and she fell onto them.

The doors had closed. A white line still gleamed from the top. It got lost behind white fingers that tried to pull it wider, then was unbroken, all the way to her Chips. His head laid on its ear, his left arm stretched out towards her. His body stuck inside the line.

'Oh God.'

'Will we be sacked for this?'

'No. But if he dies, there'll be a stack of forms.'

'Terence!'

Jinx's eyes filled and blurred. She crossed her hands over her mouth.

'Did he just say "Terence"?'

'They do that when they're about to…'

'Stupid door… There, that's got it.'

'Terence.'

Four hands swooped down and cupped each end of the body. A red line ran up and over Chips's new tummy.

'I've got him… Go and get her, will you?'

Fists banged on cage doors. Jinx pressed her face further into her unbitten leg. Bonbon had told her about that, the name thing. She'd heard it at the doctor's... Those others had said a name, just before they died, she'd said. What would Bonbon say when she heard about Chips? She thought about her Outside and her Chips, Bonbon and Blankey. Meeting every day. Even when they did get home, how would they be happy without ever seeing Chips again? Tears zipped down her leg and joined up between her feet. She would stay with those lovely thoughts of her Outside... Chips would be alive in her head if she didn't start to get used to what was around her. She squeezed her eyelids together and covered her ears with her hands. Bonbon and the others would rescue her before she'd even had the time to make this place into memories, she thought, and then they would collect Chips, and lay him to sleep somewhere much nicer than this place. Maybe she could keep him with her, and cuddle him and talk to him and stroke his belly...

The banging continued.

Jinx peeled herself out of her body again and crawled under her chest bones. That had worked really well when she'd been with those two white-plastic he-ones. Maybe it would work now to block out the banging.

She sat like that for *ages* until she started to wonder when the others would come and if she should be making sure she could walk so she'd be ready for the rescue. Her stomach folded and bubbled. Chips would never be rescued. She sniffed. But he would want her to get out of there.

The banging was louder now. It seemed like more than one door was being banged against. It couldn't hurt to take a little look at who was making all that noise. Especially as *they* were going to be rescued too.

Jinx opened her eyes, went to the front of the cage and peered through the bars. The banging stopped. She looked into the cage in front of her, then the one above that *and* the one above that.

Then all the cages either side of the cages in front of her. She shook her head and stared again. Her legs were filling up with bath water so hot that she wanted to kick it out of them and as it got to her tummy she wanted to open her own belly button and let the water pour over the floor, but she didn't. It filled her arms and squeezed her hands into fists, then rose up through her neck, pulled on her hair so hard that her head jerked back, stuck its fingers in her mouth, held on to her throat and squeezed: 'NO!' she screamed. 'NO!'

The faces stared, eyes wide as the word was repeated over and over again.

'You were the only thing left to hope about!' she cried at the faces. All those faces from the previous room. All those faces who'd now been crammed together into groups of four and five, forced to live silently in the same tiny cage. Loop and Mop and Lamb and Osmo and her Bonbon. Her Bonbon in a different cage; a cage high up from the floor and so far towards the right that Jinx almost couldn't see her. 'Bonbon!' she shouted as she smacked the glass door in front of her. 'Bonbon, get me out of here!' She felt her way across the door to an airhole and pushed her mouth up against it. 'Can't we even get out?'

Bonbon shook her head and pointed to a big gold thing that hung from the lock of her cage. 'Padlock,' said the inside of Jinx's head and realizing what this was she cried again.

'But we can't stay like this forever! What happened? What are you doing here?'

The faces stared back at her without blinking.

'Tell me! Mop… tell me what happened!'

Mop pointed to his mouth and shook his head.

Jinx looked around her own cage, her mouth open and panting. Littlers that she'd never seen before sat rocking, or twisting their bodies weirdly or chewing their own hands.

The breaths stopped.

She flicked her gaze up to the other cages, one hand over her throat. 'I can talk!' she said aloud just to make sure. 'I *can* talk, can't I? Can all of you hear me?'

The rows of heads nodded.

Jinx was silent for a moment as she padded her fingertips over her throat and thought about her new voice. But what was the point in talking if no one could answer? 'Irony,' said the inside of her head. 'Although that means I can talk to *them*? Do you think that means I *can*?' She jumped to the front of the cage.

The heads nodded again.

Her eyes skipped over them… She tried to see up and down the corridor as far as she could. But who could she talk to? 'But who can I talk to?' she yelled.

The others shrugged, except for one who banged on his glass cage. She looked at him, Tuft, and watched as he pointed back towards the lift, then strolled up and down his cage with the thumb and baby finger of one hand held against his ear and mouth. Two others in his cage stopped eating their hands and watched him. He moved his lips as if he were talking to his finger. 'I don't understand.' Jinx shook her head. 'Who are you trying to be?'

Moira's vacuum bot went zooming along the corridor before she'd had the chance to get out of the lift. She giggled. Funny little thing it was. In fact, she was really quite pleased to have it around sometimes, even though it wasn't alive. Especially after what had happened this afternoon with poor Lewis; crikey! Who'd have thought it? They knocked him out completely, banging his head against the ground like that… He could have choked to death. What frightened her the most was the thought that had gone into it, quite frankly. It was all very premeditated. Rolling the flakes in the vinegar just after she'd cleaned… How had they managed to think that up? Good job she only ever used vinegar. She'd never forget Lewis's video call from the basement corridors, looking into the screen with yellow crust all around his mouth and in his hair. She chuckled. He could be a real shit sometimes. And funnily enough, she was *sure* that they sensed it, the fact that he could be a shit. That was why they'd chosen him. It could have just as easily been her… Ha ha, all that yellow gunge crusting around his nostrils! Poor little mites. She would have kicked off too if she'd been stuck underground and force-fed memory suppressants. Poor, poor things. And the worst thing was, they almost made it! She would have told them if she'd known what they were planning: you can only open the glass door with your chip *and* your thumb print. They should really have waited somewhere until someone opened the door; but then they would have been seen by that someone. Doomed from the start. Poor, *poor* things.

'Moira?'

Moira jerked her head. The suction pack was on as well as the vacuum bot – maybe it had got something stuck in it? Sometimes it squeaked…

'MOI-RA!'

She spun around. That was definitely her name, but… there was nobody there. Only those poor things chewing on their feet and dribbling onto the floor. One littler stood right up against her door with her lips pressed through the airhole. The one next to her sat rocking with her back to the glass.

'Moira! I'm here, look!'

Her eyes flicked back to the one who was standing up. Her mouth dropped open.

'Yes. Me. Jinx,' said Jinx, standing back to rub her throat, wondering if Moira could really hear her. 'Hello?'

Moira switched off the suction pack and blinked into the cage. 'Hello?' she tried, getting closer to the littler, her own voice bouncing off the glass doors all the way along the corridor. She looked back towards the lift, then reached behind her and turned the suction pack back on. 'Are you talking? How… how can you talk?'

'Erm… I don't know,' replied Jinx. 'But I only found out today.'

'Shit! You speak really well! You speak English like me! How'd you learn that in one day?'

Jinx thought for a moment as to what 'English' was. Hmmm… 'I speak every day, but never in front of the biggerers…' She opened her eyes wide. 'Can you really hear me? It feels a bit like I'm dreaming.'

'Ha! You don't say!' laughed Moira, as quietly as she could. 'Yes, yes. I can hear you. What was that word you used? Biggers?'

'Big-ger-rers,' Jinx pronounced carefully. 'Don't you know that word?'

Moira stuck her lips out and shook her head. 'No. No I don't. I guess it's like littlers but bigger.' She laughed again before repeating to herself. 'Biggerers.' Then: 'Oh shit!' she turned and pressed the black clippy square on the cage she had been cleaning. The shutter slid back up and four littlers stared at her, their pupils like portholes. 'Sorry, guys,' she said. 'Wait, they can't talk?' She turned back to Jinx.

'No… Only me, I think.'

'But that's amazing!' Moira's eyes gaped as she said 'amazing'.

'I need your help,' said Jinx.

'What happened to your belly?'

Jinx looked at her belly and felt her eyes go blurry again. 'They did this.' Sniff.

'They did?'

Jinx nodded.

Moira covered her mouth and gasped. 'Does it hurt?'

Another nod. 'And then they… Then they…'

'They what?'

'They killed Chips.'

'Who's Chips?'

'Chips is…' sniff, 'my… darling.' She held her cheeks, her chest jumping as she breathed jerky breaths. 'They shut him in a door.'

'Who shut him in a door? The guys from here?'

A nod.

'Oh, that's awful.' Moira's gaze twinkled all over Jinx, her mouth moving without knowing what words to make. She hadn't heard about a death… Maybe all the Lewis stuff had overshadowed it, but, even so… 'I haven't heard of anyone dying. Maybe he'll be okay?'

Jinx shook her head. 'He said something in front of them. He said "Terence".'

Moira's eyebrows made dents in her forehead. 'I would have definitely heard about that…'

Jinx sniffed. 'Really?'

'I'm pretty sure, yes…'

'But he spoke!'

The wrinkles deepened. 'But *you're* speaking!' Moira shook her head, her stare travelling down to Jinx's feet and back up again to the mouth. The talking mouth. Shit. Jinx really was like Moira. Exactly the same but much smaller, *obviously*.

Jinx's eyes brightened. 'I *am* speaking!' She looked up at the others. Ed nodded at her, eyebrows raised.

Moira followed her gaze. Ed's neck stiffened.

'Does that mean he might be okay?'

Moira blinked back at her. 'Like I said, I'm sure I would have heard about this. I've been here all day.' Her eyes narrowed and got closer to the cage. 'I really wish there was some way I could help you all to get out of here…'

'That's why I called out to you.' Jinx wiped under an eye with the heel of her hand. 'Please help us. It's so nasty here.'

'Oh you poor dear…' Moira sighed, putting her head against the glass. 'I just don't know what I can do. They're such a big company and… And I have a kid and…' She tailed off and they looked at each other for a while, her head still resting against the bars. After a moment or two, she stood up straight and wiped her nose. 'And he would be *horrified* by all this. What is it that you want me to do?'

Jinx scrunched her mouth up to one side of her face and let her gaze creep from Moira's mouth to her ear.

'Will you let me use your talky thing?'

'My what?'

'The thing that you talk into in the other room, while you're cleaning.'

Moira realized what she was talking about and pointed towards the ceiling. 'They'll hear you,' she mouthed. 'Oh no, that's not *me*,' she winked. 'I don't have a talky thing.' Winking again.

Jinx screwed up her face. 'Yes you…' then lowered her voice as Moira put her finger to her lips again. 'Do,' she breathed, wondering why that bit of the conversation was naughtier than the rest.

'Who do you want me to call?' Moira whispered.

Jinx opened her mouth and closed it again. This was the bit she wasn't sure about. 'Someone who can help?'

'Someone who can help…' repeated Moira, her eyes looking up to the side as she thought about who might be able to help.

'My She-one maybe?'

'Your *what?*'

'My *She*-one.'

'What's a shiwan?'

'The biggerer that I live with. My She-one.'

'Oh… Right.' The eyes twinkled. 'It seems that some words *are* different. Do you have her number?'

'Her what?'

'The number of your shiwan?'

Jinx blinked.

'What about her address?'

'—'

'Her name?'

'*She*-one.'

'Oh, I get it. That's her *name?*'

'Yes.'

'And her last name?'

'I don't know, Moira. I really don't know.'

Moira smiled. It was nice to hear this little person say her name. It seemed so personal like, like if her pet cat were to call her by her name or even her *dentist* instead of saying 'Mrs Croft'; if he said 'Moira', she'd be more comfortable about having his hands in her mouth. It was a bit like a hand-squeeze; or saying: 'I'm not talking to anyone but *you*.' Moira had a thought and flicked on the black box clipped to Jinx's cage. 'Here it is!' she frowned. 'Susan Marley, does that ring any bells?'

'—.'

'No?'

'What's a "bell"?'

'Oh, I mean that I think your *shiwan* is actually called Susan.'

Jinx thought. 'I've heard the word used at home but I never really knew what it meant.'

'Well, that's what it means!'

'Susan.'

Moira pressed the screen on her wrist and bleeped it to the clippy thing.

Jinx watched the wrist and hand twist upwards and wondered what other things she could make them do now that she could speak to their owner.

'Can you put Bonbon in my cage?'

'What?'

'She's up there.'

Moira turned around. Bonbon gazed down at her. 'Oh right! You two came together a couple of days ago, didn't you?'

Jinx nodded. 'She's my other darling.' Her face crumpled again as she started to cry.

Moira looked between the two cages. 'Why have you been separated?'

Jinx shrugged.

'I can't open these cages, I'm sorry…'

'Okay… Doesn't…' sniff, 'matter.'

'Please don't cry.'

Jinx held her breath and nodded until another sob pushed its way out of her.

'This is awful. You know what? Don't worry…' She lowered her voice. 'I'm gonna take care of everything.' She put her hand flat against the glass door. 'Just you be strong, okay?'

'Yes.' Jinx looked at the massive hand. 'Be strong,' she said.

'Sure?'

More nodding.

Jinx watched Moira walk back to the lift until she couldn't see her any more. When the lift doors closed, the cages opposite and beside her clapped so much that Jinx was sure Moira would turn around and come back again. Jinx put the back of her hand to her face – she must have looked so red, she thought, as she tried to smile up to the others, hoping with every thought in her head that Moira would find the She-one.

Susan had tried to go to work, spent three hours pretending not to cry at her desk and was eventually sent home by Lydia, her supervisor. She had once read a book at a library desk where a watcher sat at the end of each row to make sure the readers were wearing gloves and had masks over their noses and mouths. The book had been so sad that the watcher had asked her, ever so nicely, to either put on the goggles that he was holding out to her, or maybe come back when she was feeling better. She had taken the goggles. But after about ten minutes, the letters became all magnified and weird through the tears that were gathering inside the lenses. She decided that she would have to come back another time. It had taken her four more visits to read the last thirty-nine pages of that book. She couldn't remember feeling so sad because of the written word. Until today. Today she sat on the kitchen floor and read the letter right to the end. She let her tears splash all over the paper that had been scrunched up by Mrs Lucas's own hand. Mrs Lucas had refused to believe it. What a waste of ink, what a waste of paper, what a waste of words. She'd thrown it into her garden to waste it. To treat it with as much respect as it deserved. What a waste of time, she must have thought.

How wasteful it was to read a letter while letting tears re-liquefy the ink, magnifying then splodging each word. He'd spent his whole life perfecting the curve of every 's' and the loop in every 'l', and this was to be their final show. What a *waste*, Susan had thought; and who was the show for? The life that was *joined* to his. Maybe that's why she'd thrown it away, because with this wasteful letter, her life would be wasted too.

'All that love,' blubbed Susan. 'Such a waste.'

The lines repeated, over and over; re-writing themselves in front of her eyes. Maybe *that's* why Mrs Lucas had thrown the letter away; she couldn't stand it reading itself to her any longer. But had he written like that because he was going to die? Maybe he'd been a real meanie all their lives and had only *just* come across all the lovely things he could have said, stored somewhere in a dusty part of his brain. Maybe *that* was why she had thrown out the letter. No… No, she couldn't believe that either. There were layers in that letter that seemed to coat every word, like a very old house that had been painted many times. It *was* just a normal house. They *were* just simple words. But the charm of the years locked into that house seemed to transform it… 'We had such a nice time, whenever we went to St Ives for an ice cream. That was *our* place, we used to say. Don't go back there alone, will you?' And the tears welled again as the lines read themselves over and over…

She came home to sit on the stairs and re-read the letter. Every so often she would get up and look through the window to see if the house next door would give a sign that Mrs Lucas was back. Susan would probably run outside and throw her arms around her the minute she saw her shuffling up the driveway. Poor Mrs Lucas. *Poor* Mrs Lucas.

She grabbed the phone. She would try again. Not for Bonbon and Jinx, but for Mrs Lucas.

'Billbridge & Minxus headquarters, reception, how can I help you?'

'Hello. My friend had her littler stolen—'

'Hold on a minute, Madam, stolen by whom?'

'By you, and—'

'She wouldn't have been stolen, Madam, there was obviously a reason why she needed to be brought in for examination.'

'She didn't show any signs of communication, but her owner is one hundred and thirty years old.'

'Are *you* the owner?'

Susan smirked. 'No, that's why I said "My *friend* had her littler stolen".'

'I just needed to verify. I can't discuss this situation with you if you are not the legal owner.'

'The owner is currently trying to talk her husband out of euthanasia.'

'—.'

'When she gets home, the house is going to feel very lonely.' Susan gulped. 'So…', sniff, 'given the fact that…' sniff, 'her littler didn't show *any* signs of communication…' sniff, 'I was hoping that you could tell me…' sniff, 'when you're planning to return her.'

'I'm sorry,' the other said slowly. 'I can't talk about this with you.'

'Well, what *can* you do for your customers?' Sniff. 'All I've had from you people for the last *three* days is no, no, no, no… Why are you even *there*?'

A long exhale fizzed through the line. 'I have a daughter,' said the woman. 'And I live alone,' she said. 'I need this job. There is a one in five chance that this phone call will be re-listened to tonight and if it is, I'll have a written warning. I'm really putting myself on the line here so that I can tell you I can't give you information because I'm not allowed to access it. It's a secret. But I wish I could,' she sighed. 'I'm sorry. I really mean that.'

Susan's lips trembled. 'Thank you. That's the most human response I've had in three days.'

She couldn't blame that lady; in fact, that lady made her understand that *all* of the ladies who answered the phone bobbed together in the same boat. Maybe if they had read the letter, that would have changed everything; that would have made them realize just how much of a joke their situation was compared to what *really* lay in store for them... Or to someone they had tied their lives to. What would she do if that were Hamish? Because it *would* happen; one or other of them would go first and that would be it. Such a waste. Life was too short to get cross with each other, even if they *did* have one hundred years left.

She was still wondering if she or Hamish would go first, when the phone rang again. She picked it up, making her eyes all wide and waving her hand next to them to dry them out. 'Hello?'

'Hello? Are you Susan?'

'Speaking.'

'Um... Hi. You don't know me but... I made a promise to someone that I would call you.'

Susan turned her mouth upside down. 'Oh, really?'

'I know I'll be found eventually and that I'll lose my job over this but...'

Susan sat up straight. 'What do you mean?' It must have been the lady she'd spoken to not two minutes before. 'No... No, don't lose your job. I'll just wait for the email!'

'What?'

'I don't want you to lose your job. You have a daughter to think about. It's the company that's got the problem, not you.'

The front door opened and Hamish walked in. Susan frowned a frown at Hamish that was meant for the person at the other end of the phone. She got up so that he could sit on the stairs to take his shoes off.

'I don't have a daughter!'

'You just told me that you have a daughter, didn't you?'

'Um… I think you think I'm someone else.'

'You're not the lady from Billbridge & Minxus.'

The line went quiet for a moment. 'How do you know that?'

'Because I just spoke to you,' she said to the back of Hamish's trousers as they walked up the stairs.

'No… That wasn't me…'

'Really? Who's the message from?'

'Jinx,' said the voice.

'What?'

'Jinx told me to ring you. She needs your help to get out of here.'

'Jinx? What… My Jinx?'

Hamish's trousers turned and descended four steps.

'Yes!'

'She told you that? She's been clapping?' Her voice started to tremble again.

'No, she didn't clap. She spoke! She asked me for help and… I have to pass her message on, even though I'll lose my job.'

'She what? Did you just say that she spoke?'

Hamish jumped the stairs two at a time and put his ear next to the other side of the phone.

'Yes!'

'You're joking?'

'No! She told me to call you so you'd come and rescue her. You need to know, they have voice recorders in that room. As soon as someone realizes that she can talk, I don't know what's going to happen to her. They don't want them to *clap* let alone talk. And she talks *well*; just like you and me. I've never seen that before. Never, never, never…'

'But no one gave us the address; we don't even know how to get there,' Hamish cut in. 'Hello? Hello?' The line was dead.

Susan's mouth dropped open. 'You scared her! Ring caller ID!' she said, fumbling with the phone to try to do exactly that. 'Ring caller ID!'

'Well, give me the phone, then!'

The phone started ringing in her hands.

'Hello?' she said, turning to Hamish and putting her finger to her lips.

'Sorry. It's Moira, the lady from before. The man's voice scared me. I didn't realize that I was talking to two people.'

'I know. I've just told him off.'

'Will he come too?'

'Well… Where, exactly? We don't know where to go; no one will give us the address.'

'That's no surprise. In fact, *this* is the reason why I'm going to lose my job. I'll most probably be taken to court as well. If the company gets away with this, it'll have to change its geographical location. I'll be completely unemployable…'

'Oh gosh, well… No. I had no idea. No, you mustn't do that.'

'I'm hoping it won't get away with this. I'm going to take that risk because what goes on here is sick, you know? A *human* spoke to me today. She told me that she and her friends don't want to be in prison any more because they tried to clap their hands; how dumb is that? I feel like I *have* to do this. Does that seem strange?'

'No, that's very admirable,' said Susan. 'Good for you.'

'Meet me in the eighty-ninth.'

'The eighty-ninth? Wow, is that where it is?'

'Yep. I'll bleep the exact address to this number; is that okay?'

'The eighty-ninth is… you know; dodgy and… I don't mean to be rude but, you could, you know… be anyone, couldn't you?'

'Ah… I get it.' The line was silent for a moment and just as Susan was about to say something the other blurted: 'Bring people! In fact, bring as many as you can.'

'People, why?'

'The more people that witness this, the better. Can you do that? Can you bring people?'

Susan's gaze leapt about the hall. 'I'd have no idea where to start looking for…' A crumpled sheet of paper lay on the bottom step. Greying heads bobbed like balloons as they took sips of tea in Susan's mind. 'I think I probably can,' she said.

'Can you be there at nine?'

She looked at Hamish. He nodded. 'Yes. But how will we get in? What will we… I mean… Will you let us in?'

'Let me worry about that.'

They hung up and Susan scanned her wrist for Meredith's number, called it, then strode between the kitchen, hall and living room telling her exactly what had happened. Could she round up the others? Could she get them there by nine? Susan would bleep her the address. Yes, she was pretty sure that she could trust this person, she sounded really convincing… Oh really? A set-up? But who would want to do that? Well, surely if all of them arrived together they'd be all right. It didn't matter if it *was* a hoax; it was worth taking a look. Yes, she did realize that they were all quite elderly. Yes, she had had her own reservations to start with. No! She was sure that they wouldn't line them up and push them into a mass grave! Well, *yes*, the company *did* seem to want them out of the way, but mass murder? Well, yes, her exact words were 'bring lots of people'. And yes, the eighty-ninth was dodgy. No, she'd never, ever heard of a talking littler. Susan pinched the bridge of her nose and walked to the kitchen to look for Hamish. Then back to the hall. Empty. Then another look in the living room; maybe they'd crossed paths along the way? Well, if Meredith didn't want to put the others in danger, wasn't she slightly curious herself? A little? Would she perhaps send word out to see what everyone else thought? They'd have to leave in an hour. Not much time, no. Where the hell was Hamish? Susan opened the dining-room door – odd that it was closed… She looked inside; Hamish stood by the window with his wrist up close to his lips. He turned and looked at her with eyes so wide and so frightened that she said: 'Excuse me one moment, Meredith.' She strode over to him. 'What's wrong?'

'Me… Oh, erm… Nothing,' he said to her. 'Yes, yes, it is Susan,' he said to his wrist.

'Who's on the phone?'

He ignored her question, apparently listening to the other person. Then: 'Susan, who are you talking to now?'

'Meredith. Hamish, she doesn't think we should trust the call.'

'Meredith doesn't trust the call,' he repeated to the wrist.

'Hamish, who are you…' He held a finger up to her.

'Susan, who was the call from?'

'Meredith.'

'No!' he said, with a little, sweet laugh that she'd never heard before. 'The lady who called us about Jinx!'

'Oh!' Susan scrunched her eyes shut then flung them open again. 'Moira! It was Moira!' she said.

Hamish nodded deep nods as he listened to what was being said to him. 'Okay: tell Meredith that this is *not* a hoax and that Emma Howards is going to call her in just a minute to confirm this.'

'Right,' Susan repeated this to Meredith whose voice became all high-pitched and clipped. 'That changes the situation, somewhat,' she said. 'I'll be waiting for her call.'

Susan hung up and tapped the end of the phone against her teeth for a moment. Emma Howards. She watched Hamish as he did strange things like standing with his hand behind his head and his elbow in the air. His cheeks were blotchy and his eyes jumpy. She turned to leave and do something important like phone someone else but found herself walking in a little circle until she was looking at him again. Now he was running his finger backwards and forwards along the edge of a chair back. She frowned. She'd never seen him interacting with other people; only Mrs Lucas, but that was different, she was *their* neighbour; this new person was someone from Hamish's world… She smiled at the way he listened to her so hard that his irises flicked about like dragonflies in a jar. This was what he was like with other people. It had been so long since they had been two separate people that she'd completely forgotten.

'Hang up,' he said to his wrist before heading for the door.

'Who was that?'

He looked at her with his 'people' face, all dancy and listening. 'Erm… Emma. One of my clients. She used to work for Billbridge & Minxus, so, she knows Moira.'

'Really? That's quite… handy.'

'Well…' Hamish started to explain then changed his mind. 'She'll be here in twenty minutes. She's going to help us.'

CHAPTER 22

Susan had let Emma sit in the front seat. From there she was able to notice that every time Emma turned her head towards Hamish to talk to him, her lips were shaking, but not just the red part, the bit that went down towards her chin and the bit that went up towards her nose. Where her Cupid's bow was, Susan thought, wondering if Cupid had a shaky aim and conjuring up the loveliest picture in her head of the cherub leaning out of his cloud with one eye closed and his tongue hanging out as he tried to concentrate on not shaking.

Susan decided to ask her a question. 'Was it long ago that you left the company?'

Emma turned to look into the back seat. Susan saw the full shakiness of her face. 'Erm… Well actually, not long after you adopted Bonbon and Jinx.'

Susan raised her eyebrows. 'Oh right! Hamish told you about them, did he?'

Emma twisted right round in her seat. 'There's a bit more to it than that—'

'You, erm, don't have to tell her,' Hamish interrupted.

'What's the point in *not* telling Susan? There's no going back now, really.'

Susan smiled at Emma, grateful that she had called her 'Susan' and not 'her'.

'I'm in the same situation as Moira now.' Her bangles jingled as she waved her hand to indicate the space around her, her same situation. 'I'm probably going to get into a lot of trouble, so I don't have to keep secrets any more.' She looked at Hamish. 'Dr Wix has been my confidant during these last two years and… Well… The reason I *know* him is because I was checking up on him, actually.'

Hamish let out one of those sweet laughs again. On hearing it, so did Emma. Susan watched them and decided that she had better do the same.

'I chose you both to be Bonbon and Jinx's family.'

Susan let her mouth fall open.

'I needed a family that would fit specific criteria. Preferably a couple, so there would be more eyes kept on the littlers and more money in the house.' She looked up at the roof of the car as she counted on her fingers. 'Preferably young; I didn't want them to be outlived by their family and… What was the last one? Oh yes. Preferably childless; I didn't want their arms getting pulled off by kiddies.'

'Childless? But the whole point of the "Little Love" scheme is to make kids care about something other than themselves.' Susan scrunched her fingers into fists; when had she picked up this habit of making them into speech marks?

'You've been watching that documentary.'

A nod.

Emma took a deep breath. 'This company is so full of lies that you would *not* believe it. What you're living now is just the very surface of everything it's done and got away with. Its lawyers are among the highest paid in London… Where was I?' she said, looking at Hamish. 'Ah yes. Hamish will be the first one to tell you how children behave towards anything that is smaller than they are.'

'Would I?'

'I hope so,' she replied. 'They usually want to hurt it or love it. And when I say love I mean in the way that they would love a *doll*.'

'I thought there were follow-up visits?'

'There are. That part is *not* a lie. And some of our inspectors' reports would make you wince. But does the littler ever get taken away? Once. That happened only once in my time. The Toe Biter of Michigan, remember him?'

'But he used to bite toes.'

Emma shook her head. 'He was tied to a broom handle and laid on the floor while the kids took it in turns to put ice cream on his genitals then let the cat lick it off. Can you imagine how a cat's tongue must feel to them? Eventually he leaned over and bit one of their toes *really* hard. He got taken away because the family thought he was dangerous for kids. *Then* it was all over the press and the company had to make out that he was an exception who had overridden his anti-aggression feature.'

'Does that exist? The anti-aggression thing?'

'There are measures in place to make them more placid than, shall we say, a *normal* human being…'

'But they're capable of overriding it?'

'Exactly! Pain is pain, at the end of the day; it can only be endured for so long. There's a difference between being spontaneously aggressive and being desperate to switch pain off.'

'I knew it! And all this communication prevention crap, it's because they're worried they'll tell us something compromising, isn't it?'

'Susan's been honing her own little conspiracy theory for quite a while,' said Hamish. 'I *think* she might be on to something, actually.'

Susan tipped her head to one side; did he really think that? He'd never said that to her…

'I would heartily agree with her,' said Emma, nodding heartily. 'Part of the reason they're so, shall we say, *stupid* when they first come out of the centre is because of the memory suppressants.'

'Really?'

'Mmm-hmm.' Emma's wrist started to beep. 'It's Meredith,' she said before answering. 'Hello? Where are you exactly? Oh right… Are you in convoy?'

Susan had recognized Emma immediately when she'd come running down the stairs earlier and found her sitting well forward on the sofa, clutching her bag on her lap. She got to her feet and leaned over the coffee table to shake Susan's hand, her fox tail swishing round to the side of her head as she bent forward.

'I know you from the meeting, don't I?'

'Yes. You were there this week, weren't you?'

'That's right.'

Susan rubbed her hands together; this was the part where you'd usually say: 'Hamish has told me all about you.' But he hadn't. So instead she heard herself saying: 'Hamish hasn't told me *anything* about you.' She giggled and Emma giggled too. 'Obviously, he has to keep your relationship hush-hush.' She giggled again. Emma didn't giggle. Hamish's face did that thing where it went all expressionless. Finally, Emma giggled and Susan joined in to be polite; but had thought she'd probably embarrassed Hamish. She twisted her hands. What a stupid thing to say. 'Did you manage to speak to Meredith?' she chirped, hoping to cover up her last remark.

'Yes! She's trying to round people up as we speak. Moira has been working for that company since… I can't even remember. She's been there for years.'

Susan put on a serious face. 'Will she really lose her job over this?'

Emma nodded. 'Yes,' she said in a low voice. 'I'm afraid so… But I'm not surprised. The fact that Jinx is talking is unbelievable. It's really something that we've all been waiting for them to be able to…' She searched for the word, opening and closing her hand in front of her. '*Prove* their equality, if you like.'

'Equality?'

'They are *human*, Susan. They have the same capacities as we do.

The only difference is they're little and they can't talk to us.' She rocked back on her heels, angling her wrist upwards to check the time that glowed orange through her skin. 'It's a two-hour drive, we should probably get…'

'Of course, of course,' Hamish said, getting to his feet and putting his coat on. 'We should get going.'

* * *

'I've come to collect Isabel,' he said into the intercom.

'Oh…' said a rasping voice. 'Right, well… I'm afraid Isabel's already gone.'

'I think she came back again.'

'—.'

'Hello?'

'Yes, I'm just checking. No… Nobody's buzzed her in.'

'Oh.' Drew stuffed his hands in his pockets, leaned back to glance up at the windows, then pressed the button on the intercom again.

'Yes?'

'Are you sure she's not there?' Just as he'd finished the sentence, a young man in a cap walked up to the doors, changed his rucksack to the other shoulder and stuck his thumb in the thumb-reading box. The door clicked and he pushed it open.

'Sorry, do you mind if I…'

'Oh, um…'

'I've come to collect Isabel; I'm in a bit of a hurry.'

The young man smiled on hearing Isabel's name. 'Sure,' he said. 'You're not her usual, are you?'

'No,' said Drew, as he followed the young man through the doors, his eyes darting over the room. It was still horribly dark in there, it always had been. He noted that the lino had changed colour since he'd come with Isabel to see Hector, then jumped up the staircase that hung like a uvula in the gaping, disinfectant-smelling mouth of the lobby.

At the top, a tiny chair sat on a metal runner: Isabel's stair lift, he thought; she'd definitely come up here. Drew barged into the door that led to reception as he'd always done, back in the day. It didn't budge. He tried the handle then knocked on the rectangular window that opened up one side of the door; metal wires framed invisible squares along the inside of its glass.

A white-coated blonde wrinkled her brow at him through her glasses before indicating that she wanted to see his badge.

He shrugged his shoulders; he didn't have one.

Her lips made mumble shapes and she walked away.

The young man who'd let him in had reached the top of the stairs. 'Sorry,' said Drew. 'She said something to me but I couldn't hear her – would you mind?'

The man stopped and looked at him. 'Not *really*,' he said. 'I'll go and check with my grandfather if you want. Just wait a minute.' He turned away, then back again. 'Sorry, who should I say…'

'Is Mark Hector your grandfather?'

The other nodded. 'Yes.'

'Tell him it's Drew.'

The young man nodded again, then disappeared through the door. Poor kid. Couldn't blame him for doing his job properly. He traced the marbly lines in the new lino to Isabel's little chairlift. She was probably in there right now demanding to see the clone. Silly girl. There was no way they'd let her talk to it… erm, her… surely? Good God, she'd be lucky if they let her go! He'd never bashed down a door before; would he be able to? Maybe with Watty's help. Watty… He felt down his jacket and reached into an inside pocket to take out his phone. Just as his fingers closed around the phone, something knocked on the window. Drew looked up.

* * *

Now, in the car, Hamish had the weirdest feeling that he'd become polygamous. Every time he glanced next to him, he was sure that his armpits got a little wetter. And when Susan's voice piped up from the back seat, the sweat would suddenly feel cold and his chest would deflate slightly. It was as if she were the first wife and all he wanted was for her to leave him alone with the second, *new* wife. Not necessarily for anything *untoward* but just so that he could be with her and, and be the Hamish who was respected; the Hamish who had saved the day by delivering the news that had changed everything. 'I'm sorry,' he'd managed to say, before Susan had come bounding down the stairs. 'I shouldn't have… you know.'

'I think it was inevitable,' she stammered, looking down at the sofa before lowering her bottom onto its edge.

'"Entirely forbidden" is the phrase I would have used.'

'That's partly why it was inevitable.'

'I should never have called you.'

She flicked her eyes everywhere but towards his. 'I'd like to think you're glad you did.'

He pushed his hands into his pockets and looked at the floor.

'Anyway,' she went on, '*I* was going to call *you* before I leave.'

'You're planning to leave?'

Her eyes held his for a second. She took a breath to answer.

Then Susan arrived. And two worlds were suddenly in the same room.

The gnome inside Hamish's head closed his eyes and gritted his teeth as Hamish thought about the comment Susan had made; the 'hush-hush' one. It was no good, he couldn't think about that. 'Emma, do you have Moira's number? We could call her to say we're nearly there.'

'No. I've never had Moira's number.'

'Didn't you know her very well?' Susan piped up again.

Ever since she'd set eyes on Emma, Susan had worn her 'like me' badge. Hamish imagined how she would stick her head out to the side as she asked a question like that; her eyes all wide as if what the other person had to say was the most interesting thing ever… It was his fault. It was certainly his fault… It was so rare that they were around other people, he'd forgotten the way she interacted with them. Except for Mrs Lucas, but she was different, she wasn't a threat. Susan was much more natural around Mrs Lucas.

'We weren't *allowed* to know each other very well.' Emma twisted right around again to answer Susan. 'Only on a professional level. We were all chipped the day we started working for Billbridge & Minxus. They wanted to make a, kind of, network of colleagues. The irony being that it was to prevent us from networking.'

'Gosh, really?' gasped Susan, as if that were the most awful thing anyone had ever said.

Hamish put one elbow on the window sill and hooked his fingers over his lips. Stop it, he said to himself. Stop being so bloody analytical. Susan just wants a friend…

'Yep, really. All verbal exchange was recorded and monitored to check that we weren't being slanderous. Wow, it feels so weird to talk about this!'

Emma was really doing a cracking job. So patient with Susan… answering all her questions… Oh stop it, Hamish! Stop it!

Hamish put both hands on the steering wheel and peered ahead.

'Um, Emma?'

'Yep?' Then: 'Wow. They didn't waste any time, did they?'

'Who?' Susan leaned forward and squinted through the window.

About thirty grey and white heads glowed in the headlights.

'What are they doing in the middle of the road?'

'This isn't a road; it's the driveway to the centre.'

Hamish wrinkled his head. 'It can't be, we've been on this road for miles. We've been all across a huge industrial estate and now through the woods.'

'I'm telling you, you don't turn off from this road, the company *owns* the road. The entrance to the centre is just behind on the other side of these woods.'

'Impossible.'

'Is it?'

'Yes.'

'*Is* it?'

'*Yes!*'

'You have reached your destination. This information has been brought to you by WayToGo.'

Emma gave him an I-told-you-so look. Hamish smirked.

Susan noticed the I-told-you-so look. And the smirk. She also listened as they bickered about whether or not this was the right road. Not only did she notice but it struck her as rather *familiar*. *Susan* never got a smirk when she told him he was wrong. *Susan* got a sigh or a huff or… or *nothing*. She slit her eyelids so the couple before her became a scene in an old movie with a letter-box screen. They looked the part, Susan thought, turning her eyes away and looking out of the window. 'It's ten to nine,' she said, getting out of the car and walking over to the crowd of glowing heads. She heard the other two doors slam and felt relieved that they hadn't lingered in the car.

'Meredith!' she called.

'Susan!' Meredith trotted over. The others, hearing Susan's name, started to gather round. 'What's going to happen? Do you think we'll be able to get them out?'

'I'm not sure,' said Susan. 'But the most important thing is that you see us going in.'

'Should we come too?'

'I don't know exactly what the lady has planned.' Susan avoided her name, although she didn't really know why. 'All she said to me was to bring people, the more the better.'

'Is it true that your littler can talk?' said one, who Susan recognized to be the paisley lady who had offered Mrs Lucas her spare chair at the meeting.

'That's what I've been told,' Susan smiled.

'What are we doing here exactly? Do you think we'll have to go in?'

'Okay everyone.' Emma's voice sang out from just behind Susan and the glare from backs-of-silver-heads subsided as they turned their shadowy faces towards her. 'I can tell you now that *unfortunately* you won't be able to come inside. Your purpose is to observe, take photos, record us going into the building; whatever you have to do. When my colleague arrives, we'll all walk together to the centre. Tonight is unplanned, yet, in a way, it's been on the cards for a couple of weeks now. This is not a prison break, it is unlikely that any littlers will be getting out, but if you could all do your utmost to make sure that this cannot be erased from history then we're more likely to beat the company and *hopefully* get your loved ones back.'

'Good. That's exactly what I wanted to say,' said an approaching voice that Susan recognized. As she turned to see who it was, she caught Hamish staring at Emma with a weird look on his face… It was a bit like that time they'd had aperitifs at his boss's house and had been shown a book collection that was much bigger than Hamish's. Awe-struck, that was probably the term, she thought, as she squinted into the trees.

A woman with a red Puffa jacket strode out from behind a low branchful of leaves, glancing from side to side and then behind her. 'Emma,' she said, holding out her arms. 'What are you doing here?'

'Moira!' Emma took the hands and squeezed them. 'We're really gonna do this.'

Moira turned her mouth upside down. 'I can't come,' she said. 'I was just going to let her in and tell her where to go. My son is in the car with my sister.' She tilted her head to where the car was. 'We're leaving as soon as she's in.'

Emma nodded. 'I don't blame you at all.' Then: '*I* can still get in, right?'

'I'm not sure,' said Moira. 'Do you still have your thumb?'

Emma laughed. 'Yes! But maybe they updated something or…'

Moira shook her head. 'Nope. Still held together with string and sticky tape. They don't need anything but lawyers.' She narrowed her eyes. 'What about your chip?'

'Yeah.' Emma dug around in her pocket. 'I thought it might come in handy.'

'Then we shouldn't be talking, you know,' she grinned. 'I'll have to hack mine out later.'

Emma made a yuk-face. 'I did it. It's not so bad…'

'Yeah, I'm really looking forward to it.' She turned to Susan. 'You ready?'

'I really don't mind going instead…' Hamish chimed in.

'No,' said Susan, locking Hamish in a rigid stare. 'Jinx asked for *me*.'

Hamish rolled his eyes and was about to say something when Moira cut in.

'That she did. She asked me specifically for her *shiwan*… Apparently that's what she calls you.' Moira waved one finger in the air as she turned to walk away. 'Follow us to the gates, everyone!' she called. 'Take pictures, videos. Anything you can.'

The crowd lowed and rustled. Zips unzipped and old digital whirrs and bleeps flared flashes.

Hamish caught Susan by the elbow. 'Are you sure you don't want me to go?'

Susan pulled her arm away. 'I'll be fine,' she said, her eyes catching the glowing clock face on her wrist. 'Maybe we should record ourselves going in?'

'Good idea,' replied Emma, dabbing at her wrist until it beamed fluorescent green.

The group walked together to the gates where the LOG members were told to stay and wait. Only Moira, Emma and Susan climbed over and crossed the forecourt.

'Okay,' said Moira as they got to the glass front of the building. 'Susan, if for some reason Emma can't go through, do you see that door at the back of reception?'

Susan looked through the glass entry doors into the dim reception area. 'Just about, yes.'

'The button you need to press is the brown one on the right of the lift. That will stop at every floor to the basement. The doors will open once onto an empty corridor. The second time they open you'll be at a room where the littlers go when they first arrive, and the third one is the silent room where Jinx is.'

'Right. Okay,' Susan said through a barely opened mouth, sure that if it opened any wider her heart would come tumbling out of it.

'Is the security bot still there?' asked Emma.

Moira nodded. 'Yep. And they've got another one.'

'Shit. There are two?'

'They shouldn't have a problem with you because you've got your chip. They might not go a bundle on Susan.' Moira shrugged. 'But anyway, they're still in the room out the back. You should have just enough time to go down, get Jinx and come up again.'

'And what if we don't?' said Susan.

Moira pressed her lips together while she considered this. 'Just be quick, okay?'

'Fine,' Susan nodded.

* * *

'She's not here.' Mark Hector opened the door and wiped his forehead at Drew.

Drew squinted for a moment. Gosh he'd aged. The stretched skin on his face pulled his eyelids taut, revealing heavily mapped eye-whites. And he had a stick. 'I don't believe you,' he said, turning sideways and barging through the gap he had made in the door.

'Oh no you don't!' Mark Hector put his hand out to grab Drew's sleeve; Drew curled out of the way and strode through the corridor. The layout hadn't been altered in the slightest; he knew these rooms as if he'd built them. 'Isabel!' he shouted through a doorway before continuing along the corridor, opening doors, making piles of paper scatter and surprising people who hobbled along the corridor in white coats, grey hair tussocking out from their hair nets. Some faces he sort of recognized, some were *completely* unknown, and apart from the young man who'd let him in, everyone seemed so *old*. 'Isabel!' he shouted from each doorway. 'Isabel!'

'She's not here,' said Hector.

'Isabel!' cried Drew, as he swung open a door. A balding lab technician dropped and caught whatever he was holding. 'She must be here somewhere.'

'No, Drew… Not in there!'

Drew glanced back at Mark Hector before opening the door. Nothing. An empty room. That was strange; why hadn't he wanted him to come in here? Then he remembered, there was another room that led from this one. He crossed the empty space and opened a second door in the far right-hand corner. 'Isab—' he started. There she was. At eye-level, right in front of him, in some sort of glass box. She turned as she felt the light from the door shine on her naked back and squinted up at Drew with lazy eyes. They must have given her something… Drew reached behind him to turn the light on as Hector's stick struck its way across the previous room.

'Get out of there,' he barked.

Drew gasped. A row of Isabels turned towards him as the light filled their tanks. His eyes wandered up to another row, and *another* row above. Then to the opposite end of the room where more little Isabels stood naked, their faces pressed against their glass doors, their stares reflecting the daylight-bulb rather than the sparks that flickered in the real Isabel's eyes.

Drew looked at Mark Hector, hand still over his mouth and eyes wide open. He shook his head. 'Why?'

'Ha!' wheezed the doctor. Of all the questions…

'Apart from anything else, why take such an enormous risk? This will *ruin* you.'

The doctor's eyes snapped back onto Drew's, each wrinkle in his head uncreasing as if every drop of water in every cell was freezing and expanding his skin. No. There he was *thoroughly* mistaken… There was no way that he'd invested all of this effort, brainwashed his whole team, worked all of these *years*, risked his whole *career*, to have some little gay *shit* tell him, with such conviction, that this would *ruin* him. 'It will not,' replied Dr Hector, tapping his walking stick as he said 'not'. 'This has *completed* me.'

Drew baulked. The man was mad.

'If anything happens to me, you certainly won't get out of this unscathed.' The sides of Hector's mouth frothed with each sibilant.

'This has nothing to do with me.'

'I did you a huge favour, Drew Mahlik, and you know it. *You* are at the root of all this.' He splayed his stick over forty-five degrees, indicating the rickety beings for which Drew was responsible.

'You can*not* compare that with… with *cloning*! You're in breach of, well, everything! Look at them.' Drew gestured around him. 'Is this how they're destined to live from now on? Not that they'll live for very *long*… What on Earth are you going to do with them?'

'They are prototypes of the race that will save humanity.'

'This is *in*humane…'

'Like keeping Isabel prisoner, you mean? That poor girl has *nothing* but a couple of gays and a dead dog—'

'Where is she?' shouted Drew. 'Where is she? Have you hidden her in one of these cages?'

'*No!*'

'Where is she, then?' Drew leapt from cage to cage. 'Isabel? *Isabel?*' The dozy eyes glazed back at him.

Dr Hector sighed. 'Drew?'

Drew crouched down to scan the cages at ground level.

'Drew?'

'—.'

'Drew, this is important; when was the last time you saw her?'

Drew looked up, balanced on the balls of his feet, his eyes searching for the memory; when had he last seen her? 'Don't pretend to be all concerned about her… I can tell you right now, she'll never work with you again.'

Oh, he'd got well ahead of himself, thought Dr Hector; wasn't he clever? He furrowed his head and held up a palm. 'Drew, she's not *here*. She left about an hour ago; your Watty came to pick her up.'

'—.'

'I know you think I'm a big meanie, but I'm very fond of Isabel.'

'—.'

'Why don't you go home? She's bound to come back at some point.'

'She really isn't here, is she?' Drew replied, reaching into his inside pocket. 'Six missed calls,' he announced as the phone started to flash.

'That's what I've been trying to tell—' Drew held his hand up and Dr Hector held his tongue between his teeth.

'Hello? Watty?'

'Are you at the lab?'

'Uh huh. I don't think she's here.'

'She's not! She waited for me to leave then got Reg to take her home.'

Drew's eyebrows jumped up. 'She what?'

'Yep. Little madam.' Then: 'Are you okay?'

'I can't believe it.'

'I'm parked outside if you want to come down.'

'Watty, I've seen them…' Drew glanced over his shoulder towards 'them', before dodging past Mark Hector and swishing out of the room.

* * *

'Ready?' Moira pulled Susan under the sensor just in front of the doors and waited while it scanned her own head. A small hatch opened in front of them with a black box inside. Moira held her thumb over it. The doors swished open and Susan felt herself being shoved through them before they swished shut again, locking her in with white noise. Susan held her breath and looked around her. But nothing happened. She watched through the doors as Emma held her chip up to the sensor, hoping that she wouldn't have to go down alone, or worse. If Emma set off an alarm, she'd be trapped in there. Camera flashes blinked in the distance as the LOG collected evidence that they had gone inside. In case they didn't come out again… Moira's words swirled in Susan's head.

The doors swished and Emma came in.

'Oh, I'm so relieved,' whispered Susan.

'I think it's recognized me as ex-personnel.'

'What does that mean?'

'I don't know, but it was written in scary red letters.'

'Maybe it was just in case you didn't know.'

'That must've been it.'

They glanced back at Moira as she jogged back to the gates and on to her new life.

They crossed the reception area to the lift, each holding her glowing green wrist outwards.

'Do you think there are lasers here?' Susan asked as the lift doors shut behind them.

'Lasers?' Emma laughed. 'What, like in those old films made

about a hundred years ago? No… They have a technology called "Ripple" but as we've been bleeped in we shouldn't set that off.'

'We have to be quick, though, right?'

'Yep.'

'Oh.' Susan started as a high-pitched ringing vibrated the air around her ears. 'Is that *your* phone?' But rather than the interchanging bursts and silences of a phone cry, the ringing continued as one long scream.

'Shit.' Emma's eyes darted over the ceiling of the lift. 'We've been detected.'

'Ripple?'

'No, as ex-personnel. I guess the system allows a little time for an override before…'

Susan stuck her fingers over her ears – the alarm was really quite shrill. 'We can't go back now.'

Emma shook her head. 'Someone will be on the premises in about ten minutes.'

'That's not enough time.'

The doors opened at the first corridor. Susan looked at Emma.

'This one's usually empty.' She gritted her teeth while the doors shut again. 'It used to be the room they used for inspections. They'd reprogram the lift so it would only go down one floor and then the inspectors would never have to know about the floors below.'

The lift hummed down towards the next floor. The alarm tapered out.

'Okay. This is us. I think we should just grab Jinx and head down to minus three. The last floor.'

Susan looked at Emma. 'Only Jinx?'

'Yeah. She's the one who can talk.'

'What about the others?'

'We can't take them all.'

'Maybe two or three?'

Emma thought for a second. 'Fuck it. We'll grab as many as we can.'

'Yes!' Susan stiffened as she considered the opening doors, then covered her mouth. Five cages stacked one on top of the other appeared in front of her. The occupants sat rocking or twitching. One knocked at his glass door with his forehead. 'Oh my gosh,' she said. 'What's wrong with them?'

'We have to hurry.' Emma strode past Susan and into the corridor. 'Shit,' she said as she about-turned and got back into the lift.

'What's wrong?' asked Susan, still walking into the corridor. Emma grabbed her hand and pulled her back. A tall being clunked stiffly into her peripheral vision. 'Fuck!' she said, jumping back into the lift.

'Susaaan!' screamed a little voice as the doors were closing.

Susan jerked her head back towards the doors. 'Did you hear that?'

'It must have been Jinx,' Emma breathed, her eyes wide open.

'I can't believe it, that was *my* Jinx,' said Susan, still facing the direction of the voice.

'They must've picked her up on the voice recorder and so one of them came down to check it out.' She looked at Susan. 'They get quite confused about things like that. That one probably would have stayed there until someone came to deal with it in the morning, you know, *guarding* her… Even though she's obviously not going anywhere.'

'Would have?'

'They'll be after us now.'

'Oh.' Susan thought for a moment. 'But they can't get at us without the lift?'

Emma shook her head.

'We'll just have to jam the lift at the bottom floor.'

'You're right. Let's do it.' Then: 'Do you know how to jam a lift?'

Susan stared at Emma, her thighs shaking against each other and her breath scratching at her throat. Coloured blobs kept floating past her eyes. Oh God; keep up, heart… If her legs started to get wobbly, and her hearing started to dim, she'd faint right there, and probably wet herself. She slouched back against the lift wall and repeated the question: did she know how to jam a lift? The whole thing seemed so ridiculous that her mouth wouldn't stay in a serious shape any more; she laughed so suddenly that a drop of spit flew out of her mouth, her legs bending underneath her, her whole abdomen heavy with laughter. And Emma was doing the same thing. Holding her stomach and bending forward until she was crouched on the ground.

They laughed until there was nothing left to do except try to breathe while scanning the other's bluey-white face. Susan put a hand to her cheek, wondering if she looked as pale as Emma. 'Why does the lift take so long between floors?' she finally asked.

'Because where we're going is very deep underground. Listen: we can't hear the alarm at all now.'

Susan inhaled slowly as she scanned the air for soundwaves. 'No.' She shook her head. 'But why so deep?'

'This is where the littlers go to retire.'

'The retirement centre? That's *here*?'

'Yup.'

The lift stopped and the doors started to open. Susan got to her feet and stepped out into a dimly lit corridor with white walls and dark green lino. Several aisles led off from it; her eye was drawn to one of the cages that stood just inside the next aisle along. A face looked at her through the bars, ligaments spaghetti-ing through its thin skin from its ear and across its neck. There was no cheek to cover its teeth, and drool flowed out over its exposed gums, down its chin and towards its shoulder. Its left eye, which was completely exposed, had dried up and crusted over, and instead of hair, its head was covered with tufts of fluff that sprouted out of shiny pink skin like feathers on a baby bird.

In the cage below, a little being pushed half of itself up. Its body was enormous on one side, too big to extend upright in the cage; the other side was the size of Jinx. Or Bonbon. It was this side that walked towards her as the other half dragged itself along to follow. Half of the head lolled on its shoulder, unable to perch upright inside the low-ceilinged cage; one eye struggled to blink as the weight of the larger half pulled back its eyelid. It looked at her, licking its teeth, its one big foot so swollen from lack of movement that some of the skin had cracked and was weeping clear liquid. 'Hello, fella,' she smiled, tapping on the wall. 'You poor thing.'

The lift beeped in the corridor behind them. Susan ran to stop it from going back up. Emma was already there.

'Someone's called it back up,' said Emma, hovering between the lift doors.

Susan looked back at the cage with the half-and-half littler inside. 'I have an idea.'

Five minutes later, she'd grunted and roared and rattled the door off its hinges. The littler inhabitant poked the large half of his face out, pouted his lips and started to whoop.

Susan jumped then turned in a circle as a few more littlers joined in. She stuck her fingers in her ears and grinned at Emma who stood watching from between the lift doors, her hands pressed against each one to stop them from closing.

'Oops, sorry,' she called, jogging back over to the lift. 'We'll need a couple more,' she said. 'To keep the lift well open.'

'Right,' said Emma. 'One thing we don't lack is cage doors.'

Susan turned back to fetch another. The half-and-half thing had shuffled out of its cage. She crouched down in front of it, telling herself that it was human; and it certainly wasn't an 'it', he was a *he*. 'My name is Susan,' she said. 'Nice to meet you.' She held her hand out. He tried to pick up his big arm but it was too heavy, so he gave her his little hand and laughed as she shook it.

'He just laughed at me!' Susan called back to Emma.

'Most of them are unsuppressed down here: There's no need for it. Their brains are probably dead, anyway.'

Susan looked at the walls of cages that made corridors so long that the ends tapered into darkness. 'The rest of their lives,' she said to herself.

The two of them took it in turns to grunt and wrench three more doors from their cages, the four newly freed littlers following them backwards and forwards to the lift. 'It's not an exact fit. We'll have to keep an eye on it,' Emma said as she stood with her hands on her hips. 'What do we do now?'

Five pairs of eyes blinked back at her. One, with a face covered with hair and little stumps instead of hands, and another whose legs were fused from groin to knee, had jostled to sit on Susan's foot, before putting their arms around each other and settling down together. They looked so sweet, thought Emma, wondering how long it had been since they'd had a cuddle.

'How could anyone leave them here to be forgotten about?' said Susan.

'They are the company secrets. Whenever something goes wrong in the lab… Well, as you can see…' Emma nodded her head towards Susan's foot, feeling at least three sets of ears inclined in towards her.

'But there are so many of them.'

'Don't forget, they're from all over the world. The *developed* world.'

'Really?'

'Mmm-hmm – company headquarters.'

'Why don't they…' Susan made a neck-slicing gesture with her hand.

'M-U-R-D-E-R.' Emma spelled out the word. 'They are human, remember. That would be entering into a whole new level of bad.'

'*This* is hardly living.' Susan looked around her for a moment, then back down to her lap as the half-and-half one shuffled over and rested its head on her knee. 'I know what we have to do.'

'What?'

Susan held her arm up and eye-flicked her wrist. 'Upload a film.'

Emma slapped her hand on her forehead. 'Yes! But we should be quick.'

'Right.'

'With commentary; don't forget to explain what we're doing here.'

'Absolutely. And give the address!'

My name, he thought through fluttery eyes; yellow lights dimmed somewhere beyond the cage. The eyelashes interlaced back together over slit lids. Eyelashes, interlaced, lids… How was he thinking these words? Glass flew, spraying ticks of light that bit his face and hung on. How lucky that it didn't hit his eye. He turned to her, she had no steering wheel to crush her legs, and there she slept, cheek down, closed eyes like curving scolopendras. A tick had got her cheek, up towards the left cheekbone like a dot of lip liner.

I can't feel my legs.

Her hair spread from her head as if it were being flattened by the wind to that big white balloon.

I can't feel my legs.

Sir, we're going to try and take you out of the car.

Eyes opened again. Dim lights. Roaring and metal being wrenched from metal. Whooping and women's voices. Women. Women using proper syntax and worldly vocabulary.

Eyes closed.

I can't feel my legs.

We're going to lift you out of the car, Sir.

Dead? What do you mean, dead? Nobody dies in this day and age!

We can't save your leg. We have four of your size in the storehouse in London – would you like to keep the same coloured bodily hair?

But people can't just die – bring her back! Give her something, you must have something from your bank to save her. A heart? Do you have a heart?

That was six months ago, Sir. You were at her funeral…

This isn't my leg… It's shorter. Where's my wife? Tell my wife that this isn't my leg…

She passed away fourteen months ago, Sir.

I've decorated her room. White lace and one of those husky-dog rugs. But not real husky-dog. She loves animals too much, don't you, love? Where is she? She was right here…

She's been dead for two years, Sir.

Should we give him pills?

I don't want pills…

Give him the pills. YOU CAN GO HOME, SIR. Your daughter has a gift for you. Nadine, you know Nadine? She has a gift for you.

A gift. From my daughter.

I'll love him. He'll be my best friend. I have so much spare love now that… Well, you know what happened the other day, to my wife?

That was three years ago, Sir.

Eyes open. What were those women doing? Such a noise…

My name.

He looked to his left. Littlers shuffled past his cage and along the corridor. *Have you seen Jinx?* he wanted to call. He squinted. No wire metal criss-crossed over his vision – the cage door was gone!

It was my name.

He held his stomach and pushed himself to his knees, gripping the side of the cage to pull himself upwards.

When I was a full-human, Terence was my name.

* * *

'He's made about thirty. I can't… I can't quite get my head around it; they're all *Isabel*.'

'Bloody hell, Drew, are you absolutely sure?'

'Watty, I saw them all. A whole roomful of them.'

'And they were *exactly* like Isabel?'

'Yep… Well, they're *clones* of her so you could say that they *are* her.'

'But… what does he want them for?'

Drew watched weeping willow leaves tickle over the car and thought about Dr Hector's lips, all bulgy and plastic-looking. 'Apparently, they're the race that will save humanity.'

'But how can they? Aren't they likely to develop lumps and bumps and… eventually they'll just warp and die?'

'Exactly.' Drew rested his elbow at the base of the car window and hooked a finger over his lips. 'I reckon he's still fiddling with embryos.'

'You mean he's going to, somehow, mix the clones with the embryos?'

Drew shrugged. 'He might do. He might be doing it already.'

'Crazy man.' Watty chewed the inside of his cheek and drummed his fingers on the steering wheel. 'Quail can't go back there.'

'God no…'

'She's only seen one… What should we tell her?'

'Pfff… No idea. This'll torture her.'

'Mmm,' Watty nodded, his eyes checking the right mirror as he flicked the indicator on. 'Maybe we could keep this to ourselves.' He slowed the car down and started to turn right.

* * *

Susan approached a cage. Inside stood a bald littler with so many tumours on him that when he walked to the front of the cage, he used his hands to carry a great mass that grew from his hip. She cringed as he lifted his arm to reveal a knot of lumps, red and infected from where they'd been squashed between his arm and his body. A bulge of skin hung like a beret over one of his eyes. The light from her wrist shone over him before she twisted the lock on his cage and lifted him down to the floor. She aimed her wrist towards the top row, which stood at least ten cages up. Eyes reflected sparks of light, then closed or looked away. Good Lord, when had these beings last seen light? Or even the ground?

Next to the beret's cage, a pretty littler with straight red hair sat on the floor, holding on to her own feet and swinging herself onto her back then rocking back onto her bottom. She laughed when she saw Susan, who stood with her wrist aimed at her. 'As I said before, we are at least half a kilometre underground. There isn't one ray of natural light…'

For the next ten minutes, the two women trod through the corridors with slow, wide strides as their wrists absorbed the bulging eyes, burn scars, lost limbs, fused fingers, clubbed feet, double heads, wart clusters and hairy growths. Emma filmed rows of older ones, poised like stone Buddhas, their gaze milky and unfocused behind wiry white sprigs of hair. The younger-looking ones jumped up to peer at the glowing wrists, climbing out of their cages as soon as the door was unlocked. An increasing line of newly freed littlers swayed behind Emma like a tail. Most of them followed her; some of them stayed in their cages, too used to the small space to want to come out. They cowered as Emma held her arm up to film herself. 'It's okay,' she said to them, retracting her arm and peering into her wrist, before recording the address of the company. 'We're stuck here right now,' she said, as she heard Susan say the same thing.

'You done?' Susan appeared in front of her, a line of little people hobbling behind. 'Look who I found!' She turned to the side so that Emma could properly see the littler who was sitting on her shoulder, her fingers woven into strands of Susan's hair and clinging to her jawline.

'Blankey!' cried Emma.

Blankey peered down at Emma, then toppled forward as she craned to see the littlers that bobbed around Susan's feet.

'Oops!' Susan caught her. 'She's very floppy,' she said, transferring the drooping bundle from her shoulder to her hip. 'But she looks *so* much better than when I last saw her.'

Emma peered into each of Blankey's eyes, pinched the skin on the back of her hand and checked over her arms and legs for… Susan didn't really know what she was looking for. 'They've probably given her something to numb her brain.'

Blankey let her head flop onto Susan's hoodie.

'Do you want to take her?' Susan offered her hip.

'No.' Emma stroked the side of Blankey's cheek with one finger. 'I'm just relieved she's okay.'

'If she's down here that means they were never going to give her back, doesn't it?'

'That's exactly what it means.' Emma swung backwards with her hands on her hips and smirked. 'And I think I know *why*. They've worked out that she's his late wife.'

Susan squinted. 'Sorry?'

'Blankey came from the cells of his late wife's body parts.'

'*Whose* late wife?'

'Terence Bennett.'

Susan gaped her eyes.

'That's why he took her,' Emma continued. 'That's why they can't give her back to Mrs Lucas.'

'Because he'll take her again.'

'Or someone else would realize and make it public.' Voices. Emma looked up. A few more littlers shuffled towards them from the opened cages. Some of them held hands. One limped and held his arms around his stomach. Or hers. Emma couldn't quite make it out… 'I'm not sure if they'll let him go home now – Mr Bennett – after all of this. I asked Hamish about mental health outpatients but…' She folded her arms. 'I mean, Dr Wix… He said it depends on the case.'

'But what a bloody stupid thing to do. Adopting out his dead wife's extra-created descendant to his next-door neighbour.' Susan stopped and folded her lips inwards. 'Ah. Was that down to you?'

'Yep,' said Emma. 'My fault.' Her armpits started to prickle. 'And the fact she's down here means that *they* know it was my fault…'

So who are Bonbon and Jinx? Susan wanted to ask, her eyes dancing over Emma's face. Instead she offered: 'Surely it was an accident…'

'Don't you think he'll ever be allowed home?'

The question arrowed through the air and pierced their low tones. The women started and looked up.

'Did you hear that?' queried Susan.

Emma took a step and looked about her. 'Hello?'

'Because he's not bad enough to be taken away forever.' The limping littler hobbled towards them. 'He's just ill, really.'

'Are you…' Emma started.

'Jinx's boyfriend?' Susan finished.

'Jinx!' he shouted. 'Where is she?'

Susan nodded towards the ceiling. 'The floor above. We're going to rescue her later.'

'Really?' he wheezed. 'When? Ooooh…' He closed his arms further around his stomach.

Emma bent towards him. 'What happened to you?'

He screwed up his face for a moment before exhaling slowly. 'I can't really remember…'

'But you look much better than when I last saw you,' said Susan. 'Has this happened while you've been here?'

'Yes. This morning.'

'They probably gave him memory suppressants.' Emma stared into each of his eyes then sat back, holding her cheeks. 'I can't believe he's talking.'

'I don't think they did,' said Chips. 'My memory is much better. I can remember so much more than I ever could.'

'So they never intended to return Chips to his owner either?' Susan frowned. 'If he's down here, I mean.'

'My owner,' Chips laughed, then clutched his stomach again.

Emma winced and knitted her fingers. 'As soon as you're out of here, we'll find you a new home.'

'You can live with me,' said Susan, nodding.

Chips closed his eyes. 'He's a good man and he loves me. He's just ill,' he hoarsed up at them.

'But he obviously doesn't feed you properly.'

'He gave me my humcoat before you gave Jinx hers.'

Susan bit her lip.

'And Bonbon. She was always cold…'

'You're right, Chips, you're absolutely right.'

'And he only took Blankey because he loved her. That's not a bad thing, is it?'

'No,' the two women said together.

'And I wouldn't be here without him. He gave me life. I'm happy to be alive, even if I get a bit hungry, sometimes.'

Emma frowned. 'What do you mean?'

Chips opened one eye and focused it on Emma. 'You know where we come from, don't you? I heard you talking about Blankey…'

'My colleague looked after you. I didn't have anything to do with your files.' Emma's face collapsed into wrinkles. 'Gosh, don't tell me you're his son or something… Are you?'

'I'm him,' Chips winced.

Susan baulked. 'His son, seriously?'

'No… I'm *him*.'

Emma held her hands out and sat like that for a while, her opened mouth stretching out her scowl. 'Impossible.' She folded her arms.

'Do they do that?' asked Susan.

Emma snapped into a standing position. 'Obviously they are taking from live participants now.'

'No… I think they must have…' Chips began.

'Must have what?' Emma enquired.

Chips blinked at her, then turned and vomited on the floor. Two littlers shuffled over to him and took it in turns to rub his back. Susan took a sheet of Fibre-Web from her pocket, leaned forward and wiped his mouth. 'We can talk about this later. Don't worry…'

'All my memories came back. I'm him. I really am him.'

'Okay, it's alright,' Emma lulled. 'I just can't get my head around it…'

The lift bleeped again. 'We'd better do something with this,' Susan held up her wrist, 'before they climb down to get us.'

Susan folded the scarf she was wearing and guided Chips over to it. He lowered himself onto it, wincing as he bent.

'You're right,' said Emma, walking to the lift and checking the doors. She stopped to hold her temples. 'I just can't believe it…'

They uploaded their films to every social network they could think of; then to every news site and every politician, mailed them to every person on their contact list, asking them to pass it on; displayed it on comments boards and posted its link in discussion forums. Every two or three minutes, the lift would beep as the security bots called it back to the top and the two women would look up, making sure that the cage doors hadn't slipped or crumpled, before turning back to their wrists.

'Where else can we send it?'

Susan's wrist flashed purple. 'Shit, it's Hamish… They must still be outside. How long have we been here?' She dabbed the screen. Emma smiled and looked away.

'Hi. Yes, we're fine. Sorry, who's calling up the lift? I *know*, Hamish, but we haven't decided what we're going to do yet. Yep, sure, hang on.' She held her arm out to Emma. 'He wants to speak to you.'

Emma touched her wrist to Susan's, then held her arm up to her ear. 'Who's calling up the lift?'

'Security.' Hamish's voice was hushed and serious. 'Should I call the police?'

'The police? No… Why? What could they do?'

'Susan's just told me that you're both alright. I know you probably told her that to keep her calm…'

'We're fine. We make a good team.' Emma looked at Susan. 'Hamish, did you get the footage?'

'Yes, it's horrific. Everyone is standing here watching it as we speak.'

'Tell them we need it to go viral.'

'I think they're on the case.'

Emma grinned into the phone. 'If people start to go home, don't hang around out there alone, will you?' Her eyes landed on Susan as she said the 'will you'. Susan stared at her with her head on one side, biting the skin around her thumbnail as if she were lost in a film.

'How long do you think you'll be down there?'

'We're a bit unsure about the security bots; if they were real people we would probably just let them take us.' She looked at Susan. 'Wouldn't we?'

Susan blinked, as if someone had interrupted her during a really good scene. She nodded, then got up to check the lift.

'Hamish, did you hear what I just said?' Emma jammed her finger in her ear as several voices started to speak at once.

'Sir, I'm going to have to ask you to hang up the phone.'

'Why?'

'What's happening here is a private matter; I can't risk you communicating the events that you're witnessing to anyone outside of—'

The line went dead.

'Hamish?'

'It's still jammed.' Susan sat back down and nodded towards her wrist. 'What happened?'

'We were cut off,' Emma replied. 'Security are trying to call the lift up.'

They spent the next ten minutes opening cages, then they un-jammed the lift and squashed themselves and the littlers inside. Two littlers made a chairlift with their arms and carried the one whose legs were fused from the knees up. The others moved to make space for them inside the lift. Chips lay in a cradle that Susan had made with her forearm, his eyes trained on Blankey who peered at him from her shoulder.

'We can't stop at the next floor, can we?'

Emma chewed the inside of her cheek. 'We'll have to come back.'

'But we need Jinx to tell her story…'

'I think we've told a chunk of it already.'

The lift doors opened. 'No, no… We're not getting out here,' Susan spread herself out in front of the doors as the calf-high party started to spill into the silent room. She wanted to yell out to Bonbon and Jinx that she'd come back for them, but the lift doors closed and they were scooted up two more floors before they could all burst out onto the white reception tiles.

Six people stood waiting for them, their legs at ease and hands behind their backs. They told them that they would be pressing charges for slander, that the police were involved – the cars were waiting outside – and that the littlers were the property of Billbridge & Minxus until such a time that the law decided otherwise.

'They are the property of *no one*,' Susan spat, shoulders hunched and eyebrows fierce. 'They are *human*,' she said, before asking each of the people standing in front of her who their owner was, then stopped to swap Chips to the other arm and lift Blankey down to her waist. Didn't they think that the law would 'decide otherwise' once they found out exactly how these humans had been repressed?

Emma stood at ease, stared ahead and said nothing.

* * *

In the event of their deaths, they had donated their bodies to medical research. And all their organs. Not many of Drew's were reusable – whatever it was that had driven into the passenger side of Watty's car had turned Drew's insides to soup, no, *coulis*... Watty would have written 'coulis'.

She rubbed out 'soup' with the end of her pencil and replaced it with 'coulis'.

Watty was pretty much intact. Except for his brain; his head had crashed into Drew's then back into a window... Or the other way around. Isabel only remembered the bit where she'd been told it was probably the blow to the head from Drew that had killed him.

Unthinkable, thought Isabel. They couldn't know for certain that Drew had killed Watty, could they? 'Probably,' Mark Hector had told her. 'Probably.'

She'd looked at him with clone-eyes; or the look of a person whose eyes would only really see the inside of their head, since three quarters of their world had been sucked from outside of it.

'I *know* what you saw the last time you came to the lab,' he had said to her. 'Well... she saw you too. And actually, she'd like to meet you,' he'd told her, not even a week after the crash.

Isabel sat with her lips against the pages of Watty's notebook, her stare drifting around the distended spiral of a single black paperclip, almost invisible in the grain of his big empty desk. 'Alright then,' she had said through the book.

Mark Hector smiled, nodding at the book. 'Why don't you keep writing in it?'

'—.'

He lowered his voice. 'The thing is, Isabel, if anyone found out about her, then… you know, anyone in your *family*…Well… She's not exactly *legal* as you know.'

'My family?'

'Yes, I'm sorry. Stupid thing to say… Although there is the little laundry place just up the road. Am I right in thinking that…'

'I get it; I'll keep my mouth shut.'

Dr Hector sighed. 'I know you will.'

* * *

They squinted beyond the forecourt as they were led across it towards the awaiting party that twinkled with camera flashes. Its hum held the magnitude of a much bigger crowd than the one they'd left. Wrists with glowing microphone icons were pushed up to their jawlines. Members of the LOG held up plastic cups and tried to hand them red-velvet biscuits. 'Well done!' they grinned, holding hands out towards the troop of littlers that stumbled on the uneven concrete. 'Some of them belong to LOG members,' Susan called before correcting herself. 'I mean, *live with* LOG members. We must change the "O",' she laughed as she passed Chips to Meredith before a hand on her head pushed her down into a car. Hamish's face appeared at the window on the opposite side, its nose snorting two steam-spots onto it. He said nothing. They stared at each other until the car moved away. Susan tried not to notice that his eyes kept flicking to Emma, who slid down the seat as a journalist aimed his wrist at her.

'Stop!' shouted Susan, just as they were pulling off. 'Just let me give him something!'

'What?' said a policewoman. 'No.'

'We haven't been arrested; open the door.' gurgled Emma, her chin squashed into her chest.

'And you think that breaking and entering isn't a crime?'

'We had *keys*,' she said. 'If we were arrestable, you would have arrested us.' She over-pronounced each syllable. Susan turned her head away, her cheeks bloated with laughter.

'Fine.'

The door opened. 'Take this,' Susan said, unbuttoning her coat and pulling Blankey from her hip. 'I mean, take her… Take *her* to Mrs Lucas.'

'I will,' Hamish said, still looking at Emma, then flashed his almost-panicked stare at Susan; shit, he'd let himself linger on Emma. His eyes jumped to her of their own accord, reaching for her face like a drowning man grabs for a buoy. The buoy rolled away, she looked at her knees. Stupid, bloody eyes; they'd lingered again. This time he held Susan's stare. 'I will,' he repeated. The car door was closed and they regarded each other through the window; Susan stared unblinking, as if she'd just caught her partner with another woman.

* * *

'Do you think they'll ever meet again?' Isabel scraped sugared icing from a stale bun with her index fingernail.

'Who?' said Reg.

'Watty and Drew.'

Reg held his breath and jigged his gaze over her.

'Like in heaven.'

'You've never believed in heaven…'

'Or reincarnation, then…'

Reg pressed his lips together and straightened in his chair. 'You know, Quail,' he said, tracing a circle on the table with a dough-coated fingernail, 'you'll always have a home here, with me. Why don't you stay?' He nearly added: *it's what they would have wanted*; instead he said: 'It would be a pleasure.'

'No,' Isabel replied. 'But I won't be very far away.' She kinked her head in the direction of the lab. 'None of us will be very far away.'

Reg scrunched up his eyebrows… *Us?* he'd wanted to ask. She hadn't been quite right since… well… since the accident.

'I think I'll write it as a request – you know – in the notebook. Whoever finds it, when I'm gone, might be far enough into the future to bring them back.' Her pupils climbed up to the right as she thought this. 'And I'll add that they're never to be separated again.'

'Alright, Quail.' Reg's mouth stretched into shapes of words before letting out a sigh. 'Just you remember that I'm here.'

Reg saw her twice, maybe three times after she left. He tried to contact her, but she never answered his calls; occasionally sent an email… He had an inkling about her new family, the clones; since that time in the coffee shop; the last day that they had all eaten cake together… She finally had some friends, he thought to himself. Maybe she was happy, at last. Good on her.

Isabel kept her promise and kept her mouth shut, primarily because she loved them. She'd given them all names, taught them how to read, write, *speak*… She wrote about them in her notebook, Bonbon, Mop, Fola, Lamb, Jinx… All of them. She gave them cuddles each time they returned from whatever procedures they'd undergone, and turned a blind eye when they were taken away. She turned a blind eye because Mark Hector had taken the little fistful of dog hair that was taped into the back cover of the notebook, and brought her best friend back to life. She turned a blind eye because he was the only person she knew who would have the guts to bring back the rest of her family, the same way he'd brought her new family into the world. She'd told him that each of her daddies had had body parts cloned, for later in life, and wondered aloud if it was possible to make up the rest of them? He'd said nothing… That was better than 'no'. That meant that maybe he *would*; one day.

A WORD FROM JINX...

I can see him from the booster seat in Susan's car. He's often here, looking exactly the same as he did before. He always looks like he's searching for someone... Sometimes, while he's searching, he sees me and he waves. I wave back. I'm not sure if Susan has seen him here; I get the feeling that's why we come to this place in particular, to see if we can see him. Although mostly it's because Mrs Lucas likes the food from here; Jerry used to come with us when he was... well... when he was alive. It's really funny, actually, as soon as my memories started to resurface, he and I managed to trace a link back to 1998; I knew the sister of one of his best friends' cousins. She was a dancer at the theatre company I used to volunteer for when I wasn't on tour with the ballet...

I love remembering myself as a dancer. This is the part of my life that I try *so* hard to think about. I love that memory of being the master of my body; of making it look like it could fly. I still try to dance like I used to, but my new body just won't let me. Bonbon loves these memories as well; although they're not as clear in her own mind. She remembers that she used to like watching me dance, but... It's just not all that clear, really. Talking helps. Talking helps a lot. I call it 'practising memories'; it's always the well-practised ones that seem to stay in my head. Well practised then and well practised now... Through talking and, and *walking*, funnily enough; and asking people things about *things*, I've managed to trigger so many memories and as soon as I remember one with Bonbon in it, I tell her straight away. That's why Bonbon's a bit behind. She can't quite manage to talk yet. Many of us can now and many of us can't and, well, she's one of those who can't. The other batches tend to struggle a lot; they say that our batch was 'defective' and if it hadn't been for that, there would have been no 'product recall' and no one would have known the truth.

Bonbon is definitely a Batch Twenty. I know her voice is *in* there, because we've laughed together, the three of us, and then Susan and I spend about an hour trying to make her laugh again… But I should know better really. It's not something you can do automatically the first time; it has to come with a wash of emotion; with something that just *has* to be said. She understands. She told me about the littlers at the hospital who were about to die in front of her. We think that their emotion was so strong that they were able to say their last thought out loud. Probably calling out for someone they really loved. Or maybe even their own names when they were full-humans, like Chips did. Who knows…

Bonbon is so focused on the real stuff, the *practical* stuff. Being able to see into our past has shown me that she's *always* been that way. She, well *he*, he was very much an action–reaction kind of person, which is weird when you consider that *I* was the scientist. When there was a problem, he liked a solution; he needed money so he opened that launderette-library place; when someone was sad he liked to make them laugh, when someone was hungry, he liked to give them cake. All very practical; that's why she can't pull the emotions together to speak. It seems that her little voice inside her head, *him*, is always telling her: 'but why on Earth would you get in such a state?' She laughs, though… That's nice. It's always lovely to hear Bonbon laugh.

I haven't told her this, but from what I've seen, there is *one* thing that might get her in such a state: if anything were to happen to me. Of course, neither of us wants *that*… But Susan and I thought about pretending to her that something horrible had happened, just to get her to talk… But that's a stupid idea. 'Tempting fate,' Mrs Lucas had said, making her eyes go all serious the way she does. 'Plus, you'd devastate little Bonbon.'

None of us wants that.

I was very different when I was a full-human. I was always looking to go beyond my limits *regardless* of what my head said. I'd use my whole body to show my feelings as if it were a cage and all that emotion would escape through the bars like tiny birds. It was as if I were dancing with the wasted energy of those dead children. That was me when I was fully charged. *That* was when my body told my mind that the only way, the *only* way was to take home the embryo. Well anyway, that's how I remember it.

And then there's the other one; the little girl. That's why we're little, apparently. Her memories are harder for me to catch; like thousands of flying feathers. But… when there are many of us there are more hands to catch them and, and sometimes we jump at the same time to catch the same one. Sometimes, the memories aren't words or pictures, but sadness or, or anger and we get angry! But not with each other, only with the world. Bonbon is much better at catching these feathers than I am. She often goes to see Windy just so they can talk about their memories of the little girl; *Isabel.* I find it hard to see Windy without wanting to cuddle her. I've talked to Bonbon about this and she says that I love Windy as if she were my parent *and* my child. I think she's right. I agreed with her straight away, the first time she said it.

It's not the same love as I feel for Chips…

I told Jerry that we should take his cells and make him into a littler. That way, he and Mrs Lucas could stay in love until *she* died; then we'd just do the same to her. We'd write a note and slip it in their dead hands, requesting that they never, ever get split up again.

Just like Isabel did with us.

Jerry laughed. So did Mrs Lucas.

Susan didn't… Neither did Bonbon. It's weird, but Bonbon spends a lot of her time worrying about death. Sometimes she says that things were easier before, when she didn't know so much and so didn't have so much to lose. I know *why* she's worried about death… She's worried about losing me again, and for good the next time around. She has flashbacks about the car accident. I don't remember any of it; I think my brain has blocked it out completely. But she does. I tell her that we just have to write it all down, so others can see our story when we're gone; we are, after all, just a story that we're living. Nothing else… When Jerry died, I cried and cried; so much that Mrs Lucas gave me a cuddle and said: 'I'm just so glad that he came home first. Otherwise the ending would have been all wrong.'

We can write. We probably could, even before we had our memories, but nobody ever gave us a pen. Not that many people *have* a pen these days. Bonbon writes all the time. She said that she can remember herself writing and that was *her* way of letting the birds out of the cage. The others can write too; and all of us *love* to read. We're always sharing information about what we've read, and sometimes someone will say: 'I've read that before!' when they haven't; well, not *this* time around…

'Do you need me to come with you, Susan?'

'Yeah. Just give me two minutes, will you?'

It's so nice to be able to go to the shops. People still look at me strangely when I start talking to them, but the whole scandal has been such a big story that… well… I just think it will take a bit of getting used to, that's all. After a while, people won't even blink when we walk into a shop and start asking for grapes.

Mmm, grapes. I could eat grapes *forever*. I can't decide if I prefer grapes or custard. Once I tried them both together. It was quite nice; better than flakes. Yuk! Bonbon and I *hate* flakes. But Chips still eats them, every day…

Most people recognize Susan. They often ask how the new centre's going; has she adopted many out… And she always gives the same answer: there are still plenty of them looking for a nice home. A *nice* home, we have to stipulate. We've had some real weirdos wanting to come and take the retired littlers home. 'You mustn't be so judgemental, Jinx,' she says to me when I screw my face up after a visit from a potential adopter. But it's not me being judgemental. It's Bonbon who tips me off. She's got a real eye for nasty people…

Unlike before, the contract is made between the littler and their new biggerer; the littler can choose who they want to live with and can choose if they want to leave. Or they can choose to live at the centre. Some of them will never find a home, poor things. It's a sad truth, but they're just too disfigured. Or too traumatized. It's usually one or the other…

Ah ha! That's why she wanted two minutes to herself! She's seen him and she's gone to talk to him. *Susan*, how many times have we gone through this? Oh well, she looks as though she's keeping her cool. Maybe one year apart has done her good. Maybe they can be friends again. It would be nice if he came over every so often to see us… We do miss him sometimes… But then, we do have a new man of the house who's taking up more and more room every day.

It turns out that 'Chips' was a really good name for him… It's one of his favourite foods; *one* of them… We share a sunshine-coloured basket that smells like custard. He talks *all* the time and uses long words that make me shut my eyes and really concentrate to recall their meaning. Recall. That's one of Chips's words. It's not very long but it's a word I wouldn't usually say… He remembers everything about his past life, well, his current life. He visits his old owner sometimes and reads to him or reminds him of his memories. 'Giving him back himself,' as Chips would say. I've left Chips and Bonbon at home today. I'm trying to make them fall in love with each other. I think it's working; I often catch them cuddling, and once I came home and found them kissing. Bonbon tells me that she loves Chips but Chips is still a bit unsure… The biggerers think we're a bit weird for trying to set up this 'triangle' relationship, as I call it. But all three of us have agreed that it's a good idea; much less complicated than one of us getting left out.

'Are you coming, Jinx?'

'You told me to wait a few minutes.'

'—.'

'And anyway, you were talking to Hamish.'

'I know.'

'What's wrong?'

'I don't know… Just still feels a bit weird.'

'I knew it would.'

'I couldn't exactly ignore him, could I?'

'No. Did he say anything about…'

'About Emma? He hasn't heard from her either.'

'Hmmm. I hope she's alright.'

'Me too.'

'Come on then, Madam… Did you pick up Mrs Lucas's list?'

'Yep.'

'There's someone bleeping out flyers about ballet classes by the entrance.'

'Really? Could you bleep one to your wrist?'

'Sure!'

We still have stuff to do. The battle's not over yet. It's hard to tell how long we're going to live and how quickly we'll get old. Windy was only eleven years old when I met her. I think about that sometimes, wondering when I'll get old or when it'll all end; only because, we are the last ones, Batch Twenty. When we start dying, it'll be the end of our race. I'd like to think that we will stay a race; although making that happen seems rather complicated. Chips told me a story about the first ever woman who was made from her boyfriend's rib. I said that I didn't really fancy making a baby like that, to be honest. 'Why not?' he said. 'I came from an amputated leg.'

He's right, he did. And he's just perfect. Like grapes and custard.

A group of us has volunteered to be part of a trial to see if there is the possibility of procreation. The trial hasn't been approved yet and we don't know if it will be. The most important thing we've learned, from our experience and from our collective memories, is to make ourselves heard because, well, we *want* to stay a race. We have the right to stay a race.

It's a new fight now.

THE END

'Funny that you should bring a child to see me, on this day of all days,' husked the mousy curls, now veined with silver.

Her vision blurred the white face that sat on Hector's grandson's lap. The white was the same as the wall behind it, the only detail that defined it as a head was the red fox tail when the little girl turned to whisper something to her daddy.

'She's always wanted to meet you. And…'

'It's better to do it just before I die because, well, I'll be gone. Children have large mouths.' Isabel squinted. 'I've always wanted to meet a child. Pity I can't really see her.'

The child leaned forward close enough for Isabel to see that her eyes were pink and gleaming wet. A dark shape was placed next to her thigh and the eyes blurred backwards again with a sniff.

'What is this?' asked Isabel, teasing the shape's fur with her fingertips.

'Jinx,' said a child's voice.

'It's one of her teddy bears—'

'How does she know about Jinx?' Isabel interrupted.

'I brought her back,' said the little girl. 'For you.'

'But how did she…' Isabel started, then paused, her milky eyes quivering. 'Is my notebook next to me?'

'Yes,' said Hector's grandson.

'I want her to have it.'

'Oh, but she's only three…'

'Hector will give it to her when she's older. I want her to have it.' She tried again to squint at the girl. 'Emma, isn't it?'

'Yes,' said the little girl.'

'Emma, I want you to have this. Will you look after it?'

The fox tail bobbed with deep nods.

'Good girl,' said Isabel. 'Thank you.'